STARSHIP RAIDER

BOOKS BY JAROM STRONG

Paragon Space

Starship Salvager

Starship Raider

Starship Rebellion

STARSHIP RAIDER

JAROM STRONG

SECOND SKY

Published by Second Sky in 2025

An imprint of Storyfire Ltd.
Carmelite House
50 Victoria Embankment
London EC4Y 0DZ

www.secondskybooks.com

The authorised representative in the EEA is Hachette Ireland
8 Castlecourt Centre
Dublin 15 D15 XTP3
Ireland
(email: info@hbgi.ie)

ISBN: 978-1-83618-198-9
eBook ISBN: 978-1-83618-197-2

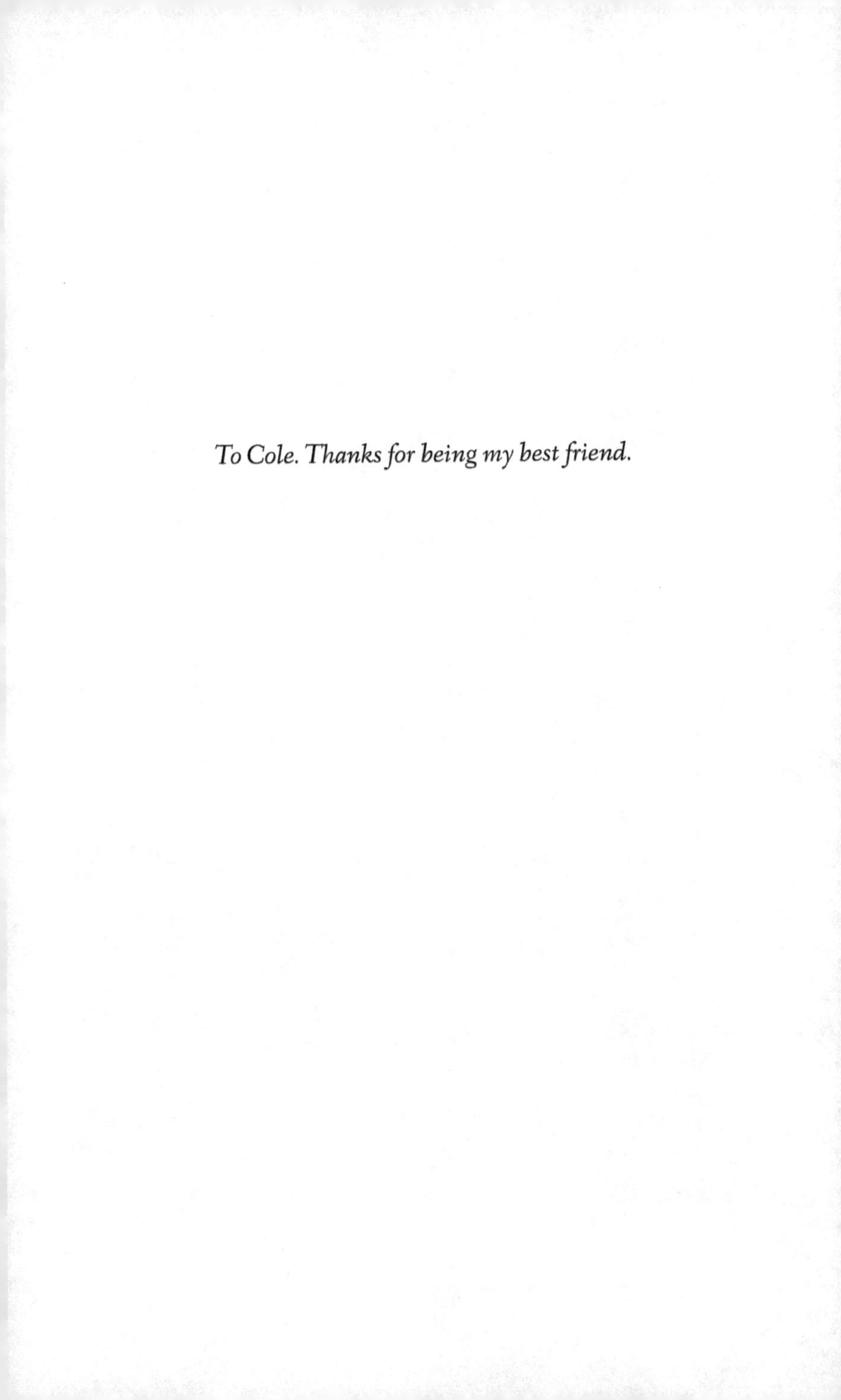

To Cole. Thanks for being my best friend.

ONE

My old man used to say that there are two kinds of pain in life: the unavoidable kind—the kind that just happens to you, through bad luck or bad people—and the stupid kind. The kind of pain that you bring about yourself, through your own dumb decisions. Usually, he'd say it while he was tanning my hide for some knobheaded thing I'd done, shouting *guess which kind this is?* over the sound of the beating.

Sometimes, when I'm hurting, I still hear his voice in the back of my head, asking me that question.

Today, the answer was obvious.

I grunted as the ripper's tailspike slammed into the side of my helmet and sent me staggering. By all rights the blow should have killed me. If I'd been wearing any other kind of exo, the creature's long, spear-like, biosteel tail would have punctured right through the armor and into my skull. I'd seen it happen dozens of times.

I wasn't wearing just any exo, though.

The Icarus's sleek surface crackled with light as the advanced energy-infused armor deflected the ripper's blow. The ripper leaped, two sets of scythe-like claws and a maw bristling with jagged jet-black teeth—all sharp enough to shear through steel with ease—arcing towards me. I used my exo's neurointerface to activate the suit's thermal blades. Two incandescent sheets of pure thermal energy coalesced at the ends of each of my arms. I made a long downward cut. The blade caught the ripper on one shoulder and cut straight through its torso, bisecting it diagonally. It landed at my feet in two twitching, sizzling chunks of flesh. The upper half tried reaching for me, claws flailing uselessly. I lifted one armored boot and slammed it down on the creature's skull with a wet crunch. It spasmed and went still.

Rose's voice sounded in my ear, focused and intense. "*More heading your way!*"

I whirled, assessing the situation.

It wasn't great.

I was standing in the center of a four-way intersection of wide corridors. The ripper I'd just killed had come from the right. More rippers, farther away, were charging down the corridors ahead of me and to my left. Gunshots echoed down the hallway behind me. I glanced over my shoulder to survey my crew's position.

Once again—not great.

"This was a bad idea!" Shell growled into the comms, her voice lurching with each jolt from her Jackhammer autorifle. Nadus was next to her, his massive Jericho CES-4 exosuit making her Hardrock 13 look small in comparison. The two of them were the farthest from me, capping off the far end of our position spread across the small stretch of corridor. Their profiles were silhouetted by the strobing muzzle flashes of their weapons as they fired down the corridor in the opposite direction to me.

"*Hey, don't blame me!*" Rose's voice was strained, her breath short. From the sound of it, she was rapidly typing something into the *Orpheus*'s navigation system. Probably trying to figure out if there was a faster way to get to us without triggering the automatic defense systems of the derelict transport we were aboard. As it was, she was stuck on the other side of the ship, keeping the *Orpheus* in the transport's blind spot. "*I never claimed it was gonna be an easy job.*"

"It'll be worth it," Rid muttered. He had his lockbreaking kit out and was kneeling next to a heavy blast door set in the center of the corridor we were defending. Sparks cascaded across the walls and floor as he made a long, careful incision with his thermal saw. "As long as I can get through this damn door. What kind of passenger transport has a heavy-duty vault anyways?"

"Probably the kind that should be *left alone!*" Bentley's voice was stretched tight with stress. He was standing next to Rid, holding a datapad with one hand and furiously manipulating it with another. The datapad was connected to a computer system in the wall of the ship by a long cable. "The security systems are weirdly tight too. The usual protocols aren't working. I'm telling you, something is off about this ship."

I turned away, fixing my attention on the horde of rippers swarming towards me from two sides. More had appeared on the right too. I backed up a few strides to keep myself from being surrounded. "You're *sure* this source can be trusted, Rose?"

"*It was anonymous. But it's a little late for second thoughts, don't you think?*"

I blinked. Anonymous? Rose had never said anything about that. "It was *anonymous?* Why would you—"

A ripper lunged at me, claws flashing.

I'd already felt uneasy about this job. Too much that was off about it. Rose had been adamant and I'd reluctantly agreed. But her sudden admission about the source turned my unease into dread.

The stupid kind of pain.

I activated my thrusters, giving me a quick burst of speed as I sidestepped the ripper and decapitated it with a flick of my wrist, then used my neurointerface to aim the Icarus's shoulder-mounted grenade launcher and fire a frag grenade right into the center of the horde. The resulting explosion would have been deafening had it not been for my exo helmet's protection. Even with the protection, I found the noise distractingly loud. On most salvage runs the life-support systems had long ago given up their ghosts, meaning that we fought in a noiseless, gravity-less vacuum. Not here. If I'd wanted to, I could've taken my helmet off and been just fine. Not that I *did* want that, of course.

Chunks of flesh and bone splattered against the surface of my exo. The rippers towards the rear—the ones who hadn't been eviscerated by the frag grenade's storm of shrapnel—staggered backward, temporarily stunned by the blast.

"How the hell are there this many of them?" Nadus growled. "This ship isn't big enough for a horde of this size."

"I don't know. But scans show more on the way."

The rippers recovered and charged again before I could reply, but I was inclined to agree. The transport vessel was a relatively small one. Making things even stranger, I'd seen no signs of struggle as we'd crept our way from the emergency airlock we'd entered the ship through to where we were now. Rippers never left behind bodies, but there was always *something* where they'd encountered prey. Discarded gear, blood-stained clothes, claw marks on the walls and floors. Usually, the life-support systems had gone offline, which obviously wasn't the case here. In fact, other than the rippers, the ship seemed to be in damn near pristine condition. None of the usual signs of slaughter or frenzied evacuation...

A thought occurred to me. "Rose. Can you tell if any—" I ducked beneath a tailspike, then hacked the end of the tail off with a quick swipe and took out two more attacking rippers on the backswing. "If any of the escape pods have been evacuated?"

"That's *what's on your mind right now?*" she snapped.

"Almost through," Rid said, voice strained. "Just need a bit more time."

I gritted my teeth. Rose was right—none of the details would matter if we got turned into a meal for rippers. "A bit more time, coming right up." I waded into the onslaught of rippers, blades whipping back and forth, felling them like wheat before a scythe. They kept charging, throwing themselves into the path of my blades with reckless abandon. These weren't the evolved ultrarippers we'd faced on the *Revelation*, able to plot and adapt and assess risks. Just the regular ol' rippers that the Paragon had been using for decades now. Mindless, soulless killing machines incapable of emotion or thought beyond the ever-pressing need to feed. Good thing too. If these *had* been ultrarippers, we'd already be dead. Instead, we were just... *probably* going to die.

The ultrarippers were all dead, though. I'd made sure the last of them were destroyed on the *Revelation*. No matter what Ramar claimed...

"*I still can't get around to the docking bay until Bentley finishes disabling the defensive battery,*" Rose said. "*Those guns will tear the* Orpheus *to shreds.*"

"I'm *working* on it!" Bentley snapped.

A ripper managed to leap over my flashing blades and land on top of my shoulders. All thoughts of Ramar and his ultrarippers were shoved violently from my brain. There was a buzzing sound as the energy flowing through the outer shell of my armor pushed against the creature. It kept its grip, though, clawing at me in a desperate attempt to hack through my exo's layers and into the flesh beneath. *My* flesh. I reached up and grabbed the ripper by the back of the neck, then slammed it against the wall.

"Door's open!" Rid exclaimed. "Let's go!"

"Bentley, can you move?" I released the corpse of the ripper I'd just flattened against the wall and turned back to the rest of the horde, making a wide slash that sent severed body parts flying.

Bentley's voice was frantic. "Not until I—oh, that's weird."

"*What?!*" Several voices snapped at the same time.

"I'm through," he said, his voice suddenly more curious than afraid. "We can go. It's just weird because the protocol that ended up working was a—"

"*Go!*" I started retreating slowly backward, cutting down one ripper after another and leaving a trail of dismembered carnage in my wake until I reached the now open blast doors and came back-to-back with Shell and Nadus.

"You guys head in," I said. "I'll drop an incendiary behind us."

"Got it." Nadus fired a few last shots from his Jackhammer, felling a wave of rippers, then ducked through the doorway. Shell went right behind him. I waited a moment, then stepped through the door.

"*Close it!*" I yelled.

Rid slammed his fist against a control panel on the wall. The doors began to slide shut. Just before they did, I fired an incendiary grenade from my shoulder launcher through the gap. There was a sudden rush of heat—detected by my exo's systems and signaled painlessly to my brain—and a burst of light as white flames enveloped the corridor. Rippers threw themselves at the door, heedless of the flames. The last thing I saw before the doors sealed was a ripper pawing weakly at me as its flesh sizzled.

"Remind me," I said grimly as I stared at the door, "not to take any more of Rose's jobs."

"*Quit whining, we're making it through alright so far. Bentley, is it safe for me to move yet?*"

"Defensive battery is offline," Bentley said. "You can move

free of fear of being incinerated. Just have a few more odds and ends I'm taking care of."

"Good. Heading over to the cargo bay. See, Lax, what'd I tell you? Easy-peasy. Now—what's in there?"

I had to hold my tongue to keep myself from lashing out at her. Rose had always been pushing me to take more high-risk jobs—but flat out *lying* about the details of a job was a new low. If I'd known her source was anonymous, I'd never have agreed to any of this. Still—we were here, and chewing her out over the public channel for the whole crew to hear would only make things worse. There'd be time for that conversation later.

I sighed and turned, surveying the room we'd stumbled into. It was dark, lit only by our exo floodlights and my flickering thermal blades, which I deactivated when I saw the room was clear. It seemed to be some sort of vault. I realized with a sinking feeling that the doors we'd gone through were the only way in or out. It was about ten meters wide and just as long. In the center of the room there were several unmarked crates.

"They're all locked shut," Shell said.

"Huh. Weird." Rose's voice crackled. *"Doesn't look like any of the escape pods cut loose. They're all in place."*

The pit in my stomach was growing deeper, but I held my tongue as Rid started cutting one of the locks off the crates. Bentley was right. Something was off about all of this. A small transport ship drifting alone in deep space. The location didn't make sense. There was no reason for it to be where it was. When a ship got hit by rippers, it generally happened near some sort of celestial body, before the ship could breach into the safety of nullspace. After that the ships would drift off course, eventually get reported, and then we'd come in. This ship was too deep. Like the *Panama* had been. Plus, its security systems were extreme. What kind of transport ship had an autodefense battery like this one? On top of that, how the hell had they been hit by rippers with such strong defenses? And if there had been no evacuation—as indicated by the fact that the escape pods were all accounted for—why weren't there any signs of struggle?

"Bentley," I said, watching sparks fly as Rid cut through the lock. "You were saying that something was weird about the security protocol. What was it?"

"It was a Paragon security system," he said, still working on his datapad. "Which normally isn't a problem for me."

I frowned. There was no reason *to* expect it. This was a privately owned ship. Why the hell would they have a Paragon security system?

"Got it," Rid grunted. He reached for the lid.

"Wait." I gently pushed him aside. "Let me. Could be trapped."

I carefully pried the lid off of one of the crates, half expecting to be suddenly enveloped in a violent explosion. I wasn't. Instead, I found myself staring down at a row of carefully stacked packages.

"*What is it?*" Rose asked eagerly.

"I... still don't know." I gingerly lifted one of the packages. They were all uniform, each one roughly the size of a brick and wrapped in plastic. My first suspicion was narcotics of some kind. That thought quickly vanished. The substance was far too heavy. I turned it over.

"Aw, *hell*," I muttered.

"*What?*" Multiple exasperated voices called out at the same time.

I held the package towards them, displaying the prominently written words: LIFEBLOOD BIOFUEL. There was some more text beneath that, jargon-filled beyond my expertise, but the part I really cared about was stretched ominously across the bottom of the label: *Property of Divinity Biotechnologies. Do not distribute without authorization.*

Nadus cursed. "We should leave."

"Yeah." I shoved the package back into the crate. "Let's go."

"Wait!" Rid's hand closed over the lid, keeping me from returning it. "Why? We're already here!"

"We *shouldn't* be," I said, prying the lid free. "I don't know what's going on here, but it's obviously a set-up of some kind. And I know better than to screw around with Divinity."

"*We're already screwing around with Divinity,*" Rose said. "*In case you forgot, we just barely finished raiding a ship full of secrets the Paragon stole from them.*"

I grimaced. Of course I hadn't forgotten. I'd hardly thought of anything else for the past year. "I know. And that's exactly why we should be trying *extra* hard to stay unnoticed. So let's pack it up, get back in the *Orpheus*, and—"

"This is Lifeblood," Shell said, her voice awed. She had reached into the crate and pulled one of the packages out to inspect.

Bentley frowned at the package. "Is that supposed to mean something?"

"It's a biofuel." Shell's tone was almost reverent. "For crops. Makes it so you can grow insane amounts of food without sunlight or water."

I glanced sharply at the package. "Seriously?"

"For Roamers it's worth more than... well, just about anything," Shell said, turning it over in her hands. She glanced at the other crates. "Are they *all* Lifeblood?"

Rid pried another lid free. "Seems that way."

Bentley's eyes were wide. "This stuff must be worth a *fortune.*"

I slammed the lid Rid had just opened back down with a scowl. "That's the problem. This is very clearly somebody's hidden stash. Somebody who will probably be immensely pissed if we—"

Rose cursed suddenly, her voice stabbing through the comms channel. I blinked. "What?"

"*Somebody just breached,*" she said. "*We've got company.*"

The pit that had been forming in my stomach dropped suddenly into a wide chasm. I groaned. "Who?"

"*I don't know. It's a big ship—scan is saying the model is an old Redhawk battleship. I mean, really old.*"

"Not the Paragon, then, or Divinity," Nadus said. I nodded, feeling a surge of relief. We still had a big damn problem on our hands no matter who it was, but just about anything was better than having the Paragon on top of us.

"Who is it, then?" Shell asked. "Pirates?"

"Either that," I said, "or it's whoever left this stuff here."

"*They're heading our way,*" Rose said.

"Right. Let's go," Nadus said.

"Wait." I grimaced. "Grab the Lifeblood."

All heads turned sharply towards me. "But you just said—"

"I know what I said," I growled as I lifted the nearest crate. It was heavy, but my exo made light work of it. "Situation's changed. If this is what they're after we'll need the leverage to keep them from shooting us down. Bentley, see if you can turn off the gravity to make it go faster."

Rose scoffed. "*We could take them, whoever they are. Their ship is* ancient. *They probably just have a bunch of old flak guns. I bet they couldn't even put a dent in the* Orpheus's *shields.*"

"That's a lot of conjecture," I said. "And the *Orpheus* isn't a fighter, she's an infiltrator. Stay hidden. We'll head to the cargo bay. If we're fast enough, we might be able to make it out before they can lock onto us. Everyone clear?"

Nods and words of confirmation all around as everybody set about their various tasks. For a brief moment, the urgency I felt was pushed aside by a swell of pride as I watched them work. Just over a year ago, most of us had never met each other. None of them had ever worked a salvage job before. Now they were an experienced, capable crew, able to rapidly adapt to changing circumstances. They'd gone through hell on the *Revelation* and come out the other end. If they could pull through that, they could pull through anything.

Then again, I'd thought the same thing about my old crew.

"Keep in mind you've still got rippers out there," Rose said. *"Looks like a decent little cluster of them survived your incendiary grenade."*

"How could I forget," I said dryly.

A rogue, likely pirate-operated warship inbound. Several crates full of illicit goods that would almost certainly bring a heap of trouble down on our heads. A horde of rippers waiting for us to open the door so they could get at us.

I turned towards the sealed blast doors, took a deep breath, and activated my thermal blades.

Two kinds of pain.

TWO

"Go!"

I shouted the word mid-swing as I hewed through the last three rippers. With the gravity turned off, their dismembered corpses simply spun in the air, twitching violently. The rest of the crew rushed behind me, using their exos' thrusters to move rapidly without gravity's hindrance.

"How we looking, Rose?" I asked.

"Scans show that's the last of the rippers. But that ship is definitely coming our way," Rose replied. *"I don't think they've detected the* Orpheus *yet, though. Bentley, you're sure the defense systems are turned off?"*

"Yeah, yeah." Our resident techie paused, using his thrusters to slow down as he glanced through a large window and out into space. "Whoa, look!"

I paused briefly to see what Bentley was pointing out. In the pitch-black of space I could see a small shape approaching, looking toy-like with the vast distance separating us. With a mental command, I zoomed in on it with the Icarus's cameras until the vessel came into focus. It was a battleship, alright, and whoever was piloting it wanted everybody to know it. The hull was pockmarked by craters and bristling with weapons. Rose had been right—the ship was ancient. Nobody had produced battleships like these since the Gideon–Redhawk war, nearly half a millennium ago, long before the Paragon had risen to power.

"Keep moving," I said, reeling my vision back to the standard setting and turning away from the window. "How's everybody holding up?"

I got a quick status report from everyone as we continued rushing down the corridor. No problems to speak of. Nadus watched from the rear, Jackhammer at the ready, while I resumed my position at the front of our formation. The Icarus's induction armor was far from unbreachable, but it gave me much better odds of surviving an ambush than anybody else.

No ambush came, though. The hallways were silent and empty, as I'd expected they would be. If any of the rippers had still been alive, Rose would have detected them and they'd have attacked us by now. They had no concept of fear or patience or strategy. Still, though—I'd lost one crew to making assumptions. I'd be damned if I was gonna make the same mistake twice.

There was a crackle as Rose spoke up. *"The battleship is sending out a general broadcast. Patching you in."*

There was a burst of static in the comms, followed by a masculine voice.

"... Am I on? No, I see the light, I just... oh, we're on! Ahem." The voice waxed deeper and strangely lyrical. *"This is Captain Zathari Renault of the* Walrus, *hailing all nearby vessels. Please deactivate all nonessential systems and prepare to be boarded."*

"Maybe they don't know we're here," Bentley said, his frail voice as nervous as ever. "As long as we stick to the quantum communication channel there shouldn't be any signals for them to pick up."

"We can hope," I said. "With a little luck we might be able to slip away before they realize we're here."

"Maybe they're just another salvage crew," Shell mused. "They could have gotten the same tip we did."

"With all of that firepower they're packing, my bet is on pirates," Nadus grunted as he swung around a corner. "Ain't too much difference between the two anyways."

I frowned back at him. "Now how you figure that?"

Nadus shrugged. "Just a matter of timing, ain't it?"

"No," I said, feeling irrationally irritated. "It's a matter of—"

"*Ahem,*" said the stranger's voice over the public channel again. "*Perhaps I should have been more clear. I'd like to speak to Lackan VanDunn, please. Sooner rather than later. I don't see the* Orpheus, *but I imagine that if we were to start blasting away at that transport you're hiding behind, we'd hit you eventually.*"

I blinked. The entire crew looked sharply at me.

"You know this guy?" Shell demanded.

"Don't think so." I furrowed my brow. The voice didn't sound familiar at all. Neither did the name, Zathari Renault. Then again, after an eight-year stay in prison, I could easily have forgotten a few names from my old life. *Lives,* more like.

"Keep moving." I found myself hissing the words as if the newcomer might hear me if I spoke too loudly. "We're almost to the cargo bay. Get loaded up and ready to leave. Rose and Bentley—hook me up to the cruiser's broadcast system so I can talk to him without our signal giving away the *Orpheus*'s location. Or mine."

"On it," Rose and Bentley said simultaneously.

"*Look, we* know *you're there,*" Zathari continued, his voice increasingly warped with irritation. "*And we* know *you* know *we* know *you're there.*" There was a short pause like he was working through what he'd said and making sure it all added up.

"Almost ready," muttered Bentley, frantically working on

his datapad while he propelled himself with his thrusters around a corner.

"So just make this easy for all of us. We have no desire to blow anything or anybody up today—just need to have a quick chat with you. So... come on, speak up."

In the corner of my heads-up display I saw a notification that a new radio channel had become available. I hesitated.

"Talk to him," Rose said. *"Buy us some time at least."*

"He must be the one who sent Rose the tip," Nadus grumbled. "Wanted to lure us out here."

"Maybe," Rid said. "But then why would he let us steal a fortune's worth of Lifeblood from under his nose?"

I synced to it, double-checked to make sure it was the right one, then spoke up.

"Alright," I said. "Fine, you got me." I just needed to buy us a few minutes. I grimaced at the thought. Small talk had never been my forte. "Quite the antique you're flying there."

I'd expected to hear annoyance, but Renault's voice seemed only amused. *"Ah, the man himself! And don't you worry about the* Walrus, *she is more than fit for the task."*

"What task is that?" I muffled a sigh of relief as I saw the cargo bay down the hall from us.

"That depends entirely on the result of this conversation," Renault said.

The *Orpheus*'s cargo bay door opened. I stepped to the side while the rest of the crew entered. "Well, Captain... Reynolds?"

"Renault," he corrected. That time he did sound a little annoyed.

"Renault," I repeated. "Renault. Sorry. Bad with names. Speaking of which, you seem to know mine. Have we met before?"

"Unfortunately, we've never had the pleasure. I'd love to remedy that, however. What say you come aboard my ship and we have a chat?"

I frowned, then switched to the private channel. "How close are they?"

"*About to be right on top of us.*" Rose's voice was awed. "*Damn, but that ship can move.*"

I switched back to the public channel. "Look, Reynolds—"

"*—Renault—*"

"Renault, sorry. I'll be honest with you. I don't know you, and my mother said never to get in a stranger's vehicle, and there's a lot of talk about pirates these days, so you'll understand if I'm a bit hesitant to take you up on that."

"*I'm afraid I don't plan on giving you an option, VanDunn.*"

Rose spoke up. "*Something detached from his ship. No, several things. They're hunter drones.*"

Aw, *hell*. So long as the *Orpheus*'s stealth shields were engaged and we weren't sending any detectable signals from it, we'd be invisible to the *Walrus*'s scanners. If the hunter drones got close enough, though, they'd detect us visually, allowing the *Walrus* to obtain a target lock.

"*Come on, Lackan,*" Renault pressed, his voice playful now. "*You know there's no way out. You have my word of honor that no harm will befall you or yours. As I said, I just want to have a chat.*"

"Look, no offence, but I don't exactly put much stock in the honor of pirates," I said. Nadus and Shell were loading the cargo truck aboard now. I grimaced. Every passing second was increasingly precious. Once those drones were in range our stealth advantage would be gone, and the *Orpheus* didn't have the firepower to take them all out.

Renault sighed. "*Pirate is such an overused, cliched word. So small-minded and desperate sounding. Like some sort of common miscreant. Buccaneer has a bit more old-timey flair to it, wouldn't you agree? Zathari Renault—King of the Buccaneers. Now there's a title with some ambition to it.*"

He was rambling. Maybe I wasn't the only one trying to buy

time. Either that, or this guy just loved the sound of his own voice. Fine by me. "Alright, then. What the hell does that have to do with me?"

Renault sighed. "*Very well, then—allow me a moment of bluntness. If I was after you—really after you—I'd have opened fire already. I'm certain you're simply hiding on the other side of that freighter and I have more than enough firepower to shoot through it. But I'm not. I want something and I believe that you can help me get it.*"

Nadus gave me a thumbs up. I breathed a sigh of relief as the cargo bay door sealed shut. "Yeah? I'm all ears, captain." A moment later there was a slight lurch as the *Orpheus* undocked.

"*As you no doubt have noticed, the tides of politics are shifting in a most unpredictable manner these days,*" Renault said. "*The Paragon is weakening, the cracks in its foundations yawning into mighty chasms into which the powers of tomorrow must flow...*"

Like I said—some people just love the sound of their own voice. I've never been one of them, though, so I let him keep talking while I tuned him out to focus on my crew. And, more importantly, on getting them all out of here alive.

"*Those hunters are getting really close,*" Rose said. "*Let's just blast away.*"

"The hunters would see us," Rid said.

Rose scoffed. "*Sure. The* Walrus *might even get a few shots off before we're out of range, but our shields can take it. Their ship is like a million years old.*"

"Doesn't move like it, though," Shell muttered. "And no matter how old their ship is, we don't have the firepower to take *them* down."

Firepower. An idea struck me. "Bentley," I said into the private channel. "Do you still have access to the transport's security systems?"

"Yeah," he said, sounding confused. "But... *oh.*"

"Do it," I said. I switched back to the public line, latching onto the last thing I'd heard Renault say before I tuned him out. Something about new powers. I spoke up, cutting off his speech. "So, you're fixin' to be one of those new powers?"

"*Me? No, I'm just hoping to align myself with them,*" he said, not seeming to mind the interruption. "*Truth be told, Lackan, I'm not here for you so much as I am for your employer. Maren Sevani, Smuggler Queen of the Albeni sector. All I want is to arrange a conversation with her.*"

"Not my employer," I said, for some reason finding myself vaguely annoyed by the assumption.

"*Associate, then.*"

I glanced over at Bentley. He didn't look up from his data-pad. "Fine," I said. "Easier ways of doing that that don't involve ambushing us in deep space."

"*Except that I somehow think she'll take me more seriously if I have her friends with me,*" Renault said. "*Not to mention her daughter.*"

"*Hunters are in range,*" Rose breathed. "*They see us now.*"

"There *you are,*" Renault said, sounding pleased with himself.

I glanced over at Bentley. He grimaced and twirled a finger. *More time.* I mentally scrambled for something to say—small talk had never been my strongest skill. Something Renault had said grabbed me, though. Puzzled me.

"I—wait, hold on, what was that you said?" I was genuinely confused.

"*I said that Sevani will have to take me seriously if I have her daughter with me,*" Renault repeated, sounding annoyed.

I forced myself to chuckle. It was fake at first. But the more I thought about what Renault had said, the funnier it became. Before too long I found myself shaking with laughter.

"*What the hell are you on about?*" Renault snapped.

"I'm sorry," I wheezed. "But you want to strike a deal with Maren Sevani... by kidnapping her *daughter*?"

"*Not* kidnapping, *per se*, *but—*"

"Captain Renault, you either don't know the first thing about Maren Sevani," I said, "or you're a far, far braver man than I am."

Bentley gave me a thumbs up.

"*The plan has some holes in it, I'll admit,*" Renault said, exasperated, "*but—well, there is no but. I've got you clearly in my sights. Power down your ship and prepare to be boarded or I'll incinerate you before you can so much as—*"

"Look, Captain," I said. "It's been nice chatting with you, it really has. I'd advise you to work on your pitch, though. And to pay more attention to your surroundings."

"*What do you—*"

"Hit it, Bentley," I said. "Rose, get us out of here."

Bentley pressed a button. I watched over his shoulder as the datapad showed the transport's automated defense system spring to life, acquiring targets. As per Bentley's instructions, it designated the *Orpheus* as friendly. The four hunter drones, however, it quickly identified as threats.

A dozen energy turrets activated at once. Within milliseconds, the hunter drones were reduced to ashes.

Renault swore. "*Target the cruiser!*" he yelled at somebody, presumably one of his officers.

"Rose, get us out of—*oof.*" I grunted as the *Orpheus* lurched again. That'd mean Rose was really giving it the throttle. The ship's gravity generator typically worked to counteract the effects of acceleration, but when you really kicked it into overdrive there was only so much you could do.

"*Already on it,*" she said.

I glanced back at Bentley's datapad. With the hunters disposed of, the transport had turned its batteries onto the

Walrus. A dozen beams of energy materialized. I was far from an expert on ship-to-ship combat, but I figured that even if the attack didn't destroy the antique pirate ship it would at least severely damage it. Either way, Zathari Renault and his misplaced ambitions would no longer be our problem.

"If this Renault guy did set this all up," Bentley said as he frowned at the screen, "he did *not* think it through very well."

Shell spoke up. "They're not even slowing down."

She was right. The *Walrus* seemed unaffected by the volley, the energy beams dissipating on its shields with a white glow. It adjusted its course slightly.

"Okay," Rose admitted. "*So, they upgraded their shields. Still, a ship that old will hardly be able to put a dent in—*"

A single burst of light flared from the *Walrus.* Some kind of massively powerful energy cannon firing. A short moment later, the transport we'd been on a few minutes ago exploded, spewing a million tiny chunks of debris into the void.

"You were saying?" Rid asked. We were all huddled around Bentley now, watching the drama unfold through his datapad.

"Holy *crap,*" Nadus muttered. "What kind of gun was that?"

I shook my head slowly. I'd figured Renault was all hot air and laughably empty threats. But I didn't feel like laughing anymore. Hell, even a Paragon battlecruiser would have to think twice before tangling with that kind of firepower.

"*VanDunn!*" Renault was shouting now. "*Where are you, you sneaky bastard? We're not done talking!*"

"*Almost to breaching distance,*" Rose grunted. I nodded. Nullspace breachers were infamously unpredictable when operating near other objects of mass. The farther away from the *Walrus* and the ruins of the cruiser we were when we fired it up, the better.

"*This isn't the end of this!*" Renault growled. "*Trust you me, we will meet again, and when we do—*"

"*Breaching,*" Rose said.

Renault's voice cut off abruptly. I felt a familiar twisting sensation as the *Orpheus* blinked from existence in the physical world and crossed into the empty void known as nullspace.

There was a short silence.

"*See?*" Rose gave a nervous chuckle. "*Easy.*"

THREE

"Just four days ago, dozens of innocent bystanders were killed during a chaotic battle between enforcers and a group of politically motivated gunmen on the citystation Gilgamesh 4, located in the Ebisu system. I'm here with the local Paragon enforcement representative, Captain Ari Denman..."

"Getting crazier every day out there," Nadus grunted beside me, taking a sip from his cup.

I nodded, not taking my eyes from the screen hanging from the ceiling in Sevani's bar. Not too long ago no reporting station would have dared suggest that there was anything wrong with the Paragon's utopia. Now even they couldn't ignore the writing on the wall.

The screen showed two women—the news anchor, dressed in a professional but appealing pantsuit, and the enforcer representative, a severe-looking woman with a weariness to her posture that not even her crisp uniform could hide.

"Thank you, Lisha," the enforcer said. "I want to begin by assuring everyone that the situation, while tragic, is well under control. The terrorists involved in this incident have been captured or killed, and while I, of course, am not at liberty to share any details, our intelligence agencies are already investigating their motivations and backing."

"Of course," the reporter said. "This attack comes as just the latest in a string of incidents beginning with the uprising on Brahma last year." An image of a Brahmian street filled with smoke, rubble, and black-clad enforcers appeared on the screen. I felt the muscles in my jaw tighten. Another image appeared—this one of smoke rising from what appeared to be a burning Paragon administrative building on a different planet. More images cycled through, one after another, each showing different scenes of chaos and carnage. The reporter continued, speaking over them. "It seems as if we hear about a new terrorist attack somewhere in the Paragon every day. Do you believe that there is any connection between these attacks?"

The enforcer representative shook her head. "Only in the sense that chaos breeds chaos. We have no reason to believe that there is any grand, unified threat to the Paragon other than the threat of disunity. These attacks are all the work of groups of cowards, working from the shadows, who hate the Paragon and hate the freedom and happiness that it has brought to humanity. They would see us return to an age of discord, when humanity was divided by planet, system, and creed. They hate us, and they hate all of *you* watching. So remember, if you hear any kind of support for these vicious attacks, for your family's safety, report it to your local enforcers. In particular, we are still searching far and wide for an armed and dangerous Brahmian rebel who goes by the name of *Artemis*."

A grainy image of a woman's face—sharp-featured and beautiful, with black hair and piercing eyes—appeared on the screen. Memories surged through me. A single gunshot echoing in a Gharseva back alley. Black hair wild as her head snapped backward. Blood pooling around her as she crumbled to the street. Eladrius, turning his aim on me.

I forced myself to look away. They'd been cycling that

image for a while now. I wasn't sure exactly how much they knew about Artemis, but nobody had come asking any questions around here yet, so I figured that we were in the clear—for now.

"She is said to be in the company of two rogue Vanguard soldiers. She is believed to be connected to the incident on Brahma as well as—" the enforcer seemed to catch herself midsentence. "As well as other incidents."

I grimaced. I had no idea how much of what had happened on the *Revelation* had made its way back to Paragon intelligence, but this enforcer certainly seemed to at least be aware of it. My guess was that the battlecruiser had sent some sort of automated signal to the Paragon when we shut down Ramar's malware.

"Turn that crap off!" Rose's voice rang out sharply across the bar. "We're here to celebrate!"

The bartender hit a button on a remote and the screen powered off with a click. I glanced over at Rose, who met my eye only briefly before looking away. She'd been avoiding me the whole journey home from our near disaster aboard the mysterious transport.

"You think..." Nadus frowned at the now blank screen. "Never mind."

I glanced at him. "What?"

His eyes were thoughtful. Guilty. "Do you ever wonder if we should, you know... be out there? Joining the fight?"

I raised an eyebrow. "Against the Paragon?"

"Yeah." He finally looked away from the screen and into his glass with a glum expression. "I dunno. Just seems like there's more we could—*should*—be doing, you know? Trying to do some good for a change?"

Guilt tugged at the corners of my mind. I did know. But I shoved the feeling away. "Yeah. But it's not our problem. We've got plenty of our own problems to deal with right here."

His eyes didn't move from his drink. "Even if everything that's happening out there is our fault?"

I stiffened. He kept talking, his voice quiet. "None of this would be happening if it weren't for us. Even if you ignore our part in the war itself. We went to Brahma looking for a payday. And now, because we were there, hundreds of rebels are dead. Including the ones you—" He caught himself and turned his eyes downward again. "*We* killed."

My thoughts were pulled inexorably back to Brahma. To the screams that Tekka's team—*my* team, people I'd spent hundreds of hours training and bonding with—had made as the ultraripper I'd unleashed on them tore them to shreds. To the way Tekka's body had convulsed when I'd put that armor-piercing round through his head. To the plumes of smoke rising over Gharseva in the aftermath of the enforcer attack on the Khendars and their rebels. And then, even further back, to the first time I'd been to Brahma. Beautiful green fields turned brown and red. Thriving cities ravaged by bombardments and rippers alike. A rebel soldier—not much more than a kid—kicking his legs wildly as his skull slowly fractured in my gauntleted fist, caving, breaking... *CRUNCH.*

My lungs constricted. My muscles tightened. My breathing shallowed.

Nadus was right. No matter how you looked at it, there was no escaping the awful arithmetic. My hands weren't just bloodied. They were dripping with blood, making a long, crimson trail everywhere I went. I wasn't egotistical enough to believe that the current unrest in the galaxy was *entirely* my fault, but I wasn't naïve enough to think my actions hadn't contributed, either.

Calm. I took a long, slow drink, letting my heart rate settle. When I felt calm again, I spoke, my voice sounding more confident than I felt. "Maybe. Or maybe it would've been someone else. Paragon's always been an unstable ultracell just waiting for the right spark to set it off. Either way, there's no point in getting involved now."

"Yeah." Nadus rubbed wearily at his brow. "Guess you're right. Just been weighing on me lately. Forget I said anything." He glanced up at the clock, then cursed under his breath, finished his drink in one gulp, and rose to his feet.

I frowned up at him. "Where are you going? Seems like I barely see you around the station these days."

He shrugged. "Just... out."

I studied him for a moment, trying to work it out. More and more over the past few months he'd been disappearing between jobs. I hadn't thought too much of it up until now. After all, that was free time. What my crew did when they weren't on the *Orpheus* was none of my business. Still—it was odd he wouldn't tell me. Or maybe Rose's little stunt just had me acting paranoid.

I nodded, and he walked out of the bar. I watched him go, the guilt that had built up during our conversation slowly growing heavier. I wanted to be irritated with him, but the harder I tried, the more I found my anger flipped around on myself. Truth was that I agreed with everything he'd said. I *did* feel responsible for what had happened on Brahma. I did feel guilty for killing Tekka, even if it had been the closest thing to the right choice I could come up with. I did feel guilty knowing that the galaxy was burning down around my ears while I hid under Sevani's wing here on Albeni 7 and pretended I had nothing to do with the chaos unfolding. With the lives being ruined daily across the stars.

"That does *not* look like the face of a man who just became rich."

I turned back to the bar to see Sevani easing herself onto the stool Nadus had just vacated. Her sharp green eyes and wavy brown hair reflected the neon-blue light from the sign behind the bar. The sign bore the name of the place: *Tyrell's Bar.*

Sevani gave a crisp nod to the bartender, and he reached below the bar for a bottle of faintly blue liquid and a shot glass. He placed both in front of her.

I grunted. "That's what Rose told you, huh?"

"She said it was a success," Sev said. "And that you brought in a good haul. I've learned better than to pry her for details."

I grimaced. "It was a good haul, alright. Too good."

Sev raised an eyebrow.

I explained what had happened, leaving nothing out. Sevani listened intently, eyes narrowing the longer I spoke. When I finished, she leaned forward onto the bar and massaged her temples with her fingers, groaning.

I grimaced. "Yeah."

"*No.*" She reached for a drink.

I frowned. "No?"

"*No.* You don't get to say that. You don't know what's going on. I do. Do you have any idea who you just robbed?"

I raised an eyebrow. "The pirate? Renault?"

She scoffed. "No. He's a different problem altogether. Fancies himself king of the pirates or some nonsense. I've lost three good ships to that poser."

"King of the *Buccaneers*," I corrected. "He made sure to emphasize that. Seems to have a little crush on you. He knew exactly who we were. Said he was trying to talk to you. Something about..." I waved my hand vaguely. "Had a hard time following it, to be honest, what with everything going on. Something about ambition. New powers in the Paragon or whatnot. Sounded like he wanted to strike some sort of deal with you, and thought that capturing us would give him bargaining power."

She waved a dismissive hand. "No. Not him. I don't know how he followed you there, or why, but that wasn't his cargo you stole."

I frowned. "Then whose?"

"Have you ever heard of a man named Adrian Vatheson?"

"No."

She pulled out her handcomputer and input a few commands. A few moments later she showed me an image of a strikingly handsome man looking to be in his mid-twenties or so, wearing a shimmering suit coat that looked like it cost more than everything I owned. "He's the Paragon's official overseer for the Boadicea system," Sev said. "Has been for nearly thirty years."

I frowned. "He doesn't—"

"Look old enough? I know. Adrian Vatheson is almost eighty years old. But when you're rich enough to get whatever medical procedure, you want..." She shrugged. "Age just becomes an idea."

I kept on staring at the picture. "But how—"

"Doesn't matter." She shook her head. "His age isn't the point. The point is that for the past thirty years now, Vatheson has used his position to court the favor of the most powerful people in the Paragon. He's built the most luxurious citystation in the Paragon—a dream destination for the rich and elite. Normally, I wouldn't care. But recently, he's started dipping his toes into the underworld. Using his influence to acquire rare goods for cheap and making a killing selling them beneath the table."

I nodded slowly. "Alright. So what's the connection?"

"This is." She hit a button. The image of Vatheson began to move.

"*Sevani,*" he said. His voice was unnaturally smooth, and the smile that went with it just a tad too wide. "*I hope you are doing well. I recognize that our business often puts us as rivals with one another, and yet I hope you know that I nonetheless hold you in high regard, as both a competitor and a neighbor. I—*"

"It... goes on like this for a minute." Sev fast forwarded. "Here."

"*Unfortunately, however...*" Vatheson's smile slipped. "*I have run into a... predicament. Just a few short hours ago, a hidden stash of mine containing... highly valuable cargo was robbed. Now, I know that you share the same respect for me that I possess for you. And so I do not for a minute believe that you would stoop so low as to steal from me. And so instead of coming to you with accusations, I come to you with a simple question. Do you or do you not know anything about these individuals?"*

The image of Vatheson vanished, replaced by a grainy image of several individuals in exosuits in a small, cramped room. No—a vault. And not just any individuals. Us.

"Dammit all," I muttered. There'd been a hidden camera somewhere in that vault, clearly hooked up to a quantum network. There didn't seem to be audio, though, and from the images alone, it was difficult to identify the exos.

"It's a long shot, I know." Vatheson's face reappeared. His expression made it clear that he thought it was anything *but* a long shot. *"I know that you've been out of the salvage business for many years now. And despite the rumors I hear of her adventures, I'm sure that you'd never allow your daughter to do something so... dangerous. But I am very eager to have this cargo returned to me, and so I simply request that if you know anything about its disappearance, you tell me. If not..."* His smile faded. *"Well. Then I suppose I shall have to begin taking more drastic measures to recover my property. And that would simply be a hassle."*

He vanished. Sev powered off the handcomputer and looked at me.

Now it was my turn to groan. I shut my eyes for a moment, rubbing my forehead.

Dammit. I'd *known* something was off about that ship. It was too untouched, too far, too *new* to match the profile of any regular salvage job. Why hadn't I just listened to my gut and turned around the moment the situation felt off?

There are two kinds of pain, boy...

"Alright," I said. "So. We give it back to him. Explain it was a mistake. Tell him that—"

Sev shook her head sharply. "It wouldn't be enough. He'd demand blood. Yours, specifically. And he might not even be content to stop there."

"Why not?"

"Because for all his talk of the property *you* stole from *him*," Sev said, "The most important factor here is who *he* stole it from in the first place."

"Divinity," I muttered.

Sev nodded, her eyes grim. "Vatheson can get away with just about anything because he knows all the right pockets to funnel cash into. His enterprise is built on Paragon corruption. But there's no bribing Divinity. I don't know how he got this Lifeblood stuff from them in the first place, but you can bet your ass that if they find out he has it—*had* it—there'll be no escape for him."

Which explained why Vatheson was so desperate to get it back. As much as the Paragon liked to pretend that they ruled the galaxy—or the relatively tiny portion of it humanity had colonized so far, anyways—it was an open secret that they danced to the Divinity Corporation's music. We all did, one way or another. Divinity produced all the technology that made the Paragon run. Rippers, ultracells, Vanguards, this Lifeblood stuff. And they were *extremely* jealous guardians of their secrets. There was a reason that the Paragon had been so adamant about covering up the *Revelation*'s mysterious disappearance. If I was in Vatheson's shoes I'd be panicking too.

I gave a weary sigh. "So what do we do?"

"Nothing. You lie low. If he suspects anybody, it'll be all of you—and he'll be certain to be surveilling everything he can on this station. Sending his spies to poke around. My people are loyal, for the most part, but I'm not so cocky as to believe that at least some of them won't turn informant for him for the right price. Starting now, I'd say nothing on this station is secure."

I cursed under my breath. "What about the cargo?"

"I'll work something out. Best bet will be to move it as discreetly as I can, then either stash it somewhere in deep space or simply jettison it. The only certain thing is that you absolutely *cannot* sell it. To anyone. That's exactly what he'll be watching for."

So just... sit around here?"

"Yes."

I nodded. "Sounds good to me. I don't think I'm the one you'll have to convince, though."

Sev turned towards her daughter, narrowing her eyes. Rose showed no indication that she thought anything was amiss. "She told you the tip was anonymous?"

"Yeah. Eventually. Think she knew I'd veto the job if she told me up front." I turned back to my drink. "Clearly, somebody set us up. I just don't know who."

"Obviously not Renault," Sev said thoughtfully. "Have Bentley do a clean sweep of the *Orpheus*. Renault must have managed to slip a tracker on you somehow. It's the only way he could've followed you out there. But I agree. Somebody wanted you to take that cargo."

"The real question," I said, "is who would even know it was there in the first place."

Sev nodded. "I'll put some feelers out. See what I can find. In the meanwhile, talk to Rose. See what else she knows." She drew her lips to a thin line. "As much as I hate to say it, she's far more likely to tell you than me."

I sighed. "Maybe. She's never outright lied to me about something before, though. Not like this, at least."

Sev studied Rose, her eyes dark and serious. For my part, I found myself struggling to wrest my gaze from Sev. Maybe I'd just been too infatuated with Kessa back in the day to notice it, but Sev was strikingly beautiful. I felt guilty the moment the thought struck me and turned quickly back to my drink, shoving the thought aside.

"She's just straining at the leash you've put on her," Sev said quietly. "All that girl wants is to prove she can make it on her own. To take risks and have adventures."

"Like we did," I said. "You can't blame her, really."

"No, you can't. That's what makes it so damn frustrating." Sev chuckled. "It's my fault, really. The stories I used to tell her about our adventures... I *may* have overromanticized them. Just a little."

"They *were* romantic," I said. I flushed slightly as I saw the odd look Sev was giving me. "In a general sense, I mean. You know. For all I liked to complain, those were good times. The best times."

Sev smiled. "Yeah. They were."

We sat in silence for a few moments, our smiles slowly fading as we rolled over that last word in our heads. *Were.* We'd had our adventures, sure. And then they'd come to a grim, abrupt end.

"She really is good," I said. "And the rest of them are too. At least as good as we were. I wish I could tell them to have at it. It's just..."

"It's more complicated than it was for us," Sev finished for me. "Especially after last year."

"Yeah. It'd be one thing if we were just regular vultures. But if word gets out of what we did—what we found out on the *Revelation*..." I trailed off, feeling vaguely sick as I thought through—for the thousandth time—what the consequences of our secret being unleashed would mean. Not for me—but for everybody else. The Paragon wouldn't rest until they'd hunted every last one of us down.

I shook myself. "What really matters right now is keeping our heads low. Keeping out of trouble." I jerked my head towards the black screen. "War might be just around the corner, but I'll be damned if I'm getting pulled into it again."

Sev's vivid green eyes turned thoughtfully to me. "Is that why you turned down Ramar?"

Ramar. Yet another name to feel guilty about. I took a slow sip from my drink, hoping it would wash away the vaguely sick feeling I got whenever I thought about the rogue scientist. It didn't.

After I'd saved him from the *Revelation,* he'd vanished into the void—which was fine by me. In fact, I'd managed to almost forget about him until about a month ago, when he'd suddenly walked back through the doors of Tyrell's Bar.

"I thought you wanted me to say no to him," I said.

"I did. And I'm still glad you did. I was still surprised by it, though. Especially after that whole speech he gave you last year. You know, about your part in all this not being over and what-not." She shrugged. "What did he want, anyways?"

I grimaced, thinking back to the conversation. "He wanted my help. Said he'd found out what happened to the *Panama.*"

She paled. "Oh."

"Yeah." I sighed. I'd had just about the same reaction when he'd told me. "He thought there might be a chance that somebody had gotten ahold of the ultrarippers that were on there. Wanted me to help him find out."

She swirled her drink in her cup, staring thoughtfully—morbidly—into it. "And... were you tempted?"

"No." I regretted the lie the moment it was out of my lips. "Yes. How could I not be? But..." I glanced back towards Rose and the rest of the crew. *Green dots, flashing red.* "I've dragged them into enough trouble as is. I'm trying to keep them *out* of it for a change."

"I would argue that it was Artemis who dragged you all into trouble last time," Sev said, raising her glass and taking a long drink. She made little attempt to hide her distaste as she said the name. I didn't particularly blame her. I hadn't liked Artemis at first, either. It had taken nearly dying together a few times to get her to open up her steely exterior and show her more human, vulnerable side.

Sev started to speak but hesitated, giving me a sideways look. "I never could figure it out. Did you and her..."

"Nothing ever happened," I said, a bit more sullenly than I'd intended to.

"Ah." She gave a grin that was equal parts mischief, alcohol, and... something else. Relief, maybe? "So you just *wish* she'd rubbed off on you."

I glared at her.

She winced. "Too soon?"

I said nothing, turning away to glower into my cup. It wasn't too soon, really—or at least, I felt as if it shouldn't be. A full year had passed since our disastrous adventure on the *Revelation*. A full year since Artemis had been killed. Far longer than Artemis and I had actually known each other. Yet I still felt a pang of regret whenever I thought back to her. She'd deserved better than to die on that Brahmian backstreet. But if everybody got what they deserved—well, I suppose I'd have died a long time ago.

"No," I said, finally. "But... well, Artemis was. I wasn't ready to move on yet. All those years in prison, I never really processed what happened with Kess. Not in any way that let me move forward, at least. I was a walking disaster."

Sev grinned wryly at me. "*Was?*"

I chuckled. "Fair. But... yeah. That stuff you told me, that night I called you from Brahma. And getting off the cans. And being, you know, here. With you, and the crew. It's all helped."

"Yeah. I do. It helps to have someone to talk to." Her smile faded. "Honestly, I didn't really have that until you showed up again. After I got Rose back, I just tried to suppress it all. The grief, the pain. It paid off. But until you showed up, I felt... alone."

I nodded solemnly. I knew all too well what she was talking about. I'd never been alone for so much as a moment during my eight years in prison—and yet I might as well have been the only man in the galaxy, trapped alone with my grief, trying desperately to keep it from consuming me. "It's funny," I said, glancing across the bar towards where Rid was sitting with an arm around Rose's shoulders. "Well—not *funny*. But I think Rid showing up was what saved me. Even more than Nadus." I furrowed my brow, thinking back to when I'd finally decided to stop following Venter's orders and help Rid. "Nadus gave me a way out, but something about Rid woke up that part of me that cared about other people. Guess it just... felt good to be needed again."

"I sure as hell wouldn't have made it without Rose," Sev said. "For the same reason. Knowing she needed me gave me a reason to keep going, even when I didn't want to."

I turned back to my drink, savoring it and then holding it up. "The hell is this stuff, anyway?"

She smiled. "House special—my husband's special mix. Tin Can Blues, he called it."

I glanced at her. Even after a full year since telling me of his existence, Sev was usually reluctant to discuss anything concerning her late husband. I knew better than to pry—after all, I hated it when people brought up Kessa—but I couldn't deny my morbid curiosity. Especially now that she'd brought it up.

"He was a bartender?" I asked.

"Right here." Sev nodded at the bar. "Before... you know. The virus, and the *Panama*."

"You never did tell me his name."

"Everyone knows his name." She raised a glass towards the neon sign. *Tyrell's Bar.*

"Ah." I stared at the flickering letters, a slight tug of guilt pulling at me. "It's funny. I always thought I knew you pretty well, back in the day. When you disappeared for long stretches between jobs I didn't pay it too much mind, figured you were up to your own mischief. Now I feel like the Sev I knew was just... a front."

Sev was quiet for a long moment. "It was never a front," she said finally. "You just knew a... different part of me. Tyrell knew I needed freedom, and I knew he needed stability. We made it work, in our own weird way. He'd laugh if he saw me now—all settled down, wearing suits, managing other people's work." She made a sour face. "All the stuff I swore I'd never do."

I chuckled. "And Kessa would laugh at me. I used to never shut up about how badly I wanted to get us out of the salvage business. Now here I am, right back in it."

Sev smiled at me. "That's fate for you, I guess."

I raised my glass. "To Tyrell, then, huh?"

Sev smiled—a heavy smile that I was well acquainted with. Heavy with memories, good and bad. "And Kess. And Artemis. And Black, and Liung, and all the others we left behind. But, more importantly... to us."

I raised an eyebrow. She clinked her glass gently against mine. "They're all gone," she said gently. "There's no bringing them back. But *we're* still here—for better or worse. So it may as well be better, right?"

"Can't argue with that," I said, and drank.

FOUR

There are two kinds of pain, boy.

"This was a bad idea!" Shell growled into the comms, her voice lurching with each jolt from her Jackhammer. Nadus was next to her, firing wildly down the corridor into the onrushing horde of rippers.

Guess which kind this is?

"*Hey, don't blame me!*" Rose retorted over the comms. "*I never claimed it was gonna be an easy job.*"

Something wasn't right. I was confused, disoriented. I tried to ground myself, to focus, but there was something coming towards me. Rippers. I pivoted to face them, my thermal blades flaring to life.

"It'll be worth it," Rid was saying. "As long as I can get through this damn door. What kind of passenger transport has a heavy-duty vault anyways?"

"Probably the kind that should be *left alone!*" Bentley shouted.

I shook myself. The transport. Of course. We had to disable the ship's automatic security system so that we could escape. Before Renault arrived.

Except that this all looked wrong. This hallway didn't look like the luxury cruiser's hallway. No fancy doorways, no carpeted floors. It was all stark, utilitarian. Familiar.

I *knew* this place. But there was no time to work out why. The rippers were almost on top of me. I braced myself, dropping into a defensive fighting stance. Something was off about them. Limbs too long. Claws too short.

Guess which kind this is?

They didn't spring for me. None of them paused to launch their tails. Instead, they just sprinted as if to go right past me, to get to my crew. I bellowed and swung, my blade passing cleanly through the first several of them—

With no effect.

The rippers ran straight through it, as if it wasn't there. Not a scratch on them. I blinked in confusion, then swung again, flailing desperately, angrily at them, but I might as well have been a child trying to beat the wind with a stick. One of them ran right through me, passing straight through my leg as if it was a hologram. As if *I* was a hologram.

"Guys," I said. "Something is—"

Screams. I pivoted. My eyes widened with horror. As immaterial as the rippers were to me, they were *not* to the rest of my crew.

There are two kinds of pain, boy.

Bentley was shouting, his voice hoarse and high-pitched as he swatted at a ripper that was pinning him to the floor, claws tearing great chunks out of his armor. Rid was gagging, his voice choked and wet, as several of the creatures burrowed into his gut. Shell gave a startled cry as a claw sliced cleanly through her breastplate, blood bubbling through the three long incisions in the metal. Nadus bellowed, Jackhammer firing wildly but ineffectively as he spun, trying desperately to shake off the rippers clinging to his back.

Guess which kind this is?

Noise behind me—heavy footsteps. Metal scraping against metal. I whirled. A monstrous shape loomed down the corridor. Far bigger than the other rippers, with two great, metallic wings extending from its back. I felt a cold chill run down my spine. One of the evolved rippers we'd encountered aboard the *Revelation*. One of Ramar's special mutants. An ultraripper.

There are two kinds of pain, boy.

"You're dead," I growled, raising my thermal blades. "All of you. You died with the *Revelation*. Blown to bits and sucked into a black hole."

The winged ripper stopped, looming over me. The unmarked flesh covering its face slowly tore open, blood gushing from the open wound to reveal its layered, metallic teeth and a long, snake-like tongue.

"*Not... all... of... us,*" it hissed.

I suddenly recognized where we were. We weren't on the luxury cruiser. And we weren't on the *Revelation*. We were on the *Panama*. The long, dark corridor stretched out vast and infinite and bloody and lined with thousands of corpses. Rose. Rid. Shell and Bentley and Nadus, rippers still feasting on their corpses. Kessa and Black and the rest of my old crew. Tekka and his team. An untold amount of rebels who'd died by my hand as they desperately tried to defend their homes.

Guess which kind this is?

The ripper reared, opened its maw, and lunged towards me.

"Lax?"

I sat up abruptly. A small glimmer of light was being cast into my room through a crack in the door. Real estate was a precious commodity on Albeni 7, but Sev had still managed to set each of us up with rooms that we could use while we were here. I squinted to see Rid's sharp features watching me through the door, his eyes concerned.

"Yeah?" I groaned.

"You alright?"

I raised a hand and wiped at my brow. It came back glistening with sweat. My knuckles were cracked and bloody. I winced and looked over at the wall beside my bed—the one dividing my room from Rid's. There was a large, blood-spattered crater in it.

"Yeah," I said. "Sorry I woke you."

He made no motion to leave. "Kess?"

"No."

"Artemis?"

I looked back to Rid. He was shirtless, and in the darkness, the glowing red skull tattoo on his neck was casting a sullen, burning light over his lean figure. All in one piece. All his guts securely where they belonged. I tried to chase away the still-lingering mental image of rippers tearing into his abdomen.

"Vanguard?" He was working through a shopping list of all my most traumatic moments. And damn me if it wasn't one hell of a list. "Or Tekka? You still feel guilty about—"

"I'm fine, Rid," I said. "Go back to bed."

He studied me for another moment, then simply nodded and shut the door.

I reached down and tugged my sheets off, tossing them aside. They were tangled and twisted and wet with perspiration. It had been months since I'd had an episode this bad. I groaned, placing my feet on the floor and my head in my hands. Dammit. Just when I thought I'd been getting better. That I was getting over it all.

I desperately wanted a can. Just a hit. Something to take the edge off, to dull the pain. Instead, though, I sat up, closed my eyes, and took a long, deep breath. I hadn't touched a can in over six months now. There was a doctor on Albeni 7—an ex-military psychologist who specialized in helping guys who'd been through hell. Guys like me. I'd seen him a few times at Sev's insistence, and for the most part it had helped. Helped to have someone to talk to. Helped to have actual medicine to take instead of the same depressants the Paragon had shoved down my throat in the Vanguard. Frigicerin wasn't meant to heal—it was meant to suppress, to keep bloodthirsty super-soldiers like me in check.

But that line of thinking wasn't helping. I pulled my thoughts back to Doc. *Breathe*, he'd said. *When everything feels like it's going to hell, step back to the beginning. By breathing. That's where it all starts. Then you can see the whole picture.*

So I breathed. In and out. Deep, heavy breaths, trying to focus as much of my attention on each inhalation and exhalation as I could and clearing everything else out of my mind. Like I was rebooting an overheated computer system. It wasn't easy, and it didn't feel natural. It felt like I was deliberately turning my back on a threat. But I'd been through this before, so I kept going.

It worked. Bit by bit, my heart rate slowed and my thoughts ordered themselves into something resembling linearity. Finally, I stood with a groan and walked towards the tiny washroom connected to my apartment. Well—tiny by my standards, at least. Most folks living on Albeni 7 were lucky if they lived within a five-minute walk of a public washroom. Water was always a precious commodity on space stations.

That was yet another source of guilt for me. My quarters might not have seemed like much to boast about, but I'd been around enough to know that by most people's standards—especially on Albeni 7—I was living a life of luxury. People who deserved better all around me lived and died in squalor. Families, doctors, teachers, the like. People who left the universe a better place than they'd found it.

My movement activated a dim light on the washroom ceiling. I glanced up at the mirror hanging above the sink. In the sullen glow my eyes looked hollow and dark. Dozens of scars across my body cast gnarled patchwork shadows. The metallic ports in my shoulder glinted dully. My knuckles were caked black with congealed blood.

All I'd ever left behind me were bodies, as far back as I could remember. Bodies across a dozen planets during the war. Kessa and my crew, taken by ultrarippers on the *Panama*. Artemis, left behind on Brahma. Tekka and his rebels, killed by my own hand on the *Revelation*. Any one of those people probably had more to offer the world than I did. Any one of them might actually have been able to help people instead of hurt them.

And yet here I was. Somehow, for some inexplicable, unknowable reason, still alive. Despite all the wars and rebels and assassins and pirates and rippers that had left so many of my friends and companions dead.

There he is, ladies and gentlemen. The Luckiest Man in the Universe.

FIVE

I fought back a grimace as I climbed the hatch that led to the *Orpheus*'s bridge. Seemed like it got a little longer every time I went up it. Maybe being a vulture was a young person's game—and I certainly wasn't young anymore.

"Rose," I said as I ascended the bridge hatch. "We need to..."

Rose, Shell, Bentley and Rid were all gathered around the large holoprojector in the center of the room. I caught a brief glimpse of what looked like ship schematics before Rose hit a button and powered down the projector.

"Yes?" she said, fighting a grin that was half embarrassed guilt—like a child caught in the middle of some small act of disobedience—and half a mischievous, challenging smirk.

I sighed. "Rose. Can I talk to you?"

"Sure." She settled back into her seat. Bentley and Shell shared an uncertain look.

"Alone," I growled.

She gave the others a short nod. One by one, they left the bridge.

"Go easy on her," Rid muttered as he passed.

Finally, we were alone. Rose raised an eyebrow. "Well?"

I stared at her a moment, then lowered myself into one of the vacated seats. "Rose... what were you *thinking*?"

She lifted her chin defiantly. "That it's beyond time for us to take some *actual* jobs."

"That's fine. But you've got to *tell me first*." I leaned forward. "You violated the trust of the entire crew, Rose. Put them all in unnecessary danger. And now we're in serious trouble."

"Not the whole crew," she said quietly.

I frowned. "What do you mean?"

"They knew," she said. She jerked her head towards the hatch. "Rid, Bentley, Shell. They agreed to it."

I narrowed my eyes.

"Don't blame them," she said quickly. "I engineered it all. None of them liked it. But my point is that they all agreed with me. Well, Bentley took some convincing, and I couldn't tell Nadus cause he'd tell you, but—"

"Agreed about *what*?" I snapped.

Rose set her jaw. "That we should be trying to make a difference. That we should be *doing* stuff, instead of just taking the lamest, safest jobs."

My fists clenched of their own accord. "How in the hell do you think that—" I paused. *Breathe. That's where it all begins.* After a moment, I relaxed my hands and sagged back into my chair, massaging my temples.

"What else don't I know?" I asked wearily.

"Nothing." She leaned forward, her eyes earnest. "Honestly. All I kept from you was that the source was anonymous. I knew you wouldn't take the job if I told you. I had no idea those pirates would show up."

"Did you know about Vatheson?"

She frowned. "Who?"

"The system overseer," I groaned, "whose hidden stash of smuggled rare goods we just robbed?"

She shrugged. "No. But there's no way he knows it was us. Is there?"

"He'll find out, Rose." I studied her, trying to wrap my brain around how somebody so sharp could do something so damn *stupid*. "This isn't some backspace crime boss we're talking about. This is a man with powerful connections and a hell of a lot to lose. The last kind of enemy we need right now. We won't even be able to sell the Lifeblood. Not while he's looking for it, at least. I..." I trailed off as I noticed Rose's expression turn sour. "What?"

She grimaced. "I guess there is one other thing you don't know."

I felt suddenly queasy. "What?"

"We kind of already have a buyer lined up."

It took all of my restraint not to leap from my chair. "*What?*"

She grinned apologetically. "Surprise?"

"They're Roamers," Shell said, her voice stoic as ever. She glanced at the rest of the crew, gathered again in the bridge, as she spoke. "News of the transaction won't ever make it back to this Vatheson fellow."

I stared at the rotating image hovering before me. A Roamer homeship, fifteen kilometers long. An Exodus class vessel, built in the days before ultracells or foldgates or quantum communication, with a singular goal: to carry as many humans as possible as far away from Earth as possible. Some two thousand years later and millions of lightyears away, it was still functioning.

I shook my head. "How could you possibly know that? Roamers are as involved in smuggling as anybody. More so, even."

Shell looked to Rose, who nodded encouragingly to her.

Bentley and Rid watched on with uncertain expressions, while Nadus—whom I'd called the moment I found out Rose was planning a rogue job—studied the three-dimensional image of the Exodus ship with a curious expression. I'd been relieved to find that he, at least, hadn't been part of the conspiracy.

"Not these ones," Shell said finally. "I know because..." She hesitated, grimaced, and finally gave a resigned sigh. "Because it's the *Aboena*. My homeship."

I stared at her. "I thought you were exiled."

"I was," she said stiffly.

"When I got that anonymous tip," Rose said, not meeting my eyes, "they told me that they had a buyer who was interested in the cargo the transporter contained. They wouldn't tell us who until after we'd finished the job."

"So you're still in contact with this source?" I asked.

Rose pointed towards the comms station. I sighed and moved to the computer, scanning through a screen full of back and forth messages. The most recent:

ORPHEUS: *Why should we trust you? We don't know who you are.*

CONTACT: *I can't tell you who I am. If anybody on the* Aboena *finds out I contacted an Outsider it will end poorly.*

ORPHEUS: *Why?*

CONTACT: *Command has ordered all outside communications be terminated. But people here are starving. Dying. Desperate. They need those supplies. You will be well rewarded.*

I leaned back in my seat. "You're being played," I growled. "You know that, right?"

"What makes you so sure?" Rose asked indignantly.

"I just am." I pointed at the message. "For one thing, if this is some Roamer who's stuck on the *Aboena*, how the hell did they know where the Lifeblood was?"

"I don't know," Rose said. "But it's not impossible that they have some outside intelligence."

"How do you know they're not planning on just luring us in then killing us and taking it?"

"Isn't that a risk you run with any job?" Rose asked. "We'll be careful. Keep our guard up."

I turned to Shell, glowering. "And *you* believe all this?"

She shrugged noncommittally. "The *Aboena* cut off all contact with the outside world several years ago. Nobody knows why. But it's not inconceivable that somebody aboard could be smuggling goods in and out. There would certainly be a demand for it."

"Sure," I said. "But they reached out to *us* specifically."

Shell shifted uncomfortably. "It's... possible that they may have chosen our crew because they knew I was on it."

I raised an eyebrow at her. "You have friends you keep in touch with on the *Aboena*?"

"I *had* friends. I don't keep in contact with them. But it's too strong of a coincidence for me to ignore the possibility that somehow somebody on the *Aboena* knew I was flying with Rose."

"Or, again," I said, "that somebody *outside* the *Aboena* already knows about all that and is playing us."

"The message definitely came from the *Aboena*," Bentley said. "I was able to trace the message. Whoever sent it used a personal communication device, though, not an official ship array. Meaning it wasn't an official transmission. Which..." He glanced around, his face growing slightly red. "I suppose we already knew, but..."

I turned my attention back to the hovering image of the

Aboena. I couldn't shake an ominous feeling when I looked at it. A dreadful inevitability.

"Nadus," I asked softly. "What do you think?"

He finally lifted his eyes from the blueprints, settling them on me. I could tell just from looking at him that he had the same bad feeling I did.

"It's your call, boss," he said. "But if what they're saying is true... if those people really need that Lifeblood..." He shrugged, looking back down to the holoprojector. "Then it seems like the best chance we've had in a hell of a long time to do some actual good for a change."

Silence fell, all eyes watching me.

I wanted to say no. I knew that *something* about this was going to explode in our faces, and that when it did, we'd have nobody but ourselves to blame. But... dammit, Rose just looked so *excited*. So eager. They all did, in their own various ways. Bentley for the money. Rid because it was what Rose wanted. Shell because, despite her best efforts to hide it, I could tell she was having a hard time rejecting a call for help from her home. And Nadus for the same reason that I did, deep down. That gnawing feeling of guilt. That little worm boring into our brains, whispering constantly: *you ruined the universe.*

Seemed like anything we could do to fix it again—even if it was just a little bit—and even if it was probably a trap—was worth a shot.

"Two things," I said.

Rose perked up, her eyes incredulous.

"First," I said, "if we do this, nothing else gets hidden from me. Second, I get final say. If we get there and I think it's too dangerous, we turn around and I don't want a word of complaint out of any of you. If this mystery contact changes the deal or tries to screw us, we walk away. Understood?"

Nods all around, none of them more eager than Rose's.

"And third," I said, looking Rose in the eyes. "When this *does* blow up in our faces, I reserve the right to say I told you so."

She grinned. "You've got a deal."

I turned back to the *Aboena*, stared at it for a long moment, and then released a long burst of air through my nostrils.

"Fine." I straightened. "Set it up."

Rose gave an excited whoop and hugged Rid, who mouthed *thank you* at me. Shell's shoulders sagged slightly in what I'd learned was a sign of relief. Bentley beamed in such a way that if I'd been a fanciful person I'd have sworn I could see little cartoon credit symbols in his eyes. Nadus just nodded slowly to himself, not taking his eyes from the *Aboena*.

Rose moved over to hug me, but I stopped her with a raised hand. "Don't be celebrating yet," I growled. "We've gotta have *maximum* operational security here. Nobody knows where we're going but Sev. I don't want anybody to even know that we're leaving until we're long gone." I grimaced. "Except for, you know, the mysterious contact we have no way of vetting."

Rose straightened and gave me an overexaggerated salute. "Aye-aye, cap'n."

I gave an exasperated sigh to cover up the amused smile that was at great risk of creeping onto my face. "Alright, get to work. Everyone knows their jobs."

They did. Within moments, only Nadus and I remained at the projector, with everybody else busily making preparations.

"Is this a bad idea?" I asked.

"Yeah." He nodded, then grinned wryly. "But it's the worst kind of bad idea. The kind you really have no choice but to go through with."

"Sure feels that way," I muttered.

He slapped me on the back and turned away. "We'll make it through. We always do. And maybe—just maybe—we'll have made the universe a slightly better place when we're done."

I nodded slowly. I didn't believe it. But it was a good thought nonetheless.

He left me alone. I gave the *Aboena* one final, scrutinizing, accusatory stare. *What are you hiding?*

It didn't answer, of course, but if a holographic blueprint of a spaceship could look smug and secretive, well, this one did.

There are two kinds of pain, my old man muttered in my ear. *Guess which kind this'll be?*

SIX

Times run differently on a space station. With no day or night to govern their sleep cycles, folks just settle into whatever rhythm works for them. Because of this, most stationside businesses don't really have a "closed" period.

Tyrell's Bar was the rare exception. Once per twenty-four-hour wake cycle, it would shut down for two hours. Some of this was used for deeper cleaning that was hard to do with customers around. But for most of it, the bar sat empty and dark, despite the customers that otherwise would certainly have filled it—and, by extension, Sev's pockets.

Except today. Today, I sat there, waiting beneath the neon blue light behind the bar. I didn't have to wait long before I heard the door open and close behind me.

"You're lucky I think before I shoot, or you might have a hole in the back of your head."

I chuckled. "Luckiest man in the universe, I've been told."

Sev's footsteps clicked on the floor as she walked across the room and slid onto the barstool next to me. She raised an eyebrow at the two empty glasses and bottle of Tin Can Blue I'd set out on the bar. "I see you've prepared."

"Well, ambushing you during your alone time like this." I shrugged. "Figured I may as well make it at least somewhat enjoyable."

She eyed me, then shrugged and lifted the bottle, removing the top. "Well, then. To what do I owe this ambush?"

"We found a buyer," I said.

The bottle wavered.

"Just wanted to give you a heads up," I finished.

She composed herself, then finished pouring two drinks. I raised an eyebrow. "You really have changed. Back in the day I think you'd have socked me right there and then."

"Maybe," she admitted. "And maybe I'd have enjoyed it. But I've been in business long enough to know that when someone with your experience admits to doing something so catastrophically dumb after being specifically told *not* to do it, there's usually a good reason for it." She took long drink, wiped her mouth, and gave me a warning look. "And so, with that in mind, I am allowing you the opportunity to prove me right. *Before* I punch you."

I filled her in. Again. She listened carefully. Again.

"You know you're getting played, right?" she asked when I'd finished.

I lifted one palm in a gesture of helplessness. "That's what I told them."

"Yeah, but then you agreed to go along with it anyways."

"They're all convinced." I raised my glass to my lips. "Even Shell thinks there may actually be something to it. Honestly, that's half the reason I'm willing to see it through."

She nodded thoughtfully. "I still think it puts you in an unnecessary amount of danger."

I shrugged. "I agree."

She side-eyed me. "I still think it puts *my daughter* in an unnecessary amount of danger."

"I agree with that too. But honestly, at this point I think

she'd just go off and do it on her own if I refused to sign off on it." I stared down into my drink. "I'm trying my hardest, Sev. I really am. To keep them all safe. To keep them out of the way. But it seems like the harder I try, the harder they—*she*—pulls away."

"Of course she does. It's like we talked about before. She wants to be out there, making a difference. Making a name for herself. Carving out a legacy. You can't do that while you're hiding from the universe."

I grimaced. "Yeah. I guess not. And I guess I lost my appetite for all that a long time ago."

"I don't blame you. It fills you up fast." She cast her eye around the bar. "I can honestly say that I didn't set out to become the de facto ruler of Albeni 7. But after... well, you know. Everything that happened to me. To *us*. I guess it sort of just happened."

I frowned. "Rose said you literally killed the resident smuggling master before you."

"Yeah, but not to take his place." She shrugged matter-of-factly. "He just needed killing, in the way that some people do. I had people to protect, Rose chief among them, and it eventually reached a point where killing him was the only way to do it."

I nodded somberly. "You've really gotta tell me that full story."

"Sometime. But not tonight." She rolled the base of her empty glass around on the surface of the bar. "So. It sounds like you're going to the *Aboena*, then."

"Yep."

"And I can't talk you out of it."

"You can talk *me* out of it. It's your daughter I'd be worried about."

She snorted. "Right."

We sat in silence for a few moments. Finally, she sighed and shook her head. "It's funny, but when you told me about what happened with Vatheson's Lifeblood—the first time, I mean, when you stole it—I was almost excited."

I raised an eyebrow. "You that eager to start a war?"

"No. But..." She shrugged, seeming almost embarrassed. "I thought that maybe—just maybe—you'd actually hang around here for a while."

I wasn't sure what to say to that. I half expected her to follow up with a sarcastic barb. Half *hoped* she would. Instead, she looked wistfully around the bar. "Honestly, Lax, sometimes I feel as if you're the only person I can be... *myself* around. When I stepped up and took charge of Odyssey Logistics, I learned very quickly that I had to take most of myself and shove it into a box. Take what worked and leave what didn't. But sometimes..." She shrugged. "I don't know. I guess I just miss the old me. That cocky, chip-on-her-shoulder pilot with the whole universe as her stomping ground. I'd mostly given up on her, until you walked out of the grave and through that door last year."

I studied her for a moment as she stared straight forward. In the darkness of the bar her face was outlined in vivid blue, contrasting the deep shadow that hid the rest of her face. I saw no sign of the smirk she usually wore. Just... thoughtfulness. Remembrance. Regret, maybe.

"You ever think of just... leaving it all behind?" I asked quietly.

She looked at me. "Leaving it for what?"

"I dunno. Anything. Peace."

She laughed. "Peace. I don't know if I believe in such a thing. Maybe it's out there, somewhere. Hidden away like a pirate's buried treasure."

I grinned. "Figure it's at least worth looking for."

"Maybe." She sighed. "And sure, I've thought about it from time to time. About what comes next, at least. But next isn't here yet. Not because I don't want it to be. But because people here rely on me. Nobody else can do what I do here. Not yet. And until somebody else can, I have a responsibility to take care of these people. No matter how much I might detest the fact. It's like you and the crew, just on a larger scale."

I nodded slowly. "Let's make an agreement, then. You do what you've gotta do, and I'll do what I've gotta do. And when we're done..." I shrugged. "Maybe we find that peace out there somewhere."

She raised an eyebrow. "Like buried treasure?"

"Like buried treasure."

She raised one finger like a hook. "Argh?"

I chuckled, then raised my own finger and hooked it around hers in some sort of child's idea of a pirate handshake. "Argh."

We lingered for just a moment with our hands touching, then broke apart in embarrassed giggles that were decidedly unbecoming of a smuggler queen and a veteran Vanguard. Sev brushed a strand of hair away from her eyes and for just a moment I thought she was blushing. My own face felt a bit hot.

"I should go." I stood up, finishing my drink in one swallow, then clinked the empty glass on the bar. "Thanks for the drink. I'll keep Rose safe, like always. You have my word."

"I know."

I turned and headed for the door.

"Lax."

I paused, glancing back at her and expecting some final sarcastic retort. "Yeah?"

She smiled. A small, sad sort of smile, but earnest through and through. "Keep *yourself* safe too."

I nodded and walked away.

———

Normally, I can't help but feel a bit of a thrill while setting out on the *Orpheus*. Maybe it's just the fact that I can still never quite believe I have my old ship back. Or maybe it's the allure of a new adventure, even if it was suppressed beneath several layers of exhaustion and stress. Still—each time we set out, as I watch Albeni 7 grow smaller, then vanish as we breach into nullspace, there's a small part of me that feels renewed. Invigorated.

Not this time. With each second that brought us farther from Albeni 7, I felt my stomach drop a bit lower. When we breached into nullspace, heading towards the foldgate that would take us from the Albeni system to the Alpha Centauri system, the complete darkness enveloping the *Orpheus* held a dreadful finality.

You're making a mistake. I knew it on a deep, instinctive level. But the decision had already been made. And Nadus was right—if Shell's people really did need this cargo, this could be a chance to make a difference for good. To go somewhere and leave behind something other than blood and broken corpses.

So, I did what I do best with unpleasant feelings: suppressed. I shoved them into the cluttered recesses of my mind and focused my attention on the task ahead of us. Theoretically, it was simple. All we had to do was reach the *Aboena*—which, according to our mysterious contact, was currently in a deep orbit in the Erikson system. That meant we'd have to go through the Alpha Centauri gate system. Once we reached the *Aboena*, though, all we would have to do was sneak up to the ship, dock, unload our cargo, get paid, and then fly away.

I had finally managed to convince myself that it just might turn out to be that easy when we reached the Albeni system foldgate.

"Well," I muttered, staring out the *Orpheus*'s front viewport with the rest of the crew, "That went to hell even faster than I figured it would."

"We don't *know* they're here for us," Rose muttered. "Could be a random patrol."

Nadus shook his head. "Sending *that* on a random patrol would be like using an orbital missile system to kill a spider."

"Well, maybe it's a really big spider," Rose muttered.

The object of our attention was a hauntingly familiar one. A massive rectangular shape perched menacingly above—or below, or beside, depending on your point of view—the long queue of vessels waiting to pass through the foldgate and on to their various destinations. It was

dwarfed by the massive foldgate and dwarfed most of the passing ships in turn.

A Paragon battlecruiser. We were still a long ways away from it, but even here, I could make out the name of the ship printed in bold letters along its side: *Leonidas*.

"They're broadcasting," Bentley said. His eyes were focused downward as he clutched the headset attached to the communications computer to his head. "Sending out a general message that no vessels are allowed through until they've received explicit authorization from the *Leonidas*. Then it looks like they're hailing individual ships and forcing them to stop so they can search them."

"What kinds of ships are they stopping?" I asked, though I had a sinking suspicion I already knew.

"Let me check." He input a series of commands, then narrowed his eyes as he scanned the resulting data on his screen. "It's not exact, but there seem to be two main commonalities in the ships getting stopped as opposed to the ones being allowed to pass through. They're all either registered to Odyssey Logistics, or they're smaller ships with stealth capabilities."

Dammit. Damn *all* of it. I leaned against the console, holding back a growl. Vatheson had moved quickly. Sev had said he had influence within the Paragon, but being able to get an entire battlecruiser to attend to his bidding—especially when there were so many problems happening in the Paragon right now—was *way* more than I'd expected him to be able to do. I wasn't sure if he'd sent any more communications to Sev, but the fact that he was specifically targeting ships registered to her company seemed to indicate that he'd given up on civility.

"Mom's gonna be pissed," Rose muttered.

"You think Vatheson's behind this?" Nadus asked.

I nodded. "It's the only thing that makes sense. Like you said—this isn't random. They're looking for someone—or some*thing*—specific. And I'm betting it's us."

"Can we sneak past them?" Rid asked.

Rose squinted at the *Leonidas*. I could tell she wanted to try. She shook her head, though. "We could try. But there are way too many eyes up there."

"So..." Bentley licked his lips nervously. "What do we do?"

I gritted my teeth. No way forward. And if Vatheson had the resources to blockade the foldgate, it would only be a matter of time before he was searching Albeni 7 itself. Which meant going back wasn't an option, either.

"Whatever we do," Rose said, "we better do it quick." She input a command into her console and then pointed at the holo-projector. "They're starting to notice us."

The holoprojector showed a map of the ships around us. The "queue" of waiting ships was quite long, with each vessel leaving at least a kilometer between themselves and their neighbors. A distance like that might sound like a lot of room, but trust me, in space, it's like breathing down somebody's neck. There were five vessels—three of them freighters transporting freshly harvested minerals and the other two cargo vessels—in front of us, each represented by a blinking green dot on the map. One green dot was rapidly moving along the line *towards* us, though. Rose pulled up a databox tagging the dot. A Paragon gunship, similar to the one that the crew had escaped the *Revelation* on.

"They're hailing each ship one by one," Bentley said. "Collecting their information, then giving them instructions."

Rose turned to me. I stared through the *Orpheus*'s front window. I could just barely make out the steady glow of the gunship's thrusters now, propelling it through the void from ship to ship. Pretty soon it would be close enough that if they already knew where we were, activating our stealth systems wouldn't do us a lick of good.

"Get us out of here," I said. "Before they lock us in their sights."

Rose hit a few buttons and the *Orpheus* veered away from the foldgate.

Bentley peered out the back window at the now receding foldgate. "So we just... give up?"

"Consider it a tactical retreat," I said, trying not to show my irritation at the predicament. "Call Sev. I assume she already knows about this, but just in case she doesn't..."

Rose cursed. "We might have a bigger problem."

I whipped my head towards the rear window, expecting to see the gunship turning to give chase to us. It was still on the same trajectory, though. I frowned. "What?"

"Wrong side," Rose said.

All heads turned to peer through the front window—the one that was now looking *away* from the foldgate. Between the stars I spotted a tiny speck moving towards us.

I glanced down at the holodisplay. Another ship had appeared—this one approaching from the opposite direction of the foldgate and the battlecruiser. A databox appeared next to it. An old Redhawk warship.

"You have *got* to be kidding me," I muttered.

The communications computer lit up, making a gentle chiming sound. Shell, sitting closest to it, glanced at the screen. "Incoming message."

"Ignore it. Go around." I shook my head. I had no patience for pirate antics today. Renault might have us pinned between his ship and the *Leonidas*, but if there was one fundamental truth about space, it was that it's *really* damn big. Plenty of other directions to go.

"Well, he's nothing if not persistent," Bentley mused.

"And crazy," Shell said. "Never heard of pirates willing to go anywhere near any strong Paragon presence. Their entire survival depends on not getting on the Paragon radar."

"Used to be that way, at least," Nadus said. "The way he talked last time makes me think he's trying to change things up."

Ambition. I shook my head in exasperation. Right up there with the worst of the vices, in my book. Sure as hell among the most annoying, at least. The incoming message chime was still going. I reached a finger to mute it. "Well, he's sure as hell not gonna change anything on his own. Even if he does have a—"

"Um..." Rose's mouth fell open slightly. "He's not alone."

My finger froze above the mute button. I glanced sharply towards the holodisplay. Five more dots had appeared, each one approaching us from a different direction and closing in rapidly.

I gritted my teeth, considering our options.

They weren't great.

There'd be no hiding from Renault this time. In the time it took us to get to breaching distance he would be able to fire on us with time to spare. The only other option was going back the other way—towards the *Leonidas* and its searching gunships.

I didn't like either choice. But of the two, one seemed far less likely to be fatal.

The *incoming message* tone continued chiming gently.

I sighed. "Answer it."

A familiar, cheery voice crackled to life. *"Why, Lackan VanDunn! Fancy running into you here! What say you and I have a short chat, hmm?"*

SEVEN

The *Orpheus* shuddered slightly as it docked.

I stood before the cargo bay door and waited, letting my hand rest on the handle of Peacebreaker. When it came to ship-to-ship combat, we were hopelessly outgunned. In close quarters fighting, though, I'd be damned if I wasn't going to hold on to whatever power I had.

"*Sealed and locked in,*" Rose's voice said on the overhead speaker. "*You sure you wanna go through with this?*"

Hell no. But I didn't see a choice this time. Renault had caught us with our pants down. We could have tried to make a run for it, but... well, after seeing how quickly the *Walrus* had disposed of that transporter, I didn't feel like taking a gamble. And if that was a gamble, attracting the *Leonidas*'s attention was just straight-up suicide.

The only remaining alternative? Humor the bastard. He insisted he meant us no harm—even as he threatened us. It was time to see what exactly he *did* mean.

I sighed. "Yeah. Let's get it over with."

The airlock opened, followed by the cargo door beyond it. The docking bay before me was small and cramped. Every available space was jammed full of various goods, cargo, and supplies. Bulging sacks hung from the ceiling, stacked crates lined the walls. Standing in the center of the room was a group of ten pirates, each one as varied from the others as the squad of uniformed enforcers would have been identical.

The one in the center—a Vanguard with a badly burned face—stepped forward. He was wearing a dark-blue combat suit and holding what I recognized as an LPS-13 Haymaker shotgun in the crook of his arm. Same technology as Peacebreaker, except on an even larger scale. Perfect for clearing a ship corridor of hostiles. The rest of the pirates seemed to have taken the same combat philosophy to heart, bristling with pistols, shotguns, submachine guns, shields, and melee weapons. All designed to minimize collateral structural damage while maximizing threat. Perfect if you want to clear a hallway full of combatants without damaging the ship you're trying to steal from them.

Ugh. *Pirates.*

The Vanguard cleared his throat. "VanDunn?"

"Yeah."

"Name's Flint," he said, his voice deep and gravelly. "Cap'n wants to talk to you."

I gave a weary shrug. "Let's go, then."

One of the Flint's companions eyed Peacebreaker, holstered on my hip. "Your gun."

"My gun comes with me," I said calmly.

The pirates all looked uncertainly at Flint. He just shrugged and turned away. "You feel like taking it from him, be my guest."

Evidently, they didn't feel like it. They shuffled after me as I followed Flint out of the docking bay.

The corridors of the *Walrus* were just as crowded and grungy as the docking bay. Pirates stopped what they were doing as I passed, watching me with wary eyes. Truth be told, there was nothing especially marking them from any other run-of-the-mill backstation criminals. They were grimy and scrappy and desperate. Most of them looked like they'd seen more than their fair share of combat. Some of them were even wearing the remains of old military uniforms. I saw two men, one wearing a tattered old Paragon officer's coat while the other was shirtless with a large tattoo reading FREEDOM FOR BRAHMA across his back, sitting at a table playing cards together.

Eventually we stopped in front of a large, decorative door. Looked like it had been looted from some other, fancier ship and installed here. The Vanguard pounded twice on it. A few seconds later, it swung open, and I ducked through and into the room beyond.

I'd expected to find myself in a grungy bridge, filled with screens and computer equipment. I couldn't have been more wrong. The room appeared to be some sort of observation deck, with large windows in all directions allowing me to look out into the surrounding stars. It was about twenty meters long and half as wide, with a velvet carpet running down the center. At the end of the carpet was a large, throne-like seat, elevated above the rest of the room. Trophies and treasures were pooled carelessly at the foot of the seat like a dragon's hoard. A coterie of finely dressed pirates stood proudly around the throne, fixing me with steely scowls.

Zathari Renault himself was sprawled across the throne, one leg draped over the armrest in what looked like a carefully practiced pose of self-assured apathy as he lifted a bottle of wine to his lips. He looked to be in his late thirties, with wild black hair and a trimmed goatee. As I entered the room, he shoved the bottle of wine into the hands of one of his sycophants and rose to his feet, spreading his arms and causing the tails of his blood-red coat to flutter majestically.

"Welcome, Lackan VanDunn," he declared with all the pride of a new father showing off his child, "to my kingdom!"

I blinked.

I'll admit that I wasn't sure what to feel in that moment. On the one hand, I found all of the showmanship to be ridiculous. But on the other, I was forced to admit that it somehow *worked*. The figure standing before me wasn't just some man in a silly coat. He was a Pirate Lord of Yore, draped in the glorious loot of his many victories, surrounded by his loyal crew, seated upon a throne of stars. It was like a picture out of some old children's book. The very image of what a buccaneer was *supposed* to be.

His smile only widened with each passing second it took me to gather my thoughts. It was a strange smile—quite unlike the polite, tolerant masks of pleasantness that I'd grown accustomed to receiving from powerful people. There was no falseness whatsoever about Renault's pleasure. His was a mad grin brimming with unrestrained zeal.

"Quite the room," I finally said, glancing around. "You're not worried about the windows taking a hit?"

He waved a dismissive hand. "There are deployable blast shields," he said. "Besides, this room is really just for show. Nothing of vital importance would be lost if it *did* take an unlucky hit. Still, though, an impressive setting for striking deals, no?"

"It is," I admitted. "You really took your king of the pirates thing to heart."

"*Buccaneers*, VanDunn." He grinned. "*Buccaneers*. And if you're going to do something, there's no point in doing it half-way. Is there, men?"

"No, captain!" they shouted in a discordant chorus.

"How rude of me," Renault said, turning and gesturing towards the handful of men and women gathered behind him with a wide, sweeping wave of the hand. "Allow me to very briefly introduce you to my court. Each of the women and men before you are proud officers of my fleet—some captains of their own ships."

I scanned his entourage. They were all suitably pirate-like, clad in mismatched uniforms decorated with various plundered accessories. One was wearing a black leather jacket bristling with spikes on the shoulders and elbows, while another wore composite combat armor that had been inlaid with gold designs. All of them bristled with weapons. Apparently, they'd all taken to Renault's example of debauchery—I felt decidedly under-dressed in my simple T-shirt and thin jacket.

"Quite a little army you've got thrown together," I said. "All this just for little ol' me?"

"Not *just* you." Renault settled back into his seat. "In case you didn't notice, there are quite a lot of Paragon ships buzzing around the foldgate. Quite inconvenient."

I frowned. "And you're, what, planning on going after them?"

"No. But if they came after us, I wouldn't want them to be disappointed. Fear not, though—we are currently speeding *away* from them. And the *Leonidas* seems to have no intentions of budging from its current position, so you and your crew are safe." He gave me a wry look as he said the last word, making the unspoken part of his message clear. Safe—from *them*.

I narrowed my eyes. "Alright. You wanted to have your little chat, face to face. Here's my face. There's your face. Let's have at it. What do you want?"

He settled back into his seat, gesturing towards a bench near me. "I've been deep in thought since our last, uh... *encounter*."

I remained standing, raised an eyebrow.

"You played me well, I admit," he continued. "I had you right where I wanted you, and still you managed to slip away. Lucky on your part. Which I mean as a compliment. But I think you'll agree that there's no slipping away this time."

I did agree. Not happily, but still—it was impossible to deny that he had all the cards this time. Trouble was that I knew what those cards were.

"Fine," I said. "You got us. Outgunned, outnumbered, and outmaneuvered. But if you think this is gonna help your sad little cause, I don't think you listened to a word I said during our last little chat."

He cocked his head. "How so?"

"Because you don't know Maren Sevani," I said calmly. "And I do. And I know for a fact that trying to strongarm her into being your ally is a stupid, pointless play."

"Well said!" He grinned. "Which is why it is a different offer I bring to the table this time." He gestured towards a bench behind me. "You're sure you don't want to sit?"

I lowered myself slowly onto the bench. Renault cleared his throat, as if preparing to give a speech he'd spent a considerable amount of time rehearsing.

"Luck's a funny thing," he said after a moment. "People often confuse it with coincidence. They could not be more different. Coincidence is simply a cosmic oddity. Luck, however, is the good fortune bestowed upon those who have the flexibility of mind and the readiness of means to seize upon the coincidences that come their way."

I folded my arms, waiting for him to come around to his point. Judging by the slight changes in stance his subordinates made, they were used to his speeches. None of them showed any signs of annoyance, though. They were all focused on me, their eyes skeptical, searching.

"When last we spoke," Renault continued, "I genuinely had no idea what job you were undertaking. I was able to find you only by carefully spying on you beforehand. I assumed that the job would be like any other a vulture expects. A ship with a few ultracells and a few rippers."

He leaned forward, eyes glinting. "So imagine my curiosity when after your very well-executed escape from my grasp, after I haplessly destroyed the vessel you'd been aboard, the entire underworld suddenly goes into panic mode as a certain crooked

Paragon system overseer begins frantically searching for a lost cache of undisclosed contents. Followed by, only a short while later, a blockade being placed upon the only way out of the Albeni system—with the Paragon seeming to be in search of a vessel matching yours."

"What're you getting at?" I growled.

"I'm getting at the fact you've made yourself a very powerful enemy." Renault made a chiding *tsk* sound. "Adrian Vatheson is nobody to be trifled with. He'll find you eventually. I assume that's why you're trying to get rid of the offending cargo as quickly as possible."

I said nothing. By the way he smiled, that was all the confirmation he needed.

"I have no idea who you managed to talk into buying it," he continued, "but that's also none of my concern. My concern is that in case it hadn't become abundantly obvious, you have no way of getting it *out* of the system, even with your friend Sevani's considerable resources. Not quickly, at least."

"And why's that your concern?" I asked coolly.

"Because the way I see it," he said, crossing one leg over the other, "*Your* powerful enemy also happens to be *my* powerful enemy. Currently, I believe Adrian Vatheson to be the greatest threat to people like you, me, and your friend Sevani. You think it's a coincidence that it's only recently that he's begun ramping up his activity? Becoming bolder, more aggressive? Sending Paragon battlecruisers to intrude on his rivals' territory? He sees the writing on the wall, same as you and I. He knows what's coming. And he knows that when the Paragon crumbles, somebody will need to step in to fill the void. *All* of it."

I scoffed. "If you think he's so scary, why don't you ally with him, instead of us?"

"Because he is, frankly, a bastard." Renault shrugged apologetically. "He's Paragon stock. There's no other way of looking at him. He values one thing and one thing only—power. And he has no intention of sharing any of it. An alliance with him would be no alliance at all—it would be subservience at best. And I think you'll agree with me that we've had quite enough of subservience to the Paragon."

I nodded slowly.

"So!" He perked up, holding up one finger. "My offer is this. I can provide you the means to transport your ship through the foldgate and to wherever your ultimate destination is. Specifically, we have a large mineral hauler which we have converted to be able to conceal ships much larger than yours for discreet transport."

Hiding the *Orpheus* in a mineral hauler did seem like it could work. I gave it a moment's thought.

"And your price?" I asked.

His grin returned. "That's the best part. No price."

I glanced around at the surrounding pirates, trying to gauge their reactions. I expected to see derision. Contempt for their captain's weakness. But I saw nothing of the sort. Any skepticism or distrust was directed at me, in protective solidarity with their leader.

My eyes settled on Renault again. There had to be something I was missing. "What's your game, Renault?"

"Game?" He put on an exaggeratedly offended expression. "Do I look like the type that plays games?"

I raised an eyebrow.

He sighed. "The game is the same matter I tried discussing with you during our last encounter, VanDunn. A storm is about to break upon us all. It's only a matter of timing. Which leaves men such as ourselves with one simple decision to make: will we *ride* the storm—channel its power and chaos—or will we succumb to it, and let it drag us into whatever murky depths it will?"

I said nothing.

"When the Paragon crumbles," he continued, "—and it *will*,

eventually, one way or the other—people like you and me are going to be in strange circumstances. All of a sudden everybody is going to be asking the question: well, who's in charge now? And the answer, I believe, will be quite bloody. People all over—people like Vatheson, with deep pockets and all manner of Paragon weaponry to call upon—will leap at the chance to carve a place for themselves in the new order.

"Here is the dilemma I see for myself. I have a frankly ridiculous supply of firepower. More than I know what to do with. However, I have no infrastructure. As my situation stands right now, if the Paragon were to collapse, bringing down galactic commerce with it, I and mine would find ourselves suddenly deprived of ships upon which to prey."

I nodded slowly.

"Maren Sevani, on the other hand," he said, "has the *opposite* problem. She owns a great deal of infrastructure. Has deep connections across the stars. However—and I know this for a fact—she has very little means of protecting that infrastructure. When the storm arrives, all that she's built up for herself will be swept away.

"So—what is my game, you ask?" He spread his arms wide in a gesture of goodwill and supplication. "Simply that you consider the precarious perches upon which we all reside. And how much stronger we would all be were we to combine our respective strengths." His smile widened. "For now, though, please—simply take this humble offering and remember that should you or yours ever need an ally, we are ready and willing."

Darkness enveloped the *Orpheus* as Rose carefully steered us into the interior of the mineral hauler. One of the massive containers—built for holding mind-boggling quantities of minerals harvested in the Albeni mining stations—had been cleverly modified to allow a smaller ship to latch on to its interior.

"You're sure they're not gonna just..." Rid grimaced. "I don't know, haul us off to wherever they hide out? Hold us for ransom, or just blow us up, or—"

"If they wanted us dead we'd be dead already," I said, watching the stars wink out one by one as we moved deeper into the container.

"This must be how they move between systems," Rose mused. "My mom's been trying to work that our for ages now." She grinned mischievously. "And it was right under her nose the whole time. They basically do the same thing she does—just on a bigger scale. Smuggling entire ships instead of just supplies."

The *Orpheus* rumbled as it locked into place.

"And we're sure it'll work?" Bentley asked. "That they won't stop this ship all the same?"

"So long as we keep the *Orpheus* in stealth mode," Rose said, "we're well concealed. And this hauler isn't associated with Odyssey Logistics, so they should let us pass unimpeded."

The communications system chimed as a transmission rolled in. Bentley hit a button to let it through. Renault's voice crackled to life. "*All strapped in? Ready to go?*"

"We're ready," Rose said.

"*Good. Stand by.*"

The entire ship shook as the heavy door closed, sealing us inside of the container. A few moments later, the *Orpheus* jolted as the freighter started to move.

"No turning back now," Nadus muttered. "That's for sure."

———

The journey trapped inside of the container felt somehow more surreal than even a nullspace trip. It was the noise, mostly. After so many years you get used to the sounds that your ship makes.

The freighter, however, constantly groaned and shifted, especially as it accelerated and decelerated during its approach to the foldgate. Every time we slowed, I felt my heart rate quicken, expecting the container door to be blasted off and for Paragon troop ships to come tearing after us. But they never did.

I wanted to radio Renault and get an update on our progress. I wanted to radio Sev to fill her in on the situation. But sending any sort of signal would've compromised us to scanners. So I contented myself to waiting, seated in the back of the bridge away from the rest of the crew.

"Did he say anything about how he got such heavy firepower?" Nadus muttered to me, sitting down near me.

I shook my head. "I didn't take the time to get a breakdown of his operation. But he's organized. Hell of a lot more organized than I thought he was."

Nadus nodded appreciatively. "You don't attract that many followers without at least a few redeeming qualities."

"Yeah." I furrowed my brow as I recalled everything I'd seen aboard the *Walrus*. "He's given them an identity. They work more like a small army than a bunch of cutthroats with a ship. I've never seen pirates with so much..." I hesitated, looking for the right word. "Unity?"

"Times are changing," Nadus said. He studied me seriously. "I'm not saying that Renault is a trustworthy ally, but... if the Paragon *is* falling apart... well, there might be some truth to what he's saying about people like us needing to group together."

I looked sharply at him. He raised his hands defensively. "I'm not saying we need to join his fleet or anything. Just... we should keep our minds open."

"Just the other day you were talking about wanting to make a difference for good," I said. "Fighting the Paragon. Righting all our wrongs, all that stuff. You really think ganging up with a bunch of pirates is the way to do it?"

"I think that you've gotta start somewhere," he said. He shrugged. "That's what this is all about, isn't it?"

I narrowed my eyes. "This is about getting ourselves out of the mess Rose got us into. After that, we're done. We can go find someplace else to do some good. Someplace where we're not—"

I cut off speaking as a strange sensation passed suddenly through me. Like I was in two places at the same time. Evidently, I wasn't the only one who felt it.

"Whoa." Bentley jolted in his seat. "Did you guys..."

"Yeah." Shell nodded. "I felt it too. We just passed through the foldgate."

"So..." Rid looked around nervously. "Guess that means we're clear, right?"

A few more minutes passed. Finally, the freighter groaned as it decelerated.

Renault's voice sounded as Bentley opened up the communication channel again. *"Alright—we're through and safe. You should be able to get from here to your destination free from fear of further harassment... by Paragon ships or pirates."*

The freighter rumbled.

"The doors are opening," Rose said. She manipulated the controls and detached the *Orpheus* from the container, steering us towards the exit.

"We're heading out now," I said into the radio. "And... thanks."

"My pleasure, VanDunn. Just remember what we discussed."

I glanced at Nadus, then sighed. "Will do."

The *Orpheus* veered out of the back of the container, then around it. The claustrophobic darkness of the container opened up into the Alpha Centauri system, bustling with traffic moving from one foldgate to the next. The freighter continued on, surging ahead into the darkness. Rose started plugging in the coordinates for our destination.

I glanced through the rear facing window. Through the Albeni system foldgate I could still see part of the *Leonidas*.

"Let's hope that's the last we see of them," Rid said, watching over my shoulder as the *Leonidas* slipped from view.

I nodded my agreement, then turned in the other direction. There was only one way to be sure of that—and that was to finish our business. Nadus was right. There was no turning back now.

"On to the *Aboena*," I said.

EIGHT

"Like all Roamer homeships," Shell said, standing over and staring down at the hovering image of the *Aboena* projected by the bridge holodisplay, "the *Aboena* was built during the Exodus to carry humanity unfathomable distances. The vast majority of its passengers were asleep, frozen in stasis until their journey's end. The crew had a different charge: to stay awake with the *Aboena*, year after year, generation after generation, until she had reached her destination. They maintained the systems. Watched over the engines. Ensured that the stasis pods continued to function correctly. Back then this was all new, experimental technology."

I nodded along. Shell's face was stiff as she spoke, but I'd known her long enough now to see the emotions she was suppressing as she spoke about her homeship. Fear. Uncertainty. Guilt. I eyed the white tattoos etched along her arm, remembering the stories she'd said went with them. The ripper attack she'd fought off. She'd made it clear to me from the beginning that she had no desire to talk about the conditions surrounding her banishment from the *Aboena*, and up to now, I'd had no reason to ask. Not my business. But now...

Shell pressed on. "The *Aboena* had a three-hundred-year journey to its destination—the planet Redhawk. Once they arrived, some of the crew decided to join the passengers on the surface, joining the colonization efforts. The rest, however, had grown too attached to their ship. So when the foldgates were build and they were free to leave, they began their long roaming." She shrugged. "They've been doing it ever since. Sometimes they trade with other Roamers. Sometimes they trade with Outsiders. But the bottom line is that they go where they please and they care for their ship."

Bentley frowned. "So... why did they cut off contact, then? With the outside world, I mean. You said that several years ago they stopped communicating with Outsiders. Stopped trading. How can they expect to survive?"

Shell narrowed her eyes, staring at the projection of the *Aboena* like she was trying to intimidate it into talking to her. "I don't know. That all happened after I was banished."

"Surely you must have *some* sort of idea, though," Rid said. "I mean, how are they feeding everyone?"

"They're probably not." Nadus folded his arms. "They're probably starving. That's why they need this Lifeblood so badly."

"Sure," Bentley said. "But... again, *why?* What's the point of hiding?"

Shell grimaced. "Roamers put the safety of their homeship above everything else. It's been bred into us since the beginning. All I can say is that if they've cut themselves off so severely... Command must believe it's necessary to protect the *Aboena*."

I studied her carefully. Something in the way she held herself made me think there was more she knew. But I didn't want to press her in front of the crew, so I moved on. "You've mentioned this 'Command' before," I said. "What exactly do you mean by that?"

Shell settled into a seat. "The chain of command on the *Aboena* isn't structured like any other ship," she said. "You have to think of it less like a ship and more like a mobile space station. A population center. As such, there's no one person calling all the shots. No captain. Instead, there's a group called Command who makes all of the most important decisions. Where the *Aboena* will go. Who they'll trade with. They establish laws the Aboenians have to follow."

"Alright," Nadus said. "So who decided who gets to be in Command?"

"They're chosen by vote," Shell said.

"Vote?" Rose looked back at us from her place in the pilot's seat, her face skeptical. "That doesn't seem like a very effective way to run a ship."

"That's your exact problem," Shell said. "Again—you can't think of the *Aboena* as a ship, running under a captain with specific orders. It's a small nation drifting through space." She gestured towards the schematics. "Massive chunks of the ship aren't even occupied. Most of the populace and crew are concentrated around here." She gestured towards the front end of the ship. "And the rest are scattered throughout. Most of the interior sits empty, though. Which is how we'll be able to dock without Command knowing." She pointed towards a specific point near the back end. "This is where we'll go in. Our contact will meet us there."

I nodded. "That's right. We'll dock, get our payment, unload, and be out of there without needing to so much as step foot aboard the ship, all before anybody even knows we were there. Assuming everything goes according to plan."

"Because things *always* go according to our plans," Bentley said.

"Hey." Rose spoke up. "I see her."

There was a rush of movement as we scrambled to get a good view. I let everybody else go first, walking behind them and peering out the *Orpheus*'s front-facing window over their heads.

She didn't look like much.

Not from here, anyway. Just a small white mote caught in the dark eye of the universe. A child's toy abandoned in the void, insignificant and alone.

The Aboena. One of the first ships mankind had built capable of faster-than-light travel. A relic of an age of exploration and uncertainty.

Shell's home.

"That," Bentley said, "is completely, utterly, incomprehensibly insane."

"What is?" Rid asked.

"*That.*" He pointed through the *Orpheus*'s bridge window at the distant speck that was the *Aboena*. "Just imagine what it must have been like, back in the Exodus. Boarding one of those ships without knowing what you'd find on the other end of the journey. Not knowing what would be happening to the rest of humanity while they were asleep. Hell, for all they knew they'd be the last of their species alive when they reached their destination."

"Hell of a lot of faith," Nadus said.

I stared at the ship, watching as it grew slowly bigger. An ominous feeling settled in my gut—the same one that had been growing in me since I'd agreed to this damn job.

I glanced at Shell. She'd lingered behind with me, eyes downcast as if she hardly dared to look at her old home. I hesitated, then spoke quietly enough that only she could hear.

"Shell," I said. "Why did the *Aboena* go into isolation?"

"I already told you," she said quietly. "I don't know. I haven't spoken to anyone from the *Aboena* since I left."

"I know you know *something*, though," I said. "Something you're not telling me. Why?"

She frowned. "It's... nothing. Just a baseless rumor I heard. I didn't want to scare everyone."

"What rumors?"

She finally looked up at the *Aboena*. Her eyes fixed on the distant speck, filled with... it was hard to say exactly. Trepidation. Anticipation. Maybe a hint of longing.

"The rumors are spread by smugglers," she whispered, not taking her eyes away from the window. "They say that the Roamers found something. Something drifting in space. When they brought it aboard, Command ordered that they seal off all contact. To keep anybody Outside from finding out what it was —and to keep it from getting Outside."

The ominous feeling in my gut tightened into a cold spike. Damned if I knew why. Of all the problems we had to deal with, that seemed like the least of them. And yet, something about the words made me deeply uneasy.

I jolted slightly as Shell shoved me. She fixed me with an annoyed glower. "See? This is why I didn't want to say it. It's a foolish rumor. Not worth fretting over."

"Yeah." I shook myself. "You're right."

Rose looked over her shoulder towards me. "Well? Now what?"

I straightened, shoving away the uneasy feeling. "Like I said before—we get in, unload our cargo, get paid, and blast off. No sticking around for any longer than we absolutely have to, no matter what we see. Got it?"

Nods all around.

"Good. Rose, you have our instructions?"

"Sir, yes sir." Rose's voice carried a heaping spoonful of sarcasm. I decided to ignore it.

"Alright then," I said. "Let's see how big this sucker really is."

. . .

So, look. There's only so many ways I can say this. I'll keep it simple. There's big, and then there's *big*.

The *Aboena* was BIG.

As Rose took us closer I somehow expected it to stop growing. It didn't. By the time we were gliding stealthily along the hull as per our contact's directions, it had grown to godlike proportions, stretching out too far to see both ends of it at once. Looking up at the mass of steel looming above us, it was impossible not to feel a sense of reverence—as if we were hiding in the shadow of an ancient leviathan god.

I found myself thinking back to what Bentley had said about the Exodus. The insanity of boarding a ship and blasting off towards a planet no human had ever seen before. Not knowing what would await you when you arrived. Not knowing what would happen to your old home during the voyage or what the fates of the other Exodus ships would be.

"You're sure they can't detect us?" Bentley asked Rose as she maneuvered the *Orpheus* around a structure of some kind protruding from the *Aboena*'s surface.

She shook her head, smirking. "Not unless they have better technology than the Paragon itself. And judging by how ancient this ship is, I *highly* doubt that."

"It's just that... well, last time we judged a ship by its age," Bentley said, "we almost got incinerated."

"True," Rose admitted, peering up at the venerable behemoth looming above us. "But, look. There's old, like that pirate's Redhawk, and there's *ancient*, like this. That ship right there is literally older than any human civilization besides Earth. Honestly, I'm baffled they can even keep it flying."

"They keep it updated," Shell said. She was seated in the corner, fidgeting with the handle of her long knife. Her muscular arms were still bare, revealing her strange, white geometric tattoos. "And every Roamer is a mechanic first and foremost. We literally learn to read from ancient maintenance guides. There is no higher priority than preserving the home-ship." She shifted uncomfortably. "Which is why *everyone* knows not to question Command. Whoever this contact is must be truly desperate."

"Anybody would be desperate in their situation," Nadus said. "From what the contact said, they're in dire straits without this Lifeblood."

"Or they just know they've got some grade A suckers in their trap," I growled. "Keep your guard up. Watch for any approaching ships. Keep a sharp eye on the security systems. Who knows what they'll try."

I gave one last look to the looming mass of the *Aboena* and grimaced. I tried to tell myself that this was just a trade deal. Even if it was a bit shady. We'd go aboard, meet this mystery contact, get rid of our cargo, and fly home.

It didn't feel that way, though. *I* didn't feel that way. I had the same eerie feeling I always had right before I boarded a dead ship full of darkness and danger.

"Alright, Lax." Rose's voice stirred me from my grim stupor. She rose from her seat. "Shell, Bentley and Rid have things under control up here. Let's head down and—"

"No way." I pushed myself up. "You're staying up here. Shell, you're with me."

Shell frowned, then got to her feet. Rose blinked in surprise. "But—"

"No buts, Rose." I moved towards the hatch. "You stay up here. Nadus and I—"

She darted in front of me, blocking my path and baring her teeth. "This is *my* deal," she growled. "I've been handling it from the start. They reached out to *me*. *I'm* the one who's been talking with them. You can't just take this away from me like that. And don't give me that 'need you in the cockpit crap,' I've heard it too many times."

"Rose, I *don't* need you in the cockpit," I snapped.

She said nothing, her mouth hanging open slightly. I kept talking, the words bursting out in a low snarl. "I'm trying to *protect* you. That's *all* I've tried to do from the start. I need you *safe* and I need you somewhere you can't screw this up any more than you already have. Somewhere *out of the way*. Do you understand?"

I regretted the words the moment they were out of my mouth. I'd reprimanded her plenty of times before, but never like that. Rose stared at me in shocked silence, her mouth gaping slightly. Then she snapped it shut and nodded sullenly.

"Good." I moved past her and towards the hatch. Shell followed me, her face expressionless as ever. Bentley and Rid watched me with wide eyes. It did *not* make me feel any less guilty. Which in turn made me feel even angrier. "Keep a sharp eye out," I said as I went down the hatch. "The sooner we close this deal, the sooner we're done with this mess."

"That was not handled well," Shell said softly when we were on the second deck.

"You disagree with me?" I grunted. "If Rose had just come to me—if *any* of you had just come to me—"

"You know why she didn't come to you," Shell said flatly.

I sighed. "We'll talk through this later. You ready for this?"

She stiffened slightly. "I had hoped not to get involved."

"You don't need to get involved. I just need you with me as backup. After Nadus you're my best fighter. Nobody I trust more to have my back. If they try to pull something..."

She nodded. "I'll be ready."

Nadus was waiting down in the cargo bay, staring at the crates. I sat on top of one of them, sighing.

"Hell of a weird job," I muttered.

He grunted. "We've worked weirder."

I lifted the lid from one of the crates and peered at the packages of Lifeblood inside. I should have been excited. This was quitting money, after all. Like I'd always wanted. Enough credits to do... well, basically anything within reason. If I wanted to, I could leave Rose and the crew to their adventures and go settle down somewhere. Keep my head nice and low. Far away from the wars and the power struggles and the pirates and the vengeful smugglers and the rippers.

I sighed and shut the lid. I wouldn't be doing any of that and I knew it. The crew needed me. Or maybe I needed them. The thought of being alone again, even if it meant escaping all the madness that had become my life, became more unbearable the more thought I gave it. Sev's face popped into my mind, her features outlined in blue beneath the bar sign. *You do what you've gotta do, and I'll do what I've gotta do. And when we're done... Maybe we find that peace out there somewhere. Like buried treasure.*

The *Orpheus* shuddered slightly as it docked. The vague smile that had started to form against my will on my lips shattered as I was thrust back into the present moment.

I took a deep breath, turning towards Nadus. "You ready for this?" I asked.

Nadus nodded.

"We're sealed in," Rose's voice said over the intercom. *"Pressure readings look good. You guys ready?"*

I stood up and turned towards the airlock at the far end of the cargo bay, letting my hand rest on Peacebreaker's familiar grip. "Yep."

The airlock doors started sliding open. Bitterly cold air rushed through. I winced and pulled my light jacket tighter around me. The doors halted with a heavy metallic thud that echoed sullenly.

Beyond the doors, it was utterly dark.

I glanced behind me. Shell was positioning herself near the back of the bay, hidden in shadow with a marksman's rifle tucked under her arm. Nadus was standing by the crates, near where a thermal shotgun was tucked away. He gave me a nod. "We've got your back."

I took a few cautious steps forward, my hand never moving from my pistol's grip, and came to a halt right at the edge of the loading ramp. The only light came from behind me, warm light from the *Orpheus*'s interior spilling over into the cold emptiness of the *Aboena*. The floor was spotted with bits of rust. The air was frigid and smelled faintly of mildew.

"Hello?" I regretted speaking the moment the word left my mouth. It was hardly more than a whisper, and yet it felt profanely loud in the ancient silence.

There was no reply.

I held up my radio. "Rose," I whispered. "Where are—"

I cut myself off as I heard a distant noise. Footsteps, echoing in the darkness. A moment later, a dim, orange light flickered to life at the far end of the loading bay. It held still for a moment, then began moving closer, swaying slightly as it did. Three more lights appeared behind it.

Nine figures emerged from the shadows, walking slowly towards me. They seemed to be as apprehensive as I was. Their orange lights cast an eerie, primitive glow over the loading bay, making me feel like I was in a wild cave rather than a space-age starcraft. I didn't pay it too much mind, though. My attention was drawn to the approaching strangers.

They reminded me a bit of the pirates, clad in mismatched outfits salvaged from a dozen different sources. If the pirates had looked rough and tumble, though, the Roamers looked positively wild. They wore tattered, patchwork coats, covered in old stains and decorated with strange symbols and words I didn't recognize. Some of them had their faces covered, either by cloth wrappings or ancient-looking gas masks. Those whose features weren't concealed looked ghostlike in the flickering orange light, their gaunt visages wreathed in shadow.

They were all armed. My eyes flitted from one weapon to another as they drew closer. Some of them had firearms—pistols, shotguns, and assault rifles of makes I didn't recognize that looked like they'd been carefully maintained over generations. Others carried more simple and yet brutal-looking weapons—axes, swords, and spears that seemed to have been crafted from salvaged ships' parts, though they looked no less deadly for it. One of them even carried what looked like a small crossbow. So far, none of them were pointed at me. But that could change in an instant.

"You seeing this?" I hissed into my radio. Rose should be able to watch them through the cameras built into the *Orpheus*'s cargo bay doors.

"*Yeah.*" She sounded a bit unnerved. Hell, I probably did too. I'd expected to find people like Shell. Precise, efficient, calm and collected. All words that I'd have picked out as stark opposites to the madmen creeping towards me.

"That's close enough." I raised one hand towards them, palm out and fingers outstretched, while I kept the other firmly on Peacebreaker.

They halted.

A long, silent moment passed. The Roamers watched me like wolves afraid their prey might bolt away if they moved too quickly. I lowered my hand, eyes flitting between them, watching for any signs of aggression.

When it became clear they had no intention of speaking first, I cleared my throat. "You here for the Lifeblood?"

They made no reply. I grimaced as an uncomfortable thought crossed my mind: did they even speak our language? Galactic Basic was what humanity had used since the foldgate network had been created, but these folks might be a bit out of the loop.

My knuckles whitened around Peacebreaker's handle. I turned my head from side to side, surveying each of the shadowy figures. I found no help there. They just watched me, hungrily.

"Well?" I growled. "We gonna deal or not?"

"You're a stubborn man, VanDunn."

The voice came from behind the line of Roamers. I narrowed my eyes, trying to locate the speaker. Another figure emerged from the shadows behind the line of lantern-bearing Roamers. Tall and lanky, bundled in a long, thick coat. His face was hidden in the darkness, but his voice was familiar. Horrifyingly so.

I blinked, trying to make sense of it. "What in the..."

"But I meant what I told you back on Albeni 7." The figure took another step forward, letting the sharp white light from the *Orpheus*'s interior wash over his face. Ramar Vent—the man who had stolen fire from the gods by creating a new strain of rippers—the man who had made an entire battlecruiser disappear almost without a trace—the man who was, unintentionally, the architect of the worst moments of my life—stood before me, hands at his side, his face an unreadable mask.

"You're a part of all this now, whether you want to be or not." He gave a thin-lipped smile. "So yes, by all means—let's deal."

NINE

My hand didn't move from Peacebreaker.

For just a moment, I wasn't on the *Aboena* anymore. I was on the *Revelation,* staring at the strange man we'd found marooned aboard a lost ship who claimed to know the secrets that had plagued us for so long. I was back on Albeni 7, listening to him try to convince me to go off with him in search of the rippers that had killed my crew.

Ramar raised an eyebrow at me. "May I come in?"

The question dragged me back into the moment. I narrowed my eyes at him. "What the hell is going on?"

"*Lots* of things are going on, Lackan," Ramar said calmly. "You'll have to be more specific."

"You know damn well what I mean," I growled.

Ramar sighed. "Very well. I'll explain. Perhaps inside?"

He took a step forward. I noticed one of the nearby Roamers tense, his eyes fixed on Ramar. As if he were worried the scientist were going to bolt.

"Like hell." I shook my head. "You're not stepping a foot on my ship until I get some answers."

"You'll have to ask a question, then," he said coldly.

I gritted my teeth, unsure of where I should even start. "Are you the one who's been contacting Rose?" I finally asked.

"I am," Ramar said.

It took all of my restraint not to simply draw Peacebreaker and shoot him on the spot. Instead, I gritted my teeth and asked another question. "Why?"

"Because I needed the Lifeblood," Ramar said. He side-eyed the Roamers. "*Need*, I should say."

"You said the Aboenians were starving," I growled. "That you were a Roamer, trying to save your people. How much of that are your lies?"

"Half of it." He folded his arms. "I'm obviously not a Roamer. But the Aboenians are in desperate need of help. I hope that I can provide it to them—with the Lifeblood you've brought me." He glanced past me, into the *Orpheus*'s interior. "You *did* bring it, no?"

I glanced backward, towards Nadus. His eyes were narrowed at Ramar same as mine.

"You realize how much heat you've brought onto us?" I asked, turning back to Ramar. "Do you have *any idea* what kinds of problems you've caused?"

"Yes," he said. His voice held not so much as a hint of remorse. "I've put you in the crosshairs of Adrian Vatheson—Paragon overseer turned smuggler. I imagine the fallout has been... unpleasant."

"Un*pleasant*?" I took a step forward, causing the Roamers to tense. "You might've started a war. You've put everything Sevani has built at risk."

"An unfortunate consequence," Ramar said. "But I'm afraid it was necessary."

I stared at him, unsure of what to ask next. I had dozens of questions and was too pissed to think through any of them properly. How had he even known about the Lifeblood? Why the hell did he care about these Roamers? Was this where he'd been since visiting me on Albeni 7?

He spoke again before I had a chance to. "I understand that you're angry. I don't blame you. But I already tried asking you for help before."

"Yeah," I said. "I said no. And I meant what I said. I don't want to get pulled into all of this. I never did. And I sure as hell don't want to have my crew dragged in behind me."

Ramar took another step forward. "And I meant what *I* said, Lax. The things happening here—the things I've uncovered—" He glanced over his shoulder at the line of Roamers behind him. "There is something very important and very, *very* strange happening aboard this ship," he said softly.

"There are strange things happening everywhere right now, Ramar." I folded my arms. "What's this really about?"

"This is about finishing my work," he said.

Green dots, flashing red...

I pushed the memories away, feeling a surge of anger. "We finished your work. The *Panama* is destroyed. The *Revelation* got obliterated and sucked into a black hole. Your ultrarippers are all dead."

Movement behind the Roamers. Footsteps, echoing slow and menacing through the darkness. The other Roamers tensed, standing straighter as the footsteps drew nearer. Ramar's usually stoic face paled slightly.

"Not *all* of them," he hissed.

The newcomer stepped into the light. He was big, so far as regular humans went, though still several inches shorter than me. The mantle of bristled grey fur around his shoulders made him loom even larger. There was something predatory to the slow, deliberate, almost *lazy* way that he moved, as if he were conserving energy for a sudden and frenzied burst of violence. He held no weapon, but a long knife identical to Shell's was

The Roamer with the breathing apparatus perked up, tearing his eyes from my gun as Cairn tossed the chip over his shoulder. He snatched it out of the air, then pulled out a battered-looking handcomputer. "Just a moment," he said in a wheezing Aboenian accent as he stepped away.

Cairn gave a long, happy sigh. "Life really is simpler when you cut straight to the chase, eh?" He grinned at Ramar. "Well, so much for your leverage. I guess you should have chosen a better man to depend on."

The words stung. I pushed them away. I didn't like dealing like this. Backstabbing wasn't my style. But then again—was it backstabbing if I'd never agreed to the deal in the first place? This entire endeavor had been founded on false premises from the beginning.

"Done." Dak stepped back into the light and tossed me the routing chip. I snatched it out of the air, then stared down Cairn as I reached for the intercom system near the airlock door. "Bentley," I said. "Has the transaction gone through?"

He spoke a few moments later, sounding shaken. "Uhm... yes. Eight hundred thousand."

"Good. Get ready to launch."

Rid's voice spoke up. "Lax, maybe we should—"

I slammed a button to mute him, then turned to Shell and Nadus. They were both staring at me. "Let's get it unloaded," I grunted.

A few of Cairn's men moved forward. I put a hand on Peacebreaker as I stepped backward towards the cargo. "Stay where you are. Nobody sets foot on my ship. The cargo's coming out."

Nadus looked like he wanted to say something but chose not to, helping me move the crates. Shell hung back, keeping an eye on the Roamers. Ramar watched in a daze, while Cairn and his men muttered quietly among themselves. I resisted the urge to ask Cairn what he intended to use the Lifeblood for. The messages from Ramar—back when he'd been anonymously corresponding with Rose—had made it seem like it would be going to help poor, starving Roamers. Nothing about Cairn's bearing made me think he was that type of person, though.

Not my problem.

Protect the crew.

I slid the last crate off of my cargo truck and onto the floor of the *Aboena*'s loading bay with a grunt, then pushed the truck back into the *Orpheus*'s cargo hold. I wasn't sure how they were planning on moving the crates, but that wasn't my problem to deal with. With the Lifeblood unloaded, I approached Cairn and Ramar.

"I don't know what you guys have going on here," I said, "and it's not my concern. But I better not see anybody coming after us."

"Our deal is done," Cairn said. "You needn't worry."

"Good." I turned away. "We won't meet again."

"For your sake," Cairn said. Something in his voice made me pause and look back at him as he continued speaking. "I pray not. But then again..." He grinned. "It's a crazy universe out there, getting crazier every day. Who knows what fate holds?"

My eyes flitted from his to Ramar's. The scientist had composed himself and was watching me with a cold, calculating gaze—as if he were in the process of planning his next move.

I turned away and walked into the *Orpheus*.

"Seal the airlock," I said into the intercom. "We did what we came to do. Let's go."

I watched the *Aboena* grow steadily smaller through the bridge's rear window. There were no signs of pursuit. Barely any indication that the ship was even alive.

The command deck was silent. Rose hadn't so much as

looked at me since I'd snapped at her before the negotiation with Ramar and Cairn. Rid was sitting nearby her, glancing nervously back and forth between the two of us. Bentley was staring mutely at a computer screen, while Shell was sitting near me and watching as the *Aboena* gradually grew farther away. Nadus emerged from the hatch, then sat heavily in one of the seats near the central projector.

I let the silence drag on a few more minutes as I tried to figure out what to say. I could barely even figure out what I thought. I couldn't shake the feeling that what I'd done was wrong. I'd clearly abandoned Ramar in a dangerous situation. Selling the Lifeblood directly to Cairn had somehow undercut whatever position Ramar had held. For all I knew, I'd just condemned him to a grisly death.

Not all of them, Ramar had said. The words echoed endlessly in my brain. He really believed that some of his ultra-rippers had somehow survived, and that these Roamers had something to do with them. I wasn't sure what the Lifeblood had to do with any of it. But Ramar didn't do anything without a purpose. Seemed like he'd counted on me helping him somehow.

You should have chosen a better man.

But... dammit, that was on *him*. I had never agreed to do anything but sell the Lifeblood. I had no obligation to Ramar or his crusade—and I was done fighting other men's wars for them.

Finally, I spoke. "We would have been pulled into whatever plot Ramar is up to. This is for the best. We got our money, and we got rid of the Lifeblood. Now we head back to Albeni and—"

"And lie low?" Rose said sullenly.

"Yeah." I gritted my teeth. "Lie low."

Bentley perked up suddenly. "We just received another message. From—well, from Ramar."

Dammit. I sighed. "What does it say?"

He frowned. "It just says *HELP*."

Nadus glanced at me, raising an eyebrow. I grimaced and shook my head. "He's just trying to lure us back."

Rose shook her head. "You are *unbelievable*."

"What's unbelievable," I growled, "is that you really think that man is—"

"Hey. Another message coming in." Bentley leaned in. Then swore.

"What?" Rose and I snapped simultaneously.

"It... oh, see for yourself."

He turned the screen around. I leaned in.

SORRY ABOUT THAT. GOT HIS COMPUTER. HE WON'T BE BOTHERING YOU ANYMORE. YOU DON'T MIND IF I KILL HIM DO YOU?

Rose folded her arms and glared at me.

I closed my eyes and let out a long, ragged, exasperated breath.

It's not my problem.

It wasn't. This was Ramar's fault—not mine. I shouldn't feel guilty about it. And yet... I did.

You should have chosen a better man to depend on.

I glanced towards Nadus. He was staring out the back window towards the *Aboena*.

"What do you think?" I asked.

He gritted his teeth. "I think Ramar's a bastard. I think he lied out his ass to get us here in the first place. But..." He met my eyes. "I think that if he's doing it, he's got a reason for it. And I think that if we want to do some good, we've got to start somewhere."

I looked away from him, towards the gradually shrinking *Aboena*. We could fly away right now and be done with all of this. No more Ramar. No more Vatheson. With eight hundred thousand credits to divide among ourselves. It was one hell of a haul. All I had to do was ignore that damnable, piercing, *guilty* feeling in my chest.

I looked at the rest of my crew. They were watching the *Aboena* too, their expressions ranging from angry to remorseful. Even Bentley—the one person I'd expected to side with me on this—looked deeply uncomfortable as we flew away.

I sighed.

"Turn around," I muttered.

Rose raised an eyebrow. "What? I couldn't—"

"*Turn around.*" I climbed to my feet, swore viciously, then stomped towards the hatch. "You guys wanna be heroes? Fine. Let's be heroes. Take us back to the docking bay."

TEN

"You're sure you can get us in without alerting anyone?" I asked, shrugging into the thickest coat I owned—which still wasn't very thick, but it would do better against the *Aboena*'s bitter cold than the light jacket I normally wore.

Shell nodded. "Most of the ship is uninhabited. Basically, you have a few clusters of high-density population towards the front of the ship and a few inhabited areas around the most important maintenance and cargo areas while everything else is empty. With a little help from Bentley, I'll be able to get us in at the same docking bay as before."

Bentley looked up from his datapad. "I'm happy to help, but... this ship is quite literally two millennia old. I doubt my expertise will be applicable."

"We'll be able to work it out together," Shell said.

Rid started to climb into his exo. I held up a hand. "Wait. No exos."

He frowned. "Doesn't that kind of put us at a disadvantage?"

"We're not looking for a fight," I said. "We just need to pick up Ramar. We are *not* going to get involved."

Rose smirked. "I thought he wasn't our problem."

"He isn't," I grunted. "But I won't leave him to die."

"Should I reply to the message?" Bentley asked.

I gritted my teeth and turned towards the hatch. "Not yet. Not until we're ready to mobilize, at least. He'll just want to extract some sort of ransom."

"Are we willing to pay that?" Rid asked.

"Willing? No," I growled. "But if it'll help us keep negotiations open until we can pull Ramar out, maybe."

Shell followed me down. "So your plan is just to storm aboard, find Ramar, and break him out through brute force?"

"Pretty much," I admitted.

Shell frowned. "You can't fight them all."

"*Docking now,*" Rose said over the intercom.

The *Orpheus* rumbled once again. I strode up to the Icarus. "I don't need to fight them. Just need to intimidate them."

"Cairn didn't seem like the intimidated type," Nadus mused, hitting the button to open up his Jericho armor on its mounting frame.

"Most people don't seem that way," I said. "Not until they—"

I heard a grinding sound as the airlock doors began to open. I frowned. "Rose, we're not geared up yet."

"*What do you mean?*" She sounded confused. "*I didn't open them.*"

Bentley's voice sounded over the intercom a moment later. "*Wait. Somebody else is accessing our system. They've taken the—*"

I didn't pay attention to the rest of his sentence. Something small and round flew through the gap in the airlock door, bounced, rolled, and came to a halt a meter away from my foot.

My eyes widened. "Hit the—"

The ball exploded. Not in fire or light. The only sound was a slight whoosh of escaping air. A vaguely orange substance filled the air. My mouth, nose, and eyes were suddenly full of a harsh, sweet taste.

Nadus frowned at the ball, one hand on his weapon. "What the..."

I felt it at the same time as him. A deep, overpowering exhaustion. I tried to stay on my feet. Drew Peacebreaker and aimed it vaguely at the airlock. It was almost all the way open now. I heard footsteps pounding on the floor. Saw figures striding through the haze filled air towards us. Tried to focus—to settled Peacebreaker's sights on the nearest one—only to feel my legs buckle beneath me and the world to swing wildly sideways.

Someone was talking. A familiar voice, I thought. *There are two kinds of pain, boy...*

Nadus sagged to his knees, then toppled forward onto his face. Rose's voice was saying something frantic over the intercom, but I couldn't make out the words. Boots walked past me and towards the stairs up to the second deck. I tried to aim Peacebreaker, only to feel something heavy press down upon my wrist.

I looked up to see Cairn stooping over me, one boot pinning my arm to the floor.

"Why, Vanguard," he said, his grin wide and toothy and predatory. He took a long, deep breath, then exhaled, orange mist rushing from his nostrils. I squinted at him, trying to force the blurriness into focus. He was breathing this stuff like it was regular air. So were his cronies. "You're back already? Did you truly miss me so much?"

"You..." I tried to put the words together. "What..."

"Oh, don't worry," he said, trailing a finger through the orange mist. "It's not fatal. Just... *inconvenient*. For you, at least."

He carefully pried Peacebreaker from my limp fingers. He held up the gun, admiring it for a moment, and then held it up.

"Here you go, Dak," he said. "A fitting reward for a task well performed."

The masked Roamer reverently took my gun from Cairn's hands. My eyes drifted past him, towards Nadus's stretched-out form. His eyes were closed. I couldn't tell if his chest was moving. I tried to move towards him, but my limbs wouldn't obey me.

"Don't worry about your friends." Cairn grinned down at me. "I'll see that they're taken care of. Now—sleep well. And thank you for the ship. Once again, it's been a pleasure doing business with you."

I reached for him. Tried to grab him. To hurt him. To kill him. But he was intangible. Or maybe I was.

There are... two kinds... of...

The world went dark.

ELEVEN

Slowly, feeling returned to my limbs and lucidity to my brain.

I wiggled my toes. Clenched and unclenched my fists. Rolled my shoulders. Sat up. Groaned. Everything seemed to be in working order.

My head was pounding, every thought accompanied by a pulse of deep pain. But I *had* to think. Had to work through what had happened. It was all fuzzy and distant and unreal. I was alone in a dark void.

Calm.

Focus.

Breathe.

Remember.

I remembered the airlock doors opening suddenly. Remembered something shooting into the cargo bay. A hissing sound. A harsh sweetness that filled my mouth and my nose and my eyes. Cairn kneeling over me, grinning that predatory grin of his.

Don't worry about your friends. I'll see that they're taken care of.

My guts constricted into a tight knot.

Green dots, flashing red...

I tried to scramble to my feet only to slip on something foul-smelling and slimy. I fell back to the floor with a thud. I reached out and my hands pressed against cold, circular walls surrounding me. I tried to get up again, leaning on the walls for support, but they were coated in the slime too. I slipped again. Cursed loudly.

Two kinds of pain...

My crew was going to die, if they weren't dead already. They were going to die horrible, unknowable deaths at the hands of these Roamers. And it was my fault. My fault for leading us to the damnable ship in search of ghosts better left alone. My fault for trusting a snake like Ramar. I felt my breath heaving in my chest, heard my heart pounding in my ears.

Wait. That wasn't my heart. It had a metallic ring to it. I focused, tracing the source of the sound. It was coming from the wall next to my head. A steady, heaving pounding sound. Along with a muffled voice.

"Hey! Who is that?"

I frowned. *"Nadus?"*

A pause. *"Lax?"*

"Yeah!"

"You alright?"

"Yeah. You?"

"I'm fine. It's pitch-dark in here. Can you see anything?"

"Not a thing." I felt at the walls again. "You have any idea where the hell we are?"

"No. Last thing I remember is those Roamers dragging us out of the *Orpheus*."

I swore viciously, my voice echoing up the narrow confines of my cell. "Ramar must have sold us out."

"We don't know that." Nadus groaned. "He's probably in the same situation. What about everyone else?"

"I don't know. We gotta get out." I managed to get to my feet, supporting myself by putting my hands against the wall in front of me and letting my feet slide into the base of the wall behind me. "We gotta find the crew. Then find Cairn and smash his skull in."

"Lax. Wait."

I ignored him, reaching up and clawing blindly at the wall in front of me, seeking for something I could grip. I found nothing. I kept scrambling, though, my desperation pushing me to irrationality. "There's no telling what Cairn will do to them. We have to get—"

I took a step forward and my feet gave out beneath me. I grunted and fell.

"*Lax.*" Nadus's muffled voice was harsh, insistent. "Stop. Relax. Panicking isn't going to help anyone."

My breath was ragged in my lungs. I turned slowly until I was flat on my back, staring straight up into the darkness of my cell.

"If Cairn wanted to kill us, he would have already," Nadus said, his voice echoing around me. "Obviously they want something out of us. So we've got some time. Calm down and let's make a plan instead of beating our heads against the wall."

I closed my eyes. In the pitch-darkness it made no difference, but it still felt right. *Calm. Breathe.* I focused on my breath, remembering what Doc had told me. *When everything feels like it's going to hell, step back to the beginning. By breathing.*

Bit by bit, I pulled myself together, feeling the panic bleed slowly out of me. Finally, I groaned and sat up, pushing my back against the wall.

"Thanks," I said. If it had been anybody else, I'd have been embarrassed to have been caught breaking down like that. But it was just Nadus. We'd been through hell together and carried the same scars. "Guess I'm just..."

"Don't worry about it. You know anything about these guys you haven't told me?"

I shook my head instinctively, despite knowing he couldn't see me. "Not a damn thing."

I heard some distant grunting sounds, followed by a heavy thud and a groan. "Damn. These walls are slick. What'd they throw us in, anyways?"

I reached up and felt around me, conducting a more thorough and level-headed exploration of my cell. It was circular and cramped, maybe a bit wider than a meter from wall to wall. "Some kind of storage tank, I think. Maybe an old fuel cell."

"And this... slime?"

I grimaced as I pressed the bare skin of my palm against a slippery wall. Whatever it was, it was cold and smelled rancid. "I don't even wanna know."

Nadus gave a heavy, reluctant sigh. "Well, let's see what we can do."

Not much.

In the darkness there was no way to tell how long we'd been at it. Hours, certainly. Long, arduous, cold, slimy, hours spent in increasingly futile attempts to shimmy up the narrow confines of our prison cells. We tried all sorts of different strategies. We tried scraping the gunk from the walls with our boots. Tried wedging ourselves against the wall with our feet and pushing ourselves up. Tried jumping, reaching upwards in a desperate attempt to touch the grate that sealed the top. Every attempt ended the same way: on our asses in the slime at the bottom of the cell. But that didn't stop us from trying. Over and over and over again. Up, down, up, down, up...

Noise. Something jarred me awake. I sat up. I didn't even remember dropping off. "Nadus?"

I heard nothing. He must have been asleep.

I listened carefully. I could have sworn I had heard...

Sure enough. Footsteps echoed down the hallway above us. Sounded like multiple people. I craned my head upwards.

Light. Blessed light. Even the few dim beams shining down through the bars of the grate were blinding. A moment later, I couldn't help but wince as somebody lifted the grate and shoved it out of the way.

Somebody was saying something, but I couldn't make out quite what. It was like they were speaking some strange, garbled form of Basic. Mostly likely it was whatever language the Aboenian Roamers had settled into over the millennia since the Exodus. Three figures crystalized bit by bit into view as my eyes adjusted to the light. One Roamer I didn't recognize, holding a flashlight and aiming it down at me. The second was Dak, Peacebreaker still tucked into his waistband. The third was the Wolf himself.

Dak was talking, his voice high-pitched and demanding as he gestured towards me. Cairn watched me silently, his eyes hidden in the shadows.

I rose carefully, slowly, to my feet, still glaring up at them.

"Where the hell is my crew?" I snarled.

Cairn lowered himself until he was squatting directly above the pit. "They're *mine* now, Vanguard. So's your ship. It's a nice ship. I like it. Full of all kinds of treats too. To think that I got two hundred kilos of Lifeblood, a fully stocked Blackbird stealth interceptor, three slaves, and two Vanguards to play with all for the price of eight hundred thousand credits?" He grinned manically. "Why, it's been a long, *long* time since I had this lucky of a day."

My fingers formed white-knuckled fists. My breath was hot and angry through my clenched teeth. Hungry, violent rage surged futilely through my veins. And Cairn could tell. His smile only broadened as he watched me grow increasingly agitated.

"When I get out of here," I snarled, "I'm going to kill you."

He chuckled softly. "You know, I think I would be saying the exact same thing were our positions reversed. It's funny, but I empathize with you. I really do."

He stared down at me for a moment, then turned to his companions and said something in sharp Aboenian. The two Roamers shared a glance, shrugged, then proceeded down the hallway. Cairn waited until they were gone to resume speaking.

"I remember a time," he said, "when I thought that all I wanted was to live in peace and silence, away from the rest of humanity and their toils. That's all any Roamer wants, really. Any good one, at least."

I ground my teeth. "There a point to all this?"

His eyes glinted with amusement. "Perhaps I'm lonely, Vanguard. It's a heavy burden, being powerful. Maybe I simply seek companionship from the similarly afflicted."

I scoffed. "Do I look powerful to you?"

"You look like you've worked very hard to *avoid* power." He leaned over me, peering down. "Or, rather, you *sound* that way. I spoke to our mutual friend at length about you, after your departure. Had to make sure you wouldn't cause any problems for me in the future. In the end I decided you simply provided too good an opportunity to waste. My, my. The things he said about you. The places you've been, Vanguard. The things those angry eyes of yours have seen."

A chill ran down my spine.

"That's right," Cairn said softly. "I know about that battle-cruiser of yours. It's a hell of a story. Truth be told, I can't believe you survived all of it. But our mutual friend had... *ample* reason to be truthful with me."

My brain short-circuited for a moment. Ramar had told Cairn about the *Revelation*? I had a hard time believing that anybody could get that man to spill his secrets, no matter what kind of torture they put them through. The only reason Ramar would tell somebody would be if he thought he had something to gain from it. Maybe this was a final, desperate play by the scientist to get his leverage back. Or maybe Ramar was dead, and Cairn had figured it out some other way.

Cairn watched me carefully. "You could have done all manner of things with the secrets you found aboard that ship. You could have taken the weapons of the Paragon and turned them against whoever you pleased. You could have become a force to be reckoned with. And yet you chose to destroy them, instead." The amusement in his eyes faded, leaving them cold and dangerous. "Why?"

"Because I've seen what they can do," I growled. "The destruction."

He narrowed his eyes. "That's the *point*. That's what any good weapon does."

"A good weapon destroys what you want it to," I said. "Rippers destroy *everything*."

"Only if you're not strong enough to control them," Cairn said.

I frowned up at him in confusion. "*Nobody's* strong enough to control them."

He grinned. "Not yet, maybe."

"You've seen what rippers can do," I growled. "Regular rippers. I know that the *Aboena* got hit once. Shell told me the story. Only an idiot would think they can control that kind of chaos."

That struck a chord. He looked up, staring somberly out into the darkness. "I suppose that's the difference between us then, Vanguard. We've both seen carnage. Both seen chaos. Both seen the effects of raw power. Yet you run from it." He looked back down at me with a lurid grin. "While I choose to *embrace* it."

He sighed and climbed to his feet. "And that, in the end, is why I am going to win. And you are going to die. Because that's what happens when you run from what you are. You're a

Vanguard. A living weapon, made for one purpose and one purpose only: to kill. Do you really think you can hide from that?"

I ground my teeth. "Pull me out of here and we'll see."

"That's the spirit!" He gave a harsh laugh. "There's the beast of destruction I was expecting. Keep that. Embrace it. Stoke that flame. I'll need it for... well, you'll see soon enough. But I have other matters to attend to, first, before the day of my Proving comes. I've a pilgrimage to complete, to receive my gift from the Stranger. And I must decide what is to be done with the rest of your friends. I hear the girl's mother should be willing to pay a handsome price for her recovery."

White-hot rage lashed through me. If I'd had more energy, I'd have leaped at Cairn then and there, clawing desperately— and probably futilely at him. But I was defeated, and I knew it. For now, at least.

"After that, though..." Cairn turned away. "What fun we'll have, my Vanguards and I. Try to keep your strength, Vanguards." His voice faded into echoes. "You'll *need it*."

The door shut.

The light went out.

"I don't like him very much," Nadus said sourly.

I shook my head, still reeling from the conversation. "How much of that did you make out?"

"Enough. He knows about the *Revelation*?"

"Yeah."

"Maybe Ramar was right," Nadus said. "Maybe we should have... well. Too late for that now."

"Wait." I narrowed my eyes. There was something Cairn had said that had been itching at me. Something about...

"He said he had three slaves and two Vanguards," I said slowly. "And later on he said *the girl's* mother would be willing to pay a hefty price."

There was a moment of reflective silence. "Which means he doesn't know about Shell," Nadus said.

I nodded, another detail springing to my mind. For the first time in—well, however long we'd been trapped in this pit—I felt a surge of hopeful energy infuse into my voice. "The gas. The stuff they knocked us out with. The Roamers all seemed immune to it. They were breathing it like it was nothing. Maybe Shell was safe from it too.

"Even if she did escape," Nadus said skeptically, "what could she even do? She's just one person."

"Just one person," I agreed. "But she knows the ship. She knows the way they work. She told me she used to be a Marshal—some kind of enforcement officer." I squinted up into the darkness, as though by trying hard enough I could bring back the light that had briefly illuminated my cell. "Who *is* this Cairn guy, anyway? Is he in charge?"

"If he were in charge, he wouldn't have had to meet with us in secret," Nadus observed.

I nodded along. It was a good point. "True. Maybe he's hiding from Command too." I perked up slightly. "Maybe that means that if Shell finds them, she can send help. After all, she used to work for them, right?"

"Maybe," he said cautiously. "But if they were to find out, they might see us as the bigger threat. We're the Outsiders, after all. But—there's no harm in hoping, right?"

"I sure as hell hope not."

We went silent for an indeterminable amount of time. A thought struck me.

"Hey. Back on Albeni, before we got into all this. You disappeared. Where were you?"

There was a long silence. "You'll think it's stupid."

"So?"

"You'll think *I'm* stupid."

I gave a harsh, humorless laugh. "I'll think *you're* stupid? I'm that one that got us into *this* mess."

Another silence. This one shorter. "I was with the Order."

I frowned. "Order? You mean..."

"Yep."

My mouth hung open. The Sacred Order of the Stars—the church that Nadus had been involved in when he'd busted me out of prison. The same church that Ramar's spy, the Penitent, had disguised himself as a priest of in order to keep an eye on us. I remembered Father Eladrius's warm smile and wise eyes—and I remembered how cold and empty those eyes had been when he'd gunned down Artemis. I knew that the church itself hadn't had anything to do with Eladrius, but still, the association haunted me.

Nadus laughed. "See? I told you. You think I'm an idiot."

"I *know* you're an idiot," I said. "But not about this kind of thing. Guess I'm just... surprised. After, you know..."

"After the guy who converted me turned out to be an assassin?"

"Yeah."

Nadus sighed heavily. "That threw me for a long time. Couldn't wrap my head around it. Eventually I found the local Albeni chapter and went there to try to dig up what information on Eladrius I could find. Looking for closure, maybe—or revenge. I don't know. Doesn't matter anyways, because I never found anything. No records, nobody who knew of him. What I did find was a buggy electrical grid, a worn-out heating system, and a feeble old priest with a bum prosthetic leg. Didn't seem like anybody else was gonna help, so I lent him a hand. And one thing led to another, then another. The meetinghouse is all working now, so whenever I'm onboard we'll go find other work to do for people who can't do it for themselves..." His voice trailed off for a moment. "I dunno. Seems silly now."

I nodded slowly to myself. "Must've felt nice. Doing some good. Making a difference."

"Yeah. It did. I... look. It's as much my fault as yours we got into this. I pushed you into it. I guess that being with the church, seeing how bad the people on Albeni have it... it made me realize how damn lucky I am. *We* are." His voice went soft, soft enough I had to strain to hear him. "After all the stuff we did, we don't deserve to be alive. But we are. I figured that maybe this was why. That by coming here, we could make a difference for good. I mean... there's gotta be a reason for it, right? Some way we can make it all right?"

I stared into the darkness. "I don't know, Nadus. I just... don't know."

———

Time passes differently in a dark pit in the corner of oblivion.

I'd thought it was bad on Albeni. Or in prison. There, time had been at least a tangible concept. A measurable, observable phenomenon. Here it was an alien theory, and trying to track it made me feel like a primitive scholar using sticks and stones to measure the speed of light.

Having Nadus there kept me sane for a while. We talked and reminisced and even laughed, because laughter was about all we had left. We dug through old memories neither of us had thought about in years. Relived boot camp, sprinting up and down Mud Hill together. Refought dozens of battles. Remembered friends lost and forgotten.

Eventually, though, the words went dry. Conversation faded into long, empty, desolate silence. Knowing that he was still there—that I wasn't utterly alone in the darkness—brought some small amount of comfort. But not much.

I kept trying to escape for as long as I had the strength. No matter how hard I tried or how patient I was, though, I couldn't figure out how to move that grate. The walls were too slick for me to be able to apply the right amount of pressure. Time and time again I climbed up to the very top, only to eventually fall after repeatedly failing to lift that damned piece of metal. Eventually I gave up.

After that I hallucinated, my mind filling in the dark gaps of my existence with fragmented memories. I sat with my old Vanguard company. Listened to Kessa talk in excited circles about a book she'd read. Spent hours with every member of my crew. Endured spiteful rants from Venter, my old frigicerin supplier in prison. I shared a drink in Tyrell's Bar with Sev and was surprised by how much I missed her. How much I wished I could just talk with her one more time, about... well, anything.

I even saw my old man once. I expected him to mock me. To shake his head in disapproval and mutter something about types of pain and natural consequences. He didn't, though. He just stood above my grate and stared down at me with a blank expression.

"Well, Pa," I said, unsure if my lips were actually moving or if my words existed only in the confines of my addled brain, "here I am. All these years later. Are you happy?"

He watched me a moment longer, then turned around and walked away. Not so much as a word spoken.

"*I hope it was worth the credits!*" I yelled after him.

"Vanguard."

I started. There was light. A figure was standing above me. Not my father. The Wolf. In my fever-dream state he seemed larger than life, his form taking up the entirety of my blurred vision. Something about him seemed different from the last time I'd seen him, though. Something in the shape of him. The way he held himself. The dangerous glint in his eyes.

"It's time," he said.

And again my vision went dark.

TWELVE

Something cold and metallic was wrapped around me. Sudden pressure as I was yanked upwards. And then—light. Blinding, all-encompassing light. I flailed, lashing out at anything within reach. My fist struck flesh and I heard an angry shout. A moment later I felt a sharp pain in my arm.

I went limp. I was being dragged along the corridor floors, through light and dark, through dream and reality until it all became a blur. Roamers pointed and laughed at me. Kessa gave me a sad but encouraging smile. My mother turned her head away in shame. The Wolf watched me with a deep, burning hunger in his eyes.

Get up, Sevani was saying, her voice fierce and unmistakable, lined with steel and venom. *Get up.*

Rid watched me with dull, lifeless eyes as I was dragged past where he was nailed to a wall. Shell and Bentley were there too, their naked bodies bearing the marks of horrible torture. Dak walked beside me, leering down and patting his hand on Peacebreaker's handle. My father was next to him, staring straight ahead as he walked, refusing to look down at me.

"Look at me, you bastard," I snarled.

Get up, Lax. Get up.

But he didn't. He stopped moving, falling behind the ghostly retinue. Another took his place. Tall and spindly, lined with jagged biosteel spikes, pale skin mottled with blood. It leered at me. Demonic, nightmarish wings looming behind it.

"I... killed you all," I said through gritted teeth.

Not all of us.

"Lax, get up!"

Sharp pain in my arm. Fire in my veins. I bolted upright, grabbed the nearest person, only to grunt in pain as somebody struck me in the face with dazzling force. I let go of the person I'd grabbed as I sagged back to the floor.

"Easy. Easy, Lax."

I looked up. Nadus was kneeling over me. "Sorry about the hit. You were gonna kill Rose."

I blinked. Rose was standing next to him, holding her arm and breathing heavily. She gave a sigh of relief. "I was worried you were... gone," she said, her voice ragged.

I shook myself, looking around. The three of us were alone. No Roamers, no hallucinations, no rippers. Just four metal walls and two metal doors.

"Where..." I could barely croak the words. "How..."

"Here." Nadus pressed a canteen to my lips. "Easy now. Take it slow."

The water was lukewarm at best but it didn't smell like urine, which made it just about the best damn thing I'd ever drunk. I forced myself to imbibe it slowly, though, one sip at a time. When I'd drunk the water, Nadus handed me a protein block.

"To answer your question," Rose said, "we don't know where we are. And the Roamers brought us to wherever here is."

I looked Rose up and down. She was still in the same clothes she'd been wearing on the *Orpheus*, albeit now dirty and ragged. I had a thousand questions. They came out all at once in a jumbled mass. "You alright? They hurt you? Where's everyone else? What happened after—"

"Shh." Rose squeezed my hand. "I'm alright. Nobody hurt me."

I took a deep breath. *Calm.* If Rose was alright that meant there was hope for the others.

"We saw everything that happened in the cargo bay," Rose said. "Watched it through the security cameras from the bridge. We almost did an emergency airlock break and vented the cargo hold, but you and Nadus were still unconscious in the docking bay. We had to surrender."

I looked around to make sure there were no cameras watching us. "What about Shell?"

Rose frowned. "What about her?"

"Cairn came to gloat," I said weakly. "A while ago. Made it seem like they hadn't caught her."

Rose shook her head. "They kept me in a different location than everyone else. Cairn made it seem like they were going to try to ransom me." Her eyes grew hopeful. "But if Shell really is loose somewhere..."

I nodded, finishing off my protein bar and speaking around a mouthful of the chalky substance. "She's just about the only person in the universe who might actually have a chance at helping us now. She must just be biding her time." I frowned. "How long have we..."

"About three weeks," Rose said. "Since they captured us."

So long. No wonder I'd been hallucinating by the end of it.

"Here." Nadus pressed another protein bar into my hand. "Keep eating. Need to get your strength back. No telling what these bastards have in store for us."

I ate the second protein bar, chasing it down with water as

Rose and Nadus continued talking. I was already starting to feel better. Light, food, water, room to stretch my legs, and friendly faces all made for a potent medicine.

"Any idea what happened to Rid and Bentley?" I asked wearily.

Rose shook her head. "No. I..." She paused, seeming to search for words. A ripple of emotion passed suddenly through her optimistic demeanor. She fought back a sniffle. "I don't know... what..."

I hesitantly reached out with one hand to comfort her. As soon as I did, she moved and sank suddenly into my arms, sniffling. I stiffened with surprise, then pulled her into a hug, holding her gently as she fought back sobs.

"I'm sorry," she choked. "I'm... we should never have come here. I shouldn't have taken us here. Shouldn't have lied to you, made you..."

I wasn't sure exactly what to do. It had been years since I'd hugged anyone. I settled for just squeezing her tighter. I was surprised at the relief I felt. I hadn't realized how heavy of a burden Rose's anger and disappointment in me had been. There was no denying that we were still in a hell of a bad situation. But as I held Rose, suddenly the world seemed to shift just a bit more towards being right again.

"Hey. We're gonna make it," I said gently.

She pulled back from me, wiping a tear away and giving me an unbelieving look. "How can you say that? They have our ship. They have Rid and Bentley. Shell is lost. We have no way of signaling to anyone for help."

The relief I'd felt succumbed to guilt. Here Rose was blaming herself for what was still undeniably my fault. It had been my choice to come back for Ramar. I'd agreed on coming to the *Aboena* in the first place, despite knowing better.

I looked up at Nadus. His eyes were grim with determination.

"I don't know," I said. "But no matter what it takes, we're getting out of here. We'll find the rest of the crew. Hell, they might find us first."

She gave another sniffle and wiped at her eyes. "What about the *Orpheus*?"

I took a deep breath. Truth was that thinking about Cairn and his goons rifling through the *Orpheus*—through all that remained of my old life—made me sick to my stomach. But I'd lost the *Orpheus* once before and lived with it. I could do it again.

"It's just a ship," I said. "Getting the crew back together comes first. After that... well, we'll see."

All three of us tensed as we heard a sudden metallic whirring sound. A moment later, one of the doors leading out of our room slid open. We stared at it, but nothing came through.

Nadus and Rose climbed to their feet. I followed suit. My legs were weak from lack of use. It took me a few minutes to steady myself.

"Coast seems clear," Nadus said.

I looked around our room. No signs of a watching camera or anything like that.

Rose looked to me. "You ready?"

I took a long breath, then nodded. "Yeah."

Rose turned and strode through the doorway, Nadus right behind. I followed after them.

"What the hell..." muttered Nadus.

The doorway led into another room, about the same size. The room's walls were lined with hanging weapons. Swords, axes, clubs, hammers, spears. All of them looked as if they had been fashioned from melted-down spare parts. A pair of large blast doors were sealed on the other side of the room.

An eerie feeling crept into my gut. They wouldn't lead us into a room full of weapons unless they wanted us to fight something. And they wouldn't want us to fight anything they weren't certain we would lose to.

"Listen," Rose said. I perked my head to the side. After a few moments, my brain locked onto the sound. Voices. Distant, loud, muffled, intermingled. Emanating from the other side of the door. A crowd.

The eerie feeling solidified into dread. *Proving.* Was this the Proving? Were we the ones being Proved? Against what?

"What the hell is going on?" I muttered.

"Dunno," Nadus said grimly. He studied the rack of weapons, then grabbed a long war hammer that looked as if it had been plundered straight from an ancient battlefield on Earth. "Better gear up, though."

I glanced through the weapons. Damn, what I'd have given to have the Icarus with me. Or even Peacebreaker at my side.

But I didn't.

Resolve filled me suddenly. I didn't have guns. My friends were scattered and lost. But I had a rack full of weapons in front of me, my best friend at my side, and Rose to protect. Like Rid always said—you have to play the cards life deals you.

And if there's one hand I know how to play, it's a fighting hand.

I grabbed a spear. Then a long, thick bladed sword. Then I stuck the haft of an ax down my belt. There was nobody around telling us to take just one. After a few minutes, each of us was holding a weapon in each hand. I met Nadus's eye. He stared grimly back at me.

The crowd outside grew louder, then fell silent. A single voice spoke in Aboenian.

"Whatever is out there," I said, "just stick together. Rose, stay in the back and support as best you can. Nadus and I will take the brunt of it."

She nodded, lips curled in a snarl. That girl had plenty of fight in her but even more common sense—most of the time, at least. There was no logic in throwing her in front when there were two Vanguards available to take the heavy hits. That was what we were built for, after all.

The voice speaking from the other side of the door reached a thundering crescendo, resulting in a torrent of wild shouts. There was a heavy mechanical grinding noise as the blast doors began to slide open.

Light surged through as the gap between the doors widened. I lifted the sword, shielding my eyes. The crowd began chanting.

"Now what?" Nadus asked.

"Nowhere to go but forward," Rose said through gritted teeth, and strode ahead into the blinding light. Nadus and I shared a glance then followed.

Our surroundings revealed themselves gradually as my eyes adjusted to the light. We were standing on a wide, open floor made out of paneled grates. Strange, alien-looking crimson vines clung to the bars. Six steel pillars extended from ceiling to floor at various points. The walls and ceiling were built out of the same panels as the floor. Floodlights shone from the other side of the grates, turning the crowds of Roamers behind them into dark silhouettes. Their cheers rose to a furious pitch as we entered the arena.

"They're everywhere," Nadus muttered. I glanced down, then up. He was right. Below us Roamers were peering up, and above us they were crouching to look down.

There was a harsh thud from behind. I turned to see the door that we'd entered the arena through seal itself shut.

"There goes one escape route," I muttered. My heart hammered, like it always did just before a fight. My knuckles whitened around the sword and spear I'd taken from the crude armory.

"Something tells me we won't have much luck using the

other one," Rose said. I followed her gaze to see an identical set of blast doors on the opposite side of the arena from us.

I squinted past the flaring floodlights and into the crowd. It didn't take long to find who I was looking for. Cairn was standing with his arms crossed on the other side of the wall, only a few strides away from where the announcer was still ranting. Our eyes locked through the bars separating us.

"Welcome, Vanguards," he said with a wide grin. "And friend."

My eyes flitted down to the spear in my hand. With a good enough throw I reckoned I could get it through the grate and pin the smug Roamer bastard to his seat. End this show before it started. But something made me stay my hand. Maybe a keen awareness that my strength was limited right now, and I needed to spend it wisely. Killing Cairn might be cathartic but it wouldn't save me. Wouldn't save Nadus and Rose.

Besides that, there was something... *different* about Cairn. I frowned, trying to put a finger on it. Maybe it was just that I'd been half delusional when I last saw him, but he seemed... bigger. In more than just a physical sense. He loomed larger than life next to the other Roamers, pulling all of them into his orbit.

And his eyes... those seemed different too. I blinked in confusion as I studied them. They seemed almost to glow, glinting with a faint, white, otherworldly light.

What had he been doing while we were locked away?

Cairn's smile turned knowing, as if he could read my thoughts. He turned to the announcer and nodded. The announcer said something to a small Roamer next to him, who hit a button on a control panel.

The blast doors on the opposite side of the arena began to grind open.

"Eyes front," Nadus said, raising his hammer and spear.

I felt suddenly exhausted. Two weeks of languishing in the

darkness, only to be thrust into *this*. Surrounded by strangers who wanted me dead. About to face... anything. Probably one of those rippers Shell said the Roamers had managed to trap into a section of the ship. Or multiple. Only thing that seemed certain was that Cairn had no intention of letting any of us leave this arena alive. He just wanted to leverage our deaths to entertain his followers.

I glanced at him again. Cairn simply looked amused. I spotted Dak next to him, Peacebreaker still resting at his side. He was positively giddy, his breathing apparatus's tubes inflating and deflating quickly.

A sudden surge of hate filled me. Those bastards had taken my ship. My gun. My crew.

I turned sharply away, stepping up next to Nadus and Rose. "Whatever it is," I said quietly, "we can take it. We've been in worse spots. Just stay calm and focused. Rose, get behind us. Use your spear to take jabs when you see an opening. Nadus and I will try to keep its attention."

"What is it?" Rose asked. I could hear the fear bubbling just beneath the surface of her voice.

"Dunno," I said, not taking my eyes from the doors. Damn, but they opened slowly. Dramatic effect, I guessed. All I could see through the gap was darkness. "Probably a ripper—"

There was a sudden screeching of metal. One of the blast doors was thrown violently from its hinges. A massive shape lurched into the arena.

Nadus swore.

The ripper spread its six sinewy legs, looking around itself, trying to make sense of the overabundance of stimuli. It raised its metallic wings protectively.

I felt an icy chill run down my spine. Not *just* a ripper. One of Ramar's enhanced ultrarippers. The ones that had been on the *Revelation*. And the *Panama*. The ones we'd come here searching for.

I killed you all.

The nightmare finally fixed its eyeless gaze on us. This one was different from the ones I'd seen before. A sheet of glistening black biosteel had grown over the top half of its face, encrusting its skull.

Not all of us.

The pale, sickly-looking skin that was stretched tight over the ripper's face split to reveal a massive, gnarl-toothed maw.

It charged.

THIRTEEN

"*Split!*" I yelled, bolting off to the right.

Nadus pivoted to the left, Rose staggering after him. I screamed at the top of my lungs, trying to keep the angel's attention on me. I wasn't sure how intelligent it was, or what its targeting priorities would be. Regular rippers were predictable, stupid. They just charged at the nearest warm body. Based on every experience I'd had, plus my conversations with Ramar, the ultrarippers seemed smarter.

The ripper lunged for me, sweeping out with one of its front claws. I dove out of the way and rolled into a crouch just in time to see it reposition and aim its tailspike at me. I lunged sideways and the spike speared the grate beneath me. I heard shouts of horror intermingled with delight as I rolled again, rising into a fighting stance with the sword in my left hand and the spear extended in my right.

The nightmare repositioned, circling me slowly. I moved with it, my eyes flicking back and forth between its legs and its tail. It started advancing. I inched backward, keeping the distance as best I could until—

The pillars. I felt a spike of panic as my back pressed against one of the metal beams supporting the arena. The ripper saw its chance and lunged, claws swiping. I ducked as the creature's biosteel claws tore cleanly through the beam, shrieking over my head in a shower of sparks.

I hacked upwards with the sword as I scrambled away and felt the blade bite flesh, then pivoted and slipped around the pillar, putting it between us. Black blood was pouring from a long gash I'd left in the creature's arm, and I could hear cries of disgust from below as the foul ichor splattered down through the grates onto the heads of the watching crowd of Roamers. The ripper ignored the wound. Even as I watched, it was healing, the fibers of its body reknitting.

A thousand questions battled for my attention. Where had it come from? How had they captured it? Were there more of them? Why hadn't they overrun the entire ship?

Figure it out later.

The ripper moved around the pillar and towards me with frightening speed.

Survive now.

I lunged forward with my spear, but it maneuvered one of its biosteel wings into the way, deflecting the point in a shower of sparks. It flicked its wing to the side and I cried out in frustration as the spear was jerked from my hands. So much for range. I clenched my teeth and gripped the sword in both hands, point extended outward.

The nightmare tensed its back legs, getting ready to pounce. Before it could there was a flicker of movement as a spear thudded into its back. It spasmed, a gnarled shriek catching in its throat as it pivoted towards the source of the attack. On the other side of the arena, Nadus was standing, teeth bared and his hand still extended from hurling his spear. Rose was nearby him, holding her own spear at the ready.

The ripper charged towards them. I sprinted after it, clutching my sword in both hands. No time to go back for the spear. The angel lunged at Nadus, who expertly sidestepped its first claw swipe and then swung with his hammer, knocking a follow-up attack out of line. He retreated again, ducking and weaving past a flurry of clawed swipes, then managed to catch the ripper's head with a surprise hammer strike. Sparks flew as the head of Nadus's massive hammer *slammed* into the layer of biosteel the nightmare wore like a helmet. The creature reeled back, hissing in frustration.

I yelled in fury as I chopped at its tail. The blade cut through flesh but snagged on one of the ripper's biosteel bones. The ripper pivoted, slamming one of its wings into my side and sending me staggering away.

Rose gave a frenzied battle-cry and lunged forward, jabbing with her spear. The point caught the ripper in the side. It turned to face the new threat, drawing back its tail.

"*Rose!*" I shouted.

Nadus lunged and grabbed the tail, straining to keep it from striking. The ripper lashed out at Rose with its claws instead. She leaped adroitly backward, narrowly avoiding the slashing talons but losing her spear in the process. I breathed a sigh of relief.

The ripper swung its body, sending Nadus flying into a pillar near me. I held my sword up and stepped forward. The ripper crept back, watching us carefully as it waited for another chance to strike.

"We're making no progress at all," Nadus groaned, staggering to his feet and picking up his hammer.

"And we're down three spears," Rose said, stepping behind me and holding her sword out in front of her.

They were right. The wounds I'd dealt to the ripper's arm and tail had both already mended. The strange biosteel growth around its head had protected it from Nadus's hammer. My spear was lying somewhere behind us, while Rose's had been cut in half by the ripper's claws, leaving its point in its side.

Nadus's spear, however, was buried deep in the ripper's back. I could see it trying to heal the wound but unable to, flesh wriggling unnervingly at the haft of the spear. The ripper's movements were awkward and uneven as it tried to circle us despite having six feet of metal rod piercing through its torso.

"Rose," I said. "We'll keep it busy. Grab my spear and get it to me—it's somewhere behind us. We need to slow it down. Strike deep and hard and leave the weapons in the wounds so it can't heal. Otherwise it'll just keep healing and we'll just get worn down."

Rose nodded breathlessly.

"Go," I said.

I lunged to the right, lashing out with the point of the sword. The creature blocked with a wing. I jumped back before it could counterattack, making an opening for Nadus, who stepped in close and swung the hammer—directly at the broken haft of Rose's spear. The haft vanished into the ripper's side like a nail into a board. It hissed in fury and spun to face Nadus. I ducked out of the way of its swinging tailspike.

"*Lax!*"

I turned to see Rose throwing my spear towards me. I caught it in one hand, pivoted, and hurled it with all of my strength into the ripper's center of mass. The creature spasmed as the spear point plunged through its back and out of its breast.

The crowd bellowed. I couldn't tell if they were rooting for us or against us. Neither, most likely; they were probably just excited by the sight of blood. I pushed them out of my mind. So far as I was concerned, there were only four of us here: Nadus, Rose, the nightmare, and me.

"Felt that one, huh, you bastard!" Nadus screamed, swinging with the hammer again. He caught the ripper in the face again, tearing flesh from metal bone with a shower of blood and sparks.

The ripper staggered backward, claws tearing at the spears

protruding from its flesh. Nadus and I backed away, stepping out of range of the wildly flashing claws.

"We gotta finish it," he said. "It's now or—"

The ripper lunged with a surge of terrifying speed. Nadus and I both went diving in opposite directions. I felt a sharp pain in my side. Rolled to see the ripper above me, claws flashing down towards me, its face a horribly mangled mess of torn flesh and glinting biosteel. I screamed as I hacked out with the sword. The ripper's claws sliced through my blade but it was enough to knock the killer blow out of line with my head. Instead the claws plunged through the bars of the grate below us. The ripper snarled as it tried to free itself, its claws caught at an awkward angle.

It opened its maw, teeth dripping with saliva. But my attention was drawn up. There, in the center of the biosteel growth around its head, there was a gap. Tiny and narrow, right between where the creature's eyes should have been.

The nightmare's head plunged down towards me. And I thrust upwards with the fragmented remains of my sword directly towards the gap. The ripper's head jolted as the blade caught on it, sinking half an inch of steel through. Black blood sprayed onto my face. The ripper squirmed and struggled. I twisted the sword back and forth, trying to push it deeper. But the blade was too thick to puncture all the way through. The ripper's head pushed down, fighting against me, teeth inching closer to my face.

Nadus bellowed as he swung his hammer again—this time with the spiked side of the hammerhead. The spike sank into the ripper's shoulder. Nadus twisted the handle of the hammer, hooking the spike beneath the ripper's shoulder-bone, and grunted as he pulled the ripper off of me, spilling it onto its back.

I rolled out of the way just as the ripper finally managed to tear its claws free of the grate. I blinked. Most of the Roamers below me were cheering, thrashing about wildly in their excitement. One, however, was simply standing in place, staring at me. A tall, muscular woman with dark skin. Familiar-looking.

I frowned. "Shell?"

"*Lax!*"

Nadus's voice jarred me. I threw myself sideways, avoiding the ultraripper's claws by far too close of a margin, and rolled to my feet. I resisted the urge to look for Shell and turned my attention back to the threat. Blood was still gushing from the wound I'd dealt to its eye. *So close.* I just needed something else narrow enough to fit through that hole.

Nadus backed up, trying to stay clear of the thrashing ripper's claws. I noticed a streak of blood running down his arm. The nightmare righted itself, then looked back and forth between the two of us, trying to weigh the greater threat.

I drew the ax from my belt, hefting it. It was short but sturdy, with a heavy, thick head. Wouldn't do much against the biosteel, but it was all I had now.

The ripper turned to me, settled back onto its haunches, and tensed its tail, preparing to strike. I fell into a low crouch, ready to spring the moment the tail started to move.

The ripper made its shot. The long black spike shot forward. Not towards me, though. Just a pace or so to the right.

Towards where Rose was standing a few feet behind me.

I bellowed and dove towards the tail. Too late to intercept the spike. But quick enough that I knocked the blow off course. The spike veered and slammed into a pillar, embedding itself in the steel.

Nadus gave a shout and attacked the ripper from the rear, pulling its attention away for just a few moments. I lifted my ax and chopped at the tail, striking right at the joint between two of the long bones. Blood sprayed as the axe-head hacked the tail clean through.

The ripper turned towards me, snarling.

The spike was still embedded in the steel pillar, a hand-hold's worth of bloody tail still wriggling on the end of it. I grabbed it and pulled. It stuck tight.

The ripper tensed to leap.

Come on. I heaved with all my strength, bracing one leg against the pillar. *Come on, you bastard.*

The nightmare jumped, claws extended, soaring through the air in an arc directly at me.

The spike came free.

I spun, bellowed, and lunged forward, directly into the ripper's charge.

Lightning pain across my arms. Down my leg. A flash of sparks as the long black tailspike glanced off the surface of the ripper's face plating, biosteel scraping against biosteel—and sank deep into the central gap.

I grunted as the full weight of the ripper struck me, lifting me from my feet. A moment later we both crashed into the floor, the ripper's momentum sending us rolling. There was a loud metallic bang as the ripper slammed into the wall.

Pain. Pain everywhere. I pushed myself through it, climbing to my feet, staring down at the ripper.

It climbed slowly to its feet, its movements unco-ordinated and jerky. The long tailspike had vanished almost entirely into the wound. I could see the gleaming black tip protruding out the back.

It turned to me. Opened its maw. Tensed. Spasmed.

Then collapsed.

FOURTEEN

I fell to my knees. Nadus grabbed my ax from where it had fallen to the ground and stood over the ripper, hacking at its neck until he'd torn its mangled head from its body. My ears were full of noise. In the fury of the battle I had somehow forgotten that we were surrounded by a crowd of bloodthirsty onlookers. Their wild cheers blurred with the sound of my own blood rushing in my head.

I stared down at myself. Blood was running down my body in thick red streaks, intermingling with the thick clots of black blood the ripper had sprayed onto me. The nightmare had scored several long, deep cuts on my arms, my side, and my left leg. I felt weak, lightheaded.

I killed you all.

Rose was kneeling next to me, saying something. Nadus bellowed and tossed the ripper's head. It bounced off of the floor with a wet squelch and rolled to a stop.

Not all of us.

"Lax!" Rose shook me. "Can you hear me?"

"Yeah," I said numbly.

"You've lost a lot of blood," she said. "Are you gonna be able to heal?"

I blinked down at myself. The cuts were long and deep, and there were a lot of them. But I could feel the tissue starting to reknit itself. Much slower than the ripper, but still. "Yeah," I said, fighting a wave of delirium as the world wavered around me. "Think so." I blinked downwards, towards the mass of Roamers below us. Was that Shell I had seen? Or just a Roamer who looked similar? "I thought I saw—"

My legs buckled. I started to fall, then felt strong hands catch me, holding me up. Nadus. His voice sounded far away. "Hang in there," he said. "I have a feeling we're not done here yet."

"What more could they throw at us?" Rose asked incredulously. "Was that..."

Right. She hadn't been on the *Revelation* with us. "One of the special rippers," Nadus said, his voice taut and grim. "Guess Ramar was right after all, huh, Lax?"

The crowd fell suddenly silent. Nadus cursed under his breath. I looked up to see somebody entering the arena. Cairn.

He shut the door that led into the audience area behind him, then glanced at the announcer and nodded once. The man started speaking in Aboenian, his voice just as pompous and ceremonial as before. He didn't seem disturbed by our show of strength in the least.

"Now what?" Nadus growled under his breath.

"Well fought, Vanguards." Cairn glanced towards the ruined body of the ultraripper. "I was worried you wouldn't make it for a moment or two there. How disappointing that would have been."

I let a low, feral growl escape my lips. "Is this what you kept us alive for? Some cheap entertainment?"

"It's more than that, Vanguard." Cairn slowly stripped off his coat with its heavy fur mantle, letting it fall to the blood-spattered grate beneath. "I told you before. This is my Proving. Only the strongest opponents will do. You should feel honored to be worthy."

Nadus scoffed. "*You're* going to fight us?"

Cairn's face twisted into that wide, wolf-like grin of his. "No, Vanguard. I'm going to kill you."

He pulled his shirt off, exposing his lean, muscular torso, then did a slow spin with arms outstretched for the benefit of the cheering crowd. I tried to blink away the blurriness in my eyes as his back turned towards me. There was a long, pale scar running the length of his spine. Beyond that, there was something about his whole physiology that just seemed slightly... wrong. Uncanny. Inhuman. I couldn't put a finger on what exactly it was, though.

"Stay with him," Nadus said softly to Rose. "Keep him awake. Don't let him drift off."

"What are you doing?" Rose asked as Nadus laid my head gently in her lap.

"Giving this asshole an encore," Nadus said. He stood up, tearing off the tattered remains of his own shirt. His left arm was streaked with blood where the ripper's claws had nicked him, but other than that he seemed to be more or less unharmed.

An uneasy feeling settled into my gut. I tried to sit up, only to feel pain lance through me.

"Easy," Rose said. "He's got this."

It certainly looked that way. Cairn was big, alright—but only by a regular person's standards. Nadus still towered over him by at least six inches. The size difference became even more obvious as Nadus approached the Roamer, stopping a few strides away. Somehow, though, that only added to my sense of dread. Why was Cairn so confident?

"Are you ready?" Cairn stretched his neck one way, then the other, his movement leisurely. Careless. He treated Nadus to a leering grin. "I can give you time to recover, if you need it."

Nadus only narrowed his eyes.

Cairn kicked something towards the Vanguard. It bounced with an angry metallic ring, landing at Nadus's feet. The ax Nadus had used to behead the ripper.

The crowd began to murmur, their voices low and anxious. I caught a glimpse of Dak's eyes, wide with uncertainty. However confident Cairn seemed, his followers were significantly less so.

Nadus glanced down at the ax. He scoffed. "You think I need that to kill you?"

"No," Cairn said. "I think you'd need a lot more."

Nadus chuckled. "Cute."

He struck blindingly fast and without warning. The blow apparently caught Cairn by surprise, because he made no effort to dodge. Nadus's fist connected with Cairn's nose in a wet crunch and a shower of blood. The Roamer staggered backward. Somehow, though, he managed to stay on his feet, catching himself against a pillar.

Nadus was on him immediately, fists moving in an endless barrage of blows. Cairn grunted in pain as two lightning-fast punches slammed into his body. He tried to block, to dodge, to escape, but Nadus was too fast, too strong, and too angry to let him go. Cairn was shoved back into the pillar, his body shaking as blow after blow slammed into him.

"*Kill him, Nadus!*" Rose yelled. The crowd was silent, save for a few cries of dismay and disappointment.

Cairn himself made no noise. His teeth were gritted in determination as he tried in vain to avoid the onslaught. I saw desperation in his eyes. Fear. Uncertainty. The bravado was gone, replaced by pure survival.

But he stayed up.

Nadus slammed an elbow into Cairn's temple, slamming his

head into the beam. The ringing sound of the beam reverberated through the entire room.

But Cairn still stayed up. His eyes were flickering, his face torn and bloody and misshapen, but he stayed up.

Nadus stepped back, grabbed the Roamer by the jaw with his left hand, and drew back his right. Cairn flailed, eyes mad with rage, but there was no escape from Nadus's vise-like grip.

"You messed with the wrong crew," Nadus growled.

Cairn's eyes widened.

Nadus's fist slammed into Cairn like a sledgehammer, right on the Roamer's upturned jaw. There was a horrendous cracking sound as bone shattered.

He went down.

The floor rattled as he fell face first, blood splattering. He didn't move.

"*Finally,*" Rose muttered.

The crowd erupted into angry shouts as Nadus turned to face them, blood dripping from his knuckles.

"This is what you wanted!" he screamed, his face flush with anger. "Isn't it? A trial of strength? Well, you damn well *have it!*" He pointed down at Cairn's unmoving body. "There's your leader. Your champion. Your *strongest.* So what does that make us?"

I wasn't sure how many of the Roamers understood his words, but the message seemed clear nonetheless. Uncertain murmurs rippled through the crowd. The announcer leaned over to several other older-looking Roamers and began a hushed deliberation. Dak had leaped to his feet and was staring at Cairn with shocked, unbelieving eyes. He seemed almost to be fighting tears.

"Maybe *now* they'll let us go," Rose said.

Nadus turned back to us, grinning. "That wasn't so bad. Especially not compared to—"

A shocked gasp ran through the crowd.

Nadus turned. I followed his gaze to see Cairn's body stirring.

Rose's mouth fell open. "What the..."

The Wolf pushed himself slowly to his hands and knees, coughing blood. The entire right side of his face had been flattened, and there were fragments of broken bone protruding from the torn skin. As we watched, though, the crushed bones began reforming themselves, the structure of his face slowly realigning.

The crowd fell silent.

Nadus narrowed his eyes. "What is this?"

Cairn climbed slowly to his feet. He was coated in blood, and his legs trembled slightly. That faint light I thought I had seen earlier was stronger now, radiating pale and ghostly from behind his eyes. I felt like I was looking through a foldgate at two distant stars.

"Strength," hissed Cairn.

Nadus snorted, then threw a punch with his right hand. No nonsense. Straight, fast, and powerful, aimed right at Cairn's still reforming jaw.

Cairn caught it.

The shock of the impact sent tremors through his body. But he caught it. With only the open palm of his left hand.

Excited whispers began to circulate in the crowd.

"What's going on?" Rose hissed at me.

I said nothing. Could say nothing. Could only stare at Cairn and those glowing white eyes.

Nadus growled in frustration and confusion, then swung with his left. Cairn blocked that blow too, smacking it away with his right hand. Then he punched Nadus in the stomach.

There was a cracking sound. Nadus staggered backward, eyes bulging. The Roamers cheered wildly as Cairn wiped blood from his face, spat out a mouthful of scarlet, and grinned, his eyes glinting with murderous, luminescent bloodlust.

"Let's try that again," he said.

Nadus took a few deep breaths, grimaced, and put his fists up. He circled warily this time, eyes watching Cairn with crystalline focus.

I pushed myself to my knees. My legs felt like they were on fire, but I had to move. To help. There was something at play here we didn't understand.

Nadus feinted left then stepped right and tried to hook Cairn in the ribs. The Roamer avoided the punch easily, stepping inside of it and delivering a series of quick, brutal jabs to Nadus's torso. Each blow sent shockwaves through Nadus's body.

Nadus tried to escape, but Cairn pursued him doggedly, never giving him a chance to breathe. Nadus tried to counterattack but Cairn was untouchable, slipping in and out of reach with inhuman speed. Nadus tried to block but Cairn's blows were like bullets, fast and constant and inevitable. Finally, Nadus changed tactics, abruptly abandoning his pugilist's stance and trying to tackle his opponent to the floor.

Cairn was ready, though. He twisted out of the Vanguard's grip, wrapped his own arms around Nadus's torso, lifted him, and slammed him to the floor with a crash that shook the whole arena. Before Nadus could get up, Cairn was already on top of him, raining down blow after blow.

If the crowd had been excited before, they were ecstatic now. Their screams were like hammers bludgeoning my skull, growing louder and louder with each hit. They didn't matter, though. All that mattered was Nadus. I gritted my teeth and pushed through the pain, charging at Cairn. He looked up too late and I managed to grab him by the torso, using my momentum to lift him and hurl him away. He slammed into a pillar, bounced off, spun in the air, and crashed to the floor.

My legs and lower back were screaming with pain but I ignored them as I pursued the Roamer. I scooped up from the floor the ax he had offered Nadus. I wasn't sure if there was some sort of rule I was breaking barging in like this, but I was beyond caring. I just wanted Cairn dead.

He was climbing back to his feet when I reached him, looking dazed. I swung the ax directly at his head. He threw himself out of the way, the blade missing him by mere inches. He rolled, evading another strike, then sprung to his feet.

"*There* it is!" He spat the words at me, specks of blood spraying from his battered madman's leer. "*There's* the rage!"

I growled and swung the ax in a low uppercut at his torso. He stepped into the swing, catching the ax, then lashed out with one foot and kicked my already injured left leg out from under me. I fell to one knee with a sharp cry, which was cut off abruptly as he punched his fist into my midsection, driving the wind from my lungs. He grinned madly, reared his head back, and slammed his forehead down into my nose with blinding speed.

Pain. Blinding, crushing, agonizing pain. The back of my head slammed into the floor. Cairn's boot caught me in the ribs, flipping me violently onto my stomach. My blurred vision caught another glimpse of the woman who was not Shell beneath me, clutching something small and round in her hand.

Cairn hooked his foot under me and rolled me onto my back again. I groaned, blinking upwards. He loomed over me, ax in hand, looking like some sort of ghastly demon with his eyes aglow and his face coated in blood.

"Just so you know," he hissed, raising the ax above his head. "This isn't personal."

I raised my hand in a pathetic warding motion, too exhausted to reply. I was still bleeding profusely from the deep cuts the ripper had scored on my limbs. It was taking all of my energy just to stay conscious.

The ax spiked down towards my face.

Movement from behind Cairn. Nadus, face battered and bloody, charging and bellowing.

Cairn spun, the movement blindingly fast, the ax rapidly changing trajectory.

Something, somewhere, *exploded* in a roar of sound and a flash of light. The arena erupted in screams.

For just a moment all I could see was white. I blinked it wildly away. When I could see again, Nadus was kneeling next to me, his breathing slow and heavy.

He coughed a thick wad of blood. My eyes drifted downward. Something was sticking out of his torso. I blinked, trying to make out what it was, and the world came into sharp focus.

No.

The ax that Cairn had been holding—the one he'd taken from me—was embedded deep in the center of Nadus's chest. I stared, my brain steadfastly refusing to make sense of the image. Trying desperately to explain it away. To believe anything *but* that Nadus had a foot of steel buried deep within his sternum.

Screams. The arena was alive with them. Not the frenzied roars of glee from before. Terror, panic, agony. The air was sharp with the smell of burnt metal and thick with smoke. All I could make out around us was a sea of dark, writhing figures. I was dimly aware that somebody had set off an explosive of some kind, but the information seemed trivial.

My eyes drifted back to Nadus. He was staring down at the ax in his chest. It didn't look real, somehow. I tried to say something. Anything. No words formed, though. All I could do was watch as my oldest friend tried desperately to breathe around the chunk of steel embedded in his lungs. Watch as his Vanguard healing tried desperately to repair the damage.

A shape loomed in the smoke. A wrathful, hungry demon, striding towards us.

"Hey."

Nadus. My eyes flitted back to his.

"We tried, didn't we?" He groaned.

I frowned. "Tried what?"

"Tried..." He rolled his tongue around his mouth and spat a thick wad of blood. "To make up for it all. Make a difference. Leave something... *good*... behind..."

The shape loomed closer. Cairn. His flesh was raw and red and torn from the explosion. His eyes were wild with rage.

My eyes flitted back to Nadus.

"Yeah," I said weakly.

He grinned. A bloody, broken-toothed grin. His cybernetic eye had been knocked loose and was misshapen. His good eye was bloodshot and distant.

He pushed the ragged words through torn lips. "I'll see you on the other—"

His voice cut off abruptly as Cairn grabbed him by the back of the head, pulled him away, and slammed his face into the pillar with a horrible, meaty thud.

Again.

Thud.

And again.

Thud.

And again.

CRUNCH.

The floor suddenly collapsed beneath me. I fell, smoke swirling around me, and slammed into something hard. My vision blurred. Somebody was standing over me, holding what looked like a plasma cutter in her hand. Shoving me. Rolling me.

I passed out.

FIFTEEN

There are two kinds of pain, boy.

"Will he survive?"

Guess which kind this is?

"He always does."

There are two kinds of pain, boy.

"Are you sure you're ok?"

Guess which kind this is?

"Yeah. I'm fine."

There are two kinds of pain, boy.

"I should have been there sooner. Faster."

Guess which kind this is?

"Maybe if I had been, Nadus would—"

Nadus.

My eyes shot open. Bright lights assaulted my retinas. A wave of pain crashed through my body. I shot upright, groaning through the pain.

"Hey!" Hands on my arm. Rose. She was wearing a dark gray jumpsuit and a concerned expression. "Relax. You're still hurt. Bad."

My thoughts felt broken, fragmented. Rose was here. Wherever here was. I was in a bed, in what seemed like some sort of medbay. Shell, wearing a set of tattered combat fatigues and a jacket, was sitting in a chair next to Rose. But all of that was just an idle observation, immediately discarded. I felt a surge of dread as the image of Nadus—his face away from me, his head bloody and misshapen—flickered in my brain.

"Nadus," I groaned. "Where is he?"

Rose said nothing.

I grabbed her by the fabric of her jumpsuit, pulling her close and looking her in the eye. Pain lanced through my body at the movement but it was overpowered by the sudden rage swelling in my chest. I snarled the words. "Where. Is. He?"

The corners of Rose's mouth tugged downwards. A tear glistened in the corner of her eye. She stared down at the floor.

"Lax," Shell said. "Nadus is..."

She didn't finish. She didn't need to.

Nadus was dead.

The anger left me all at once, like oxygen being cycled out of an airlock. I let go of Rose, my hands dropping to my side.

Nadus was dead.

I felt numb. Hollow. Weak. The information seemed at odds with my perception of reality. It contradicted everything I knew to be true. But it was true. I'd seen it happen. I had watched Cairn crush the life out of him. And I'd lain helplessly on the floor as it had happened.

I wanted to feel rage. Wanted to feel grief. Wanted to feel anything. But I couldn't. It just... didn't make sense. Nadus had been with me before anyone. Before Kessa, before Sev, before Rid or Rose. He had been the one to save me from prison, to give me a second chance at life. Back in the Vanguard we'd trained together, suffered together, fought together, across a dozen different worlds.

And now he was dead.

"What happened?" I asked finally, my voice barely audible in my own ears.

Shell's voice was weary. "What do you mean?"

I looked past her. We were in a long, dimly lit room lined with beds and shelves full of medical supplies. Some kind of a ragtag medbay. A few people I didn't know—Roamers, though they were dressed differently from the ones I'd seen, with cleaner clothes and tidier haircuts—wandered about, checking on resting patients. A handful of men and women wearing gray tactical armor were gathered by the door. When they saw me speaking, they muttered to each other and one of them said something into a comms device.

"In the arena," I said. "There was an explosion. I thought I saw you beneath the floor, with the other Roamers. Did you..."

Shell's eyes flitted up to the other Roamers. "I arranged a distraction," she said quietly. "And used it to save—" She cut herself off, gritting her teeth. "To get you and Rose out."

I frowned at the other Roamers. "Where are we?"

"We're in Command territory," Shell said. "We're safe from Cairn. For now."

I looked at her, her form crystalizing in my mind as if I was seeing her for the first time. She was sitting down on a chair next to my bed, shoulders drooped and arms hanging down between her knees.

I nodded slowly. I should have felt at least some relief. Rose was alive. Shell was alive. We were out of Cairn's reach. But I took no joy in any of it.

I'll see you on the other end...

"Rid and Bentley," I said.

"Cairn's holding them somewhere," Shell said grimly. "We're trying to find out where. And what's happened to them."

Cairn. Merely hearing his name was enough to make my muscles tense. The image of him rising from the floor, bones mending themselves before my very eyes, flashed through my mind. I saw his cruel, bloodthirsty grin. Remembered the sheer joy that had been in his eyes as he had grabbed Nadus and—

I shook myself, trying desperately to chase away the memory of the last few horrible moments in the arena before I had passed out. I didn't have the strength to face them right now.

The doors to the medbay opened. My eyes were drawn to a cluster of Roamer soldiers entering. They looked nothing like any of the Wolves I'd seen. Where Cairn's men had been ragged and wild-looking, these were dressed in crisp but simple matching sets of gray, form-fitting tactical armor. At their head was a tall, dark-skinned woman with a shaved head and a set of sharp, white tattoos on her temples that reminded me of the ones Shell wore. She wore armor like the other soldiers, but her breastplate and right shoulder pauldron each bore several bands of white filled in with unreadable text. I blinked in confusion at her. There was something keenly familiar about her—as if I'd seen her before.

She said something in Aboenian to a man who seemed to be the head of the medbay. After a brief conversation, she nodded, and several of the armor-clad men moved towards me.

One of the soldiers gave Shell a sharp look and snapped something at her in Aboenian. She cast her gaze down at the floor.

Another soldier moved to unlock the wheels of my medical bed. I waved him away. "Don't bother, I can stand on my own two—"

My legs buckled as I tried to put my weight on them. I sagged back into my bed, teeth clenched. Dammit. Those cuts were deeper than I thought.

The Roamer woman—their leader, evidently—nodded to her men, who proceeded to roll my bed out from its place next to the wall. She said something in sharp Aboenian to Shell, whose face soured as I was pushed out of the medbay and into an adjacent room. I found myself tensing as soon as the door closed, separating me from my crew once again.

The other Marshals left, leaving me alone with the woman. She leaned backward against a table, studying me. I tried to meet her eyes, to look impassive, but I couldn't keep myself from glancing nervously at the door. She just kept staring at me, one hand resting solidly on the butt of a pistol strapped to her waist.

"My name is Captain Tetra Lazerin," the woman said eventually. "I'm a Marshal of the *Aboena* High Command Security Crew. I've been assigned to investigate an incident involving the loss of your ship, the *Orpheus*, along with the theft of your cargo and death of your crewmate." She nodded to one of her men, who handed her a datapad. She frowned down at it. "Your name is Lackan VanDunn. Vanguard, decommissioned after the fall of Brahma and the cessation of the so-called Last War."

"Yeah." I eyed the door again.

Tetra sighed. "You're safe here, as are your companions."

I looked sharply at her. "Two of my crew members are still missing."

"So I've been told." Tetra glanced out the window towards Shell. "Your Roamer companion," she said in a careful, clipped tone, "claims that they are being held in custody by Cairn."

Fury welled up inside of me. "That bastard killed my friend. Stole my ship. He—"

Tetra held up a hand. "You're upset. I understand. But I need the whole story. From the beginning."

"Why?" My tone held more disdain than I'd intended to inject it with. "You gonna go to the Paragon?"

Tetra's face had already been hard. Now it was iron as she glared at me. "I have no doubt that you are aware we have no affiliation with the Paragon or its member organizations, Mr. VanDunn. Out here we solve our own problems. This incident may have been in direct violation of a Command Order, and I am responsible for conducting an investigation. If I find that the Wolves are in need of discipline, I will see that it is done."

I narrowed my eyes. "Discipline? Did you not *hear* what happened? Those bastards don't need discipline—they need to be put down."

"That's not your decision. Things are done differently among the Roamers. You're not in Paragon space anymore." She raised an eyebrow. "Not that it seems to ever impact your course of action anyways. So again: please explain to me, in your own words, what happened."

I wasn't even sure where to begin, or how much it was safe to say. The fact that Cairn had made us fight a nightmare for the entertainment of a crowd of cheering Roamers seemed to imply that their existence was no secret here. But I wasn't sure how much to reveal I knew. And I sure as hell didn't want to start diving into what had happened on the *Revelation*.

Tetra must have noticed my hesitation. Her face softened slightly and she gave a sigh.

"I understand you are overwhelmed. I gathered enough from your companions to know that you've been through hell these past weeks. But if there is going to be justice, I need to know exactly what happened." She leaned closer, looking me in the eyes. "Look," she said. "I believe you. I'm on your side. You can trust me."

I studied her for a moment, trying to figure out why she looked so familiar. It struck me in two parts. First, was the observation that she looked strikingly similar to Shell. And secondly, that I *had* seen her before. Beneath the arena.

I narrowed my eyes. "You were there. Below the—"

"*Quiet!*" she snapped, her voice drowning me out. I choked mid-sentence. I caught a glimpse of one of the guards outside glancing curiously at us, then back away.

Tetra waited a moment, checking subtly over her shoulder

to ensure nobody was listening, then leaned back and spoke softly, not looking at me. "You must say nothing of that to anybody. I wasn't there." Her eyes flitted back to me, cold and commanding. "Do you understand?"

I nodded slowly.

"Now." She crossed her arms. "Let's try again. The entire story, leaving nothing out."

I hesitated. Where to start? "My pilot, Rose, got a tip that—"

"No." Tetra shook her head. "The *actual* beginning."

I frowned. "You know about..."

"I know some of it." Her eyes drifted to Shell. "She told me some of the basics. That you raided a Paragon battlecruiser. And found things... *similar* to what you encountered in the Wolf's arena."

That gave me pause. If Shell had told her all that, she must *really* trust this woman. "The winged ripper," I asked quietly. "Where did Cairn find it?"

"I'm asking the questions," Tetra snapped. "Now. The story."

I told her. I didn't see much point in leaving out details. It felt blasphemous, somehow, divulging secrets I'd held for so long to a woman I'd just met a few minutes ago, but I was too exhausted to come up with any sort of clever lie. Tetra listened intently, interrupting me only occasionally to ask clarifying questions.

"When Cairn visited you in your cell," she said, "near the beginning. Before he disappeared. Did he say *anything* about what he was going to do?"

"Yeah. I think. He mentioned getting ready for the Proving. And..." I frowned, trying to force my weary brain back. "Something about a pilgrimage. He had to go get a gift from someone."

She stiffened. "The Stranger?"

"Yeah," I said. "That was it."

Tetra furrowed her brow for a moment, then nodded and

smoothed her expression back into its old unreadable state "I see. Continue."

I shrugged wearily. "You know the rest. I was in there for what felt like an eternity. Then I got dragged out and woke up in a room with Rose and…"

I'll see you on the other side.

"That was when you were forced into the arena," Tetra said. "To fight the winged ripper."

I nodded. My heart was starting to race.

"After you killed it," Tetra said, "Cairn challenged you. Reports about what happened next have been… *confused.*" She lowered her voice. "I was… occupied, so I was unable to see what transpired for myself. Some say that your Vanguard friend killed him. Gave him a brutal beating. But then that he…" She hesitated. "That he healed himself. Like a Vanguard, but faster."

"Yeah," I said, my voice hoarse. "That's exactly what he did. I know it sounds crazy. But I saw him heal. Way faster than a Vanguard can. Even faster than a ripper. His bones snapped back together. His jaw reformed. He got back up, and then…"

My voice trailed off.

Thud. Thud. Thud.

CRUNCH.

"I think I know what happened after that," Tetra said. "Thank you for your cooperation." She straightened. "You'll stay here in the medbay until our physicians are sure you've recovered. After that you can stay with your crew in the Outsider quarters."

She turned to leave. I held up a hand before she could. "Wait. You said I could ask questions."

She hesitated, then nodded and returned to her place leaning against the table. "Yes."

"Cairn. What is he?"

"A radical," Tetra said. "He believes that the Roamers

should take a more... militant approach to our Outsider policy. And, as you no doubt noticed, he is far from the only one who sees things that way."

I clenched my teeth. In my mind's eye I could still see Cairn rising as if from the dead, bones cracking back into place, torn flesh reknitting itself impossibly fast. "You know that's not what I mean."

She folded her arms, studying me for a long, silent moment before speaking.

"I don't know."

I frowned. After all of her carefully guarded answers, the candor of her admission surprised me.

She opened her mouth to speak, then turned sharply to the side as another one of the Marshals opened the door and poked his head through. "Command wants to see you," he said.

"Fine," Tetra said. "Almost done here."

The Marshal lingered long enough to give me a withering glare before retreating. Tetra turned back to me.

"Speak to nobody of what you've seen," she said, her voice low and serious. "Say nothing of the winged ripper. Say nothing of Cairn's... oddity."

I gave her a confused look. "Why not?"

She sighed. "In case you haven't heard, we don't accept Outsiders aboard the *Aboena* anymore. For reasons... *related* to the things you've seen."

I nodded slowly. "You don't want word getting out. About the rippers."

"The rippers," she agreed. "And other things. Command is not likely to be pleased that you somehow infiltrated our midst, even if Cairn was involved in luring you in. Not to mention your other companion, Ramar, who is still unaccounted for."

I perked up. That was news to me.

"My advice," Tetra said, straightening, "Is that you speak as little as possible. The less Command thinks you know, the more likely they are to grant you leniency."

"Wait." I tried to stand before receiving a painful reminder of why I was in this gurney. "What happens next?"

"You will be brought before Command," she said, opening the door. "They will hear your case and pass judgment."

"When?"

"Soon." She gave me one last look. "Until then, stay here and do *nothing*. Do you understand?"

No. I didn't understand anything. I gave a slow, numb nod anyways.

"Good." She straightened, turned, and opened the door. "Rest and recover. You will be kept informed."

She left. The other soldier lingered a moment longer to treat me to a disdainful scoff before he followed, muttering something in Aboenian under his breath that sounded anything but complimentary. More soldiers came in after and wheeled me back into the main room of the medbay.

Tetra was saying something in stiff sounding Aboenian to Shell without meeting her eyes. Shell simply nodded in response before the armor-clad Marshals left the medbay.

I made no effort to stop Tetra from leaving. Every part of me —body, mind, and spirit—felt drawn and haggard and numb and empty. As if everything inside of me had been violently scooped out and dumped back in that arena.

Shell turned to me. "I have a *lot* I need to tell you."

I nodded numbly. "Yeah. I..."

Green dots, flashing red...

One of the guards by the door approached us, snapping something in Aboenian at Shell. She nodded, then rose to her feet. With a shock of cold dread I realized that her hands were manacled together.

I blinked at her. "What are... They're arresting you?"

She shrugged. "There was a reason I didn't want to come back here."

The guard took her by the arm, leading her away. She spoke over her shoulder at us as they went. "Rest up. Do whatever they say. I'll see you guys again soon—I hope."

"Wait!" Rose sounded frantic. "How do we—"

Too late. Shell was gone.

Another guard approached us. "You two will stay here," he said stiffly. "You'll be carefully monitored. You are *not* welcome guests. You will be provided with food and whatever else is necessary, but you are not at liberty to leave these confines." His eyes flitted to me and Rose. "When you are recovered you will be escorted to new quarters."

"Where are you taking Shell?" Rose snarled.

He fixed a cold gaze on her. "She is a traitor," he said. "An outcast who has returned against Command's orders—and that's only the beginning of her crimes. She will be punished accordingly."

"She was just trying to help us," Rose insisted. "You can't—"

The guard held up a hand, cutting her off. "There will of course be a trial. She will not be killed outright, if that's what you're afraid of. You will see her again."

He returned to his post at the door, muttering something in Aboenian to his companions. One of them gave a short, grunting laugh.

"Bastards," Rose muttered. She glanced at me. "She'll be alright, though, right? Cairn shouldn't be able to reach any of us so long as we're under Command's watch."

I nodded weakly.

She hesitated. "Are you..."

"I'm fine," I said. But my voice felt hollow to my own ears. I was... tired. So, so tired. I felt as though the foundations of my soul had been worn down to dust. I cupped my face in my hands. "I just need... a moment..."

Rose and Shell were alive. *I* was alive. I should have been grateful, surely. Should have been conniving, figuring out our next move. How to get out of here and find Rid and Bentley. But I couldn't muster the energy. Couldn't work my way around the one thought that my brain had room for, that was pushing out everything else.

Nadus was dead.

SIXTEEN

"MOVE YOUR FEET, PISSHEADS! UP THAT HILL!"

Terror. Adrenaline. Resentment. Hate. I moved, too exhausted now to know why, calling upon every ounce of will I had to put one foot in front of the other, over and over again, each movement taking me just a bit further up the steep slope. There was no ground. Just mud, churned into thick sludge by thousands of desperate feet, clutching at me with each step I tried to take.

"KEEP MOVING! FASTER! GET THOSE FEET UP!"

The drill sergeant's voice echoed thunderously in my ears. Somebody was wheezing next to me, his thin, prepubescent body racking with desperate sobs. Only one word was intelligible. *Home.*

Home. For the briefest of moments I remembered that place. The small but comfortable cottage. The vast fields of wheat rippling in the wind. Green trees and bright sun. My mother's laughter drifting across the evening air.

The crying boy fell to his hands and knees, shaking with sobs. "*I wanna go home. I wanna... I wanna go...*"

Home. I missed that place. It had only been a few months

since I'd been there but it felt like an eternity. There were no green trees or golden fields here. No laughter or sun. Just brown mud and gray rain. I felt tears well up in my own eyes. I hadn't asked to come here. To this cruel, hard place of screaming drill sergeants and tasteless protein goop. To be tortured and worked and abused.

Self-pity consumed me. I almost collapsed next to the sobbing boy. But then another memory tore through my brain. My father's face, impassive as the Vanguard recruiters tore me from the seat of the truck next to him. Not even looking at me. Making no reply as I screamed desperately at him to help me, to save me, to tell me what was going on.

The tears were gone. The self-pity was gone. Where they had been I felt a surge of bitter, determined hatred.

I gritted my teeth.

"GET UP! GET UP, YOU PATHETIC PRICKLICKER!"

There was a jagged, electric crackling sound. I glanced over my head to see another boy—not the one next to me—screaming in pain as a drill sergeant easily four times his size jammed the sizzling end of a shockstick into his bare back. The sergeant's face was lit into a hungry, wide-toothed grin as he pushed harder. "IS THAT BETTER? HUH?"

It didn't look like it was. I forced myself to start moving again, only to hesitate as I glanced down at the boy next to me. He was in the fetal position now, bare skin almost completely covered in mud, arms held protectively over his head as other boys crawled over him in their desperation to escape the sergeant's shockstick.

The sergeant grabbed the boy he'd been shocking by the neck, lifting him effortlessly, and shoved him violently backward, sending him careening down the hill to collide with several other climbers. Then he turned, his eyes settling on the boy next to me.

He snarled.

"Hey." I lowered myself, patting the boy's shoulder. "Hey. Get up!"

He only whimpered. I looked up. The sergeant was striding towards us, but he wasn't having a much easier go of the muddy terrain than we were.

"HEY!" I grabbed the kid's ear and jerked it upwards. His whimper bit off in a sharp cry of pain as he looked up at me. His face was black with mud except where his tears had cut long, winding streaks.

"I..." he sniffled. "I want my mom. I want my dad."

I extended my hands towards him. "Screw 'em. They're not here—*we are*. You wanna get to the top of that hill?" I jerked my head towards the drill sergeant, who had been briefly distracted by an opportunity to torment another fallen boy. "Or do you wanna talk to *him*?"

The boy wiped a muddy hand across his nose, wiping away snot and leaving streaks of dirt as he looked over his shoulder. Then to the top of the hill. Then at me.

His eyes hardened. He grabbed my hand.

I groaned as I pulled him up with me. We were the same age—none of us recruits were older than ten—but I'd always been bigger than my years. That was what Mother had said, at least. The kid staggered to his feet. We scrambled up the hill, occasionally pausing to help the other along. The drill sergeant's voice became lost behind us as we made ground, leaving behind the other recruits.

"*One... step...*" I groaned. "*At... a... time...*"

Suddenly we were at the top. We both collapsed. I started retching, ejecting what little contents my stomach held into the mud. Soon as the smell hit him my companion starting vomiting too. When we'd both emptied our insides we fell onto our backs in the mud, feeling the cold rain on our faces and listening to the clamor of the rest of the boys catching up to us.

"I'm Nadus," the kid wheezed.

"Lax," I said.

"HEY! WHO SAID YOU COULD TAKE A NAP?"

I craned my head to see another drill sergeant stalking towards us and the several other boys that had fallen around us. He held his shockstick menacingly. "Get the *hell* off of my hill! Back down to where you started!"

I let my head roll limply back until I was staring blankly up into the sky again. *No.* I didn't have the energy. Didn't have the fight. I'd spent it all on the climb up. I was too exhausted even to blink as the raindrops splattered against my face. Somebody was screaming as the shockstick found its first victim. I'd be up soon. But I was tired. So... *tired...*

The rain stopped. No—somebody was standing over me. The boy I'd helped up the hill. Nadus. His face was haggard but grim with determination.

"Come on," he said. His voice was barely audible. He stretched a hand out to me. "One step at a time."

I grabbed it. "Thanks. I—"

I froze.

Nadus's grip was cold and metallic. Where the boy had been just a few moments ago now stood a full-grown Vanguard clad in a battle-scarred Jericho exosuit. His face was hidden behind the badly scratched visor.

The exo's armored gauntlet tightened. My fingers crunched like dry twigs. Pain forked like lightning through the splintered bones of my hand and up my arm. I gave a startled, twisted cry, sagging to one knee in the mud.

The Jericho's visor lifted. Nadus's face was a canvas of torn flesh, bloody tissue, and broken bone, almost unrecognizable as human. His nose had been flattened into pulp, and a dark hole peered out lifelessly where his cybernetic eye had once been. Bits of metal gleamed through pale yellow splinters of fragmented, caved-in skull.

The ruined flesh stretched into a broken smile of jagged teeth, hanging lopsided from a displaced jawbone.

"*You're welcome,*" he said.

One step at a time.

Walking wasn't comfortable, but it didn't hurt anymore. Each stride felt stiff as my slashed muscles continued to reform themselves. I could move again, though. Which was something.

Nadus would have told me to celebrate whatever small victories I had. Nadus would have told me to focus on what I could control. Nadus would have told me to be easier on myself, and not to push myself so hard.

But Nadus wasn't here. He hadn't been for almost three days now. So I did none of that.

"Hurry up, Vanguard." The gray-clad guard behind me sounded annoyed. "This is not a recreational walk. Command will not wait."

I raised my wrists, dangling the heavy manacles they'd placed on me before escorting me out of the medbay. "I kinda got that idea."

Ahead of me, Tetra raised a calming hand to her subordinate. "Calm, Gladen. He is injured. We have time. Command is probably still busy discussing the news from Outside."

The guard—Gladen—muttered something accusatory in Aboenian. Tetra's eyes narrowed. She gave a sharp rebuttal, then turned her eyes front.

I cleared my throat. "News from Outside?"

"The Paragon has declared martial law throughout the entire Redhawk system," Tetra said absently. "They've locked down the system's foldgate. Which means the *Aboenu* will need to replace several trade partners."

It was strange to realize that the universe hadn't stopped

spinning while I was locked in that dark pit. An entire system under martial law was the biggest political upheaval since the Last War itself. What else had I missed?

Sev. A pang of guilt struck me. She was probably sick with fear and fury. And she didn't even know where we were. Maybe the Roamers would let me reach out to her. I cleared my throat. "I need to—"

"Hurry *up*, Vanguard," Tetra said in an exasperated sigh, quickening her stride.

I clenched my teeth and did my best to keep up. Tetra had frequently acted like that during the past days my crew had been imprisoned—*housed* was the word the Roamers kept using —by Command's Marshals. She would be gentle and empathetic one moment, harsh and unyielding the next. From what I'd seen, it felt almost as if she were trying to prove something to the other guards.

When I paid close attention, I found that I could scavenge small scraps of meaning from their strange language. I wasn't too surprised by the fact. After all, it was based on the same old earth tongues as Galactic Basic—the common language devised after the foldgate network linked humanity's scattered planets. But what few words I could make out gave me precious little information, and what information I *could* glean, I was too exhausted to put together.

So I followed them mutely through the twisting, narrow corridors of the *Aboena*. This area of the ship—Shell had called it simply "Command territory"—was much cleaner than the other parts I'd been through. There was no rust or lichen clinging to the walls. The people we passed were dressed neatly but simply. They made room as we passed, watching me with leery eyes and muttering to each other. They reminded me of Shell much more than Cairn's wild followers had.

"My companion," I forced through gritted teeth. "Shell. Where is she?"

Gladen raised an eyebrow at Tetra.

"High-security confinement," Tetra said briskly. "Command will pass judgment on her in their own time. Not today."

We passed by another group of Roamers—a small family, with two young children. The mother ushered her children's wide-eyed countenances hurriedly away from me, while the father studied me with a barely concealed look of terror.

"They think I'm gonna bust out of these chains and start rampaging?" I muttered.

"They're not afraid of *you*," Tetra said. "They're afraid of what you represent."

I didn't get a chance to ask what she meant by that. We came to a halt in front of a set of doors, larger than the others I'd seen. Bold lettering I couldn't read stretched out above the doors. A set of guards—more heavily armored than the others I'd seen and bearing menacing-looking assault rifles of a make I didn't recognize—opened the door and stepped out of our way. Tetra proceeded through. I hesitated, feet frozen to the floor just outside.

"But *today*," Gladen hissed in my ear, "it's *your* turn for judgment, Outsider."

He shoved me. A few weeks ago I'd have fought him—let him see how little his force worked on me—then walked in myself. But today, even if I'd had the strength, I didn't have the will. I felt numb and aloof. My weak legs buckled and I staggered through the doorway.

I stumbled to a halt next to Tetra, who was standing at crisp attention in the center of a large, spacious room. We were on a long, rectangular platform, which was surrounded by three raised tables. Three Roamers sat behind each of them, looking down at us with expressions ranging from mild amusement to imperious disapproval. More of the heavily armored guards stood at the foot of each table.

So, this was the 'Command' Shell had told us so much about.

The elected co-captains of the *Aboena*. The most powerful people on the ship. If I hadn't already been scowling, I'd have started then. All the effort I went through to stay away from the powerful and important, and yet here I was again, dragged before them. Something about the crisp, militaristic trim of this room made me feel as if I was back in the Vanguard corps, standing before a tribunal for court martial. Except if that had been the case, Nadus would have been with me. Seated behind me, lending his silent support.

I glanced backward. Of course, Nadus wasn't there. He was dead, as I had to continually remind myself. Instead, I was treated to a glimpse of Gladen's smug face as the doors shut, sealing him outside—and, more importantly, me *inside*.

I turned my attention back to the Roamers seated above me. Despite it all, I found myself feeling almost amused. After all, what was the worst they could do to me? Throw me in a cage with a ripper?

My amusement vanished the moment I recalled that the absolute worst they could do wouldn't be to me—it would be to my crew. With a snap of their fingers, these people could order the deaths of my friends. The ones that weren't already dead, at least. I tried to shake myself out of my stupor. *Come on, Lax. Pull yourself together. Focus. Control yourself.*

The Roamer sitting in the middle started speaking—in Aboenian, of course. He was an elderly man, with dark skin and a bald pate rimmed with white tattoos. He wore a sharp white uniform evocative of a high-ranking naval officer. His voice was calm but authoritative.

"What's he saying?" I hissed to Tetra.

She didn't respond. The Roamer finished speaking and another began. This one was a very attractive middle-aged woman, dressed in a brightly colored robe of some sort that hugged her figure tightly. Probably high fashion around here.

I studied each member of Command as the woman

continued speaking. The man sitting next to her was dressed in similarly provocative colors. Two others wore dark, conservative clothing; the three in the center were dressed in white uniforms; and the last one was wearing armored pauldrons on her broad shoulders.

One seat was empty.

"Lackan VanDunn," the elderly Roamer said. It took me a moment to realize that was *my* name, not Aboenian gibberish.

I straightened.

"You are accused by many witnesses of trespassing, attempted theft, and conspiracy to commit murder and overthrow Command," he said. "Do you confess to these charges?"

I blinked. Conspiracy? Theft? I glanced at Tetra. She did not look back at me, eyes still fixed straight ahead.

"No," I said. My voice sounded weak and raspy, fading into the spaciousness of the large room.

He sighed. "Your claim of innocence is noted. You may now explain your actions. Be brief but clear. How did you come to our ship?"

I opened my mouth, then hesitated. How much to say? Was it more dangerous to reveal too little or too much?

Tetra leaned into my ear.

"You're simple traders," she whispered. "Cairn lured you here, then betrayed you. You know nothing of any strange rippers or powers."

I blinked, staring at her. She clenched her teeth, then stepped back and abruptly drew a shockstick and jammed it into my side. Pain arced through my muscles as the shockstick crackled. I fell to my knees, crying out.

"*Speak*, Outsider!" she barked, voice echoing.

The elderly Roamer raised an eyebrow at the show of force, but made no attempt to rebuke Tetra. I gasped for air, then climbed slowly to my feet. Tetra stared at me, looking for all the world like she wanted nothing more than to give me another taste of her shockstick.

"My crew and I," I said slowly, looking from Tetra to Command, "we're... traders." I sucked at my teeth, settling slowly into the lie. I had no idea what game Tetra was playing, but something told me she was the closest thing to an ally I had right now. "Just simple traders. We came here to strike a deal with a man named—"

There was commotion in the back of the room. Heads turned. Annoyed voices muttered in Aboenian. A new voice spoke up over them—loud, harsh. Familiar.

My blood ran cold. My mouth hung open and empty.

Cairn emerged, walking with slow confidence to the vacant seat. He paused behind it, treating the other Roamers to a disdainful sneer one by one. There was no sign that just a few days ago, his face had been beaten to a broken pulp.

Thud.

His eyes moved slowly. Maybe it was the fear and fury that was suddenly rushing intoxicatingly through my head, but I swore I could still see that cold, dangerous, faraway light glinting deep behind his pupils. Nobody else seemed to react, though, other than to glare sullenly at him.

Thud.

Finally, his gaze settled on me. His sneer twisted itself into a narrow grin.

Thud.

"Hello again, Vanguard," he said. He ran one hand over the side of his seat and winked at me. "Quite a fancy chair, isn't it?"

Crunch.

The weariness was gone. That layer of numbing apathy I'd been trying to fight my way out of for the past few days since Nadus's death suddenly crystalized and shattered, replaced by burning, incandescent rage. I charged, a bellow building up in my lungs and tearing itself free. I don't know what my plan was, or how I intended on getting up to him—all I knew was that no matter what it cost me, I wanted that bastard *dead.*

It didn't end up mattering. Tetra was ready. The moment I moved she lashed out with one foot, striking me with devastating force in the back of my already crippled leg and driving me to one knee. A split second later, pain crashed throughout my body as she rammed the point of her shockstick into my neck.

I shouted, spasmed, and fell over onto my face. I reached out, trying to pull myself back to my feet, to get at the bastard that had killed Nadus, only to feel another shock run through my body as she pressed her shockstick between my shoulder blades and pinned me to the floor.

"Stay *down,* you idiot," she growled.

The order was hardly necessary. I couldn't move an inch. My muscles seized as electricity surged through them. My furious roar broke off into a sharp, ongoing cry of pain. She kept the shockstick down a few seconds longer, waiting until I could smell burning flesh before she removed it. By that point any fight I'd had in me was long gone. My eyes flickered, my muscles felt limp and useless, and based on the warmth spreading through my pants, I suspected I'd pissed myself.

Somebody grabbed me by the feet, dragging me. I managed one look upward before they pulled me from the room. Cairn was watching me, eyes shining with barely contained amusement. He flashed a grin. "Nice try, Vanguard," he sneered. "Next time, perhaps?"

The doors shut, sealing me out of the room. The guards who had been dragging me let go and my feet thudded deadly to the floor. I blinked, groaned, and rolled over onto my back. Someone was standing over me. Gladen.

"That was fast," he said.

. . .

I had just regained control of my legs—*again*—by the time the doors opened and Tetra came through. She gave a short nod to Gladen and strode past, down the hallway in the direction we'd come from.

"On your feet, Outsider," Gladen grunted as he helped me up. I glanced over my shoulder to try to get a glimpse of Cairn. The doors closed again before I could see through them. Gladen shoved me, sending me staggering down the corridor. "*Move.*"

My rage had cooled into an icy, bitter hatred. My head was spinning, and not only because Tetra had damn near electrocuted me to death. From what Tetra had said earlier, I'd figured Cairn just got a bit more influence within his cabal by joining the Wolf's *inner circle* or whatever she'd called it. She had said he got a vote on who the Wolves sent to Command. Not that *he'd* be going.

Tetra was several strides ahead of me. I quickened my pace, falling into step just behind her.

"What the *hell* just happened?" I growled.

"I saved your life," she said without looking back. "Twice."

I reached back, prodding tenderly at the burned flesh on my back. "Didn't feel that way."

"Another second and those guards would have shot you to pieces," she said. "They have little regard for Outsiders, and less for puppets. I had to fight to get Command to see you at all."

My heart fell. "And then I screwed it up."

"Almost."

I hesitated. "And the second time?"

"Cairn attempted to convince Command that you and your crew came to rob him," she said, lowering her already carefully quiet voice as we passed by another set of Marshals. "And that you should be executed. I presented enough conflicting evidence to make his claims disputable."

"What's that mean for my crew?" I asked, not sure I wanted to hear the answer.

"It means that for now," she said, "you're safe."

"What about Shell?"

Tetra stiffened. She glanced subtly over her shoulder, making sure that Gladen wasn't in earshot. He'd fallen behind slightly, reading something off of a handcomputer. "She will be judged separately," she said. "Her crimes are greater and her status... more complicated."

"Crimes? She saved her friends from being butchered." I raised an eyebrow. "Something I seem to recall she had some help with."

"Do *not* speak of that." Tetra's face betrayed no emotion. "I have enough scrutiny on me as it is. The fact remains that she stands accused of a long list of crimes. Trespassing. Unlawful transportation of Outsiders into the homeship. Theft. Murder. Sabotage. And that's before considering her prior crimes."

I frowned. "What prior crimes?"

She looked sharply at me. "She hasn't told you?"

"All she told us was that she didn't want to come back here."

Tetra's expression was sour. "She shouldn't have. She should have stayed far, far away. All of you should have."

"Bit late for that." I hesitated. "Whatever she did before, is it enough to..."

"I do not expect that Command will show leniency to her." Her voice was stiff.

I cursed under my breath. "And you're alright with that?"

She narrowed her eyes in an expression that reminded me of Shell. I'd certainly struck a nerve. "Do you want me to hit you again? If so, please keep talking. I'll be more than happy to oblige."

I didn't want her to hit me again. But I had a narrow window of opportunity to communicate and she was the only person who had shown an iota of sympathy to our case so far.

"Look," I said. "I don't know half of what's going on here. And I don't care to. All I care about is getting my crew—what's left of them—out of here. *Alive.* And if you think you can stop me—"

"*Shh.*" She looked back sharply at Gladen. He was still looking down at his computer. "Calm yourself. I'm on your side. But the situation is complicated. Even if we somehow free your companions, there will be nowhere to go. There are only two ways off of this ship: the Trader vessels, which Command has had on lockdown for years now, or Cairn's smuggling ships."

"Just point me in the right direction," I growled.

Tetra scoffed. "If I knew where they were docked, I'd have put a stop to them long ago. Cairn has been making a mockery of Command's authority for years."

I frowned. "I thought he was a part of Command. He was in the trial."

"He is now." She grimaced. "That 'Proving' was his way up. A show to gain support so that he could be voted into power."

My eyes nearly bulged. "So that disaster in the arena was *allowed?* Command is aware that he has rippers?"

"They've chosen to turn a blind eye," Tetra said carefully.

"Why the hell would they do that? Do they have *any* idea of what would happen if a ripper got loose?"

Tetra pursed her lips. "It's a complicated, delicate situation."

I gave a frustrated growl. "Fine. I get that. But I *don't care.* All I care about is getting out of here. So if Command won't let us go and Cairn wants us dead, what other options are there for me and my crew?"

She opened her mouth to respond, only to pause. I heard rapid footsteps behind me as Gladen caught up, a suspicious look on his face.

Pain exploded in the back of my head as Tetra struck me with the butt of her shockstick. I grunted and staggered against the wall, ears ringing.

"I told you," she growled. "*Shut. Up.*"

Gladen doubled his pace. He slid to a halt and said something in Aboenian. Tetra gave a short, terse response and continued walking.

When my vision cleared, Gladen's previously stoic gaze was almost apologetic.

"Whatever you're doing to anger her," he said, "for your own sake, *stop*."

"Trust me," I growled. "I would if I could."

SEVENTEEN

There are two kinds of pain, boy.

We tried, didn't we?

Not all of us.

Green dots, flashing red…

I jolted upright, coated in sweat. Blinked blearily around me. I was in the medbay, sitting in my undersized bed.

"Can't sleep?"

I glanced to my right. Rose was sitting up in her own cot a few spots down from me, her blankets gathered in a bunch around her knees. It was hard to tell in the near darkness, but I thought I could see wet streaks on her pale cheeks.

"Not really. You?"

She gave a dry, humorless chuckle, shaking her head.

"Figures." I swung my legs to the floor and leaned forward, groaning. "Maybe it's the food. Whatever this fruit stuff they've been feeding us is, I'm about sick of it."

"How are they even growing it?" Rose reached towards her bedside table, hefting a small piece of pale, white-looking fruit. The stuff was all we'd been fed since arriving in the medbay. It was bland and overly chewy, but I figured it was better than protein blocks. "Are they using the Lifeblood for it?"

I frowned. She brought up a good point—one I'd been too distracted to think of. "Maybe. But... from the sounds of things, they've been living off of it for a while now."

Rose turned the fruit over in her hands. "So... they didn't even *need* the Lifeblood, then?"

I shook my head. "I have no idea."

Rose stared at the fruit a moment longer. A look of rage passed suddenly over her face. She drew her fist back and hurled the fruit across the room. It splatted against the far wall.

Rose took a deep breath, then hid her face in her hands.

"I wish I'd never responded to that message," she whispered.

I wasn't sure what to say. *I wish so too. Maybe that way Nadus would still be alive.* But that didn't seem like it would be particularly helpful. Instead, I let out a heavy sigh.

"You thought you were doing the right thing," I said. "There's no going back now."

She nodded sullenly. "My mom is probably pissed."

I chuckled. "Yeah. Hell, even if we make it out of this, I've half a mind to send you lot home and run for the stars myself to escape her wrath. Doubt these Roamers can do anything worse to me than whatever she's got waiting."

She gave a half-hearted smile. "She talks a big talk about that. But she'd never hurt you."

"Don't be too sure. I know your mom pretty well too, you know. Or, I thought I did. Did you know she kept you and your dad a secret from us?"

"She told me." She hesitated. "She also told me that she never meant to hurt you by doing it. She just wanted to protect everyone."

"I get it." I shrugged, looking away. "Still hurts."

She was quiet for a moment. When she did speak, it was

quietly. "You know, I think you coming back is the best thing that's happened to her in a long, long time."

I turned sharply back to her, frowning. "What do you mean?"

"She works herself too hard," Rose said. "She blames herself for everything that happened. She puts all her focus in me and into her work. Thinks she can't allow herself any personal happiness. In the year since you showed up, though..." She shrugged. "I don't know. She's happier. Lighter. Feels a bit like she did before everything went to hell. Almost."

I nodded thoughtfully.

There was a whirring sound as the door to the medbay opened. I turned sharply towards it, frowning. There was no such thing as night or day out here, of course, but so far it had seemed that most people kept to the same schedules. And this was right smack dab in the middle of when most people were sleeping.

Several Roamer guards, dressed in heavy gray armor, stood outside. These ones wore helmets that covered their faces.

Rose and I shared an uncertain glance. It had been two days since my visit to Command, and we'd heard nothing from Tetra since then. Were these guards working with her? Or was this something else?

One of the guards stepped inside and tossed me a pair of manacles. "Put these on," he said roughly. His voice wasn't familiar. He sounded nothing like any of the other Command Marshals we'd talked to. If anything, he sounded more like...

A chill ran down my spine. He talked like one of Cairn's Wolves.

"What's going on?" I asked, not moving.

"Transport." He took another pair of handcuffs and tossed them to Rose.

"To where?"

"Command has decided to grant you mercy," he said, without putting much effort into making it sound believable. If anything, he sounded almost amused by the prospect. "We're taking you to your ship."

I didn't move. A quick glance at Rose told me she didn't find the story any more believable than I did. "Seems an odd hour for..."

He drew a pistol and held it menacingly at his side. "Come on. Put on the manacles."

I studied him, then his companions. If I was quick, I could take him before he could raise that pistol. Might even be able to get a few shots off at his buddies before they took me down. But I wouldn't be able to protect Rose while it happened.

I clamped the magcuffs around my wrists. Slowly. When I was done, he stepped closer, yanking on them to make sure they were tight, then repeated the process for Rose. Finally, he waved us towards the door with his gun. "Alright. Move."

I took the lead. The other guards parted to make room for me. There were six of them in total. They were clad in the same heavy armor I'd seen the other Command guards wearing, but their weapons were more varied. Two had assault rifles, one had a shotgun, while the other two had only short blades. One of them had a black shoulder pauldron. That one was slightly smaller than the others and trailing behind at the back.

As I glanced at them, they held up a single finger, then lowered it.

I blinked in confusion. A harsh shove from behind jolted my attention away. "Move," the lead guard growled.

I glanced once again at the guard with the black shoulder pauldron, then at Rose. She raised a questioning eyebrow at me.

"*Wait*," I mouthed. She gave an almost imperceptible nod.

We moved.

. . .

"I don't think they're taking us to a docking bay," Rose hissed.

I was inclined to agree. With each step our ominous procession seemed to go deeper into the ship, rather than up towards its surface. I thought so, at least. The *Aboena* was a maze, and the farther away we got from Command territory, the more twisted and convoluted it became. Where the halls of the Command sector had been clean, well lit, and frequented by various other foot traffic, the tunnels beneath them were dark, dank, narrow, and increasingly cold.

"Where are we?" I asked the head guard, not expecting an answer.

"Keep moving," he snarled in response.

I did. Carefully. At every corner we turned, every slight pause we made, I looked for a chance to fight back. It never came.

Finally, we stopped in front of a door. The guard at the front of our little group entered a code into a control panel next to the door, then pushed it open.

"In you go," he growled.

I walked in carefully. I found myself in a small room, lit only by a single flickering overhead light. There were three other people in the room. Two of them were Wolves. If I hadn't recognized them by their wild, mismatched attire I'd have recognized their faces from the ambush on the *Orpheus*. I tensed. I'd known that this was a trap of some sort, but having it confirmed still brought a rush of adrenaline to my body.

The third person in the room was Shell. Her hands were bound by a magcuff wrapped around a pillar in the center of the room. Her face was bruised and torn, her clothing red with blood. She looked up weakly as we were forced into the room.

"Hah!" One of the Wolves—a beefy-looking man with blood-covered knuckles—grinned at us. His accent was so thick I could barely understand him. "About time! This is much more fun with an audience."

"Shell!" Rose's voice was taut with equal parts worry and anger. "Are you..."

"I've been better," Shell moaned.

Rose growled and tried to leap forward. One of our guards grabbed her from behind, restraining her. "Easy there," he snarled. "The show hasn't even started yet!"

The sight of Shell's battered face was enough to send hot fury through my veins. I forced it back, though. *Wait for the right moment.*

The large Wolf grinned. "Not what you were expecting, eh?" he said. He turned and stooped, picking up an ax that had been leaning against the wall—not unlike the one Cairn had struck Nadus with in the arena. "Do not worry. We can be quick."

Another surge of anger shot through me. I clenched my teeth.

The captain of our guard—if they even were guards—stepped forward, saying something in Aboenian. He and the big Wolf started talking animatedly. Their tone veered from annoyed to confused to angry.

I glanced at Shell. She was watching us, leaning weakly against the pillar. When I met her eyes, though, I saw a flicker of raw fury in them.

Movement on my right. I glanced over to see the guard with the black shoulder pauldron approaching me. I tensed. The rest of the guards didn't pay any mind, though, their attention seeming to be mostly focused on the heated discussion happening between the guard leader and the leader of the Wolves.

The guard casually slid a security chip into place in my magcuffs. They beeped once and opened, clattering to the floor.

All eyes turned to me.

Wait for the right moment.

Three weeks of pent-up rage—of waiting for the right moment—suddenly welled up inside of me and burst out.

I bellowed and charged.

EIGHTEEN

The guard nearest to me—not the one with the black shoulder pauldron—turned a shotgun towards me. I slapped it out of the way and shoulder-checked him, sending him hurtling into two of his buddies. Another guard raised a pistol. Rose reached out and caught his arm with her manacles, restraining him. I lashed out with one foot. There was a cracking sound as his knee bent sideways.

A gunshot boomed, painfully loud in the small confines of the room. I expected to feel a bullet tearing through my flesh. Instead, there was a cry of dismay as one of the Wolves toppled over with a bullet hole between the eyes.

I didn't take the time to figure out who fired the shot. There were bodies everywhere, shouting and grunting. The three guards I had knocked down were recovering, the one whose leg I'd broken was flailing on the floor, and the fifth dropped with a choking sound as our masked rescuer fired a shot into his neck. That left the captain, who had backed up against the wall and was scrambling to draw a pistol.

The beefy Wolf growled and lunged at me, swinging the ax towards my head. I caught the haft in one hand and kicked his legs out from beneath him. He grunted as he slammed into the ground, then scrambled to reach for a fallen weapon—the shotgun. I beat him to it, kicking him in the gut and slamming him against the wall. He gave a choking cough and started retching.

I grabbed the shotgun from the floor and whirled, aiming it at the captain just as he finally got his weapon free. We fired at the same time. A bullet *cracked* the air next to my ear. The blast of pellets from the shotgun slammed into his torso and sent him wheezing to the floor.

One of the three guards lunged at me with a long knife. I caught his wrist, pulling the knife away from my body, then let his momentum carry his body into mine, pinning him against me. He grunted as he came to an abrupt halt. I wrapped one arm around his torso then flung him upwards, slamming him into the low ceiling and letting him fall back down, twisting the knife from his grip as I did so.

The other two guards stared, knives of their own held at the ready. They kept their distance, though, their stances nervous.

I glanced down at the Roamer groaning at my feet. He was reaching groggily for a pistol that had fallen to the floor in the chaos. As I watched, his head turned up towards me. His helmet had fallen off and I caught a glimpse of two terrified eyes peering up at me.

I raised my foot.

Normally, in hand-to-hand combat, I hold back a bit. The way I see it there's no point in killing folks when I can neutralize them non-lethally.

But these men had taken my ship. Killed Nadus. Tortured Shell. Hell, they might have already killed Rid and Bentley. They'd almost certainly brought Rose and me down here to kill us.

With all that in mind, I felt no compulsion to hold back anything at all. I bared my teeth in a bloodthirsty snarl. The Roamer's eyes widened.

My foot slammed down. There was a cracking sound. The Roamer twitched and went still.

The other two guards dashed for the door and vanished.

I spun, assessing the chaos. The guard captain was on his hands and knees, groaning. Our rescuer was helping Shell out of her chains. The beefy Wolf was still retching on the floor. The guard with the broken leg had gone quiet, seemingly passed out from the pain.

"That settles that," I gasped.

"Almost," Shell growled, glaring at the fallen Wolf. She stooped and lifted the ax from the floor.

The Wolf looked up. His eyes widened. He shouted something in Aboenian that was abruptly cut off as Shell brought the ax down on his head. There was a wet crunch.

The guard with the black shoulder pad lifted their helmet. Tetra's brow was coated with sweat. She looked around at the carnage.

"We need to go," she said. "*Now.*"

"Just... need... a... *there.*"

Tetra gave a satisfied grunt. The darkness retreated to the corners of the room as a dim, flickering light overhead activated. She stepped back from the control panel she'd been tinkering with, wiping grease from her hands.

"Where are we?" Rose asked, looking around. The room we were currently in was small and narrow. A set of thick pipes extended through the walls above us, radiating heat. I guessed this was an ancient maintenance room of some sort. It must not have been a particularly important one, though, because it looked like it had been years since anyone had stepped foot in here. Lichen coated the walls, and I thought I saw a skitter of movement as some tiny animal scurried away from the light.

"Free territory," Tetra said, sagging against the wall and

sinking to the floor. She winced. In the dim light I noticed red staining the side of her armor. After fleeing the site of our near execution we'd run through the twisting corridors for nearly twenty minutes before she agreed to stop. "Only maintenance crews and Oathless come through here. We should be safe. For a while, at least."

Shell eyed the blood on Tetra's armor. "How bad is it?"

"Not bad." Tetra grimaced, trying to reach for a strap to undo the breastplate. Shell helped her, removing the chest piece, then lifted Tetra's shirt. A long cut stretched from the Marshal's hipbone across to her back. She gave a sharp exclamation in Aboenian as Shell carefully probed it.

"It's not too deep," Shell said. "You'll need to rest, though."

"I can't." Tetra grabbed a small pack and rummaged through it, withdrawing a compact medical kit. "I'll be missed if I'm gone too long."

I raised an eyebrow. "You're really going back? After all..." I gestured vaguely in the direction we'd come. "That? You just killed a bunch of your own men."

"No." Tetra took a small, gun-shaped item from the kit and held it a few centimeters away from her wound, pressing a trigger. Sharp light radiated from the device. She held it over the injury for a few minutes, moving it back and forth. There was a faint sizzling sound as the light sanitized the wound. "Those weren't Marshals. They were Wolves. They were gonna gather you all up and kill you. Out here, in unclaimed territory. No witnesses."

I studied her. "Why?"

"Because—" She breathed sharply through her teeth as she hit a different button on the device and pulled the trigger again, administering a layer of sealing paste over the wound's surface. "Cairn doesn't want you leaving the ship, and he doesn't want you talking to Command. Thinks you know too much."

"Not what I meant," I said. "Why are *you* helping us?"

Tetra glanced up, meeting Shell's weary eyes for a moment, then looked back to me. "Because nobody else is going to fix things, so I guess it's up to me. Cairn clearly wants you all dead. If I can keep you alive... well, that's a victory in my book."

I narrowed my eyes. "Let's start from the beginning, then."

Tetra sighed, then gestured towards the floor. "You're gonna want to get comfortable."

"Fifteen years ago," Tetra said, "a crew of Aboenian salvagers found a derelict ship."

"The *Panama*," I said.

She gave me a sharp, questioning look. "No," she said. "Not yet. The *Panama* was the turning point. But this was when it began. This was a small ship, unlike any other we'd ever seen. The salvagers were less than honest in their reports of what they looted from it. I was just a young recruit at the time. My squad was assigned to investigate. We never found much out, but what we *did* discover was that of the eleven salvagers who brought in the craft, all but three of them vanished into unclaimed territory, while the remaining three were found murdered. We searched for a while, but gave it up in the end. A few salvagers squabbling with each other over stolen goods wasn't anything new or important.

"Rumors began to spread, however, that what they'd found on that ship was not an item, but a person. Somebody that they secreted away with them. Some sort of miracle worker. Pretty soon people started calling them the Stranger.

"People said the Stranger could heal unhealable injuries. Cure incurable diseases. Bring back the dead. People would go on pilgrimages, scouring the ship to find this Stranger. Most disappeared. Those who came back claimed to have been touched by their power. The Stranger's followers started to call themselves *Shapers*.

"I wrote it all off. Figured it was some sudden spiritual movement that would blow over. Didn't seem dangerous, though, so we didn't put much effort into investigating. And by the time his cult formed..." She glanced sideways at Shell. "We had bigger problems on our hands."

Shell's face hardened. "The *Aboena* got hit by rippers. The war was over by then, they were just... drifting. Found a lucky target."

I nodded. Shell had told me this story before—part of it, at least. She'd been a Marshal like Tetra back then. "That was when you quarantined part of the ship."

"That was when *Command* quarantined part of the ship," Shell said, with a hard look at Tetra.

Tetra stiffened. "Command made a strategic decision to limit the casualties," she said, keeping her voice level. "A decision that ultimately saved the *Aboena*. The ship is designated into many sectors, each of which have only a limited number of ways in or out. Command chose to seal off the sector the attack had occurred in, despite the fact that there were still civilians inside."

Shell's expression darkened further. She turned away, staring into the darkness.

Tetra sighed. "My point in bringing it up is that by the time we had the resources to turn our attention back to the Shapers, it was too late. They'd become too entrenched within the ship. In fact, they'd become invaluable. They won't share how, but somehow, they'd started growing *food* in their secret places. Fruit."

I nodded slowly. "The stuff you fed us in the medbay."

"Exactly. We call it whitefruit. Command struck a deal. The Shapers would provide their whitefruit to Command. And in return, Command would grant the Shapers space, peace, and... *security.*" She emphasized the last word as if she meant something more by it.

I frowned. "Meaning?"

"Meaning that they would cut off all contact with the Outside," Rose said, eyes widening with realization.

Tetra nodded her affirmation. "The Stranger was, apparently, worried about what would happen if they were discovered by Outsiders. They assured Command that their presence would more than compensate for the lack of trade."

"Has it?" Shell asked skeptically.

"That depends on who you ask," Tetra said. "But there's no denying the miracles, as the Shapers call them. And there's no explaining them, either."

"Alright," I said. "What does all of this have to do with the rippers?"

Tetra grimaced. "That started just a few years ago. When the Shapers went out and found the *Panama*."

I frowned. "You make it sound like it was on purpose."

Tetra shrugged. "So far as we can tell, it was. The Shapers made some sort of deal with the salvagers. Got a crew to fly some of them out to the *Panama*. The salvagers I questioned said that it was as if the Shapers knew exactly where to go. Once they got there the Shapers went aboard alone. They emerged a few hours later, missing a few people, but towing several massive crates. Then told the salvagers to blow up what was left of the *Panama*."

My mind reeled. Somebody who knew precisely where the *Panama* was? After the explosion that had happened when I was aboard, it would have been knocked even further off of its path. I supposed that if someone could have gotten access to the mission data of the Paragon patrol that had picked me up, they *might* have been able to extrapolate where it would end up, but that was a big *if* stacked on top of several other even bigger *ifs*.

And that was even before I considered the fact that these Shapers had, apparently—somehow—*wrangled ultrarippers into crates*. It defied reason. Maybe they'd developed a tranquilizing agent of some kind that worked on them.

"The deal that the Shapers struck with the salvagers," Shell asked. "What was it?"

Tetra shook her head. "Those I questioned either did not know or were unwilling to confess. All I know for certain is that the looting of the *Panama* marked the start of the Wolves. The salvagers who found the *Panama* for the Stranger gradually became more violent and bloodthirsty, resisting Command's attempts at keeping the *Aboena* isolated from the Outside. Their leader, well... you already know him."

"Cairn," Shell growled.

I nodded slowly. "Alright. So what does Cairn want?"

"He wants to go on the offensive," Tetra said. "He claims he can use those winged rippers. Control them. That with them, he can destroy the Paragon."

I grimaced. Ramar had been right from the start.

"Is it true?" I asked. "That he can control them?"

Tetra shrugged. "I have no idea. But they haven't taken over the ship yet, so he's doing *something* to them."

"How many of them does he have?" Shell asked.

Tetra shook her head. "No idea. But we assume not many. Otherwise they'd spiral out of his control."

Rose folded her arms. "Our friends. Rid and Bentley. Do you know where they are?"

Tetra nodded. "I managed to figure out where Cairn holds his prisoners." She reached into her backpack and retrieved a roll of paper, which she unfurled to reveal a rough map of the *Aboena*. I studied it. Trying to wrap my brain around the *Aboena*'s layout in two dimensions made me miss the *Orpheus*'s holodisplay, but I figured it out after a few moments. The *Aboena* was roughly fifteen kilometers long. A march of that length in a straight line would take at least three hours without breaks. But I suspected our journey would take us in anything *but* a straight line. The entire ship was about to be hunting for us, if they weren't already. There'd be twists and turns to navigate, byways to avoid. We'd have to move slowly to avoid detection.

"We're here." Tetra pointed towards the front end of the map. "Well below Command's territory. Cairn has many hidden lairs, but the one he keeps his prisoners in is here." She moved her finger down and to the right. "The space is marked so you'll be able to find it." She hesitated. "I understand your desire to help your companions, but... it may be too late for them. And even if it isn't, your chances of reaching them alive are slim at best."

"We'll take those chances," I growled. "What should we do after we've found them?"

"I've arranged a meeting for you," Tetra said. "With a group of Oathless." She shifted her finger to a point roughly in the center of the ship. "Here."

I frowned. "Who the hell are the Oathless?"

"They're vagrants," Shell said sourly. "Roamers with no affiliation and no assignments. They wander the dark zones of the ship, living off of scraps."

"But their camps are well hidden," Tetra said. "They may be the only ones who can shelter you from Cairn."

Shell scoffed. "And why wouldn't they simply turn us over to him? Why should we trust them?"

"Because they have even more reason to hate Cairn than you." Tetra glared at Shell. "The Oathless say that Cairn has been hunting them. With Command forcing the *Aboena* into isolation, Cairn's Wolves had nobody to practice their killing on. Cairn has turned them to hunting the Oathless for sport." She grimaced. "So trust me when I say to trust them. There is nobody with more experience in hiding from Cairn."

"So that's our goal?" I asked incredulously. "Just... hide?"

"Until I can find a way to get you off of this ship," Tetra said wearily. "You have a better idea?"

"Yeah," I growled. "We find Cairn and kill him."

"If you see him, you're more than welcome to. And if you think you can."

"What about the *Orph*—I mean, our ship?" Rose asked. "If you know where Cairn's stowed it, maybe we can steal it back and just fly out of here on our own."

"Command has taken custody of your ship," Tetra said. "When you went to the Marshals, Cairn was forced to hand it over to them. It's too well guarded for me to get you to it."

I nodded slowly. "We'll figure that out in time. For now, let's get to Rid and Bentley before it's too late."

Tetra handed Shell her backpack. "Take this. It has emergency supplies and a flashlight."

"What about you?" Rose asked.

"I'll be fine." Tetra limped to the door. "But I need to get moving. Gladen is already suspicious of me."

"He with Cairn?" I asked.

"No. He's just loyal to Command." She glanced at Shell. "No matter how misguided they might be. I just can't ignore it anymore."

Shell nodded slowly.

Tetra reached for her, hesitated, then shook her head and turned away. "Good luck."

She vanished.

Shell deflated slightly, staring at the vacant space where Tetra had been.

Rose glanced at Shell, then towards the empty doorway. "Who... *is* she?"

"My sister," Shell said, voice weary. "Come on. Let's move."

NINETEEN

I've spent most of my life on human-built space habitats of one kind or another, ranging from smaller ships like the *Orpheus*, to large-scale battlecruisers like the *Revelation* or massive citystations like Albeni 7. I'm used to having my world be confined to a set of narrow, crowded corridors and limited resources. Living as part of a closed system.

No place that I'd ever been, though, had felt quite like the dark corridors of the *Aboena*. There was something deeply unsettling about the long, cold, narrow, drafty passageways. They felt alive, somehow, as if the *Aboena* itself was watching our progress with a careful eye.

Shell assured me repeatedly that nobody could see us. Not here, at least. These corridors were ancient and seldom traveled. Still—I couldn't quite chase away the eerie certainty that there was *something* in the shadows just behind every corner. A small flashlight from Tetra's pack was all we had to hold the oppressive darkness back.

"Why is so much of the ship uninhabited?" Rose asked, keeping her voice quiet. It echoed all the same. "After two thousand years, I'd have thought you'd have filled up every spare corner."

"The living quarters are compact to conserve energy," Shell said. "Most of the Roamers live clustered towards the front end of the ship, near Command. Then you've got the Wolves' territory—where we're headed now. Other than that, everything else is considered the dark zone—only traversed when Command need to do maintenance."

Fifteen kilometers. On a planet, it would have been a dismissively small distance. Here, though, it was everything. Fifteen kilometers of winding corridors, vital systems, storage spaces, living quarters, docking bays, and who knew what else were enough to fit an entire world inside. A nation with multiple factions. Unaligned rebels. Unsettled wilderness. Rumored monsters stalking the shadows.

I wished desperately that I'd kept going after we got that last message from Ramar. Or, better yet, that Rose had ignored his initial anonymous message. We'd be on Albeni 7 right now, warm and comfortable, plotting our next salvage job. I'd be looking forward to an evening spent over drinks with my closest friends, rather than dreading what lurked in the shadows behind me. Rose would try to convince me to go after some high-risk job and I'd talk her down to a more reasonable one while the others kept a running sarcastic commentary going. Sevani and I would complain to each other about whatever latest problems we were facing in our respective fields, then reminisce about old times. She'd smile that lopsided smirk of hers at me.

I wondered guiltily what she was doing right now. Probably trying to keep the anxiety from driving her insane. It had been over three weeks since we'd last contacted her. She was probably actively looking for us, but there was no way she'd be able to find us without a nudge in the right direction. Seeing her felt somehow as if it would make things partway right again. Hell, seeing *anyone* from outside of this damned ship would be enough to lift my spirits. Plus she might be able to bring enough firepower to actually make a difference. At the same time, though, the thought of dragging one more friend into the dark vortex of this situation was nauseating. I wasn't sure I could handle losing anyone else.

Thinking about Nadus again made my knuckles whiten around my stolen shotgun. Faithful, reliable Nadus. All he'd wanted was to help people. Me, mostly. When he found out I was imprisoned, he'd found a job and convinced Artemis to hire me. When he knew that I needed to go to some stupid, dangerous Roamer ship just to satisfy my own troubled conscience, he'd followed without question. And now he was just one more body in my wake. One more friend I'd left behind.

I realized with a start that I'd slowed down.

"Come on," Shell hissed at me. "We're almost there."

TWENTY

"Something tells me," I muttered, "that this was built far before anyone had dreamed up such a thing as a Vanguard."

"*Shh.*" Shell's voice had no humor in it. "We're getting close."

I restrained a grunt as I squeezed through the grate below me, twisting my shoulders to make myself small enough—just barely—to fit through the small hole. Once I did manage to fit through gravity did the rest of the work, pulling me down suddenly and dropping me on my feet onto a rickety metal floor.

I winced and steadied myself against a nearby wall, trying to dampen the metallic echoes. Shell whipped her head around to shoot me a glare.

"Remind me," she hissed. "How did you idiots conquer the galaxy?"

"Not by sneaking around," I muttered, reaching upwards to help Rose as she climbed down through the hole with significantly more ease than I had.

Shell snorted and turned back down the hallway, her dim light illuminating our path. The farther we'd gone from Command's territory, the more alien our surroundings had become. If you'd told me that no human had walked these corridors in a thousand years, I'd have believed you. The walls, floor, and ceiling were coated in layers of dull rust and scarlet lichen. The few lights and computer panels that still functioned flickered eerily, like ancient ghosts still somehow clinging to the present. The lichen became more abundant and more diverse in color, size, and shape. Bizarre, alien insects scurried out of sight as we stepped near them. I even caught a glimpse of what appeared to be some sort of strange, stretched-out feline watching us with large, furtive, moon-like eyes before darting silently into a vent.

Almost two thousand years ago, these halls had been constructed within Earth's orbit. Hell, some of this metal might have been mined on Earth itself. Painstakingly crafted to last for as long as it took to fling humanity into the stars. I couldn't help but feel reverent at the thought. Like I was walking on sacred ground. *Lots* of sacred ground. Despite my best efforts to keep track of the many twists and turns, it wasn't long before I felt hopelessly lost.

"Do you think..." Rose hesitated. "Do you think we're too late?"

I glanced back at her. She was trying her best to keep her warface in place, but I could see the barely restrained fear behind it. Not for herself. For her friends—and, especially, for Rid. I tried to imagine how I'd have felt if it had been Kessa being held hostage by Cairn.

Not good.

Shell spoke up. "No. Roamers waste nothing. Rid and Bentley are both healthy and capable. He'll hold onto them until he either finds a use for them or they become too great a liability." She hesitated. "In fact, he's probably hoping we'll come after them."

Rose frowned. "That's... not particularly comforting. We didn't fare very well the last time we fell into one of their traps."

I tightened my grip around my ax we had taken from the Wolves who'd been torturing Shell. "No. But there's a difference between falling into a trap and kicking the trap door open."

Shell scoffed, but I could tell Rose found the words encouraging from the way her back straightened a bit and her pace quickened. She was a fighter, that one, through and through. Like me. Running from a fight had never felt right to me.

Maybe that was why I'd felt so miserable the past year.

Ahead of us, a glimmer of light shone through a crack in a closed doorway. Shell positioned herself on one side of it. I took the other.

"Once we're inside," I whispered, "we'll have to move fast. If we overstay our welcome, we'll be swarmed by Wolves. We need to get in, find them, and get out."

"What if there are more guards than we're expecting?" Shell asked.

I shifted my weight, feeling the shotgun's cold pressure against my back, while my fingers tightened around the haft of the ax. "I'll handle them."

Shell nodded, then glanced at the door. It looked to be sealed from the inside. She took a deep breath. "Ready?"

I unslung my shotgun and nodded.

Shell shouted something sharp in Aboenian, banging the butt of her knife against the door. I heard footsteps from the other side. A moment later it shot open with a pneumatic hiss. A Roamer dressed in dark, grungy clothes peered through the doorway, a rifle held at the ready.

The end of Shell's knife disappeared into his throat. He jerked and gargled.

I darted around him and charged into the light. There was another Roamer right behind the one Shell had stabbed, standing in wide-eyed shock. My shoulder slammed into his face and sent him flying backward to slam into a wall and fall heavily to the floor, neck twisted at a morbid angle. Shell plucked a rifle from the hands of the first Wolf and tore her blade free from his neck with a spray of scarlet. He fell backward against the wall and sagged down, feet thrashing as he tried desperately to stop the flow of blood from the wound in his throat.

Shell sprinted past me. I followed her, glancing over my shoulder to make sure that Rose was close behind. She was, running as fast as she could to keep up.

The locked door had led us into another, shorter corridor with another set of doors at the end of it. This corridor was much better kept than the ones we'd been traversing, with the lichen mostly scrubbed from the walls and lights powered on.

A confused face appeared in one of the windows. The eyes went wide. Shell stepped aside, giving me room to charge past her and throw my full weight against the doors.

The Roamer who'd had his face pressed against the window gave a startled cry as he was flung like a child's toy off of his feet. I had just a moment to adjust to my new surroundings as he spun through the air.

I was standing at the end of a long rectangular room, with doors on each side. There were several tables placed around the room at which clusters of Roamers sat, eating food, playing various games, or drinking. They blinked at me in confusion. For some reason I was reminded of my last day in the Karak prison system. Maybe it was the fact that they were all sitting at tables. Maybe it was how woefully outnumbered I was—there were probably fifteen Roamers in the room staring at me. Maybe it was the fact that this *was* Cairn's makeshift prison. There were at least two major differences, though. The first was that they had guns.

One of them rose, reaching for a submachine gun on the table in front of him.

The second difference was: *so did I.*

I aimed the shotgun with one hand and pulled the trigger.

The shotgun went off just as the first Roamer finally slammed into one of the tables, flipping it over. Cards, coins, curses, and blood filled the air.

I kept moving. The shotgun bucked in my hands again and another Roamer went down in a spray of blood. Gunfire sounded beside me as Shell opened up with her stolen assault rifle, spraying a barrage of bullets into the mass of Wolves. Rose joined in a few moments later, firing her pistol wildly into the fray. A bald man with a pistol stumbled towards me and I clubbed the weapon out of his hands with the barrel of the shotgun, then brought the ax-head down on his shoulder with the other hand. He fell to his knees with a choked cry. I raised the shotgun, fired it into the back of a fleeing Roamer, then jerked the ax free and shoved the bald man with one foot, sending him flying into the path of another assailant. Though, to be fair, I don't know if calling any of these Roamers "assailants" was fair. By this point, they were victims fleeing a massacre.

One final blast from my shotgun punctuated the end of the barrage. I surveyed the carnage. Only the three of us were left standing. The room was hazy with smoke. The floor beneath us was shiny with spent bullet casings. Following the deafening sound of the gunfire, the cries and groans of the fallen Roamers were almost soothing.

"Watch those doors. Whole damn ship probably heard that." I stepped into the center of the room, identified a Roamer who looked like they might live, and knelt next to him.

"The two Outsiders," I growled. "Where are they?"

He blinked at me, pupils dilated by the extreme by shock and terror. He blubbered something I couldn't understand.

"Shell!" I barked. "Swap me."

Shell knelt next to the Roamer while I took watch. Without taking my shotgun from the door, I took a moment to grab a submachine gun and a slingpack from one of the tables.

"This way." Shell darted towards one of the doors, pausing

only to swap out her emptied assault rifle for another firearm and then proceeded through, weapon at the ready. I sent Rose through next, scanned the fallen Roamers to make sure none of them were in a condition to shoot us from behind, then followed.

Shouts rang down the hallway, followed by several gunshots. I got there just in time to see Shell quickly and efficiently dispatching two fallen Roamers. This hallway reminded me of the urban hellscape of the Albeni 7 residential zones—narrow, barren, concrete walls, featureless save for small metal doors that regularly punctuated their length. Dark brown spots of what I assumed to be dried blood lined the floor. The only light came from a dim flickering bulb in the center of the ceiling. A foul smell permeated the entire space.

"*Rid!*" Rose was already trying one door after another, frantically jostling their handles. Some opened, revealing dark and empty rooms within. Others were locked. Shell fished through the belongings of the two Roamers she'd just killed, found what looked like a key, and tossed it to Rose.

I heard voices ringing out from the main room we'd just had our massacre in. I cursed and poked my head back in. Several Wolves had entered the room, surveying the carnage with wide eyes. I killed a few with my stolen submachine gun, sending the others scattering for cover.

"We need to hurry!" I shouted over my shoulder.

"*I know!*" yelled Shell.

"*Rid!*"

I glanced over my shoulder and felt a surge of relief as Rose pulled an exhausted, dirty, dazed-looking Rid from one of the cells. He collapsed into her arms, blinking unbelievingly at her.

"Save it for later!" I snapped. A bullet slammed into the doorway near my head. "Find Bentley!"

"Here he is!" Shell pulled him from another cell.

"Can they walk?!"

I caught a glimpse of Rid stumbling forward, catching himself against a wall, then straightening with a grimace.

"Barely!" Shell yelled back at me.

More bullets rained past me, forcing me backward. I spared a look at Rid and Bentley. They looked as if they'd hardly been fed. Rose and Rid were still clutching at each other, both of them holding back tears. Bentley looked as if he could barely make out what was going on. If one thing was obvious, it was that they weren't in fighting condition. Shell had started opening the other locked doors, freeing a few stunned-looking Roamers.

I took a deep breath, then threw myself through the doorway. Bullets flew past me. A sharp pain bit at my arm as one of them found its target. I fired my shotgun mid-air, slamming one Roamer against a wall, then rolled, landed on my knees, and emptied the submachine gun. Two Roamers went down, while two more went scampering back down the hallway they'd emerged from.

I charged after them, kicking open the door and bellowing. They whirled, eyes wide. Clearly, that *wasn't* the move they'd been expecting from me. I emptied the submachine gun, then finished them off with the ax when I was close enough.

"We're clear!" I yelled. "Let's g—"

I frowned, looking around. This hallway was different than the other one. Shorter, for one thing, with no doors along the sides. Instead, it culminated in a single open door at the far end. A blue flickering light shone dimly from within the open doorway, silhouetting what looked like a person hanging by their hands from a chain attached to the ceiling, their bare feet suspended perhaps a foot above the floor.

I hesitated, then cursed and started towards it. The more prisoners we could free, the better. If nothing else, they might have valuable information. I stepped through the doorway and approached the figure. "Alright," I muttered. "Let's get you—"

I froze.

Ramar, barely recognizable beneath a thick layer of bruises and congealed blood, slowly blinked one swollen, bloodshot eye at me. I stared back at him.

"*Lax!*" Shell's voice rang down the hallway behind me. "That's everyone! We've gotta go!"

Ramar had lied to us. Manipulated us into coming here. He'd dragged Sev into a war with Vatheson. He'd put my entire crew at risk. He'd gotten Nadus killed, whether he'd intended to or not. Hell, if you went back far enough, he was responsible for getting Kessa killed too.

My blood pumped hot and angry in my veins. I tightened my grip on the ax, raising it above my head. Ramar watched me apathetically, then closed his eyes.

"They're here," he whispered.

I furrowed my brow. "What?"

"They're... *here...*"

"LAX!" Shell was screaming now. "*Hurry!*"

I cursed viciously and swung my ax. It arced past Ramar's head and slammed into the joint connecting the chain to the ceiling. I caught him as he fell. He cried out in pain.

"Can you walk?" I growled.

He only moaned.

Dammit. "Alright, brace yourself. This is gonna hurt." I lifted him and, as gently as I could, placed him over my shoulder. He was light enough that I barely even noticed his presence. When I was sure he was secure, I jogged back down the hallway, doing my best not to jostle Ramar's limp form. Even so, he gave a pained groan.

"Alright," I said, bursting back into the main room. "Let's—"

Before I could cross the central room, one of the main doors crashed open. A gunshot boomed—a familiar gunshot. A bullet whistled over my head. I spun. Several more Wolves had emerged at our rear. Front and center stood Dak, Peacebreaker smoking in his hands. His breathing apparatus heaved in and out as he aimed again.

Time froze.

I felt a surge of red-hot hatred, as overwhelming as the ignicerin the Paragon had given me back in the war. I remembered Dak's face, leering at me as I slowly faded into oblivion on the floor of the *Aboena*. I braced myself to charge. If Dak was here, Cairn might be nearby. I'd kill every one of the—

No. I ducked back behind cover. *Not now.* There was no way to cross to the rest of my crew without exposing ourselves to withering gunfire. I looked down the hall at them. Rose and Rid were still clinging to each other, while Shell was helping a still-dazed Bentley stumble out of the corridor they'd been imprisoned in.

Dammit. I searched for a way out. An idea struck me.

I motioned across the hallway to my crew to hide in the cells they'd just freed Bentley and Rid from. Rose gave me a confused look.

I took a deep breath, readjusted Ramar on my shoulder, then charged from my hallway, bellowing and firing wildly at the Wolves. They scrambled for cover, giving me just enough time to turn and bolt in the opposite direction, through a doorway and into another long corridor. I heard a cry as they gave pursuit.

So far so good. They were focused on me, and apparently had failed to notice the rest of my crew. With a little luck they'd be able to slip out while the Wolves were busy pursuing me.

And with a little *more* luck, I'd reunite with them afterwards.

"VanDunn..."

I gritted my teeth, not slowing down. The sounds of pursuit echoed from just around the corner behind us. "Stay quiet. We're almost out of this."

Ramar's only response was a twisted choking sound.

Dammit. I wouldn't be accomplishing anything if I let him die on my shoulders. I glanced around, spotted an empty, ominously dark hallway, then darted through it. I surveyed it frantically with my flashlight. There was a pile of large, round objects off to the side. I threw myself behind them, shifting Ramar to shield him from the fall, then waited in the darkness.

The footsteps drew nearer. Dozens of them, running at a frantic pace. Dim lights bounced past the doorway we'd just come through. Somebody shouted something in particularly angry-sounding Aboenian.

Ramar groaned. I clamped my palm over his mouth.

A beam of light pierced the darkness above us, sweeping across the room. I held my breath. Ramar shifted slightly beside me. The light jerked towards us, casting a dark shape against the wall behind.

I tightened my grip on the ax and tensed my legs, preparing to move. If that Roamer came towards us, this chunk of sharpened steel whipping towards his face would be the last thing he ever saw. Might be the last thing *I* ever saw too.

There was another shout. The light vanished. Footsteps cascaded down the main corridor. After a few moments, all was silent and dark.

I gingerly pushed myself to a kneeling position. Ramar let out a meager, stretched-out moan as I removed my hand from his mouth. My palm came away sticky with lumps of congealed blood.

I hesitated. *Dammit.* Every second I wasted here was another second that my crew got further away—and right after we'd finally been reunited too. But it was increasingly obvious that Cairn wasn't going anywhere—not at a fast pace, at least.

I fished through my pocket for the flashlight I'd plundered from the fallen Wolf. I listened carefully, making sure that there were no sounds of nearby Roamers before I clicked it on. It radiated a sickly yellow light onto Ramar's face. His pupils constricted as they stared into the beam.

"Well, that's something," I muttered, moving the light down across the rest of his body. But it was about all that was worth celebrating. His shirtless form was emaciated and coated with sweat, dried blood, black bruises, jagged lacerations, and raw burn marks. His face was swollen, his lips dry and cracking.

"VanDunn?" His eyes moved sluggishly past the beam of light and towards my shadowed face. "Is that..."

"Yeah. It's me." I clenched my teeth. As pissed as I was at Ramar, it was hard to hate a man who'd clearly had it so much worse than I had. "They really did a number on you."

"Where... where were you?"

"Shh." I glanced towards the dark doorway. No sound. I toyed with the idea of doubling back the way we came briefly before dismissing the idea. More of Cairn's goons would be coming that way soon. Instead, I unslung my pack and withdrew the canteen, unscrewing the cap and holding it towards Ramar's bone-dry lips. "Drink. We need to keep moving. Those bastards'll be on our tail any second."

Not that I had any idea *where* we'd be moving. I glanced down into the darkness of the offshoot corridor we'd taken shelter in while Ramar took a slow, trembling sip from the canteen. Looked like it kept on going. The fact that the Wolves hadn't bothered checking it more thoroughly worried me a bit, though. Did that mean it was a dead end? Would it lead us straight into more Roamers?

I turned my light to the round objects we had taken shelter behind, noticing a label and squinting at it. I blinked in surprise. HULLBREAKERS. Bombs built to be powerful enough to punch holes in the toughest of starcraft plating. I made a mental note to *not* jostle them any more than strictly necessary.

Ramar was drinking greedily now, the canteen tilted at an extreme angle. I gently pushed it back and helped him into a seated position, leaning his back against one of the round objects. "Easy. Don't make yourself sick. Here." I pulled a protein bar from the pack. "Get some food in you."

He reluctantly let me swap the water for the food. "I don't think I *can* move."

I took a quick sip of my own, then set the canteen aside and opened the pack one more time. One of the adrenaline shots Tetra had given us peered metallically up at me.

"We'll see about that," I said, reaching for it.

Ramar looked wearily up at me, chewing a meager bite of tasteless protein block. He blinked in confusion. "What are..."

He twitched as I pressed the business end of the adrenaline shot against his arm and thumbed the release button. There was a sharp click as four tiny needles punched simultaneously through his bare skin, delivering their payload all at once.

Ramar frowned at the now empty shot. "Adrenaline," I said, pulling it free of his arm and tossing it aside. "Once that kicks in it should give you the energy we need to get out of here. You'll hit one hell of a wall after, but that's a problem for... well, *after*. Keep eating. Looks like they hardly fed you at all."

"That was the least of my problems," he muttered, taking another bite. Might have been my imagination, but he already seemed to sitting up a bit straighter.

"Looks like it," I said, eyeing the fresco of wounds that canvased his body. "What'd they want?"

"*Now* you care?" His voice was still feeble, but venom lurked just beneath its surface.

Guilt twisted at my innards. I returned the water to him, trying to force the emotion away. "Yeah. Because now we're stuck in this together. Congratulations—your idiotic plan worked. I'm here."

He leaned forward and poked at a scabbed-over burn mark on his forearm with a grimace. "They wanted to know about rippers. The ultrarippers, specifically."

I frowned. "What about them?"

He eyed me irritably. "You still don't even believe me, do you?"

"Believe you?" I climbed to my feet. "I had to kill one of the damn things in a cage fight."

He perked up. "Really?"

"Yeah. Me and—" I cut off abruptly, the name I was trying to speak seeming to stick in my throat. The same way it still did every time I remembered he was gone.

Ramar furrowed his brows at me. "You and what?"

It was *his* fault. He'd lured us here. If he'd just respected my wishes and kept his distance Nadus would still be alive right now. We'd never have gotten tangled up with Vatheson and his schemes. My crew would be safe and sound on Albeni 7. I'd never even have had to hear the name Cairn.

I felt a sudden urge to seize Ramar by the neck and throttle him. Instead, I took a deep breath. *Breathe.*

"Me and Nadus," I said. "Cairn put us into some sort of arena. Made us fight an ultraripper with nothing but edged weapons."

"And you killed it?" He sounded genuinely impressed.

"We killed it." I swallowed a lump in my throat. "And then Cairn killed Nadus."

Ramar's face fell. "Oh."

I glared at him. "*Oh?* That's all you've got in you? Just more collateral in your great crusade against the rippers, huh?"

He stared down at the floor. "I liked him, even if he never liked me. I got to speak with him on our way back from the *Revelation.* When we all thought *you* were dead. I didn't want him to die. I didn't want any of this to happen."

I scoffed. "Yeah? Well, neither did I. Which is why I told you *no* the first time you came asking for my help. And the second time. If Cairn hadn't messaged us from your comms system, I'd never have turned around at all."

Ramar's face twisted into a grimace. "I had everything under control. I was *this* close to solving the entire problem without your help. Then you had to go and pull it all out from under me. To leave me—powerless—in *his* clutches."

"Well maybe if you'd bothered to tell me any of that, we could've worked something else out," I growled.

Ramar shot angrily to his feet with shocking dexterity, glaring up at me. "You wouldn't have listened," he snarled. "And I couldn't explain while Cairn was staring over my shoulder. Thanks to you, we're—"

"Wait." I held up a hand, cutting him off. He fell silent, eyes widening slightly as we both listened.

Footsteps. Echoing faintly from the corridor outside.

"We've been here too long." I shoved the canteen into my pack and slung it onto my back. "And the adrenaline is clearly doing its job. We can either sit here arguing until the shot wears off and the Roamers are all over us, or we can move."

He glanced towards the doorway, then nodded slowly. "Do you know where we're going?"

I lifted the ax from where I'd set it on the floor. "Somewhere that's not here."

The echoing footsteps grew louder.

"By all means, then," Ramar said, "lead the way."

TWENTY-ONE

"How did you find out about Cairn in the first place?" I whispered as we slunk through the darkness. I had the flashlight turned to the lowest possible setting, rendering the utter darkness barely discernable.

"It was Carston," he said quietly.

I frowned. "Who?"

He shook himself. "Denatus Carston. You've met. You would know him as the Penitent. Or Eladrius, as I believe he introduced himself to you."

My mood immediately darkened. If Ramar realized it, though, he didn't acknowledge it, carrying on talking as if he were describing a close friend, rather than an assassin who'd nearly killed me multiple times. "While I was on the *Revelation*, he set up an entire intelligence network collecting rumors about the *Revelation* or unusual rippers. It's how he caught onto your friend Artemis. It's also how he caught wind of Cairn and his... endeavors. Apparently, some of Cairn's Wolves did some smuggling on the side and let a few things slip. Nothing much— just rumors of strange winged rippers lurking in a ruined ship.

A harmless old starfarer's tale to most, but it caught Carston's attention."

I paused as we reached an intersection. Damn the *Aboena* and its endless gordian knot of corridors. I was completely disoriented. "So what'd you do then?" I asked, looking around and frowning. "Just... show up? Ask politely to be let aboard?"

"I contacted Cairn," he said. "And persuaded him that we could mutually benefit from forming a partnership. One that would allow me to board the ship and investigate for myself." He pointed ahead. "What's that? On the wall?"

I sighed in relief. A map, similar to the one Shell had briefed us with earlier, was printed on the side of the wall ahead. I moved closer to it. "Maps says we're here," I muttered, pointing at a red dot. "Which means that this is where we came from."

"This section appears to be rather cut off from the rest of the ship," Ramar observed. I nodded in grim agreement. Made sense. Cairn wouldn't want just anybody to be able to stumble into his lair. Tracing our path was difficult, but I managed to identify where we'd broken through and where we'd rescued Rid and Bentley.

"Shell must have led them out through *here*," I said, tapping a point that led out of this sector. "That was about where we split off."

"Any idea where she'd lead them afterwards?"

"The goal is to make it to the Oathless," I said. "Tetra—er, Shell's sister—claims we should be safe there."

"And you know where they are?"

I grimaced. "I know the general area. We had a meeting point set up. Somewhere around... *here*, I reckon."

"And you really think these Oathless can protect you from Cairn?"

I shrugged. "Hide is probably a better word for it. Sounds like they have pretty damn good operational security. Not even Tetra knows where their hideout is."

Ramar scowled. "For the people supposedly in charge of this ship, Command and their Marshals know very little of what happens on it."

"You're telling me," I agreed. "Seems like their only real power is the fact that they steer the damn thing. Everything outside of Command's territory is no man's land."

"We are strangers in a strange land," Ramar said, his voice inflecting as if he were quoting something. He moved my finger along the wall. "This seems to be the nearest exit that will point us in the direction these Oathless of yours are." He furrowed his brow. "It will likely be guarded."

"It'll definitely be guarded." I tightened my grip on my ax. "Not guarded enough, though."

Ramar scoffed. "So that's our plan. Walk right up and hack at everyone with an ax until they let us through."

"Pretty much. Unless you've got a better idea."

He shook his head. "I ran out of ideas when Cairn started poking me with hot irons."

"Alright. Come on." I turned to a door on our left and hit a button to open it. A rush of cold air struck me. "This is the quickest way."

I passed through the doorway and paused, looking around. I was on a catwalk hanging over darkness. I hesitated, then turned the brightness of my flashlight up. I let out a low whistle. On either side of the catwalk, extending down to the floor beneath us and the ceiling above us, were carefully stacked walls of narrow glass cylinders, all of them connected to a series of pipes and cables. Some of them were dark and empty. Others had dull throbbing red lights shining from screens attached to the fronts, flashing what looked like warning signs. Most of them were glowing green. Whatever their original purpose, the Wolves seemed to have co-opted them as storage for perishable items—ice, food, or medicine.

"These must be the cryochambers," Ramar said, wrapping

his arms across his bare torso as he stepped beside me. "Some of them, at least. There are thousands scattered through the ship."

I nodded, imagining climbing into one of those things and being filed into storage like you were just another piece of cargo. Embracing the long, cold sleep with no way of knowing whether you'd ever wake up—or where you'd be when you did. Goodbye Earth, one way or another.

"We're just a few chambers away," I said. "Let's keep moving."

I dimmed my light as we approached the end of the catwalk, then passed through the door at the end across a narrow hallway and into another similar chamber. I kept my light dim as we walked this time, not wanting to risk detection just for another glance at a stack of containers.

"Your deal with Cairn," I whispered to Ramar. "What was it?"

"I agreed to help him get Lifeblood," he replied, shivering. "And in exchange, he said he would dispose of the ultrarippers."

I frowned. "And you believed him?"

"Seemed like a fair trade," Ramar muttered. "He claimed he only had a few. And until you cut me out of the deal, I had the leverage to make sure he... followed... through."

I turned back. Ramar frowned, blinked, and fell to one knee, rattling the catwalk. *Dammit.* The adrenaline was already wearing off.

I knelt beside him. "Hey. You alright?"

"Yes." He grimaced. "I think I'm hitting that... *oof*... wall you described..."

"Let's hurry, then. I'll help you up." I lowered my flashlight and wrapped an arm around his torso. "We'll be out of here... before..."

My voice trailed off as something beneath us glinted black and metallic in the meager beam of my flashlight.

Ramar blinked. "What's wrong? I don't—"

I shut my hand over his mouth. His eyes drifted downward. Then widened.

This room was like the other one—except that the cryochambers had all been removed, leaving it wide and empty. It wasn't empty anymore, though.

The *thing* that had caught the beam of my flashlight shifted slightly. I moved the light slowly to the side. It was a wing. Black and glistening, attached to a mass of pale, sickly-looking flesh.

There were plenty of things I could've said to Ramar right then. *Just a few, huh?* Or *I guess we know where he keeps them now.* But even if I had dared to so much as open my mouth, I wouldn't have been able to get the words out. My mind was too full of terror. Too full of memories. Too full of sheer disbelief at what I saw beneath us.

The entire floor was covered with ultrarippers, packed in so tightly together it was impossible to tell where one ended and the next began. They seemed to be hibernating. As my light drifted across them, however, they stirred—pitch-black wings shifting, eyeless heads twisting, claws stretching lazily.

My heart was pounding so hard in my chest I was certain it was echoing throughout the chamber.

Green dots, flashing red...

Sweat formed cold beads on my forehead.

We had a good run...

My breath caught in my throat. Ramar was shaking me. I tried to move but my entire body was stiff as stone.

Not all of us...

Ramar shoved at me. The movement dislodged a single drop of sweat from my forehead. It fell silently between the bars of the catwalk. Tumbled dreamlike through the darkness. Landed with a barely audible plap on a ripper's head.

It twitched upwards.

Life returned to my limbs. I jolted to my feet, turning back the way we'd come. Ramar stumbled as he tried to run but caught himself. The floor wasn't that far beneath us. There was no doubt in my mind that the rippers could easily climb up to us. All we had to do was reach that door and—

Footsteps. Thudding from the other side. Growing louder.

Something metallic groaned beneath us as a ripper shook itself awake, wings scraping against another ripper's claws.

Dammit. I pivoted, quickening my pace towards the far door. Ramar grunted as he turned around, gasping for breath as he tried to keep up with me. I heard more movement below us. Somebody was at the door behind us. I broke into a sprint, throwing stealth to the wind.

There was a pneumatic sliding sound as the door behind us started to open. I slid to a halt at the exit and slammed my hand on the *open* button. The door began to inch open with excruciating slowness.

Shouts behind us. I unslung the shotgun from my back, turned, aimed down the catwalk. Ramar's eyes widened as the barrel lowered towards him.

"DUCK!" I yelled.

He dropped to his hands and knees, revealing a silhouette of a Roamer in the far doorway. I pulled the trigger. The dark room flared with white light for a fraction of a second. The report echoed thunderously. The figure jolted backward with a muffled cry. I glanced down. If the rippers had been stirring before, they were squirming now, each of them thrashing at the others in an attempt to escape the tight squeeze.

The door slid open just enough for me to slide through. I pulled Ramar to his feet and fled through it. I hit the button to reseal it on the other side, then dashed across the narrow passageway into the next room. It was another cryochamber. I glanced down. More ultrarippers, already stirring. Wings as black as the void. Claws to rend the strongest armor. Teeth that wanted to eat the whole world. *Green dots...*

No time to gawk. No time for fear or memories or panic.

We were almost out. I slung Ramar's increasingly limp form over my shoulder and sprinted down the catwalk. The door at the far end hissed open before I could get there and two Roamers stepped through. Their eyes widened as they saw me dashing towards them. One of them raised a submachine gun. I fired the shotgun with one hand without slowing down, sending him spinning to the floor with a cry of pain. The other one froze in fear, staring down the barrel of my shotgun as I carried on towards him. I aimed and pulled the trigger again.

It didn't move. *Empty*.

The Roamer must have realized it, because he drew a long knife and charged at me with a wild howl. I pulled the shotgun back and then drove it forward, driving the barrel into the Wolf's gut. He doubled over, eyes bulging as I used the shotgun to shove him sideways, tilt him over the catwalk guardrail, and send him tumbling head over heels into the darkness below. He landed with a muffled, fleshy thud.

The screaming started a few moments later.

I charged through the door. Across another narrow hallway and into another cryochamber full of rippers. Then another, footsteps growing louder behind us all the while. Questions I had no time to consider rushed through my mind. How many chambers full of rippers did Cairn have? How did he keep them from simply crawling up the walls and going on a killing spree? I saw no signs of restraints. No cages, no bars—not that anything that simple would have been able to restrain them anyways.

But those were questions for another time. *Almost there*. According to the map, we had just a few more chambers to clear, then we'd be able to cut through a maintenance room and back into the main portion of the ship.

Ramar staggered after me. A look over my shoulder at the sheer determination on his face was enough to confirm that he was putting every last bit of his rapidly fading energy into keeping up. A few of his wounds had reopened, glistening in my flashlight's beam.

"Almost there." I pulled him through another doorway into another ripper storage unit. These ones were fully awake. They all turned to look at us as we entered the room, their muscles tensed. They made no effort to move, though, despite the fact that any one of them could probably have leaped up to us in a single bound.

A gunshot boomed with dreadful familiarity behind us. A bullet slammed with brutal force into the doorframe no more than a few inches away from Ramar's shoulder. I glanced over my shoulder as I slammed the button that would close the door behind us and block the shooter's line of sight.

The Roamer shooting at us was short and scrawny. I narrowed my eyes as I recognized Dak's mask and breathing tubes flexing in and out. He raised Peacebreaker again and fired, the shot going wide as the recoil nearly knocked the gun out of his hand. I almost stopped in my tracks and turned to charge him, but more Roamers were filing behind him— and it was safe to assume that others were already running ahead in an attempt to cut off our escape.

The door sealed shut. Ramar's breath came in ragged gasps as we dashed across the catwalk. The rippers' heads followed us as we moved. I wasn't on the *Aboena* anymore. I was on the *Panama* again with Kess at my side, watching the rippers surround us. Why were they waiting? *Why was she smiling?*

Focus. Move. Survive. I gritted my teeth, pushing aside the memories. Pushing aside the fear. *Almost there.*

We passed through one more door. The passage beyond was different than the others we'd cut through. I looked around wildly until I spotted another door. It had a large label on it in what appeared to be an ancient text well beyond my ability to read, but the large triangular warning symbol was timelessly universal.

"Come on!" We moved through a set of heavy mechanical doors into a long, dark room full of loud machinery. Looked like oxygen recyclers hard at work. I glanced at the wall next to the door. There was a control panel there, with what looked like an emergency lockdown button.

Ramar staggered past me, then fell against the wall with a gasp. "I can't..." His breath was coming in gasping, choking sobs. "I'm... I can't feel my..."

I glanced back over my shoulder. I heard shouts echoing down the hallways. They'd lost us, temporarily, but it wouldn't take them long to be pointed in the right direction. They'd flow through that narrow hallway right into this room. Even if I carried Ramar, getting caught was a matter of *when*, not *if*.

A slight grin tugged at the corner of my mouth.

Ramar frowned up at me. "What... what are you..."

"Getting my gun back," I growled, loading the last few shells into the shotgun. I gripped it in one hand and the ax in the other.

Shouting. Footsteps. Echoing outside. Coming closer.

The Wolves were coming. Who had somehow tamed the ultrarippers and now intended to turn them loose. The same ultrarippers who'd killed my crew. Who had taken Kessa. Who had taken *everything*. And now the Wolves wanted to take everything from me all over again.

My smirk hardened into a burning, hate-filled sneer.

Ramar crawled into the corner with a groan. I hit a switch, turning off the few lights that had been on. The room plunged into near darkness. I leaned against the wall a meter or so away from the door, letting my eyes adjust to the darkness.

I heard a vicious shout. Somebody ran through the doorway. They didn't slow down, heading right for the other side. More filed in behind them. Dak, Peacebreaker clutched in his hands, came through at the rear.

I hit the emergency shutdown button on the control panel

just before they could reach the far door. The doors on both sides of the room slammed shut, trapping the last few Roamers on the other side. Red lights activated overhead, bathing the room in red. The Wolves stumbled to a halt, looking around wildly. One of them frowned as they noticed Ramar lying on the floor.

Dak spun. His eyes finally settled on me, then went wide. He raised his gun.

No. My gun. The one I'd carried for years. The one that had seen me through the best times of my life, and some of the worst.

My.

GUN.

The rage I'd been holding back for days now broke like water through a fracturing dam. I bellowed, swinging the ax in a wide, one-handed arc. There was a slight tug of resistance, then freedom. Dak stared open-mouthed at the bloody stump at the end of his arm.

I grinned.

I lifted the shotgun and fired it point blank into the torso of another Roamer who was in the process of raising her submachine gun. The blast slammed her against one of the recycler machines. I stepped past a still catatonic Dak and swung the ax upward into the torso of the next Wolf, sinking it deep beneath his rib cage. One of his companions behind him aimed a pistol at me. I jerked on the long handle of the ax, steering the Roamer coughing on the end of it between me and the threat, then pulled him close and kicked him in the midsection. The force tore him free of the ax-head with a horrible wet cracking sound and sent him hurling into his friends.

Then I was on top of them.

I lost track of the details. Lost track of where I was. Who I was. Lost myself in a storm of spraying blood and breaking bones and rending flesh. The ax swung again and again. The shotgun boomed in my hand until it was empty. I broke it in half over someone's head. Rammed the jagged, broken wreckage through somebody else's chest. Shoved them away. Gripped the ax in two hands and swung it overhead and laughed in delight as it crunched deep into a skull.

I looked around, disappointed. Nobody was left standing. Then—a flicker of movement. Dak, pawing desperately at the door, blood gushing from his ruined arm.

I grinned.

"Where..."

The ax came free with a meaty pop.

"Do you think..."

Dak turned his head towards me, eyes wide and shining red in the scarlet emergency lights.

"YOU'RE GOING?!"

I hurled the ax. It sailed through the air and struck him in the back, cleaving through and pinning him to the door. He wheezed.

I leaped towards him, bellowing. Laughing. Crying. *Three weeks.* Three weeks sitting in a hole, waiting to die, imagining what horrible fates had befallen my friends.

I grabbed him by the back of the head.

Green dots, flashing red.

THUD.

There are two kinds of pain...

THUD.

Welcome to the Aboena.

THUD.

Just come back.

CRUNCH.

I screamed. My hands were coated in something hot and sticky. I became suddenly aware of banging sounds. People on the other side of the door, trying to get it open.

I blinked. Looked down.

Dak was leaning against the door—what was left of him, at least. His head was bloody and misshapen—nose flattened and skull caved inward, bits of bone shining red through torn flesh. The door was coated with blood where I'd been slamming his face against it.

A wave of nausea swept suddenly through me. I staggered and leaned against the wall, fighting the urge to vomit.

"I..." I stuttered, not sure who I was trying to talk to. There was nobody left alive to listen. Even Ramar looked like a corpse, slumped over on his side with one outstretched arm, his eyes shut, mouth open, and chest barely moving.

The door thudded again. I shook myself. A few more seconds and this place would be swarmed with Wolf reinforcements. I'd delayed *far* too long.

I scooped up Peacebreaker, my hands shaking slightly, then rummaged through Dak's pockets until I found the spare magazines. I took a few more moments to round up some of the other fallen weapons, then lifted Ramar's unconscious form and slung him over my shoulder.

I spared one last glance at the room before heading out the far door. I saw nothing but bodies behind me. A long, unending trail of carnage, bathed bloody red, wending its horrible path from the far shadows at the end of the room to where I was now.

I turned and ran.

My footsteps felt heavy, weighed down by a weariness that felt as if it was sinking deep into my bones. Each step I took seemed to echo through the dark, narrow, lichen-coated hallways of the dark zone.

Thud. Thud. Thud...

Ramar made an incoherent groan. I absentmindedly shrugged my shoulders to rebalance his limp form. My backpack full of looted gear and weaponry clattered softly as I did so.

I kept walking. Nearly an hour had passed since we'd escaped the Wolves' den. I'd doubled back and forth enough times that I was reasonably certain nobody was following us. Now it was just Ramar and me trudging through the darkness towards where I thought Tetra had said the Oathless would meet us. One slow, weary footstep at a time.

Thud. Thud. Thud...

Dak was dead. That was an undeniable victory. Far as I could tell, he'd been Cairn's right-hand man. I should have felt some sort of righteous satisfaction. Instead, I just felt... tired. Vaguely sickened.

Thud. Thud. Thud...

I had always assumed that Cairn was exaggerating—at least to some extent—about the rippers. Figured that at the most, he had one or two rippers he'd miraculously managed to capture from the *Panama*'s wreckage chained up somewhere. That would have been concerning enough. What I'd seen—what *Ramar* and I had seen—was more than that. It was catastrophic.

Thud. Thud. Thud...

Who else knew? Was Tetra aware of just how many ultra-rippers Cairn had accumulated? Did she have any sort of plan to stop him? Was it even possible to stop him at this point?

Thud. Thud. Thud...

I gritted my teeth. *It's not your problem.* I'd lost enough in this fight already. All that mattered now was keeping my crew safe. Hopefully Shell and the others had already found those Oathless Tetra had told us about. We just needed to hunker down with them long enough for Tetra to arrange a way out for us. After that, Cairn would be her problem.

Thud. Thud...

My footsteps slowed—partly due to exhaustion and partly due to the guilt that flooded me at the thought of abandoning Tetra. She'd stuck her neck out to help us. She'd *made* us her problem. And now I was planning on leaving her with all the messes we'd made the first chance I got.

Thud...

It was better that way, though. I'd just screw everything up if I tried to help. Like I always did. Everywhere I went, no matter how good my intentions, all I left behind were bodies. My old crew. Kessa. Artemis. Tekka. Nadus. Dak. Everywhere I looked, I saw the way his eyes had widened as he stared at the severed stump of his hand. Every step I took reminded me of the sound his skull had made as it fractured against the wall.

Thud. Thud.

CRUNCH.

I paused and looked down. Lifted my boot. A small, feline-looking skull lying on the floor had broken beneath my weight. I stepped back, surveying my surroundings with the flashlight. I was standing in the center of a large crossroads. Eight paths stretched out into infinite darkness on every side of me. The floor was littered with small bones like the one I'd stepped on. I frowned as I looked closer. There was some sort of strange, plant-like growth clinging to all of them. It was a deep red color. The growth twitched as my foot neared it, shying away from the edges of my boot.

An eerie feeling crept over me as I watched the vine-like growth writhe. I'm not sure how to describe it other than a deep, unsettling certainty that someone—some*thing*—was watching me.

Thud. Thud. Thud...

I tensed. Footsteps, faint in the distance, moving towards me. Sounded like a single set. I turned in the direction they were coming from, Peacebreaker held at the ready. A dim blue light appeared at the end of one of the corridors. A moment later a small figure emerged, burdened by an oversized backpack and carrying a dim blue lantern.

The figure paused as soon as it saw me. I saw no sign of a weapon. I lowered Peacebreaker.

The stranger moved a few steps closer. It was a kid—looked to be maybe fourteen or so. He searched me up and down with wary eyes. I became acutely aware that I was almost completely covered in dried blood. His eyes drifted up to Ramar.

"Outsider?" the kid asked.

I nodded. "Yeah."

He studied me a moment longer, then started forward again. He came to a halt at the edge of the crossroads, unslung his large pack, and stooped, digging through it. He drew a long, limp, grotesque form from the pack. One of the feline creatures I'd seen lurking around, skinned and deprived of most of its flesh. Not all of it, though. The Roamer kid flung the carcass into the center of the crossroad, then reached into his pack and withdrew something long and slimy that looked like the unfortunate cat-thing's guts. Those were flung to the floor as well with a wet slap. He repeated the process in silence three more times, then straightened and turned away, beckoning with his lantern for me to follow.

He strode off into the darkness without waiting to see if I was joining him. I frowned after him. Was he one of the Oathless Tetra had told us to find? He sure as hell didn't seem like one of Cairn's Wolves. The fact he hadn't fled from me seemed to indicate he'd expected to find me—and that he thought we were on the same side. There was always the possibility he was leading me to a trap of some sort, but... well, at this point it was either follow him or wander around aimlessly in the dark until I stumbled into somebody else.

If nothing else, it meant getting away from this weird place. I looked down at the scarlet vines again. They were moving slowly towards the carcasses the kid had deposited, wrapping themselves around the bits of flesh. That eerie feeling of being observed crept over me once again.

I sighed, readjusted Ramar's position on my shoulder, and jogged to catch up to the kid. Regardless of where he was going, maybe I'd get answers out of him.

I did not get answers out of him. Not many, at least.

It quickly became obvious that his grasp of the Galactic Basic language consisted of the words *Outsider*, *no*, and *yes*. He used those words efficiently, though, combining them to communicate three distinct messages: I was an Outsider, he was not; no, he did not speak my language; and yes, there were more Outsiders ahead of us.

That was good enough for me. I matched his quick, purposeful pace, while failing to match the silence with which his feet fell, and followed wordlessly. The only sounds beside the thud, thud, thud of my footsteps were occasional incoherent murmurs from Ramar, still slumped in unconscious indignity over my shoulder.

I lost track of how long we were walking, but at some point our guide came to an abrupt halt. I looked around in confusion. The passage stretched on in front of us, and there were no doors or other features nearby to interact with. The kid looked around, making doubly certain we were alone, then stooped and banged on the floor in a halting rhythm. *Bang bang. Bang. Bang bang bang.*

A moment later, there was a clicking sound. The floor panel lifted, revealing a ladder descending into darkness. A woman's face stared up at us. The kid climbed down and walked out of sight. The woman stared up at me for a moment as the kid said something in Aboenian to her, then lifted her hands up towards me in a supplicating gesture. I hesitated, then lowered Ramar down to her. She grunted as she caught him. I climbed down next.

The woman led us around several dark, tight corners. An

orange light grew steadily brighter as we turned each one. When I reached the end I was left blinking, my eyes slowly adjusting to the light.

I was standing at the end of a long, rectangular, open space. Dozens of lanterns radiating heat and orange light hung from the ceiling. Hut-like structures made of deconstructed crates with flaps of fabric for doors, through which curious faces peered out at me, dotted the area, extending from floor to ceiling like supportive pillars. In the center was a circle of seats, with a glowing furnace in the middle. Four familiar figures were seated there.

"Lax!" One of the figures jumped up from the circle and rushed towards me. I grunted as Rose slammed into me, wrapping me in a hug. A surge of deep relief filled me as I saw Bentley, Rid, and Shell looking towards us from the circle. All safe. All together again.

Rose stepped back, looking me up and down, first with concern, and then revulsion as she realized she'd just been hugging me. "You're... covered in..."

"I know." I shrugged off my pack. "It's not mine."

"Welcome to the Oathless," Shell said as we approached the circle.

I was vaguely aware of dozens of faces watching me from beyond my crew's small circle, but I was too exhausted and too relieved by the sight of my crew to pay them much mind. Shell gestured towards an empty bench, which I sagged into. "We'd just been trying to talk them into sending a search party out for you," she said. "But it looks like you beat us to it."

"Not me." I looked around with a frown and realized that the kid who had found me was nowhere to be seen. "I stumbled across a... never mind. Doesn't matter. What matters is that I'm here." I focused my attention on Rid and Bentley. "And that you guys are here. You alright?"

Rid nodded. They both still looked gaunt and tired, but no longer quite as dead as they'd seemed in Cairn's prison. They certainly looked a hell of a lot better than Ramar did.

"Still just... catching up with everything," Rid said quietly.

Nadus. The bottom of my stomach suddenly fell out. "Did they tell you... about..."

"Yeah." Rid nodded somberly, not looking into my eyes. Rose sat down next to him and rested her head on his shoulder. He leaned numbly into her.

Bentley grimaced. Seeing him so serious—not a glimmer of a joke or snide comment in sight—felt strangely dreamlike somehow. His eyes were red. "They told us that you'd *all* died. Said we were the last ones. So I guess we're just..." He sniffled and wiped his nose. "Just glad that's not entirely true."

"They hurt you?" I asked.

"No. Not really." Bentley looked up towards where Ramar had been placed on a makeshift bed. "Not like they hurt him. We heard him screaming, sometimes. Always thought we'd be next. Guess there was nothing they wanted to know from us, though."

I nodded wearily. "Yeah. Sounds like he had a hell of a time of it."

"Sounds like you guys have too," Rid said quietly. "Thanks for the rescue."

Shell eyed me. "You look like you've been... busy."

"Yeah." I grimaced. "Ran into some opposition." I held up Peacebreaker. "Got this back, though."

Bentley's eyes widened. "That means you..."

"Killed the bastard with the breathing tubes," I said, nodding.

"Dak," Rid muttered. "Good riddance."

"That's not all, though." I stared into the lantern in the center of the room. Its warmth was seductive, beckoning me to just close my eyes and fade away. I fought the temptation. "I found Cairn's rippers."

My entire crew perked up as if I'd run an electrical current through them. They looked around at each other as if trying to decide which question to ask first. I spared them the trouble. "He has them corralled in some old cryochambers," I said. "Hundreds of them. And not just the regular ultrarippers, either. The big ones."

"How does he keep them from escaping?" Shell asked.

"Damned if I know." My eyes drifted shut for a moment. I forced them open. "There was nothing restraining them. Seems like they could have just crawled right out if they'd been of a mind to. It reminded me of..."

My voice trailed off. *No.* That was stupid. That had just been a product of the terror of the moment. The way they'd watched us going past them, unnaturally still. I felt a cold spike of dread creeping over me again just thinking about it.

"Reminded you of what?" Rose asked.

I shifted uncomfortably in my seat. "On the *Panama*," I said. "When the ultrarippers surrounded me and Kessa. They didn't attack, for some reason. Just... waited, and watched us, until the nightmare arrived."

Bentley perked up, brow furrowed in thought. "You said they did the same thing on the *Revelation*. After we, you know, left you for dead. You killed the nightmare, and then—"

"—the others just let me go." I frowned. He was right. "Do the ultrarippers have some sort of hierarchy? The smaller rippers don't eat until the bigger ones do?"

"And *maybe*," Rid said, "when you killed the nightmare, you became a part of that hierarchy somehow. You became the new boss."

Shell scoffed. "Theories won't do us any good. There could be a thousand different reasons."

"There's one person who *would* know," Rose said.

We all turned to Ramar.

In response, he did... absolutely nothing. For all he was moving he may as well have been sprawled out dead on that cot. I had to squint to make sure he was still breathing. Tetra hadn't been kidding about that post-adrenaline wall.

"Yes," Bentley said. "I'm *sure* that when we wakes up after having been tortured for several weeks straight the first thing he'll want to do is give us a nice, long lecture about ripper social structure."

"Knowing him," Rose muttered, "it actually might be."

I had to admit that I found myself intrigued by the idea. Was that Cairn's secret? Had he somehow worked his way up through the ranks of the rippers' bizarre little chain of command? I had no idea how that process would work—but it *did* have one important implication: whoever killed Cairn would take his place. If we could find Cairn, catch him away from his supporters, then maybe—

I caught myself.

That was exactly the type of thinking that had gotten us into this mess in the first place. We weren't here to solve the ripper problem. We weren't here to kill Cairn. We shouldn't be here at all. The only thing I should be spending mental energy on was finding a way to get my crew out of this mess. It wasn't our fight.

I sighed and turned back to the lamp. "It doesn't matter anyways."

Rose blinked. "Doesn't matter? Why not?"

"Because it's not our problem," I said quietly. "Cairn's probably got the whole ship looking for us by now. Tetra said she'd try to find a way out for us. So we stay here, let things blow over, and then, when the coast is clear, we make our escape."

There was a long silence. From the corner of my eye I saw

my crew exchanging measured glances with each other. I knew what they were thinking. I was thinking it myself. *That sounds awfully familiar.*

Didn't make it wrong, though. Did it?

I watched a battle of emotions play out across Rose's face. In the end, she nodded reluctantly. I found myself almost disappointed by it. But I couldn't blame her. She was probably still blaming all of this on herself. I knew all too well how a downward turn in fortune made you question your instincts.

My crew's eyes suddenly shifted to something behind me. I turned with a frown to see a woman approaching us. Significantly older than anyone else I'd seen on the *Aboena* so far, with deep-set wrinkles and mismatched artificial teeth.

Shell cleared her throat. "Lax, this is Valley, our host. She leads this camp of Oathless."

I rose, unsure of what the proper protocol was. Damn protocol. "I, uh... thanks," I finished lamely. "We appreciate you letting us hunker down here."

She sat down stiffly, waving my thanks away. "You may not thank me so much when you see how we require you to earn your keep. Shepherd here"—she jerked her head, and I saw the young man who had guided me here standing behind her—"will show you your duties when the time comes. There is nobody who knows the *Aboena*'s hidden paths better than he."

I nodded. "That seems fair enough. We shouldn't be here too long, though. Tetra is searching for a way out for us."

Valley cackled at that. "*Out?* There is no out, Outsider. Only Command or Cairn can get you *out.*"

My crew shared an uncomfortable look. I cleared my throat. "You think Tetra is lying to us?"

"Lying? No. Not to you, at least. To herself. I know her. She is an optimist. She chooses to believe in light because it is easier than accepting darkness." Valley shook her head slowly. "There is no way out, I am afraid. Not while Cairn wills there not to be.

Trust me—nobody knows better than us." Her face turned sour. "He does not forgive. Ever."

A sullen silence settled over the camp.

"Well," said Bentley. "On that pleasant note... I believe that we all deserve some sleep."

TWENTY-TWO

There are two kinds of pain, boy.

Thud.

I'll see you on the other side.

Thud.

I killed you all.

Thud.

Not all of us.

Thud.

Must have been nice. To do some good.

Thud.

You're a Vanguard. Made for one purpose, and one purpose only: to kill.

CRUNCH.

"Lax!"

My eyes flashed open. I sat up, breath heavy, forehead coated in sweat. I blinked into the darkness.

Rid was crouching near me. For just a moment I thought I was in my room back on Albeni 7. Then I looked beyond him and saw the flickering orange light of the Oathless furnace.

I took a deep breath, shoulders sagging. I groaned, rubbing the sleep out of my eyes. "How long was I out?"

"Just a few hours." Rid glanced over his shoulder towards where the others were huddled. "Tetra is on the quantcom."

I nodded. "Right. I'll be there."

He made no sign of moving away. He looked awkwardly down at the floor. "Hey. I'm sorry about Nadus. I know you guys were really close. Losing him hurts for all of us, but none of us knew him like you."

Something broke inside of me. I don't know why it was right then and there—maybe it was the straw that broke the camel's back, or maybe it was the fact that Rid was the one saying it— but it was. A lump formed in the back of my throat and my eyes suddenly started to burn. I took a slow, choking breath, trying to recover, then nodded. "Thanks. Tell them I'll be right over."

He nodded, then turned away. I spoke up before he could leave. "Hey. *I'm* sorry."

He paused, looking at me quizzically. I cleared my throat uncomfortably. "For... all this. It's my fault. What happened to you and Bentley. And everyone. I'm just glad you guys weren't hurt. I... I don't know if I could have handled that. Especially after what happened to Nadus."

"I don't think it's your fault," Rid said.

I frowned. "How you figure? I should have vetoed this whole operation the moment it started smelling sour."

He shrugged. "We thought it was the right thing to do. Right?"

The right thing. The idea seemed laughable now. Not a damn bit of good had come out this. We hadn't helped anyone. And Nadus was dead. But he'd championed the idea of *the right thing* stronger than anyone.

Rid walked towards the rest of the group. I lingered a moment longer, looking around myself. The cot that Ramar had been in was empty, and I didn't see him in the circle with the others. Odd. I groaned, rose to my feet, and joined the rest of the group, sitting down next to Shell.

She proffered me the quantcom. I glanced down at it.

CAIRN HAS GONE MAD. TRYING TO ROUTE ALL RESOURCES TO HUNTING YOU DOWN. SEARCH PARTIES ARE COMBING THE DARK ZONE. DO NOT LEAVE THE OATHLESS CAMP.

"No surprises there," I said. "Far as Cairn is concerned, we're the biggest threat to his power right now. Nobody outside of this ship knows what he's up to. If we escape, that changes."

Another message appeared on the quantcom. I read it out loud.

HE'S OBSESSED WITH LAX IN PARTICULAR. KEEPS TRYING TO CONVINCE THE REST OF COMMAND HE'S AN EXISTENTIAL THREAT TO THE SHIP.

"Congratulations, Lax," Bentley said. "Not every day you get a compliment like that."

"In a sense, though," Shell mused, "he's right. There's a reason that Command ordered the ship to go into isolation after they found the Stranger. If anyone Outside were to find out about all the weirdness happening on the *Aboena*, it would only be a matter of time before the Paragon showed up to investigate."

"Sure." I nodded. "But why *me*, specifically?"

Rid shrugged. "You're a Vanguard? You just slaughtered an entire squad of his men with an ax?"

Dak's face blipped through my vision. Eyes staring disbelievingly at the stump of his arm. Going wide as I grabbed the back of his head. *Thud. Thud. Thud.*

I looked back down at the quantcom, to Tetra's first message. *Cairn has gone mad.*

What did that mean? He'd had a vicious streak in him before, sure, but Tetra made it sound like he had become unhinged since our escape. Something had pushed him over the edge. What was it?

IS THERE ANY CHANCE HE CAN FIND US HERE?

THERE'S ALWAYS A CHANCE. I'LL TRY TO KEEP YOU UPDATED. LOTS OF EYES ON ME.

I handed the device back to Shell. "I guess we just... wait here," I said.

Rose frowned. "That just feels... wrong."

Despite my words from before my nap, I had to agree. Knowing Cairn was hunting for us while we were just... *hoping* he didn't find us made my skin crawl. But did we have any other options?

I looked up and saw Ramar hobbling back to his cot. I walked towards him as he settled down. He turned his battered face up towards me.

"Feeling better?" I asked.

He scoffed, looking away. "Somewhat. I'm not chained to a ceiling."

"Yeah." I hesitated. What the hell were you supposed to say to someone who's just finished being tortured? Especially when it was your fault?

I settled onto the floor beside him. "Look. I'm sorry about what happened. You shouldn't have lied to get us here. But I shouldn't have abandoned you here."

"I'm not interested in discussing that. It's no longer relevant." He took a slow drink from his canteen, savoring every drop like it was fine wine.

I waited until he was done. "Ramar... what's going on here?"

He turned an incredulous look towards me. "You mean you don't know?"

I sighed. "I know some of it. I know Cairn has ultrarippers that he wants to use against the Paragon. I know that he's got weird powers. And I know it all has something to do with this Stranger."

He nodded weakly. "He *must* be stopped, Lax. If the Paragon gets their hands on the ultrarippers..."

"I know," I said softly. "But my first responsibility is to my crew. I have to get them out of here."

He scoffed. "You can try, Lax. There will be nowhere safe."

I sighed. "What do you know about the Stranger?"

He shook his head. "Not much. I tried to meet them. I was unsuccessful. I have my suspicions, though."

I raised an eyebrow. "Oh?"

"I think they're an escaped Divinity employee," he said. "Everything strange about this ship—the ultrarippers, Cairn, the Shapers—all of it goes back to the Divinity gene."

I frowned. "What do you mean?"

"What I mean," Ramar said, "is that Cairn is to you as ultrarippers are to regular rippers."

I blinked. "A Vanguard, but without programmed in limitations."

Ramar nodded. "He wasn't that way before. It happened after you..." He hesitated, then sighed. "*That* was what he needed the Lifeblood for. Not feeding starving Roamers. Cairn struck a deal with the Stranger: if Cairn provided Lifeblood, the Stranger would enhance him. Cairn described it as being 'Proven.' That was why he kept you prisoners for so long. The procedure took time."

"You saw it?" I asked incredulously.

Ramar chuckled weakly. "No, regrettably. Perhaps if our deal had gone smoother, I could have arranged it. As such, though, I simply served as a consultant for Cairn leading up to his decision. Once I lost my leverage and he got what he'd wanted in the first place, he detained me and began..." His face went grim, and he held a hand gingerly over one of his many injuries. "Well. Things had never been *pleasant* for me here, but they became significantly less so."

"What'd they want from you?"

"He wanted to know how to command his rippers *without* the Stranger's help."

I perked up. "So you *do* know something about that."

Ramar shook his head. "I know that the Stranger knows something. That's all, I'm afraid. It's why I'm so convinced that the Stranger belonged to Divinity at some point. They know things—can do things—nobody else should be able to." Ramar's eyes went distant. "My colleagues and I labored for *years* to create the ultrarippers. And even when our work was done, we knew that we had simply reverse-engineered small parts of Divinity's work. What the Stranger has done is far beyond anything I even knew possible."

He started counting on his fingers. "They were apparently able to locate the ultrarippers from the *Panama*, despite the fact that not a soul knew where they were after your explosion. Even Carston and I were unable to find more than rumors about them."

Another finger. "They were able to contain the rippers. To control them. Far more efficiently than the Paragon ever was."

The next finger was broken, so he skipped it. "They have been producing a seemingly endless amount of food. The *only* way I can think of that one could produce the amount of nutrients the Stranger has for as long as they have is through some form of Divinity-cell-fueled biofuel such as Lifeblood."

One more finger. "Finally, they have successfully integrated the Divinity gene into an adult human. To the best of my knowledge, the process of creating a Vanguard must begin during the subject's childhood. The gene must have time to grow, to integrate. It's a transformation that takes years. And yet the Stranger accomplished it with significantly better results—no offence—in a matter of weeks."

I nodded slowly along. "Alright. Let's say you're right—that the Stranger is an ex-Divinity labcoat hiding out. My follow-up question is what the hell are they doing?" I gestured vaguely around us. "Aren't there better places they could be? All this talk of Proving rituals and chosen ones doesn't exactly sound like something out of a Divinity playbook."

Ramar shrugged. "Who's to say what's in the Divinity playbook? Even I'm not so bold as to assume I know their hidden agendas. But think of it this way. If you were on the run from the most powerful organization of all time, where would you go to hide from them?"

I thought about it. "I guess I'd go wherever they didn't control."

"And where doesn't Divinity control?"

I sighed. "Alright, I guess that does make some sense. But why all the mysticism, then?"

Ramar shrugged. "Maybe they think it's the best way to control the Roamers. They think they're primitive. Superstitious. Which some of them are. Cairn and his Wolves fell for the Stranger's tall tales right away. And with Command, they've been more straight forward. A simple exchange: space and secrecy for food."

"So you think the Stranger is just..." I hesitated. "Surviving? Waiting? What's *their* goal?"

Ramar stared into blank space. "I don't know. But it doesn't matter, because if Cairn isn't stopped, the Paragon will find this ship, take the ultrarippers, take everything the Stranger has made, and kill everybody aboard. And then everything I've done —everything *you've* been through—will have been pointless. The Paragon will have the ultrarippers.

I tried to imagine an army of Cairns charging onto a battlefield next to an army of ultrarippers, all of them under the Paragon's control.

It wasn't a pretty picture.

Not my problem. I clenched my teeth. My job was to keep my crew safe. To get out of here and get back to Sevani. But that looked like an increasingly unlikely possibility. Even if Tetra *was* able to find a way for us to escape the *Aboena*, how long would it be before Cairn put his plan into action? I imagined the army of Cairns and ultrarippers rampaging through Albeni 7, painting the walls scarlet with the blood of the millions of impoverished civilians trapped there.

What would Nadus have done?

You've gotta start somewhere.

I groaned, massaging my forehead. Took a deep breath.

"Let's say we *were* trying to stop Cairn," I said. "Where would we start?"

Ramar blinked.

"Killing him would make the most sense," I said. I sure liked the thought of it, at least. "If it's even possible."

"And how do you propose to do that?" Ramar gestured around us. "From *here?*"

"You got a better idea?" I snapped.

"Yes." He leaned forward, eyes growing intense. "You find the Stranger."

I frowned. "You know how to do that?"

Ramar gave a gentle scoff. "I'd have sought them out a long time ago if I did. Might've saved all of us some trouble. But I've more or less been Cairn's prisoner since I arrived here. From what I've heard, finding the Stranger isn't *impossible*—simply difficult."

"Alright. And once we find them, we, what, kill them?"

"*Shh.*" Ramar glanced around sharply, making sure nobody was eavesdropping. There were a few Roamers in earshot, eyeing us cautiously as they engaged in various tasks around their makeshift campsite, but none of them reacted. Probably didn't understand me. Ramar turned back to me. "If *necessary*... then perhaps. But I think that's far too small-minded. We don't know who they are or what they want yet. We may well discover that we're on the same side. We simply need more information." His eyes glinted with excitement. "They could hold the keys to solving so many of the galaxy's problems. Imagine the possibilities! The secrets of the Divinity gene, released for all to use. Hunger could vanish across the stars. Uncurable diseases could be cured. It would be the greatest technological breakthrough since the Exodus!"

I narrowed my eyes. "Yeah. Or, everybody might just try to make more rippers and Vanguards."

Ramar shook his head in frustration. "But there's so much *more* potential to this than just destruction. Can't you see that? Can't *they*?"

I sighed. "Listen. Before we go any further into this, I need to make one thing clear. We're *not* on the same side. Not permanently, anyways. I'm not here to solve the galaxy's problems or fight anybody's crusade. I'm here because you suckered me into coming here. And it's looking more and more like beating Cairn is the best chance I've got at getting my crew out alive. But if I see another way out—an *easier* way—I'm taking it. Understand?"

Ramar studied me for a moment, then nodded wearily. I remembered suddenly how exhausted he must feel. "Yes. I do."

"Good." I glanced towards the furnace where my crew was gathered. They were talking somberly among themselves, occasionally glancing towards us. "Let me talk to my crew. Then I'll start poking around. See if there's any chance of us finding the Stranger."

"Very well." Ramar settled back into his cot, grunting in pain as he did so. "I think I'll... try to catch a bit more..."

He was already drifting away by the time I rose and strode over to the furnace.

All eyes turned to me.

I cleared my throat, not sure how to begin. "So. I've been talking to Ramar. About the whole situation."

Rid and Bentley gave each other a meaningful look. I ignored them, continuing.

"And... I think our best bet at surviving isn't to stay here. The odds of Tetra finding us a way off—*before* it's too late outside, anyways—are slim to none. So, I figure..." I grimaced. "That our best option may be to go on the offensive."

Rid gave Bentley a smug grin. Bentley groaned. "Fine. I'll pay you when we're out of this mess. *If* we get out of this mess."

I raised an eyebrow. Rose smiled mischievously. "We knew you'd come around. You're just not a sit around and wait kinda guy. No matter how much you try to convince yourself you are."

"Don't get too excited," I said. "I haven't committed us to anything. We're just exploring options. I wanted to see what you all thought." I turned to Shell. "We're in your territory. What do you think?"

She nodded slowly, staring into the furnace. "I think you're right. Staying in place only delays the inevitable. But I don't see how *accelerating* our demise helps us, either. Cairn has us completely outgunned. How do you propose to get to him?"

"By going to the source of his power." I looked around, making sure no Roamers were listening. "By finding the Stranger."

There was a long silence. My crewmates exchanged glances.

"You know I'm in," Rose finally said. Rid nodded along with her.

Bentley sighed. "I don't like it. I was just getting used to the idea of having a chance to relax for a bit, after all we've been through. But... I suppose it makes sense." He gave a forlorn smile. "If we're going to die, we may as well go out doing what we do best, eh? Wandering the dark halls of a forbidden ship?"

"I'll tell Tetra," Shell said. She raised an eyebrow at me. "I'm assuming you have at least the beginnings of a plan on how to go about finding the Stranger?"

I glanced past her, towards where Valley was in conversation with several other Roamers.

"At least the beginnings," I said.

"We don't want to kill them," I said quietly. "We just want to see them. Learn from them. Same as any other Roamer. That's what you do, isn't it? Go on pilgrimages? Well, let us make our *own* pilgrimage."

Valley eyed me skeptically for a moment, then shrugged, turning back to the coat she was currently sewing a patch into. "Very well. Then go. No worry of mine. It is your death to die. My people will blindfold you and take you outside of our hiding place, so you cannot lead the Wolves to our door."

"Right. So we can wander the halls endlessly until they find us."

Valley shrugged again. "As I said. It is your death to die. You go out there—you die. You stay here—you live. Maybe."

"Unless we had a guide," I said, watching her carefully. "Someone who knows the *Aboena*'s hidden paths better than anyone else. Somebody who could point us in the right direction."

Her eyes flitted ever so briefly towards the young man who had guided Ramar and me here. Shepherd. He was sitting near a furnace, watching us with dark, keen eyes.

She snorted. "Sure. A guide would be useful to you. But not to me. Shepherd is useful to us. Why should I send him to die with you?"

"Because sending him with us is the only way to make

certain he *doesn't* die." I narrowed my eyes. "Do you have any idea what will happen if we don't do this? If Cairn is allowed to move forward with his plan?"

Valley eyed me. "What plan?"

"Cairn wants to attack the Paragon," I said. "He wants to fight the Outside. All of it. He thinks that with the Stranger's help, he can win. But he's wrong. Completely wrong. The Paragon will win. They will come for the *Aboena*. They will kill everybody aboard it. Including you. And including Shepherd."

She stopped working on her coat, turning her full attention to me. She folded her arms.

"Believe me or don't believe me," I said. "You know that Cairn is bad news. Sooner or later, he'll either kill you or get you killed."

"Suppose I *did* believe you," she said. "Suppose Shepherd did guide you to the Stranger. What difference do you suppose it would make? The Stranger does not bow to whims. They will not hear you. They have Chosen Cairn."

"Well, maybe they just need some better options to choose from."

Valley stared at me for a few moments, her expression unreadable. Finally, she sighed. "The boy may decide for himself. Shepherd!"

Shepherd rose to his feet, walking silently over to us. She conversed with him in Aboenian for a few moments before turning back to me with a sigh.

"He wants to know," she said, "if you plan to kill Cairn."

I studied the boy. I found no emotion in his face. Not any that I could read, anyways. Finally, I decided the truth was best.

"If I get the chance," I said. "Then you can bet your ass I plan to kill him."

Valley frowned, then turned and consulted the boy again. Shepherd made a disgusted face. My heart sank. Dammit. After what Valley had said about the Oathless having problems with the Wolves, I'd figured for certain that he had some reason he wanted Cairn dead.

"He says," Valley translated for me, "that he does not want to trade asses. But that if you are fighting against Cairn, that he will guide you."

Oh.

"I don't have a radio to give you," I said, shoving my items into the supply pack Tetra had given me. "But we'll send Shepherd back when we find the Stranger."

Ramar nodded, watching me. "I appreciate that. I wish I could come with you. But..."

"But you've taken a hell of a beating. I know." I jerked my head towards the Roamers. "Valley said they'll take care of you. I gave them some supplies as payment. I don't know that I'd say I trust them too far, but we don't really have any other choices."

"Agreed." He straightened—a movement that caused quite a bit of pain, judging by his expression. "They certainly can't be less hospitable than my last host."

"Yeah." I studied him. "You gonna be alright?"

He nodded again. "I'll be fine. I just need time to recover." He chuckled. "Who knows—perhaps, when you find the Stranger, I can make my own pilgrimage and receive some of this miraculous healing the Roamers love talking about."

"Maybe." I grabbed the assault rifle I'd taken from the Wolves and checked to make sure it was loaded. "But that's a big *if*, not a when."

"Come now, Lackan." Ramar smiled weakly. "Have a little faith."

"Nadus had faith," I said. "Didn't get him too far."

Ramar's smile faded.

———

We struck out into the darkness.

With a supply pack on my back, Peacebreaker at my side again, the stolen assault rifle slung over my shoulder, food in my belly, and some sleep in my system, I felt far more confident than I had the last time we'd ventured out into the labyrinthian corridors. Valley had given us more clothes too. Just roughly cut fabric, really, but it was one more layer against the bitter cold permeating most of the abandoned corridors.

Shepherd marched swiftly at the front of our group, taking turns with a confidence that almost made me nervous. "How does anyone find their way around in here?" I asked Shell quietly. "If you told me we'd been walking in circles for the past twenty minutes, I'd believe you."

Shell shrugged. "There are ways. Look." She pointed at a darkened spot on the wall. When I aimed my flashlight at it and squinted, I realized it was lettering, faded and coated in lichen.

"This lichen stuff," Bentley asked, his voice curious rather than whining for once. "Where does it come from?"

"Been there longer than I have," Shell said. "Feeds on the tiny bits of moisture and bacteria the life-support systems move around. Some sort of fungi from old Earth, I guess, evolved over the years. It's slow growing, but if we—I mean, *they*—didn't clean it off, it'd be everywhere by now."

Rose glanced sharply at her. "They? You're every bit as much a Roamer as they are."

"Doesn't feel that way," Shell said, looking straight ahead. "Everything has changed since I was here. Every*one* has changed."

"Even your sister," I said.

She nodded.

"No offense," Bentley said, which he usually said right before saying something extremely offensive, "but... why would *anyone* want to stay here? Everyone we've talked to seems miserable. The entire place is on the verge of war. You have *rippers* just sealed off in one portion of the ship. I mean, it's even worse than Albeni."

"It wasn't always so bad," Shell said. "And it isn't so bad now, in the living quarters. Especially among the Traders. The population is carefully controlled so that it doesn't spiral out of control like on Albeni. Everybody has plenty of room. There are large common areas. Community gardens to produce fresh food. You even got to meet people—back in the day, Outsiders coming to trade would stay in the Traders' quarters and mingle. It was how we'd learn Basic, and what it was like outside of the *Aboena*." The slow, nostalgic smile that had been building up on her face went suddenly dark. "It's out here—in the dark—that things get rough."

"The Oathless," I said. "Why are *they* down here? Did they get kicked out?"

Shell's face turned sour the same way it had the first time Tetra had mentioned that we would be sheltering with the Oathless. She sighed. "They are exiles. Like me. Except that instead of leaving the *Aboena*, as they had been ordered to, they simply retreated into the bowels of the ship."

I glanced sharply at her but said nothing. Was that why she seemed so resentful of them? Did she despise them for staying when they'd been ordered to leave? Or did she regret that she hadn't made the same choice?

Bentley shook his head. "Still seems crazy to me. To *choose* to stay up here instead of going down to the planet you've spent generations flying towards. Don't you ever wish that... you know... they hadn't? You would've been born on Brahma. Grown up with sunshine and trees."

"Wouldn't matter if I did," Shell said. "I can't change what I am."

I stiffened at the words. Cairn's lurid grin floated through my mind. *You're a Vanguard. Made for one purpose and one purpose only: to kill. You can't hide from that.*

I'd worked so hard to distance myself from that part of myself. Kessa had convinced me that I wasn't defined by my past. By the things the Paragon had made me do. The monster they'd made me. Maybe she'd been wrong, though. Maybe denying the grim reality of my true nature was the very reason I couldn't escape it. The reason that everywhere I went, that trail of bodies followed, growing longer and bloodier by the day. Friends, foes, random bystanders—all reduced to ruined corpses in my wake.

I found myself suddenly wishing for a can of frigicerin. My body still felt twitchy in the same way that it always had after a dosage of ignicerin back in the Vanguard. Except that this time there had been no ignicerin. No faceless Paragon officer in a battlecruiser high above me who had hit a button and compelled me to violence. This time there had been only me and Dak and the *hate*.

I wanted to protect my friends. Wanted to stop Cairn from launching his idiotic plan. Wanted to avenge Nadus's death. But I didn't want to turn back into the monster I'd worked so hard to evolve from.

Shepherd's voice jarred me from my thoughts. He was saying something to Shell, pointing down a set of branching corridors. Discussing which direction, possibly. After a few moments they chose the one to the right and started down it.

I quickened my pace until I was walking behind Shell. "Ask him about his experience with the Shapers."

She did. I assumed. Shepherd stiffened slightly, then gave a short, halting reply.

"The Shapers took him in when he was a child," she said after a moment. "He spent a few years with them, then left them and joined the Oathless."

"Has *he* seen the Stranger?" Rid asked.

"No," Shell confirmed after a moment. "Hardly anyone has.

He says only the highest-ranking members of the Shapers have seen the Stranger in the flesh."

"Who the hell *is* this guy?" Rose muttered. "Everyone talks about them like they're a god."

"Probably just a doctor," Bentley muttered. "Some random person with a passing knowledge of modern medicine."

Shell shook her head. "You saw the medbay. Our medicine is as advanced as anybody else's. It must be something more." She narrowed her eyes. "It's got to have something to do with the Divinity gene."

I nodded. "Ramar and I were just talking about that." I filled them in on the details of the conversation. "He thinks that the Stranger is some sort of ex-Divinity scientist in exile. It would explain why they're able to do so much with the Divinity gene."

"Just another reason why Ramar wanted to come here so badly," Rid mused. "Maybe he thinks he can learn more about the rippers."

"I thought he was already the ripper expert," Bentley said.

I shook my head. "No. I mean, sure, he knows more than the rest of us. But nobody outside of Divinity really knows how their stuff works. All he did with Project Eden was remove some of the genetic safeguards Divinity had ingrained into the rippers."

"If this is just the tech that Divinity is willing to share," Rose muttered, "imagine what stuff they have they're *not* telling everyone else about."

It was a daunting prospect to consider. Divinity stayed just uninvolved enough from public affairs to make it easy to forget that at the end of the day, they *ran* the Paragon. Every day we relied on their technology to keep the engines of civilization running, never pausing to think about what strings they were pulling from the shadows to make sure it stayed that way.

"Why'd he leave the Shapers?" Rose asked the question. Shell translated. Shepherd's face darkened.

"He left them when the Stranger started working more closely with Cairn," she said. "I guess Cairn killed Shepherd's parents, a long time ago, so he's got no more reason to love him than the rest of the Oathless."

I nodded somberly. That explained the need for revenge, at least.

"Whoa." Bentley slowed his pace, turning a small flashlight we'd bartered with the Oathless for onto the wall beside him. "What's that?"

I frowned. It was a picture of some sort. Looked like it had once been a vibrant mural of a large, blue lake, ringed by mountains. Symbols I couldn't read were stretched along the bottom of it.

"They're scenes from Earth," Shell said softly. "Some of the early generations made them. To help remember."

I swung my own flashlight, studying another mural opposite me. This one showed a shoreline city. A massive, blueish-green statue of a woman wearing a crown and holding aloft a torch rose from the water. Rid must have seen it too. He let out a long whistle. "The old earthers really knew how to put on a show. Why did people stop building stuff like that?"

"They didn't," I said, moving on. "They just don't build them in space. Not unless its somewhere rich people will see them, at least."

"My mom's always talking about that," Rose said, staring at an image of several large pyramid-shaped buildings carved from stone in a desert. I wondered idly what they'd been called as I passed them by. Rose kept talking. "She says that people on stations don't make art and stuff because they don't have time to. The station overseers keep them so bogged down with debt that all they have energy for is survival."

I felt a rush of melancholy at the mention of Sev. I wondered what was happening on Albeni 7. She was probably scouring the galaxy for us. If Vatheson hadn't killed her already, that was.

"Hey!"

Bentley's startled voice cracked in my ear. Our formation came to an abrupt halt. I barely managed to keep from bowling over Rid. I looked to the front of our group to see Shepherd holding one hand up in the air, still as a statue.

"What is it?" Bentley hissed.

"*Shhh!*" Shell snapped.

Shepherd turned slowly, eyes moving slowly upwards along the ceiling. I wasn't sure what he was looking for. I couldn't see anything other than the usual rust- and lichen-coated surfaces, and couldn't hear anything other than a slight hum of distant machinery and my crew's hushed breathing.

Thump, thump, thump...

I frowned. Had I imagined the sound?

Thump, THUMP, THUMP...

No. Something was echoing. Growing louder. Echoing faintly down the corridor. Footsteps. Lots of them. Voices, harsh and angry. The lichen on the ceiling began to tremor ever so slightly.

Shepherd said something sharply and dashed silently into the shadows.

"What'd he say?" Bentley asked.

"*Run,*" Shell snapped.

TWENTY-THREE

Shepherd's light was already just a glimmer at the end of the corridor. We sprinted after it. He took several sharp turns, waiting just long enough for us to see which way he'd gone.

I withdrew the quantcom and hastily typed into it as I ran.

BEING PURSUED. ANY IDEAS?

"Hold up!" Shell hissed suddenly. Once again, our group came to a sudden stop as Shepherd froze in the middle of an intersection, ear perked upwards. He listened for a moment. Once the echoing sounds of our own hasty passage had faded, I heard what he was listening for. Footsteps, faster now, looming behind us.

Not just behind us, though. Clanging sounds rang out from the corridor on our left. Shepherd said something that sounded like a curse and darted to the right, the rest of our group in hot pursuit.

My quantcom buzzed. I glanced at it.

NOT US. MUST BE WOLVES. RUN.

"Your sister's full of great ideas," I snarled to Shell.

"What?" She glanced hopefully over her shoulder at me. "Did she—"

"I was being sarcastic," I growled, handing her the quantcom.

Shepherd jerked a small door on the left side of the hallway open, then cursed, slammed it shut, and resumed sprinting. In the cracks around the edge of the door I saw just a glimmer of light from the other side. A rousing battle cry echoed from behind it.

"They're—*everywhere*," Bentley gasped.

It certainly seemed that way. The sounds of our pursuers grew louder with every passing minute, no matter how many tricky turns Shepherd led us down. They seemed to be all around, boxing us in, forcing us to move constantly to the right.

Finally, Shepherd came to a panting halt in the middle of an intersection, staring up ahead with a look of absolute defeat strewn across his face. He said something bitter sounding to Shell.

"They're ahead of us," Shell said grimly.

"And behind us," Rose said, craning her head.

"And..." Bentley gulped, looking from side to side. The sounds of pursuit echoed from every direction. He broke off into a string of curses.

"So what do we do?" Rid demanded. "There's gotta be *some* way out."

The footsteps grew louder behind us. Shepherd gave a defeated moan and sagged into the fetal position, hand clutched over his head. I drew Peacebreaker. "Shell. Give us something. We can't fight them all."

Shell swore, looking around wildly. After a moment, her eyes settled on a set of characters imprinted on the wall next to us.

Her mouth dropped open slightly.

She turned to Shepherd, snapping something in Aboenian. He looked up sharply. His eyes widened. He shook his head. Shell drew a pistol and aimed it at him, earning shocked looks from Bentley, Rid and Rose. Shepherd's eyes widened still further.

My heart pounded in my chest. I glanced backward, in the direction the footsteps were loudest from. I could see light now at the far end of the corridor.

Shepherd climbed to his feet, eyes fixed on Shell's pistol, then turned and began sprinting down the tunnel on the right.

"Where are we going?" I gasped as we ran after him.

"You don't wanna know," Shell growled.

There was another small door on the left. Shepherd opened it and proceeded through a cramped stairwell. I waited by the side as the rest of the crew went through one by one.

"VANGUARD!"

Cairn's voice. It boomed down the narrow corridors like the wrath of God. I spun to see light shining at both ends of the hallway.

"Ah, *hell*," I growled.

A gunshot thundered. A bullet whizzed past my head. Rid was still in the doorway, peering down into the darkness. I shoved him, sending him tumbling down the stairs with a yelp then went through myself—

Dammit. My shoulders caught on the edges of the narrow door.

More gunshots. Bullets ricocheted off of the walls around me.

No. This was not how I'd die. Trapped like a hunted animal, waiting to feel the bullet's sting or worse. I twisted, pushed, and gave a startled cry as I popped suddenly through the passageway, rolling head over heels down the set of narrow, rickety stairs. Something gave way beneath my weight with a screeching of metal. I fell, screamed, grunted as I slammed into another flight of steps, bounced, bowled over somebody, and came to a jarring halt face first on the cold metallic floor.

"*Ow*," Bentley moaned from beneath me.

Hands on my shoulders. Shell, helping me up, while Rose helped Rid and Bentley back to their feet. Shepherd was standing in a doorway to another corridor, face drawn and pale.

Movement above. I looked up to see a Wolf peering down at us from the top of the ruined stairway, a submachine gun in his hands. I grabbed everybody within reach in a massive bear hug and pulled them out of the stairwell, spilling into the corridor outside just before bullets started raining down.

I rolled and climbed back to my feet, panting. "Now where?"

"They'll be down again soon enough," Shell said. "They've boxed us in from every direction except one."

"Let's go that way, then," Bentley gasped.

Shell gestured to Shepherd, who reluctantly started moving. Shell had been right. Before more than a few minutes had passed the sounds of pursuit were already echoing behind us.

Finally, Shepherd skidded to a halt in front of a large, sealed blast door at the end of the corridor. He leaned against the wall, staring at it with dread.

I doubled over, resting my hands on my knees and panting up at the door. Something was written across it in bold, red lettering I couldn't make out. Shepherd turned to Shell, then gestured wildly at the door's control panel, shouting angrily. Sounded almost like an *I told you so.*

"Rid?" Rose's voice was weak and strained. "Can you..."

Rid glanced over his shoulder. The footsteps were growing louder. "Not without any equipment."

"You don't need any," Shell said grimly. She walked past Shepherd to the control panel.

A triumphant shout echoed down the corridor. I turned and saw a Roamer scout sprint into view at the far end of the corridor. I raised Peacebreaker and fired, sending him scurrying for cover.

"You know the code?" Rid asked, voice hopeful.

"I know it," Shell said. Her fingers moved quickly, pressing the numbers in sequence. "I programmed it."

The door began to grind open.

More Roamers sprinted into view. I fired a few more warning shots. They sent some of their own back. Bullets whistled around me, slamming into the walls and the heavy blast doors. Bentley gave a yelp as one winged his arm.

"*Go!*" Shell slid through the gap in the doors the moment it was wide enough. I kept shooting as the rest of the group went through one by one. The Wolves stopped firing as they realized what we were doing, staring with baffled expressions.

Fine by me. I slipped through the door, nearly slipped on something on the floor on the other side, then stabilized myself, not taking the time to looked down to see what it was. Shell hit a button on the other side and they began to close.

"*LACKAN!*"

Through the gap in the slowly closing doors I saw Cairn appear, his fur mantle making him loom like a giant above his men. He was too far away for me to make out the details of his face, but the white-hot fury in his voice was enough for me to picture it.

I raised Peacebreaker, holding my breath as I lined up the shot. He was walking towards us—breaking into a run—getting closer—I could see his bared teeth, could hear his angry pants as he ran—the door was almost closed—he bellowed, raising an ax —the same one I'd killed Dak with—my sights were settled square on the center of his forehead—

Shell's hand closed suddenly around Peacebreaker, shoving it downwards. Something large and metallic spun through the air towards me. I ducked as Cairn's ax whirled over my head to slam into the wall behind me. I got one last glimpse of Cairn's fury-ridden face before the doors slammed shut. There was a whirring mechanical sound as they sealed tight.

I spun on Shell, growling. "What the *hell*? I almost—"

"*Shhhh.*" Her other hand clamped tight over my mouth. Something in her eyes dispelled my rage.

"Uhm..." Bentley's voice came as a frightened whisper. "What are we standing in?"

I looked down.

My eyes widened.

The floor beneath me was coated red in dried blood and littered with debris. I lifted my foot. The item I'd almost slipped on looked like a breastplate—the same kind the Command Marshals wore. Only this one had a set of long, deep cuts through the center. No—not just cuts. Claw marks.

My blood ran cold.

Shepherd muttered what sounded like a frantic prayer under his breath.

"Shell," Rose whispered. "What is this place?

"This," Shell whispered, "is the quarantine zone."

TWENTY-FOUR

I looked around wildly, Peacebreaker raised in a white-knuckled grip. We were standing in the center of a T-shaped intersection. Throughout most of the *Aboena* there had been at least occasional flickering lights clinging to their last bits of power. Here, the only light was what we had with us. The corridors yawned deep and utterly dark at us.

"*Why...*" Bentley hissed, "*the hell... are we here?*"

"Because it was our last option," Shell said grimly, keeping her voice low. "Either tackle Cairn's entire army..."

"Or try our luck here," Rose finished, eyes wide as they flitted back and forth between the pitch-black corridors.

I heard faint, muffled shouts on the other side of the door. Something that sounded almost like laughter. A dull pounding sound as somebody beat their fists against the heavy metal.

I clenched my teeth, unwilling to turn my back on the dark passageways. "Can they..."

"No." Shell shook her head. "Only Command knows the passkey to open that door."

"*And* you," Rid pointed out.

"And me," Shell agreed, eyes dark.

Shepherd's prayer cut off abruptly. He turned towards the door and reached for the control panel, eyes bursting with terror as he mumbled something repeatedly. Rid grabbed the Roamer's wrist, wrenching it away.

"You know a way out?" I asked.

"Yeah." Shell pointed her flashlight down the hallway on the left. "That way."

"How do we know they won't just be waiting for us at the next door?" Rose's voice was trembling slightly.

"We don't," Shell said. "Which is why we won't take the next door." She took a long, deep breath. "If we go along this passage far enough, we should be able to cut straight through to where Shepherd here was planning on taking us in the first place. Or at least close enough for him to guide us back on track."

I glanced at the Oathless boy. He had sagged to the floor, crouching and hyperventilating.

"If he doesn't have a heart attack first," I said.

Bentley didn't look like he was having a much easier time of it. It looked like it was taking all of his willpower to keep from joining Shepherd on the floor. Rose had stepped next to Rid, holding his arm tightly with one hand while the other held her pistol out towards the darkness like it was some kind of holy ward against evil. Rid was taking long, slow breaths, trying his best to stay calm.

"You all know the drill," I said. "Be as quiet as possible. Nobody has been in here for years. The rippers should all be hibernating. If we're careful we can make it all the way through without so much as disturbing them." I glanced sideways at Shell. "Right?"

Shell nodded slowly. "Right."

"Alright, then." I took a deep breath, then crossed to the

wall Cairn's ax had embedded itself in. I pried it free. "Lead the way, Marshal."

Shell gritted her teeth and stepped into the darkness.

I've been on dozens of ripper-infested ships.

Some things are always the same. There are signs of carnage everywhere—yet never any bodies. Dried blood coats the walls. Discarded weapons, spent ammo casings, scraps of gore-stained clothing and armor litter the ruined hallways. The walls are marred with long scratches.

Other things vary. Sometimes you can tell that at least some of the crew managed to hold the rippers off long enough to escape in the emergency shuttles. Others, not so much. Sometimes the gravity generators are on, rooting everything to the ground, while other times the wreckage floats ghost-like in the air.

The one thing that never, *ever* changes, though, is the terror. Each and every time. No matter how well prepared I am, no matter how foolproof my plan is, I always feel the same rush of dread. The same cold fear gripping at my innards.

Except this time.

This time it was worse.

I had to force myself to keep my breathing steady and my movements calm. My body screamed at me that I should be running as fast as I could to get out. But I knew better. And, more importantly, I knew that if *I* panicked, it was game over for everybody else. The only thing that would save us right now was cool, careful, calculated thinking.

We'd make it out of this. We had to. One slow, steady step at a time. Survival was the only thing my mind had room for now. The Stranger, Ramar, Cairn, revenge—all of it seemed silly and distant. Strange, superfluous ideas I wasn't sure now why I'd ever cared about. All that mattered was getting my crew out of here—alive.

With no exosuits. No Jackhammer rifles. All we had were a handful of assault rifles, Peacebreaker, some knives, and my ax. No explosives, no thrusters. Nothing. I wished harder than I'd ever wished for anything before that I was inside of the Icarus's comfortingly armored confines.

Green dots...

"What's that up ahead?" Rid asked softly.

Flashing red...

Shell swore viciously under her breath as we drew closer to the object of Rid's inquiry. A barricade thrown together with various random objects—furniture, machinery, bits of scrap metal—blocked our path.

"Looks like some of the survivors tried to hold the rippers off," Rose said.

Shell nodded, jaw clenched. "It didn't work." There was a cold, bitter fury in her voice. She pointed at a gap in the barrier marked by jagged claw marks where the rippers had crawled through. "They probably built it here after the doors got sealed, hoping they'd open again. They never did."

"Now what?" Bentley asked. "Do we tear it down?"

"Too noisy," I said. "Can we go around?"

"We'd have to go deeper," Shell said. "But... yes."

Bentley groaned. Rose and Rid didn't look too happy. Hell, I wasn't, either. But it was better than spending twenty minutes pulling apart this pile of scrap metal.

Shell turned and began striding back in the way we'd come. Shepherd shook his head violently. "No, no, no," he whispered in Basic.

I put a hand on his shoulder and guided him gently along with us, speaking in what I hoped was a comforting tone. "Come on. I know you can't understand me. But we'll be fine. We just need to go around."

He didn't look comforted. He followed, though, one trepidation-filled step at a time. We moved slowly, every step placed with immaculate care. I kept Peacebreaker at the ready and my head on a swivel as we moved deeper into the quarantine zone, but I saw no movement. We might as well have been walking through a graveyard.

"What is this place?" I whispered to Shell as we passed through a large, open space. It looked as if it had been full of tables and chairs, many of which seemed to have been dragged down the corridor to create the barricade we'd seen.

"These were living quarters," Shell said, her eyes looking everywhere but the stains of blood scattered across the floor. "This would have been a gathering place, like I was saying earlier. People would collect here when they weren't working. Eat together, talk together. There was a garden there." She pointed towards a raised platform off to the side, covered in pots full of long-dead plants. "Down that way there was a public bath, and a mass entertainment room. People would watch old earth movies, like our ancestors did on the journey over."

I hesitated. "Is this where..."

She nodded grimly. "This is where Tetra and I grew up. I spent hours running around here, listening to Outsider stories. Getting in trouble."

I stepped over a discarded child's toy—an action figure of an armor-clad knight with a sword and shield. It had been trampled during the panicked exodus, its misshapen, flattened face staring up at me in a woeful accusation.

"Your exile," Rose whispered. "It was because of this, wasn't it?"

Shell gave a slow nod, her rifle raised as she moved around a corner into a long hallway. "When the rippers hit, and we got dispatched... my sister and I were among the first to get here. I headed up the evacuations. Tetra and her squad went in deeper to slow down the rippers. When the orders came to seal everything off, Tetra was still inside, fighting. So when I programmed the code, I made a secret code for myself, then snuck back inside."

I tried to imagine what that must have been like. Screaming mingling with gunfire through the halls. Mass panic. People running in every direction, not sure where the rippers were coming from. The final moments of dread as the horde closed in.

"I managed to find Tetra. I got her out, and some others too, just in the nick of time. And then..."

"They exiled you," I said grimly.

She nodded, eyes narrowed. "It was a direct Command order. You can get away with a lot of crap, but when Command tells you to do something, you *do it*. I didn't. And I paid the price."

"Seems like a lot of people would've paid a much heavier one if you'd complied," Rose said.

"Wait." Bentley furrowed his brow, the story apparently intriguing enough to temporarily distract him from his terror. "So why didn't your sister get exiled?"

"Because *she* didn't violate orders," Shell said, a hint of bitterness in her voice. "She was the heroic Marshal Tetra, hero of the ripper incursion, who nobly fought back the tide of—"

Something snapped. We all turned sharply only to see that Rid had stepped on a discarded piece of armor. He winced, moving his foot and carefully stepping over the macabre waste.

"Maybe we should save the storytelling for later," I whispered.

Shell grimaced. "Yeah."

I lost track of time. Shell led us down one eerily empty corridor after another. Our path was much more straightforward than the twisting, labyrinthian trails Shepherd had chosen while we'd been attempting to evade the Wolves. Then again, our goal was much more straightforward: get from point A to point B as quickly and quietly as possible. No worrying about patrolling Roamers in here. It was just us, the scattered remnants of the dead, and—somewhere—the rippers.

Those remnants became more frequent and more disturbing the farther we went. These hallways had a ghostlike quality to them that the others in the *Aboena* hadn't possessed. For most of our travels through the Exodus ship, our very presence had felt like a blasphemy. As if we were treading on sacred ground, not meant for humans—modern humans, at least. Here, the exact opposite was true. These halls *should* have been occupied. They *should* have been filled with the sounds of life.

They weren't.

I held my breath as we turned a sharp corner into a long corridor with whitewashed walls. An emergency light overhead was still running, painting the space with sickly fluorescence. A set of twin doors hung open near the center of it. I peered through them as we passed. The room inside was full of small desks, scattered chaotically and turned on their sides. The walls were laden with brightly colored posters—charts, graphs, maps of unfamiliar places. Thousands of small pieces of debris littered the floor: electronic devices, toys, books, many of them hacked into terribly clean pieces. My gut clenched as I spied a singled shoe—hardly larger than my big toe—sitting empty near the doorway.

Something *buzzed*.

I spun, raising my assault rifle. I saw no sign of hostile movement. I forced myself to calm down as I realized that it was just the quantcom.

Shell pulled the device from her pocket, coming to a halt. I read it over her shoulder.

DID YOU GO IN THE QUARANTINE ZONE?

"Guess word got out," I muttered.
Shell responded.

YES. WE HAD NO OTHER OPTIONS.

There was a short delay before Tetra's reply.

*DON'T COME OUT. CAIRN REQUESTING REIN-
FORCEMENTS AT ALL QUARANTINE ZONE EXITS.*

"*Dammit*," I muttered.
"What now?" Bentley hissed.
"Cairn's got reinforcements inbound," Shell said. "Exits will
all be watched."
Bentley let out a string of increasingly quiet, increasingly
vile curses. Shepherd gave Shell an inquisitive look. She
explained. He broke off into a string of similarly obscene
sounding Aboenian.
Rid took a deep breath. "Alright. What can we do? If we
wait them out long enough could Tetra cause a distraction?"
"I think they'll be able to wait a hell of a lot longer than we
will," I said. "We've got supplies, but not that much. And something tells me we're not gonna be able to scavenge much in
here."
There was a large floor map painted on the wall next to the
entrance to the desecrated classroom. Shell consulted it for a
few minutes. She pointed. "This is the quarantine zone," she
said, tracing a large circle on the right side of the *Aboena* with
her finger. "We entered down here. The exits are here... and
here... and here."
"No chance we could make it there before they do?" Rose
asked hopefully.

"Don't think so," Shell said.

"Any secret exits?" Bentley asked. "Come on, you grew up here. There's gotta be some sort of secret passageway, or a hidden elevator or stairway, or a damn air duct we could crawl through, or *something*."

"You really wanna be trapped inside an air duct when the rippers wake up?" Rose asked. Bentley paled.

Shell shook her head. "I was part of the team that made sure there was no way out, remember? If there was a secret way the survivors would have found it. And the rippers would have followed them."

I studied the map. *A way out*. There had to be one.

"Any idea where the rippers will be hibernating?" Rose asked. "Any power generators or anything like that?"

Shell shook her head. "Command shut down all power as part of the quarantine. They'd have killed the life support too, if they could, but the ship's emergency systems wouldn't let them."

Come on. Come on. I gritted my teeth, willing the map to give me a solution. Once we were back in the main portion of the ship, Shepherd could resume guiding us to the Stranger. We just needed to figure out a way to escape the quarantine zone without running straight into Cairn's men *or* waking up the swarm of rippers that was hibernating somewhere in this sector.

"So, we can't leave. And the rippers could be anywhere," Bentley said. "Awesome. Lovely. So happy to hear it."

"Will you *shut up*?" Rose snapped. "I swear, all you do is—"

"*Wait*." I held up a hand, pointing at the map. "Shell. Would this still be functioning?"

Shell glanced at the map with a frown. "I... maybe. It might take a little bit of tinkering..."

I raised an eyebrow. "But we should be able to get out, right?"

She nodded slowly. "It's getting back *in* that I'm more worried about."

"Wait." Rid frowned. "What are we talking about?"

I took a deep breath and pointed at the map, indicating a point on the far edge of the quarantine zone. "This right here is a docking bay."

Rose's eyes lit up. "Do you think..."

"There won't be any ships," Shell said. "But we should be able to find some emergency exosuits."

Bentley was nodding. "Right. Right! We could just do a quick spacewalk across. Come back in a different way."

Rose frowned at him. "I genuinely can't tell if you're being sarcastic right now."

Bentley shrugged. "Look, it's a crazy plan, but it's a hell of a lot better than options A, B, or C."

"Could we get Tetra to open up a different docking bay for us?" Rid asked.

Shell massaged her temples. "Maybe. But we might not even be able to get out. With no power, we'd have to manually operate the airlock somehow, then—"

Light.

It flared to life above us, so suddenly that it made all of us jump in place. I looked up wildly. All of the ceiling lights had turned on, bathing the hallways in a cheery, fluorescent glow.

Bentley's mouth fell open slightly. "I thought you said..."

"They turned the power back on," Shell said slowly, looking just as baffled.

"Well," Rose said, "hopefully that solves the docking port problem."

"Maybe Tetra did it?" Rid suggested.

A muffled, garbled voice suddenly boomed in our ears. A single word in Aboenian, repeated over and over again.

"Evacuate," Shell translated. Her eyes narrowed. "This was the message playing during the attack."

"Oh, *hell*," I muttered, the horrible realization finally creeping over me. "They didn't turn on the power to help us."

Rose's eyes widened. "They did it to wake up the rippers."

We all stared at each other for a short, shocked moment.

Somewhere, down the hall, something crashed.

"*RUN!*" Shell snapped, then bolted in the direction of the docking bay.

We sprinted after her. Shepherd fell behind, breath ragged and face flushed with terror. If he survived the day, the poor kid would probably have aged a dozen years. I grabbed him and slung him over one shoulder. He'd been about as useful to us as a sack of potatoes so far, but I'd be damned if I was leaving anyone behind for the rippers.

Bathed in the vivid white lighting, the quarantine zone was an entirely different world that somehow managed to be more disturbing than the one before. Before, we'd been forced to use our imaginations to fill in the dark shadows. Now, every last, brutal detail was laid bare, all of it telling the tale of a horrific fate that we'd soon be joining if we didn't get the hell out of here.

I heard another crashing sound somewhere on the right. I jerked my head over my shoulder and caught just a glimpse of something pale and spider-like crashing through a window, shards of broken glass showering around it.

"*Go!*" Where there was one there'd be more. I didn't want to be around to confirm, though.

"This way!" Shell turned quickly down a corner. The rest of us pivoted and followed. I had no concept of how close we were to our destination, but compared to the snail's pace we'd been crawling at before, it felt like we were flying now. Any attempt at stealth was gone, our footsteps ringing down the corridors and our breath coming in ragged gasps. The rippers were awake and they were hungry.

There was a skittering sound ahead of us. A ripper dashed

into sight, claws scraping against the floor as it pivoted towards us, opening its jagged maw wide and tensing its long, scorpion like tail to strike.

Shell and I fired simultaneously. Her small caliber pistol merely annoyed it, zipping through its shoulder and out the other end, but Peacebreaker's heavy liquid ammo slug was harder to ignore. The shot struck it straight in the torso, knocking it off of its feet and interrupting its aim. Without stopping, I fired two more shots into its head as we ran past. It thrashed but showed no signs of giving chase. The gunshots *boomed* down the hallways, momentarily overpowering the sound of the old evacuation warning. If there'd been any doubt before, it was gone now: the rippers knew exactly where we were. The sounds of claws scraping against the floors echoed behind us.

"Almost there!" Shell pivoted again, leading us through a series of sharp turns as we tried to shake off the horde of demons pursuing us. Shepherd groaned and grunted as he bounced on my shoulder. After a few more minutes of running we burst through a door and into a large, darkened room much like the loading bay we'd first docked the *Orpheus* at.

"There's a personnel airlock," Shell gasped, running along the edge of the room and opening a door on the side. "For repairs." We followed her in. I dumped Shepherd on his feet, where he proceeded to stagger against the wall with a dazed expression. Shell pointed towards a set of exosuits—light ones, not powerarmor—hanging along the wall. "Everyone find one that fits. *Fast.*"

I poked my head out the door, making sure the rippers weren't on top of us yet. The coast seemed clear for now—hopefully Shell's pathfinding had bought us some time. I turned to the spacesuits, digging rapidly through them until I found the biggest one. I pulled it on, praying to any higher power willing to listen that it would fit. It was a little tight, but I managed to squeeze into it.

"Now find a buddy to check your suit," I said, zipping up the first layer of my suit. "No point in going through all this trouble if you're just gonna die from a suit malfunction. Shell, start the airlock depressurization." Another thought occurred to me. "Will it alert Command?"

"No idea," Shell said, busy trying to climb into her suit and fire up the depressurization at the same time.

"Apparently, they didn't know when the *Orpheus* docked in the other loading bay," Rose said. "So maybe not."

"We can hope," I said. I saw a flicker of movement through the open doorway to the loading bay. A ripper skidded to a halt, looking around. I finished securing the exosuit around my body, then grabbed my helmet—blessedly oversized—and lowered it over my head, fitting it into the grooves at the suit's neck, then hit the button to seal it all tight and begin the suit pressurization. I breathed a sigh of relief as the exo's long unused life-support pack whirred to life. "Either way, we're out of time."

"Dammit." Rid looked up frantically. He—along with Bentley—was still working his way into his suit's first layer. Shepherd was even further behind, his fingers fumbling frantically with a clumsiness that told me he'd never even considered stepping foot outside of the *Aboena*. Rose and Shell were almost into theirs, however.

The ripper's gaze settled on us. It started sprinting. I raised Peacebreaker and fired. The first shot missed. The second struck it in a leg, knocking it down. It kept crawling towards us, claws flailing. I grabbed the ax from where I'd set it down and stepped towards it, swinging the weapon in an overhead strike that landed right on the crown of its grotesque skull.

CRUNCH.

"Lax!" Rose's voice. "More incoming!"

I looked up. She was right. Two more rippers were pouring into the loading bay, sprinting towards me.

I habitually tried to activate my neurointerface to tab my radio to the public channel. I dunno why—I guess something about being in a spacesuit, looking at the rippers through the sheen of my helmet, made me suddenly feel like I was in my Jericho. I immediately realized my mistake. Then, with horror, I realized that we hadn't had time to work out the radios on the suits.

I raised my visor and shouted at Rose and Shell. "Help the others with their suits! Once we're through we won't be able to talk, so—"

The first ripper lunged at me. I grunted and dodged, avoiding the claws by a matter of centimeters, then swung the ax, catching it in the shoulder and sending it spinning away. I raised Peacebreaker and fired three slugs into the center mass of the second one as it rushed, knocking it backward. Both rippers recovered and charged again at the same time, leaping high and flashing their claws. I bellowed and swung my ax in a wide, sweeping arc that knocked both of them out of the air.

I moved to follow up the attack and finish them off but more rippers were already charging into the loading bay. Three more. Then a group of five. Then dozens of them, pouring through the loading bay entrance like blood gushing from a wound.

"*We've gotta go!*" I walked backward, holding Peacebreaker up but not firing. Shooting into this horde would be like spitting onto a burning house. I made it through the doorway into the preparation room and hit the button to close it behind me.

Shell gave a thumbs up. I scanned the group quickly. Everybody looked like they were suited up. I slammed my helmet shut. "*Into the airlock!*" I yelled, unsure if anyone could hear me.

Whether they had or not, they were already moving, shuffling past each other into the small space. Rose glanced past me and suddenly pointed, eyes wide behind her clear visor.

I spun. *Dammit.* One of the two rippers I'd been fighting had managed to get a limb through the door before it shut. Within seconds, the small crack where the door hadn't sealed was full of rippers all mindlessly trying to squeeze themselves through the tiny space.

Someone was trying to say something. I whirled to see Shell raise the visor of her helmet, face frantic. "The airlock won't start depressurizing until that door is closed!"

I turned back to the rippers and leaped back just in time to avoid a claw as one of them swung at me through the crack. It was getting wider, the sheer mass of flesh trying to force itself through, slowly gaining ground.

I clenched my teeth, shoved Peacebreaker into one of my exo's built-in tool pouches, raised the ax in both hands, and started chopping. Heavy, brutal, downward strokes delivered straight into and through the writhing mass of flesh and claws.

Blood splattered. Bones crunched. My arms burned with exertion. Limbs shorn free of bodies dropped with meaty thuds to the floor. The rippers didn't care. They hardly seemed to notice. More and more of them pressed at the gap. Again and again I brought the ax down, until my brow was slick with sweat and my exo was spattered with gore.

"*Come... on,*" I growled.

It wasn't working. Not fast enough, at least. I gritted my teeth and redoubled my efforts, each sending shocks up and down my body. We did *not* come all this way just to die here. All of this effort. All of this pain. All that we'd lost. All that had been stolen from us.

I thought of Cairn. His grin as he bashed Nadus's face against that pillar, over and over again. The way he'd laughed as he did it.

I could not. *Let. Him. Win.*

I screamed, letting the rage give me one last burst of feral energy. The door closed a few centimeters more. A ripper managed to squeeze its head through, jaws snapping at me. I brought the ax down on its skull with a wet crunch, then hacked the head from the body. I couldn't tell where one ripper ended and the next began. I started kicking at the tangled mass of torn flesh, my shouts growing ragged. It was working. With each kick the mass of flesh budged backward. With each kick the door moved a bit more, the mechanism straining to close. I gave one final kick, one last bellow of rage, and the door slammed shut.

TWENTY-FIVE

I staggered into the airlock and sagged to the floor, panting. The airlock doors sealed shut. There was a hissing sound as the depressurization process started.

The surge of adrenaline that had been carrying me through the past several hours started to fade. My entire body ached. My muscles felt like they were about to turn into rock. I closed my eyes. Just for a moment...

The moment didn't last long.

Someone kicked my leg. I opened my eyes and saw Rose pointing at my wrist. I felt a sudden surge of fear as I considered the possibility that a ripper had damaged my suit. I looked down at my gore-covered wrist, inspecting it for damage. I didn't see any breaches. I did see a blocky wrist computer though.

Rose pointed at hers, indicating a specific button. I wiped the blood off of my computer's screen and mimicked her actions. After a moment, a buzzing sound cackled in my ear.

"Lax? Lax, can you hear me?" Rose's voice was garbled.

"Yeah," I said wearily. "Can you hear me?"

"Yep. That was incredible."

"Thanks," I said weakly.

Shell's voice now. "You all rested up?"

No.

"Yeah," I said.

"Alright." She hit the button to open the outer airlock door. It opened silently, and the void stared back at us. "Let's go, then."

One step at a time.

The weightlessness of space took hold of me the moment I was out of the *Aboena* and the reach of its artificially powered gravity field—the first of its kind, made possible only by the truly massive amount of power that the *Aboena*'s core generators produced. Nowadays they used ultracells for that, but of course, they hadn't had ultracells back during the Exodus.

My exo's magboots locked me silently to the surface of the *Aboena*'s hull. I looked around us in awe. I'd been on plenty of spacewalks before, but usually they'd been a quick in and out, and usually they'd involved smaller ships like the *Orpheus*.

Standing on the hull of the *Aboena* felt less like being on a spaceship than it did the surface of some strange, ancient, dreamlike planet hewn from pure steel by mad gods. Sensors and other apparatus extended from the ground like bizarre trees. In certain places there were depressions or protrusions in the hull, adding strangely uniform valleys and ridges to the alien terrain.

"Shell," I said. "Has Tetra responded yet?"

Shell suddenly started cursing viciously. I looked over to see her scrambling to pull the quantcom out of a pocket in her exosuit. I felt a pit in my stomach as I realized the problem.

"I forgot to put it inside the suit," she growled, voice cracking in the radio. "It's dead."

Dammit. Most computers break down pretty quickly when exposed to the freezing temperatures and ionizing radiation unless they're built specifically to withstand it. Clearly this quantcom had not.

"What?" Bentley exclaimed, grunting as his magboots got temporarily stuck. "So now we have *no* way of communicating with anyone on the inside? No way back in?"

The magboots locked on so long as your feet were flat, but if you rolled them in the right way they'd release. The mechanism was just different enough from how the exos I'd used before worked that I was still adjusting myself. In addition to the magboots, each of our exos had a long tether with one end attached to our belts and the other to a rolling maglock for extra safety.

Rose nudged the back of his foot, freeing him. "Ironic, especially considering you've talked of nothing but wanting to get *out* of the *Aboena* since we got here."

Shell said something in Aboenian. Shepherd gave a nervous response. They consulted together for a few minutes.

"It sounds like there's an abandoned airlock in the Shaper's territory," she said when they'd finished. "It's a bit of a hike, and we'll pass one or two other airlocks to get there, but it should be straightforward enough to find."

I grimaced. So long as we knew exactly where we were going, we should have enough oxygen to get there. "Alright. Let's move. Everyone monitor your computers. If anything's giving you a reason to worry, we'll bail and just go for the nearest airlock, no matter what's on the other side of it."

Shell nodded and continued leading us in the same direction we'd been going. The rest of us trailed behind in our strange little spaceman parade.

We spent nearly two hours hiking along the *Aboena*'s ancient surface, weaving between the various valleys and protrusions. We even passed a few windows looking into blessedly empty observation decks. In my exhausted state I was barely able to restrain a giggle at the thought of someone's reaction should they look out the window and see us. Six very lost-looking individuals in spacesuits carrying backpacks and a small army's worth of firearms. Hell, especially me. The gore coating my suit had frozen into disgusting black chunks that fragmented around my joints and clung to everywhere else. That, plus the fact that I had a large, equally blood-soaked ax strapped to my back, would have made for quite the sight. Maybe I should tap on one of the windows. See if I could get a friendly wave. *Hello, we're here to talk to you about your spacecraft insurance policy...*

"Here we are," Shell said.

I looked up sharply. Sure enough, there was a small protrusion sticking out of the hull in front of us, looking almost like a hermit's cottage. I saw the outer airlock door in the side of it, sealed tight from the inside.

"Alright, Rid," I said. "Let's see what you can do."

"No pressure or anything," Bentley said, glancing up and out into the endless, starry void.

Rid took a deep breath, reached back for the box of tools, and opened it partway, carefully rummaging through it. After a moment, he withdrew a small thermal drill.

"Alright," he said, turning to the airlock. "Let's see what we can..."

It opened.

We all stared for a moment. There were lights on inside the airlock, but no signs of people.

"Good... job?" Bentley said hesitantly.

I turned towards Shell. "Did you tell Tetra where we were going?"

"No," Shell said. "And even if I had, she wouldn't have been able to..." She cocked her head. "How..."

Rid peered carefully through. "I don't see anyone," he said.

I glanced up. There was a built-in camera above the airlock door, but it looked like it had long since ceased to function, the lens cracked and bent at a wrong angle. I frowned, wracking my brain for any possible explanation. Even if somebody had known we'd be coming here, how would they have known when to open the door?

Shepherd said something, his voice sounding reverent. Shell turned sharply towards him.

"What'd he say?" Rose asked.

"He just said... *the Stranger*," Shell said.

"How does he know?" Bentley asked.

Shell shook her head. "I don't—hey!"

Shepherd was already moving into the airlock, clambering through the door and back into the *Aboena*'s gravitational embrace. We all watched him. So far as we could tell, he didn't immediately get shot, stabbed, eaten, or blown up. All eyes turned to me.

I grimaced. I didn't like it. Not one bit. But that little oxygen tank symbol on my wrist computer was already starting to look frighteningly empty. I cursed under my breath and followed Shepherd. Everyone else filed in behind me.

Shell hesitantly hit the button to close the outer airlock door and pressurize the airlock. I squinted, trying to see through the windows on the inner airlock door. I could make out some forms beyond. Didn't look like Wolves, though. In fact, one of them looked like they were wearing an exo of their own. Had we simply interrupted somebody else's spacewalk?

Finally, there was a beeping sound as the pressurization finished. I unslung my ax and held it at the ready, while everybody else carefully withdrew their own weapons, aiming them at the door.

"If it's Wolves," I said grimly, "we're done being prisoners."

"And if it isn't?" Bentley asked.

The doors opened.

There were five of them. Four of them looked like regular Roamers, albeit much healthier-looking than most of the ones we'd seen so far. The one in the center, however, was clad in a black exosuit that concealed their face.

The Shaper held empty palms outward. "Calm. You are not in danger." A woman's voice, strangely garbled by what seemed to be breath filters built into the exo's helmet.

"Kinda have a hard time believing that," Rose snarled. "Who are you?"

"We are the Shapers," the exo-clad woman said. "And we have been awaiting you."

"Us?" I frowned. "How?"

"They said that you would be here," the woman said. "And they were, of course, right."

"They?" I asked, though I already knew. Valley's words flashed through my mind. *You will find them if they want you to.* "The Stranger?"

She nodded. "Indeed. Come."

TWENTY-SIX

I breathed a sigh of relief as I peeled off my blood-encrusted exosuit, leaving me in my slightly less blood-soaked shirt and trousers. I winced as the smell struck me. None of my companions said anything, though—probably because they weren't much better off.

"You will not need those," the Shaper said as I shrugged my pack back on and made sure my weapons were both secure and readily accessible.

"They're coming with me all the same," I said. The exo's small tool pouch had made a passable holster for Peacebreaker, so I unstrapped it from the spacesuit and attached it to my own belt. I gave her a suspicious look. "You'll have to forgive us if we're a bit short on trust these days."

The Shaper nodded. "I understand. We will not deny you. You have been through much to arrive here."

"You have *no* idea," Bentley groaned.

I glanced over at Shepherd. He had tears in the corners of his eyes—happy ones, I thought, though I'd never been much of a judge when it came to such things—and had already started speaking with the other Shapers who weren't in exos. I frowned as I studied them. They seemed perfectly normal. From everything I'd heard I'd been expecting them to have fins, or an extra set of limbs, or something. The same went for the room we were in now. It was just like the airlock prep room we'd exited the quarantine zone from.

Satisfied that we were ready to move, the Shaper turned. "Follow me. My name is Zeka—I will be your guide. For now."

I took a deep breath and followed after Zeka as she walked through the empty loading bay towards a set of large doors at the far end.

"How did you guys know we were out there?" I asked her.

"We felt your presence," she replied, matter-of-factly.

I frowned. "Look, I know you guys have this whole mysterious cult thing going, but—"

She laughed. The sound of it caught me off guard. "You have been among us not five minutes and you already doubt," she said.

Her lightness flustered me. I tried not to show it. "We need to talk to the Stranger," I said. "I know you don't let many people see them. But it's not about your miracles. Well, not entirely." Damn, I was bad at this. I found myself desperately wishing we could have somehow brought Ramar with us. He'd know what to say.

"They say that you fought the Wolf," she said. "The Wolf, who the Stranger touched, and blessed beyond any other. You have seen the miracles with your own eyes. Can you truthfully say that you have not desired to learn the truth at the heart of them?"

I clenched my jaw. Straight to the point, then. "The Wolf killed my friend. So, with apologies to this Stranger of yours, I intend to kill his little protégé right back."

The Shaper came to a pause in front of the large doors, turning to look at me. Not being able to see her expression made me uncomfortable. I had an uncanny feeling as if she could read my mind. She studied me a moment longer, then shrugged. "Such things matter little to the Stranger. Your actions are your own. If you wish to carry on in your feud, the Stranger will not intervene."

That tracked with what Valley had told us, at least, though I had to resist the urge to point out that if giving Cairn apparently supernatural healing abilities didn't count as intervening, I wasn't sure what would.

"What *did* the Stranger do to Cairn?" Rose asked, just a hint of fear lurking behind her voice.

"They blessed him," Zeka said reverently. She nodded to one of her companions, who entered a code into the control panel next to the large doors. "They touched him, and administered their sacrament unto him, as they had promised him."

I restrained a sigh. Whoever this Stranger was, they'd done a number on these people. Once we managed to get an audience with them—*if* we managed it—we'd find the truth. Hopefully. And—again, hopefully—we could use that truth to beat Cairn and escape this hellhole of a ship alive. I still hadn't written off the possibility that this was another elaborate trap. When these doors opened we might be greeted by an army of Wolves with Cairn at their head. Or a horde of ultrarippers.

The doors started to grind open. I put a hand on Peacebreaker's grip. I wasn't sure of a lot these days. But I was damn sure that no matter what was on the other side of these doors, I wouldn't go down without a fight. Not again. Not while I—

The doors opened wide enough for me to see through. My eyes widened.

Beside me, the rest of my crew gawked. Shell gasped something in shocked-sounding Aboenian.

"What... the *hell*..." Rose muttered.

The Shaper strode forward. "Come."

After a few seconds' hesitation, I followed, my hand easing away from Peacebreaker. Beyond the doors was a long hallway.

That I'd expected. What I hadn't expected, though, was for it to be *alive*.

Every surface was covered with crimson vines and verdant leaves. The floor had been trodden into a grassy path. Boughs hung from the ceiling. Gentle, golden light emanated from clusters of what looked like bunches of berries. I felt suddenly as if I'd walked from the depths of space straight into some magical land straight out of an old earth fairy tale.

"What... " Shell reached and hesitated before gently touching one of the tiny glowing orbs. "When... how..."

"It is all the Stranger's work," our guide said, not slowing down. "Where there is death, they bring life. Where there is darkness, they bring light. That is their way."

"Yeah, but..." Shell frowned, turning away from the berry and continuing down the enchanted path. "*How?*"

"The Lifeblood," Rid said. "Valley said Cairn gave it to the Shapers."

I nodded slowly. That certainly might have contributed. But these plants looked far older than three weeks. And—not that I'm much of an expert—I'd never heard of plants like these ones.

Eventually the hallway opened up into a large open area with a tall ceiling—much like the room we'd first found Valley's Oathless in. The only difference, of course, was... well, pretty much everything.

The same verdant plant life that had carpeted the outside hallway had crawled over everything in here, making the large pillar in the middle look like some gargantuan tree of paradise. Those scarlet vines ran in thick, nerve-like tendrils up the length of the pillar. Clusters of Roamers sat eating fruit and laughing together. There were a few electric lanterns hanging from the pillar in the center of the room to round out the lighting of the glowing berries. I saw something familiar growing between the glowing berries—large, white, oblong fruit.

"Hey. Look." Rose pointed towards one of them. "That's the same stuff Command fed us."

"Please sit," our guide said, gesturing towards an empty tuft of very inviting grass. "Rest. You are welcome to stay with us for as long as you choose to."

"If you insist," Bentley said, immediately collapsing to the floor.

I hesitated. I wanted to, so very badly. Every part of my body ached. But we'd come here for a reason. We'd fought Wolves, and run from rippers, and crossed half the damn ship from the outside to get here. The communication relay was part of that reason, but so was finding the Stranger. The Stranger seemed to be the only damn person on this ship who knew what was going on. If there was anyone who could stop Cairn, it was them.

"The Stranger," I said, cold anger giving me renewed strength. I took a deep breath, trying to stay calm. "We'd like to meet them."

"There are many who wish to meet the Stranger," the exo-clad woman said. "It is the greatest desire of every weary pilgrim here." She gestured towards the clusters of Roamers sitting in the room. "And yet there are few who obtain that privilege."

My heart sank. All that. Everything we'd been through. Just to be politely turned away at the door.

"I'm not sure you understand," Rose said. "We *need* to see the Stranger. We have no other options. Basically, everybody on this ship wants us dead. If you don't help us, we'll have nowhere else left to go."

"You need no other place to go." The Shaper once again gestured around us. "This is a safe place. Nobody—not even Command, and not even the Wolf—will dare to attack you while you are here. As I said—you are free to rest here in safety for as long as you wish. We will help you however we can. With enough time, we may even be able to arrange safe passage for you to the Outside."

"It's more than that," Shell said. "Cairn *has* to be stopped. He wants to use the rippers to go on the offensive against the Paragon. If he does, it'll be the end—for *all* of us. The Paragon will destroy the *Aboena* and take everything you have. Whatever weird secrets the Stranger is hiding, the Paragon will be only too happy to take them and use them against everyone else. Doesn't the Stranger care about that? Don't *you* care about that?"

"The Stranger is aware of the situation," the Shaper said coolly. "And they will not allow it to get out of hand."

The cold anger turned suddenly hot, broiling up inside of me, getting ready to break through all of my exhausted, barely standing barriers. We'd fought too hard to get here, had too much riding on this meeting, to give up now.

"Out of *hand?*" I snarled. "It's already way out of hand. Your Stranger has given apparently magical healing powers to a lunatic who wants to rule everything he sees, no matter how many people he has to kill to do it. Now that lunatic is on the Command council, giving orders. I don't know what the Stranger's plan is, but there's no way this ends well for them."

I gestured towards my exhausted-looking crew. "Now, we've been through hell a dozen times over just to find your little group, and the way I see things, it's at least partially your fault we ended up stuck on this nightmare ship in the first place. So you can let us see this cult leader of yours, or we can make sure that everyone on this ship knows why you shouldn't mess with a Vanguard."

Somebody grabbed my arm. I spun, teeth clenched, ready to lash out at anybody that dared to stand in my way. I froze when I realized it was Rose, eyes wide. She stepped back abruptly, flinching at my raised fist. Rid leaped to his feet behind her, eyes flashing at me.

"Lax," Shell hissed at me. "Cool it."

I glanced around. The other Roamers in the room were watching me with abject terror, eyes fixed on my clenched fists and the bloody ax hanging from my pack. The same look of terror that Rose was staring at me with. Rid pulled her back, putting himself between us, nervous but determined-looking.

The fight bled out of me all at once. My shoulders sagged. The exhaustion my rage had been holding crashed down upon me all at once. I felt alone and utterly defeated. My own crew was afraid of me.

You're a Vanguard, Cairn whispered in my ear. *A living weapon, made for one purpose and one purpose only: to kill. Do you really think you can hide from that?*

He was right. I'd tried to make a difference. To help people. And instead, once again, all I had to show for it was a long trail of bodies.

Zeka made no reaction to my hostility. She waited until it was clear I'd calmed myself before speaking. "I do not speak for the Stranger," she said. "I am merely a servant. If the Stranger wishes to see you, you will be notified. Until then, please, rest. You are overtired from your exertions. If you continue to behave violently, I will be forced to deprive you of your weapons." She turned her head at an angle that told me she was studying my bloodied ax. "Typically we do not allow armed travelers within our midst. I see, however, that after all you have been through you would not feel safe without them. I will simply remind you, then, that despite our mild appearance, we are more than capable of evicting you should the need arise."

I gave a slow, heavy nod. I felt foolish. Humiliated. Uncertain. Broken. I'd spent every ounce of energy I had to get us here. To meet this Stranger who apparently knew so much. The one person who would have answers about all the insanity happening here. The one person who could make it all make sense. Cairn's powers. The ultrarippers. The one person who could help us stop Cairn. And it turned out they didn't even care.

"Now," said our guide. "*Sleep.*"

She turned away. I watched her go numbly, then turned back to the rest of my crew. Rid was carefully pulling Rose away from me. Bentley was already asleep. Shepherd was gone. Shell was standing next to me, eyes questioning.

"You good?" she asked, raising an eyebrow

"I..." I raised a hand, pinching at my forehead and groaning. "I... yeah. I just need to..."

Nadus's face flashed before me. Malformed and broken and bleeding. No—it was Dak. Blood on my hands. *Thud. Thud. Thud. Crunch.* Over and over again. Someone was laughing. Cairn. No, me.

Kessa was dead. My old crew was dead. Artemis was dead. Tekka and his rebels were dead. Nadus was dead. And all of it was pointless.

I swore. Shell put a hand on my arm. "Hey. Lax."

I shook myself. *So tired.* None of it made any sense. I was tired and Nadus was dead and everything I had done had all led to this great, final, climactic moment of nothingness.

"I just... need to..."

My legs buckled. Shell caught me, lowered me down into the grass. A shiver of pleasure ran through me at the first touch. It was cool and soft as a blanket, and I was tired. So, so tired...

"I'll..." I let my head fall back. "Someone should... keep watch..."

———

"How long do you think we can keep this up?"

"You mean, how long until Sev comes in and makes us get up? Kicks us off the ship so she can go back to Albeni 7 till the next job?"

"No." Kessa nestled her head into the crook of my shoulder, wrapping one arm around my chest. "And I'd like to see her try. But I meant all of this." She gestured around us at our room on the *Orpheus*. "How long before... you know... something goes wrong?"

"Oh." I shrugged. "I don't know. Not long, probably. I'm just enjoying it while it lasts."

"Me too." She turned her head to look at me, her green eyes bright and infinite. We lay in silence together for a long time, just staring.

"This isn't real," I said, after a while. "Is it?"

"I don't think so," she said, smiling that sad, knowing smile she sometimes had.

I felt a tear well up in the corner of my eye. "I really, really wish it was," I said.

"Me too," she said quietly. "But that doesn't change a thing." She reached down and gently lifted my still bloody hand. "Long day?"

"Yeah." I stared at the caked blood. A feeling of deep revulsion welled up inside of me. Hatred. Not for Cairn. For myself. "I... I got Nadus killed. Just like I got you killed."

She said nothing. Just gently caressed the back of my hand, running her thumb along the back of it. I didn't dare look at her face. I knew that if I did I'd only see something horrible. That was how these dreams always went.

"So what do you want to do next?" Her fingers kept moving, soft and comforting across the back of my hand.

"I want to get my crew out alive," I said slowly. "I want to stop Cairn, and whatever he's doing with those ultrarippers."

"And what are you afraid of?"

"That I'll get the rest of my crew killed. Just more bodies behind me. And that..." I grimaced. "I'll lose myself in the process. I've never hated anybody like this before, Kess. When I think about Cairn... I feel like I'm on ignicerin again. Like I'd burn the whole world down if that was what it took to get to them." I thought back to Dak. The way his skull had sounded against that door. *Thud. Thud. Crunch.* The way I'd laughed as I did it. "I hated myself until I met you. Hated that all I was capable of was killing. You taught me there was more to me than that. But now..."

Her hand closed softly around mine. "Now," she said quietly, "You have to fight."

"Yeah," I said. "Somehow."

"It's alright to feel anger, Lax. It's alright to use it. You're fighting a monster, and you might be the only one that can beat him. You need every edge you can get. Just don't let it change who you are." She let go of my hand. I looked down to see that it was clean again, the blood wiped away. "Just don't forget what you're really fighting for."

I turned my head slowly until I was looking at her face. I half expected to see some nightmare or monstrosity—some gruesome memento from my past. But all I saw was Kessa. She smiled at me, her green eyes deep and radiant and more beautiful than anything I'd ever seen.

"And then," she said softly, cupping my head with one hand, "once the fight is finished, move on with your life. Be who you want to be. Be *happy*."

"I'm not sure I know how," I said. "Not without you."

"You'll learn." She kissed me softly, then nestled her head back into my shoulder. "It might take time. It might take some stretching. But you'll do it. I believe in you."

I smiled, closing my eyes and focusing on the feeling of her warmth against me. "How long do you think we can keep this up?"

"I don't know," she said. "Not long, probably. But I'm enjoying it while it lasts."

"Me too."

———

"This may be the most delicious thing I've ever eaten."

"You're just saying that cause you haven't eaten anything but nutriblocks for the past month."

"Doesn't make me wrong!"

My eyes opened slowly.

I was lying on my back, nestled by cool, soft grass, staring up into dark boughs and glowing golden berries that almost reminded me of Kessa's warm, swirling stars. I was aware instantly of where I was, though. The Stranger's bizarre, miraculous little garden of Eden. The voices I was hearing belonged to my crew, sitting together a few meters away from me and eating something. Looked like an assortment of fresh fruit.

I took a long, deep breath.

My body still ached. And I wasn't any closer to having a plan. But the jagged, razor edge of my anger had been blunted. I felt... maybe not peace. But acceptance.

If the Stranger wouldn't help us, I'd figure something else out. I wasn't sure how or what. But the fight wasn't finished. Not by a long shot.

I held up my hand. The blood was gone. Most likely I'd simply rubbed it clean on the grass as I slept. Still, though, seeing it made me somehow feel better. Lighter.

I sat up slowly.

Rid saw me moving. He grinned, then grabbed a one of the white fruits and walked over to me, sitting down by my side. "Here. Shepherd gave 'em to us." He jerked a thumb towards the kid, who was sitting in the circle eating fruit and saying something to Shell. "They're pretty good."

I took a bite. This one was juicier than the ones we'd eaten in the medbay. Fresher, probably, since we were apparently at their source. "How long was I asleep for?" I asked, wiping juice from my chin.

"I dunno. Long time, though. Hours." He gave me a careful look. "You feeling better?"

I winced, thinking back to my outburst right before I'd fallen asleep. I'd let the anger, hate, and exhaustion get the better of me. Lashed out at the one group of people left in this universe that still gave a damn about me. "Yeah. Sorry about... all that."

He waved a dismissive hand. "That's alright. We were just worried about you."

I grimaced. "I'm just... running on fumes at this point." I took a deep breath. "If they won't let us meet the Stranger, that's alright. If nothing else, it seems like we're safe here. After that it's..." I hesitated, then sighed. "It's not our problem."

Rid hesitantly reached out and squeezed my shoulder in an awkward imitation of Nadus's old favorite show of affection. It was almost enough to make me chuckle.

We joined the others. Everybody seemed relieved to see that I was no longer in a murderous rage. I ate ravenously. When I was full I sat back and listened as the crew chatted quietly about nothing in particular. Just trying to act as if everything was normal. When I closed my eyes I could almost believe it.

"Shepherd here," Shell said, jerking her head towards the now considerably less stressed Roamer, "has been socializing, gathering information. Says that we've made quite a name for ourselves. You especially. Everybody's talking about the Vanguard that slew a giant ripper, broke out of Command prison, and single-handedly slaughtered an entire squad of the Wolf's best fighters with an ax."

Shepherd perked up and said something else. Shell stiffened slightly.

Bentley frowned. "Well, don't be coy now. What else did he say?"

"Nothing," Shell said.

"*Boo!*" Rose threw a whitefruit at her. "Out with it."

"That people are also talking about a heroic Marshal," Shell muttered, sounding embarrassed. "Returned from exile to save the ship from Cairn."

Rose grinned. "Now *there's* a legend I can get behind. Next thing you know, they'll be having you pull a sword from a stone."

Shell frowned at her. "What? Why?"

Rose looked around for support. She found only more confused faces. "Old earth story," she muttered.

"Are we sure we're safe here?" Rid asked. "I mean... I haven't seen a single armed guard. If Cairn wanted to, he could just walk through those doors and slaughter everyone."

I nodded slowly. "Yeah. But he hasn't. I'm thinking he needs the Stranger too badly to risk incurring their displeasure. In fact, I'm starting to think Command does, too. It's the only explanation for why nobody's shut this little party down yet."

There was a short silence. Bentley cleared his throat. "So, um... what now?"

It was a good question. Cairn was probably out there hunting for us, still—if he didn't know we were here.

"I don't know," I said. I absentmindedly tugged at a tuft of grass, staring at the tree. Those crimson vines. I'd seen them all throughout the ship. Was this where they all originated? One massive organism, slowly spreading across the entire *Aboena?* "We're not any closer to beating Cairn. But it seems like we're safe as long as we're here. Safer than we were with Valley, at least." I sighed, looking back down at my crew. "I guess we see if we can get Ramar here. And see if the Shapers have any communication devices they'll let us use. Maybe we can contact Sev."

Rose perked up at that. "That could solve all our problems."

"Lax." Shell slapped my knee. "Someone's coming."

I sat up to see our black-clad guide proceeding towards us. What had she said her name was? Zeka?

Zeka came to a halt a few strides away from me.

"The Stranger will see you now," she said.

I frowned in confusion. "I'm sorry, what?"

"The Stranger will see you now," she repeated. "But only you. He has been watching you. He desires to see you with his own eyes."

I glanced back towards the rest of my crew. They all looked just as shocked as I felt.

I felt a grin spread over my face.

"Lead the way," I said.

"This way," Zeka said, gesturing up a flight of plant-covered stairs.

I began ascending. The grass on the stairs felt cool and welcoming against my bare soles. Lighter, somehow, as if it was lifting me up. The velvet blades curled around my feet with each step. The stairway curved around in a long spiral, lit by the strange fluorescent blooms.

I cleared my throat. Another meeting with a powerful person. More politics. One day I'd be free of it all... I hoped. But if there was ever somebody I'd needed to impress, it was this one. "So, with this... *Stranger*... is there some sort of protocol I should be following? Titles I should use? Should I bow?"

"We do not concern ourselves with such things," Zeka said from behind me. "Simply be... respectful."

Respectful. Seemed easy enough.

I found myself growing more nervous with each step I took. Everybody on the *Aboena* had talked about the Stranger as if they were some sort of deity. A mysterious, unknowable being descended from lofty heights of wisdom to bestow blessings upon us lowly mortals as they saw fit. Miracles. Any other time, any other place, I'd have scoffed at the idea. But I'd *seen* those miracles at work on this ship. Cairn's body, pulling itself back together after an unsurvivable beating. Food growing apparently out of nowhere. Ultrarippers following orders. The very plants I was walking on were an impossibility. And all of it was the work of the *thing* I was about to meet.

Focus. I paused as I reached a door. *You're not here to unravel the mysteries of the universe. You're here to make an argument. This Stranger is just a person...*

Zeka stepped around me and knocked gently on the door. A moment later, it swung silently open. Darkness loomed beyond.

... aren't they?

Zeka beckoned.

I took a deep breath, exhaled sharply, straightened, and entered. My bare feet pressed against cold metal.

The door shut as silently as it had opened, leaving me in utter darkness.

TWENTY-SEVEN

I cleared my throat.

"Hello?" I looked blindly around myself, hand stretched out wardingly. Peacebreaker's comforting weight hung at my side and yet I found no solace in it. I felt... naked. Vulnerable. As I searched through the darkness an eerily familiar sensation crawled over me. Someone—some*thing*—was watching me.

"*Step forward.*"

The voice sounded human enough. Slightly muffled. Deep enough that it sounded like a male's. The accent wasn't Aboenian, though. I wasn't sure what it was. I took one careful step towards the voice.

"My name is Lackan VanDunn," I said, trying to sound more confident than I felt. "I need to talk to you."

There was no response. I took another step. "Look, I'm not gonna pretend to understand whatever it is you have going on here. But there's something *you* need to understand. I don't think you—"

Light bloomed above me. It wasn't particularly bright, but I still had to lift a shielding hand as my eyes adjusted to the sudden transition. It was the same gentle, golden light that lit the rest of the Shaper encampment, emanating from a glowing bloom above me. After a few seconds, I lowered my hand and studied my surroundings.

I was standing at one end of a large, rectangular room. The farther half of it was concealed in shadow. Blood-red vines—thick and nerve-like—blanketed every surface I could see, swirling in a tangled spiral towards a convergence point beyond my sight. The vines writhed and twitched, parting around my feet and revealing the original metallic floor panels beneath. Other than the reminder of cold metal against my bare feet, though, there was nothing to indicate that I was still on the *Aboena* at all. I might as well be on an alien planet for how familiar my surroundings were.

I squinted into the darkness filling the far side of the room. I could make out a vague shape by the light of the blooms above my head. Long, thin, and flat. A large table of some kind, maybe.

Something shifted from the back of the room. I restrained a startled flinch. A figure rose from behind the table. My heart pounded in my chest as the figure straightened, looming with what seemed like impossible size.

"You don't think I understand the situation?"

The figure stepped around the table, moving himself closer to the light. *Breathe,* I repeated silently. *He's just a man. Just a man... isn't he?*

The figure stepped out of the darkness.

I frowned.

The figure that stepped into the light *was* just a man. He looked to be about forty or so, with long, graying hair tied in a braid behind his head, wearing a simple gray jumpsuit. His eyes were hidden behind a set of darkened spectacles. I looked him up and down, trying to find any indication that he was anything *other* than a regular, boring, middle-aged man of average height, build, and weight.

The Stranger came to a halt with his hands behind his back.

His head tilted slightly sideways, his mouth pinching in an amused smirk. "You look... confused. Am I not what you were expecting?"

No. He wasn't. But damn it all if I knew what I *had* been expecting. I cleared my throat. "Sorry. I... I guess I don't know what I was expecting. You've got quite the reputation out there."

"The reputation is not unearned." He folded his arms. "I do not often grant audiences. You were telling me that there is something I don't understand."

"Right." I cleared my throat. "I..."

Words fled me. Something *he* didn't understand? *I* was the one who didn't understand anything. I found myself suddenly even more confused than I had been *before* the Stranger had stepped out of the shadows. Somehow I'd thought that when I laid eyes on them—*him*, I guess—everything would make sense.

Focus. You're not here to unravel mysteries. I took a quick breath. *Just... breathe. What would Ramar say? What would Artemis say?*

"I'm sure you know who I am," I started.

The Stranger stood still for a moment, then nodded. "Yes. I've been watching you."

"Then you know that my friends and I are being hunted by Cairn. People say that he's your *Chosen*."

He made no response.

"I'm not gonna pretend I know what that means," I continued. "But I do know that Cairn is crazy. He's convinced that he can use those rippers to take down the Paragon. There is no version of that that ends well. Not for anyone on this ship *or* outside of it. And that includes you. Even if Cairn manages to hurt the Paragon, they'll hit back. They'll find this ship. They'll take the rippers and they'll take"—I gestured vaguely around us—"whatever all of *this* is. I don't know if you're ex-Divinity, or if you're just some kind of super-genius, but either way you should be smart enough to know that the Paragon getting their hands on the Divinity gene—raw and unchecked—is bad news." I folded my arms, feeling more confident now. "And all of that is disregarding the destruction that the rippers themselves will unleash. Millions—billions, maybe—of innocent civilians will be overrun. There is no controlled way to use the rippers. I don't know what it is you've done to keep them from overrunning the *Aboena*, but I promise it won't work on a large scale."

I came to a breathless halt, unsure of what else to say, then decided I'd covered it pretty well. I gave a short jerk of a nod, unsure if it was meant for myself or the Stranger, to show I was finished, then folded my arms. I felt surprisingly confident. Somehow I'd never believed we'd make it this far. But here I was, talking to the Stranger himself, making our case. Solving problems with words rather than brutality was new, but I figured I'd made a pretty damn good effort for a rookie at diplomacy.

The Stranger stared at me for a moment.

"Is that all?" he asked.

"I..." My confidence leaked away like oxygen from a faulty airlock, replaced with irritation. "Don't you understand? Whatever you're doing to support Cairn, you need to stop. He'll get everybody killed. What is he even doing for you?"

He shrugged. "I fail to see how that's any of your concern."

"It's *my* concern," I growled, "because he killed my friend. Because he tried to kill me and the rest of my crew. Because he's *still* trying. Because until he's out of the way there's no way off of this ship for us. So either *you* do something about him, or I will—no matter who else I have to go through."

He gave an amused scoff. "You *truly* believe that you could—"

His voice cut off mid-sentence. I furrowed my brow in confusion. He stood in silence for several moments, shoulders hunched slightly, then relaxed.

He let out a long sigh. "My need for Cairn has not yet been fulfilled, and so I cannot allow you to displace him. However, I see no need for your crew to suffer any more than you already have."

I tensed. His tone was flat, yet I couldn't help but see a threat in the words. Maybe I was just on edge. "Yeah? How you figure?"

"Cairn is... *overzealous* at times, as you have observed." The Stranger shrugged. "His grudge against you is of a personal nature. I have no interest in such pettiness. So, out of respect for the hardship you have endured in reaching me, I will help you."

"Help us how?"

"By providing you with a ship." His voice was... reluctant, almost. "And allowing you to take your crew and leave. Under one condition: that you never return."

I blinked. "*Leave?* You're not worried about news getting out?"

"I do not believe it would be in your best interest to publicize what you have seen." The Stranger turned towards the darkness. "Besides—the time is soon coming when there will be no more need for secrecy."

He began walking away. I watched him recede into the shadows, unbelieving. I wasn't sure what I'd expected to result from this conversation, but it certainly hadn't been this. This was the best-case scenario, though.

Almost.

"Wait." I took a step forward. The vines on the floor shifted out of my way. "That's not enough."

The Stranger paused, glancing over his shoulder at me. "I have given you a way out," he said, sounding bemused. "What more could you possibly want?"

I growled, "I want my damn ship back."

TWENTY-EIGHT

"You're *certain* this isn't a trap?" Bentley hissed to me, his legs pumping to keep up with my purposeful stride.

"No," I said. "But if the Stranger wanted to kill us there are easier ways." I eyed Zeka's form at the head of our little procession. I was next, followed by the rest of my crew, while several more Shapers took up the rear. "Ways that wouldn't involve putting his followers in the crossfire."

If Zeka heard me, she made no sign of it. Just continued briskly leading the way down the large, open corridor. This passageway felt significantly different from the others we'd been in. If it reminded me of anywhere, it was the corridors of Command's territory. The lights were steady and bright, the surfaces of the walls and floor polished clean. There was no sign of the mutated alien-like feline creatures or the Stranger's bizarrely pervasive tendrils. Computer terminals attached to the walls looked like they were well-maintained, if a bit archaic.

"Well, this is *much* nicer," Bentley muttered. "Why didn't Shepherd take us down this way before?"

Nobody answered, either because we were accustomed enough to Bentley's sarcasm to not take his question at face value or simply too focused on the prospect of freedom to acknowledge it. For the first time since Cairn's ambush, there was a hopeful energy to our step. The answer to Bentley's question presented itself a moment later anyways in the form of ten armor-clad Marshals striding down the hall towards us.

"Relax," I said as I noticed my crew tense. "We're under the Stranger's protection now."

The Marshal in the lead lifted her helmet as she drew close. Tetra, looking weary but relieved. She said something to the rest of her unit in Aboenian and they began walking at our group's head.

Tetra herself fell into place walking between Shell and me. "Why didn't you contact me?" She hissed at Shell, eyes furious. "I had to find out through Command that this was happening."

Shell grimaced. "Quantcom got destroyed."

Tetra sighed. "Do you have *any* idea how hard it was for me to get that set?"

"Sorry," Shell said sullenly. "I didn't have time to secure it when we evacuated the airlock."

"What's going on back at Command?" I asked.

Tetra shrugged. "They don't like it, but they're not going to stop it. They're scrambling to make it seem like letting you go is *their* decision, not something the Stranger strong-armed them into."

"Even Cairn?"

"Even Cairn." A wry smile crept over her face. "You should have seen how pissed he was, though."

A number of dangerous possibilities crept into my head. An ambush when we left the main corridor, or in the docking bay. Wolves disguised as Marshals. A hidden explosive or another chemical attack like the one that had rendered us helpless in the first place. We weren't out of the woods yet—not by a long shot. "You think he'll try anything?

Tetra shook her head. "Not while you're on the *Aboena.*

He's too dependent on the Stranger to risk incurring their wrath."

Shell scoffed. "Wouldn't be the first time he's surprised you."

"Which is why I'm here," Tetra said coolly. "You don't need to really worry until you undock. I wouldn't put it past him to send some of his hunters out to intercept you. This way."

She took us through a set of sealed doors guarded by several well-armed Marshals, then into a large elevator. One short ride later, the elevator doors opened.

This loading bay was significantly larger and better maintained than either of the other two I had been in aboard the *Aboena*. There wasn't a speck of rust to be seen. Despite that, it had none of the frenetic energy that space ports usually thrived on. Most of the docking ports were occupied and yet there was no sign of their crews or cargo. The only souls in the place were a set of several Roamers wearing faded red uniforms outside of one of the docking ports, performing what looked like a prelaunch inspection. Several more Marshals attended them, muttering sullenly among themselves.

One of them turned towards us as we approached. Gladen, I realized with a start. His eyes narrowed as they settled on me.

"Quite the tour you've received of our ship," he said accusingly.

I shrugged. "Well, there was just so much of it to see."

"The other?" Tetra demanded of her colleague. "Where is he?"

"On his way," Gladen said, not taking his eyes from me. "Damn Oathless didn't want us marching up to their precious hiding place." He folded his arms. "Tell me, Vanguard. How long do you plan on staying away? How many killers will you bring with you next time, to plunder our goods and steal our secrets?"

"I already promised your precious Stranger," I said coolly,

"that once I'm off this ship, you'll never see me again. I never wanted to be here in the first place."

"A likely story." He grimaced. "You sneak aboard our home-ship, steal our goods, murder dozens of our people, and then Command allows you to fly away free, carrying whatever knowledge you have obtained. Maybe Cairn is right. Command is growing weak."

"Enough of that," Tetra snapped. "You've done your duty, Gladen."

Gladen shrugged and turned away, leading his squad of Marshals towards the exit. Tetra watched him go, then sighed.

"The ship is more divided than ever," she muttered, leading the way towards the docking bay door. "Nobody knows who to look to for leadership anymore. Command is weak and undecided. Cairn is strong but ruthless. The Stranger only seems interested in their own experiments."

A familiar, guilty feeling wormed its way into my brain. Tetra had stuck her neck out to help us, and in return we were abandoning her with the mess we'd made—or, at the very least, worsened. *Not your problem*, I silently told myself.

"Are you going to be alright?" Shell asked Tetra.

The Marshal shrugged, trying to appear unconcerned, but there was a dark despair lurking just behind her eyes. "I'll manage," she said, lowering her voice as we neared the red-clad dock workers. "If Cairn *does* take over the ship, I might be in trouble. But for now he's just one member of Command, and there are still plenty of Roamers who see him for what he is."

"You could come with us," Rose said. "We can always use more fighters on our crew!"

Tetra and Shell shared a look I couldn't quite decipher. Some sort of sisterly understanding. "Thank you," Tetra said. "But no. My place is here. I have a responsibility to my people."

Shell's eyes grew distant at the words. Tetra studied her a

moment longer, then nodded to one of the dock workers. A moment later, the docking port door slid open.

Home.

The *Orpheus's* cargo bay had never looked more beautiful to me than it did in that moment. I had fully expected to find it empty, all of our tools, weapons, exos, supplies, and personal belongings pillaged. But other than some disarray caused by our initial skirmish with the Wolves, everything appeared to be in place.

"After Shell surrendered to Command custody," Tetra explained, "Cairn had to come up with a cover story so it didn't seem like he'd been dealing with Outsiders. Part of that meant turning over your ship to the Marshals. If it had been picked clean it would have been suspicious, so I guess he ordered his men not to loot it."

I nodded dumbly. It all felt... dreamlike, somehow. Unreal. I'd long since given up on the idea that I'd ever fly on the *Orpheus* again, resigned to the fact that we'd be lucky to make it off of the *Aboena* at all.

Rose gave a deep, contented sigh. The corners of her eyes glistened. Rid pulled her close to him. Bentley looked as if he were about to burst into happy tears. Only Shell seemed conflicted, standing halfway through the airlock and thumbing the butt of her long knife like she always did.

My crew was back where they belonged, safe and sound. All but one.

I'd thought I had started to make peace with Nadus's death, but maybe the truth was that I'd simply been too focused on survival to grieve. Standing in the *Orpheus's* cargo bay I fully expected to see him come sauntering down the stairs to the second deck with a wry grin and a dry remark.

He didn't.

See you on the other end...

Tetra cleared her throat. "Your other, uh, *companion* is on his way. In the meanwhile, I'd advise you to prepare for takeoff. The longer you wait, the greater the risk of Cairn deciding to try something."

"Yeah." I pushed the thought of Nadus's bloody face aside, took a deep breath and turned to face my crew. "We'll do a thorough inventory later. For now, Rid, make sure we're not missing anything we can't do without—ultracells, food, emergency life-support equipment. Bentley and Shell, run full diagnostics on the engines, life support, nullbreacher, and computer systems. Make sure nothing's been sabotaged or tampered with. We know they hacked us once—let's make sure there's no permanent damage. Rose, run a hull scan and make sure there's nothing attached to it."

There was a short moment of silence as they all shared slightly disbelieving looks. I don't think it was my orders that shocked them. I think they were still just making their own peace with the reality. That we'd made it. We'd survived.

We'd survived. I tried to focus on that thought. That was what mattered, wasn't it? That was the point, right?

"Let's get out of here," I said.

They burst into activity, splitting off to perform their respective tasks. I turned to see three figures stepping through the *Orpheus*'s airlock. One was a black exo-clad Shaper. The second was Shepherd, his eyes flitting about curiously.

The third was Ramar.

I searched for words to say, guilt gnawing at me. Nothing came immediately to mind. He ambled idly past me, coming to a halt in front of the Icarus, while Shepherd, Tetra, and the Shaper spoke quietly in Aboenian near the airlock.

"Seems like another lifetime," Ramar mused. "Doesn't it?"

"Yeah," I said.

"Sure would have been useful to have these the past few days, hm?"

I gave a bitter snort of a laugh. "There's an understatement."

He rapped one knuckle against the exosuit's metal surface, then sighed. "Alas, we cannot change the past."

My eyes drifted to Nadus's Jericho armor, sitting empty on its mounting frame. I said nothing. Neither did Ramar. I didn't break the silence for several moments.

"You're not coming with us, are you." It was an observation, not a question.

He shook his head slowly.

I opened my mouth to try to persuade him—then shut it. Anything I could say would have already occurred to him. He knew the futility of his crusade. There was nothing he'd be able to do. Not alone, at least. No way for one man to stem the tide of what was coming. Cairn would continue to accumulate power. He would take over Command. He would begin attacking Outsider ships. The Paragon would find out. They'd take the ultrarippers and the Stranger for themselves, undoing everything Ramar had fought for. A universe that was already on the verge of falling into chaos would be torn to shreds.

But it wasn't my problem. Keeping my crew safe was my problem.

Right?

"I'm... sorry," Ramar said.

I looked sharply at him. He continued staring at the Icarus, speaking softly. "It was unfair of me to drag you into this—again. Your responsibility is to your crew. I'm sorry I put them in harm's way."

"What are you even going to do?"

"I don't know yet. But the Shapers have agreed to take me to their encampment." He turned towards the airlock with a shrug. "Perhaps I'll have more luck speaking to this Stranger, if they'll see me."

I scoffed. "Good luck with that. I found him a bit of a disappointment, honestly, after the way everybody talked about him.

But if anyone can figure out what's going on in that head of his, I guess it's you."

He paused at the exit, glancing back towards me. He looked like he was about to say something, then stopped and left without another word.

Rose appeared beside me. "We're ready to go. Everything looks good." She frowned after Ramar. "Where is he... oh."

"Yeah," I said.

Shell had finished her diagnostic and was conversing quietly and seriously in Aboenian with her sister. They embraced tightly for a moment, then broke apart. Tetra gave me one last nod as she, Shepherd, and the Shaper left the *Orpheus*'s cargo bay.

"Ready?" I asked Shell.

She nodded, her face unreadable.

"Let's go home," I said.

I watched the *Aboena* grow steadily smaller through the bridge's rear window. There were no signs of pursuit. Barely any indication that the ship was even alive.

The *Orpheus*'s bridge was silent. Other than a few nervous, sarcastic remarks from Bentley, hardly a word had been spoken since we'd undocked from the Exodus class ship. It had only been a few weeks since we'd arrived here, but it felt like a life-time. I knew what was in those ancient corridors, now. Mostly. Nothing good.

Bentley cleared his throat. "Well. At least we got paid."

Rid snorted without humor. Nobody else made so much as a sound. Bentley wasn't wrong, though. We'd done what we came to do: exchange our ill-gained Lifeblood for credits without alerting Vatheson that we were the ones who had stolen it from him. I hadn't thought about that Lifeblood in weeks, though—much less the credits. It was a huge sum, but it seemed paltry now in comparison to everything we'd seen. And it sure as hell wasn't worth losing Nadus. Even Vatheson's wrath was no more than a distant memory.

I'd figured that when we left my thoughts would be focused on Cairn. On that stewing, burning, unfulfilled hatred still churning in my heart. But as I watched the *Aboena* slip further away, my thoughts drifted to the last conversation I'd had with Ramar before we'd left. About the Stranger.

I found him a bit of a disappointment, honestly.

I was missing something. I just... couldn't figure out what. It all felt *wrong*, somehow. We'd fought our way across the entire ship to speak with the Stranger and he'd just been... some guy. It didn't add up. I wasn't sure what it *should* have added up to, but it had to be more than that.

But I hadn't been there to unravel the mysteries of the universe. I'd been there to save my crew. And I'd succeeded. We were flying home free, reunited with each other and the *Orpheus*. I knew I should have been content with that.

So why wasn't I?

I sighed and turned towards the communication system, which Bentley was currently sitting at. "Let's start going through the comms log. I'm assuming we have a thousand messages from Sev in there."

He nodded, seeming grateful for the distraction from the room's somber mood, and turned to the screen, putting on the attached headset. He let out a low whistle. "You are correct. Let's see... *Where are you... I'm going to murder you...*"

I rubbed my temple, groaning and turning back to the rear window. Yep. This was going to be a hell of a conversation. We'd been utterly isolated from the entire world for over three weeks. Wars had been won in less time. In an age as unstable as the one we were living in, the entire universe might've changed. Bentley's voice continued behind me.

"*Damn you, Lax, I'm going to strangle you with your*

own... hm, that's a bit graphic... I told you not to go... hmm, hmm... oh."

All eyes turned to Bentley. His face had gone pale.

"What?" Rose and I snapped simultaneously.

"Uh..." He gulped. "I think you'd better see this one for yourself."

He hit a button. An image of Sev's face appeared above the holoprojector. A cold sensation ran up and down my spine at the sight. Her left cheek was splattered with dried blood. A long, shallow cut ran along her forehead. Her eyes looked sunken and hollow. In short, she looked... defeated.

"Rose... Lax... I don't know if you're going to get this." Her voice sounded flat. She wiped absently at the blood on her cheek. *"I don't know where you are, or if you're even alive right now. It's all gone to hell. Vatheson must've figured it out."*

Dammit. Damn *all* of it. "When was this?" I demanded.

"Two days ago," Bentley said. "It's the last message from her."

"It started with the blockade," Sev continued wearily. *"I know you saw that, at least. But it didn't stop there. Bastard waited until I was stretched thin as could be, trying to work around the Leonidas, then attacked Albeni 7. Hit us with everything at once. Hired local thugs. Brought in mercenaries. Hit us with massive cyberattacks. All at the same time. My boys put up a good fight, but..."* She grimaced. *"Anyways. Don't go back to Albeni 7. I managed to make it off station. Gonna take my own advice and lie low until I can figure this out."*

Sev leaned back in her seat, eyes staring out into nothing. *"I... I dunno. I don't know if anyone's on the other end of this. I don't know if any of you are still alive. I really, really hope you are. You're just about all I've got left."* She perked up, shaking herself. *"Oh. The other thing. He's not done. He's going after the Aboena. He knows that's where you took the Lifeblood. I don't know how. Maybe a Roamer talked. But if you're still there, get the hell out. Please, just... call me."*

She vanished.

There was a long silence.

"We've gotta go," Rose snarled, opening up the ship's navigation system. "Wherever she is, we'll find her. We'll show that bastard Vatheson—"

"What about the *Aboena?*" Shell was staring back at her homeship. "Vatheson's going after them? What does that even mean? What'll happen when—"

"Rose is right," Rid said. "First we find Sev. Then we can figure out the *Aboena.* Let's—"

"*Figure out?*" Bentley sounded incredulous. "What's there to figure out? We lost! We wasted more than three weeks on the *Aboena* and now Vatheson wins everything. Albeni 7, the Lifeblood, the *Aboena* and everything on it. It's over. All we can do now is get out of here before it's—"

"Too late," Rose said.

Everyone fell silent. All eyes turned to Rose. She hit a button, summoning a star chart to the holoprojector. There were three objects depicted on it. The first was the *Orpheus.* The second was the *Aboena,* growing steadily more distant from us. Finally, a blinking red dot had appeared on the edge of the map, moving slowly inward.

"What is it?" Rid breathed.

"Looks like they're broadcasting something." Bentley hit a button on the communication console. Audio started playing overhead.

"... immediate boarding. Please respond. Again: attention Exodus class vessel Aboena. *This is the battlecruiser* Leonidas *hailing you. Please power down your engines and prepare for immediate boarding. Please respond. Again..."*

My mind froze, all of the uncertainty and angst I'd been feeling shoved aside by dread.

The Paragon was here. And they wanted the *Aboena*. We hadn't even had to wait for Cairn to grow stupid enough to attack them.

Shell had gone rigid. Rose swore viciously under her breath. Rid ran his hands through his hair, eyes wide.

"So, just to be clear," Bentley said, staring at the blinking red dot. "This is the *absolute* worst-case scenario, right?"

"If the Paragon captures the *Aboena*..." Rose said slowly.

"*When*," I muttered.

"... they'll take the ultrarippers, and all of the Stranger's— weird stuff," she continued. "Which means..."

"... which means say goodbye to any planet currently trying to overthrow the Paragon," Bentley said grimly.

I saw a wall of flesh, writhing, crawling over itself in its mindless hunger. Consuming everything in its path. I saw it on a dozen planets I'd fought my way across during the Last War. And then I saw it again. Except this time led by a wall of armored ultrarippers, adapting to whatever planets they'd been dropped onto. Evolving. Spreading, uncontrollably.

"So..." Rid's throat was dry. "What do we do?"

I saw an army of armored Vanguards charging onto a battlefield, compelled forward by veins blazing with ignicerin. Except it wasn't Nadus and me in the armor. It was Cairn. A million Cairns, unkillable, insatiable, desiring only to dominate.

"Like I said," Bentley said. "We *run*. There's nothing we can do. And like Lax always says, it's not our problem."

Not our problem.

I saw Tetra, gritting her teeth as she bandaged her wound in a dank Aboenian maintenance room. *Nobody else is going to fix things. So I guess it's up to me.*

The arguing continued around me. I turned and stared at the *Aboena*, now looking small and insignificant in the distance.

I saw Cairn, grinning wolfishly down at me from his perch above my prison pit. *It's all one great, vicious, bloody game,*

Vanguard. And if you're not a player, then you're just a piece on the board.

I saw Nadus. Staring thoughtfully into his drink at Albeni 7, so long ago. *Maybe it isn't. But it's somebody's problem. So if we can help... doesn't that mean we oughta at least try? Leave something behind us other than bodies?*

"Escape?" Shell was growling. "They can't escape! If they try to run the *Leonidas* will catch them. They're too close to nullbreach. They're helpless."

"I understand that," Rose was saying. "And I *want* to help. But there's nothing we can do. We have no allies and no backup. We're completely alone now."

I closed my eyes and took a long breath. The beginnings of a plan began to form in my head.

Damn you, Nadus.

"Turn around," I said.

I opened my eyes and faced my crew. Everybody was staring at me. Nobody moved.

"Turn around," I repeated. I moved over to the communications console, ushering Bentley out of the way.

Rose frowned at me. "What... how would that..."

"We're not completely out of allies," I said. "Get us headed back towards the *Aboena*. I've got a few calls to make."

"Wait. I'm still confused." Bentley was looking at me like I'd gone insane. "Why are we going back?"

"Because *somebody's* got to save the day," I growled.

TWENTY-NINE

The airlock doors hissed open.

Two dozen Command soldiers were mustered in the docking bay. As I stepped down the ramp and into the *Aboena* once again they raised their weapons.

"Easy," I said, raising my hands. "I'm not here to fight."

One of them stepped forward, lifting a visor on his tactical helmet. Gladen. "So much for that promise of yours. You made it... what, three hours?"

"I know. Seems like I just can't leave you guys." I looked around. "I asked for Tetra to be here."

As if on cue, the doors at the far end of the loading bay opened and Tetra strode through. "I'm here," she said sharply. "What the hell do you want?"

"I wanna talk to Command," I said.

Tetra came to a halt next to Gladen, glancing over my shoulder at Shell. "What makes you think that Command will entertain such a demand at a time like this? They are busy discussing the small matter of an approaching Paragon battle-cruiser." She glanced over at Gladen. "As a matter of fact, we're all a little busy with that. Priorities have shifted very quickly around here."

"That battlecruiser is exactly why they'll want to talk to us," Shell said, stepping next to me. She folded her arms. "Because we've got a way out."

Tetra narrowed her eyes, then stepped close. "I don't know what game you're playing," she hissed. "But if this is about—"

"This is about stopping the Paragon from taking this ship," I said. "Which *will* happen if you don't listen to us."

She studied us a moment longer, then sighed. "I'll see what I can do. Follow me."

I felt a strange sense of déjà-vu as I once again strode down the corridors of Command territory towards the council meeting room, flanked by Gladen on one side and Tetra on the other. I was even manacled again—they'd insisted on disarming and restraining me if I was to go before Command. There was one big difference, however.

This time, I knew what the hell I was doing.

Tetra came to a halt in front of the doors. "Wait here until—"

"I'm done waiting," I growled. I raised one foot and casually kicked the door open, striding through. Tetra swore and scrambled after me.

Inside, I found nine faces and several rifles fixed on me. I came to a halt in the center of the room, looking back up at them.

"I'm back," I said.

Command stared down at me in bafflement, none of them more so than Cairn. For the first few seconds he looked as if he simply couldn't comprehend what he was seeing. Then his face twisted into rage. "What the *hell* is this—"

I felt the same old rush of hatred the moment I saw him. I forced it aside, though. There'd be a time for using that rage, that hatred that had been brewing in me. But for now, *I* needed to be in control. And I needed to show everybody else that I was in control. So I ignored him, fixing my attention on the elderly Roamer dressed in an officer's uniform in the center of the group.

"I'm here to save you from the Paragon," I said, interrupting Cairn mid-outburst.

He frowned, brows knitting together in confusion. He leaned over to one of the Roamers sitting next to him, muttering in Aboenian.

I turned and pointed my manacled hands out the door, cutting them off. "The vessel bearing down on you," I said, "is a Paragon battlecruiser. You won't find a more dangerous ship anywhere in the universe. There's only one possible reason they could be here: they want what you have. They want the rippers."

The elderly Roamer—*captain*, I decided to start calling him in my head—raised an eyebrow. "They *have* rippers."

"Not like yours." I pointed at Cairn without looking at him. "Not like *his*."

All eyes turned to Cairn. He said nothing. I could see him staring at me from the corner of my vision, his eyes burning with hate and his teeth clenched. I kept talking. "You all know it. Why you've chosen to do nothing about it is beyond me. But let's stop pretending that you're unaware of the crap going on around here. Cairn has an army of enhanced rippers locked away somewhere. They're called *ultrarippers*, by the way, and they're far more dangerous than even he knows. They were originally created for use by the Paragon until a mutual 'friend' of ours intervened." I finally turned towards Cairn. "And now," I continued, meeting his blistering glare, "they want back what's theirs."

"And how are you so certain," the captain said skeptically, "that they're here for the rippers?"

"In case you haven't been keeping an eye on the news," I said, "the Paragon is a bit busy right now. There's only one other reason I can think of that they'd send an entire battlecruiser to bully an out-of-the-way Roamer ship." I looked around, letting the silence last just long enough for them to lean in a bit. "And that," I said, "is that they know about the Stranger."

The captain narrowed his eyes. I was certain that they were already aware of all this. It was probably what they'd been discussing before I arrived. But that wasn't the point. The point was taking charge of the discussion and leading it to where I wanted to take it. Riding the storm of chaos.

"Why," Cairn snarled, hands clenching the edge of his table as if he was restraining himself from leaping over it, "hasn't somebody *shot* this Outsider bastard yet?"

The captain opened his mouth. I spoke up first. "Within hours, that battlecruiser will be within boarding range. They'll cut through your hull and send Vanguards with Jericho power-armor and Jackhammer autorifles into your corridors. I've seen the weaponry you use and the armor you wear." I pointed at one of the heavily armored guards still nervously pointing their assault rifle at me. "This kind of firepower won't do much more than tickle them, and that armor barely stops small caliber arms. It'll get shredded like paper by a Jackhammer."

"We are well aware of our limitations, *Vanguard*," another member of Command said. The young, attractive Trader. "And we are more than capable of—"

"No," I said firmly. "You're not." I turned towards Cairn. "I killed nine of the dreaded Wolf's best men, by myself, using nothing but an ax. You're about to be attacked by an *army* of Vanguards like me in powerarmor and very big guns. They will board the *Aboena*. They will slaughter your fighters. They will take everything of value they have. And then they'll kill the rest of you."

Cairn shot to his feet, leaning over the edge of his table. His eyes bulged with rabid fury and spit flew from his mouth as he raged. "I'll kill you, Vanguard! I'll crush your skull like you crushed my b—"

"*Cairn.*" The captain's voice cut the air. "Calm yourself."

Cairn clenched his teeth, face still a wrathful mask. He lowered himself slowly back into his seat, chest heaving, eyes never leaving me.

"I assume," the captain growled at me, "that you have come here with a proposal of some sort? Or are you simply amused by reminding us of our predicament?"

"I know how they fight," I said. "I know their tactics and protocols. I'll help you co-ordinate the defense against them. Hell, I'll fight 'em myself."

The captain scoffed. "Fighting will not be enough. It does not matter how long we keep them from boarding. They will overpower us eventually."

"Twenty-four hours." I turned slowly, meeting the eyes of each member of Command except Cairn one by one. "Give me twenty-four hours. That's all I need. Negotiate, fight, run—whatever it takes."

"And what would you want in return?" asked the Trader woman suspiciously.

"An alliance," I said.

The captain raised an eyebrow.

"No matter what happens today," I said, "one way or another, your neutrality with the Paragon is over. Fortunately for you, you're not the only one. War and chaos are breaking out across the stars. If you go it alone, you'll be picked off. Eaten. Consumed by the storm. You *need* allies. And if we can survive today, I can arrange them."

Somebody rushed into the room behind Command and said something urgent-sounding in Aboenian.

"Paragon is hailing them again," Tetra said. "Demanding a response."

The captain studied Tetra and me, then turned to the rest of the council.

Cairn looked wildly at them. "You're not *actually* considering this. He's a murderer! An Outsider! He—"

One of the other members of Command spoke up in Aboenian. Others joined in, the discussion heating up.

Cairn continued staring at the council, looking as if he was trying to convince himself he wasn't mad. He butted in at one point, snarling a few sentences before being dismissed. He blinked in shock. I felt a distinct jolt of satisfaction at the sight of his incredulous face. All of his control, all of the power and influence he'd brought to bear in hunting us down when we'd been on the ship—gone, at least for now, with one well-placed blow. Eventually he gave up on the council and turned back to glaring at me.

"The future," the captain said after a few moments, "is uncertain. We can make no promises regarding what will be best for the ship. But in the meantime, if you are willing to fight..." He shook his head, staring at me like I was mad. Which —perhaps—I was. "Well, then we would have to be much less desperate than we are to turn you away."

THIRTY

"Command is dragging out negotiations as long as they can," Tetra said as she led us through the *Aboena*'s primary corridors. The rest of the crew had joined us now that the Roamers had officially accepted our help. I hadn't ruled out the possibility of Cairn making a move on us, but I doubted he would risk incurring the wrath of the rest of Command while they were in such a tight position.

"Won't last long, though," Shell continued. "Sounds like the *Leonidas* is in a hurry."

"How close are they now?" I asked, glancing around. I half expected to see Cairn and a dozen of his warriors leap suddenly out from nowhere and mow us down, or at least to see Roamers giving us dirty looks. After all, the last time I'd been in this approximate area I'd been sprinting with a shotgun in one hand and a bloodied ax in the other. If anything, though, most of the people we passed barely seemed to notice us, too busy as they scurried about making hasty preparations for the siege.

"About a half-hour from boarding range if we keep up at this speed," Tetra said. "The *Aboena*'s putting up a good run, but there's no doubt the battlecruiser is faster."

"Why doesn't the *Leonidas* just open fire and try to cripple our engines or something?" Rose asked.

"Too scared of hitting something important," I said. "If they're after the rippers, they'll be trying to avoid collateral damage."

"This plan of yours..." Bentley gave a nervous chuckle. "Do you think it'll actually, you know... *work*? So far, as allies to hang all of our hopes on, the ones we've been saddled with seem particularly, uhm... *unsturdy*."

"Even if he *does* follow through," Rose said, "will he actually be able to make a difference against a battlecruiser? You said it yourself—there's no more dangerous ship anywhere."

"Let's just hope I'm wrong," I said. "Because I don't have a single better idea."

We stopped in front of a set of large double doors. Tetra snapped something at a set of Wolf guards, who immediately plugged in a code. The doors began grinding open.

"VanDunn," Tetra said, stepping away. "A word."

I followed her off to the side. She folded her arms, giving me the same cold, unreadable look she'd given me when I'd first met her.

"Are you playing us?" she demanded.

I frowned at her. "What do you mean?"

"You know what I mean." She scowled. "No more than a day ago you were crippled with indecision and grief. All you cared about was getting revenge and getting your crew to safety. Now you suddenly seem to have abandoned both."

I stiffened.

"I liked you before," Tetra continued. "You were easy to understand. Now you suddenly have ambitions. Alliances and trade deals. You barge into Command making demands. And in my experience, every time an Outsider comes here making demands and promising deals, they are playing us. Using the Roamer people to serve their own selfish ambitions. So I ask you, because I trust you to be honest with me: are you playing us?"

The accusation stung. Seemed like just yesterday I'd been having a similar conversation with Ramar—except I'd been on the other side of it then. Hell, I didn't blame Tetra for mistrusting me one bit.

I glanced over as the rest of the crew filed through the open door into the room beyond. Tetra made no sign to follow them.

I sighed. "Hell, Tetra. I don't know. Here's what I do know. My whole life I've been pulled from one fight to another. Always part of somebody else's plans. Always a pawn on somebody else's board. And my whole life I've been swearing to myself that I was done fighting other people's battles." I shook my head slowly. "I guess I've come to the realization that there's always gonna be a battle that needs fighting. So I might as well make it mine."

She narrowed her eyes, but said nothing, so I pressed on. "I came here with one goal—to stop Ramar's ultrarippers from hurting anyone else. Turns out that's going to be a hell of a lot more complicated than I thought. But I'm done waiting around until somebody else hands me a solution. *This* is my solution. If you count that as playing you then I can't blame you. But I'm not gonna apologize for finally growing a spine and standing my ground."

I heard excited whoops from through the doorway. I pushed them out of my mind, focusing on Tetra.

"People will die," she said softly. "*My* people."

"Yeah." I didn't take my eyes from hers. "But I think you know that even more of them will if you roll over to the Paragon's demands. All of them, maybe."

She drew her lips into a tight, unconvinced line.

"Look," I said, exasperated. "I don't like any of this any more than you do. I'm running with what I've got, just like you were. Just like you still are. I've got no way of knowing if this is all gonna turn out in our favor. I don't know what the fallout is gonna be like. I don't know if we'll even be alive to see it. But I know that if it's a choice between doing something and doing nothing—well, I'm damn tired of choosing nothing. Now." I gestured towards the door. "Can we go?"

She sighed. "Fine. But if you screw us..."

"I ain't gonna screw you," I snapped, walking past her and through the doorway. "I've got enough enemies on this damn ship as is."

I stepped through the airlock and into the *Orpheus*'s cargo bay. Closed my eyes. Took a long, deep, breath.

Home.

Rose was guiding a group of Roamer dockworkers as they very gently moved several large, round, vaguely familiar-looking objects. The hullbreaker bombs Ramar and I had seen in Cairn's storage. Rid and Bentley, meanwhile, were gearing up in their exos.

"You're *certain*," Rid muttered, "that this is the best possible way we can contribute?"

"You'll do fine," I said. "Just... don't move too quickly."

I hit a button on the side of the Icarus's mounting frame. It opened up with a grinding mechanical sound. I climbed inside, making sure my limbs were all in the right places, then nodded to Rid, who hit another button. The armor closed around me. A moment later I felt a jolt as the Icarus plugged into the port on the back of my neck, connecting me to the neurointerface. Immediately, the exo changed from a set of heavy armor into an extension of myself. It moved as I moved. Abstract functions like switching my comms settings, firing the shoulder-mounted grenade launchers, and activating the thermal blades felt suddenly as natural as breathing or moving a finger.

I gave a deep, heavy sigh of relief. I couldn't even count the number of times I'd have cut off my right hand just to have access to the Icarus over the past few days. I took a few minutes

to walk around the cargo bay, testing the exo's joints and functions, making sure the Wolves hadn't damaged anything. I
configured the exo's comms and navigational systems while I
did so, linking them to the *Aboena*'s networks.

"Lax." Tetra's voice. She was holding up a radio. "It's time.
The *Leonidas* has launched boarding shuttles."

I nodded. "Is Ramar in place?"

"He left a few minutes ago. We'll just have to hope that he
makes it. I can't spare the personnel for an escort. But he knows
where all the supplies he'll need are."

I grimaced. "No way of guaranteeing that they'll all agree to
help, is there?"

She shook her head. "No. We'll just have to hope that they
hate him enough to agree to our plan, risky as it is. But they've
been waiting for a chance like this for years now. I have a hard
time believing they'd throw it away."

"No use worrying now," I said. More for my benefit than
hers. "It's way past the time for planning. Now it's time for
action. Get everyone else in place."

She turned and strode briskly away. I took a deep breath.
Calm. You're just about to declare war on the Paragon.

No big deal.

I paused in front of Nadus's Jericho. It stared lifelessly back
at me.

"See you on the other side," I whispered.

"Tetra, do we have eyes?"

"Yes." The Marshal's voice crackled in my ear. "*Looks like
four boarding shuttles approaching. Basalt—that's the other Wolf
Command representative—wants to scramble the Wolf fleet to
fight them off.*"

"Absolutely not." I paced back and forth in my designated

waiting place. "We're well within range of the *Leonidas*'s guns. They'd get incinerated before they could so much as lock on."

"*I'll pass it along.*"

"Is everyone else in place?"

"*All defense squads are mustered and in position,*" Tetra said. "*All civilians have been pulled back into the emergency holds near the core of the* Aboena."

"Good." I switched my channel to the one I shared with Rose and my crew. "How's it looking out there?"

"*It's looking like we've got a hell of a lot of ship heading our way,*" Rose said, voice grim.

"You're sure they won't detect the *Orpheus*?" I asked.

"*Not if we're careful.*"

"Well, be careful, then. Bentley and Rid, you're ready to do your part?"

Bentley cleared his throat. "*Yes—but, I do want to point out, just very briefly, and despite knowing for a fact that nobody will listen to me, that I was never—*"

"Just make sure it gets done," I said. "And remember, all of you, don't move till the coast is clear."

Affirmations all around. I switched my channel to Shell's direct line. "Shell, how're things going down there?"

"*They're in place. Waiting for the right word.*"

"Good work. Just stay there and—"

"*I'm coming up,*" she said. "*I'm not gonna hide down here and wait while Tetra is fighting.*"

I hesitated. The plan would still work if she wasn't waiting down below. But that wasn't the point. The point was keeping my crew out of the fighting. Keeping them *alive*. Shell didn't sound like she was ready to take no for an answer, though.

"Give 'em hell, then," I said. "And don't you dare die on me. Remember: all you have to do is slow 'em down. We don't need any flashy heroics."

"Flashy heroics?" Shell scoffed. *"You're the one who insisted on holding a sector yourself. I'll check in later."*

"Roger."

I leaned against the wall behind me. If the corridors had felt narrow before, they felt absolutely miniscule now. Apparently, that was a major part of the Roamer tactics. Block off the wider hallways and force the fighting into the maze, where they could run around unimpeded and the exo-clad Vanguard troopers would be forced to rethink their tactics. Command had assured me the Roamers had their own ways of dealing with the Jericho armor. All I could do at this point was trust them. Trust them, and trust in the plan.

My heart was beating fast. I wanted a can. A drink. Anything. I saw Nadus's face, misshapen and bloody. Kessa's last, sad smile. Artemis's head jerking to the side as a bullet passed through it. I saw a bloody Brahmian battlefield, littered with bodies of friend and foe alike. Heard the roar of my fellow Vanguards as we charged into battle, feeling invincible as bullets bounced harmlessly off our Jerichos. I remembered wondering what kinds of idiots would be stupid enough to stand their ground against a Vanguard assault.

Breathe. I shut my eyes. Pushed the thoughts away. They weren't invincible. That had been the ignicerin and the propaganda talking. Plenty of my buddies had gone down. Plenty of boys from overcrowded stations or partially habitable planets who'd been sold into a life of forced servitude. Turned to monsters against their will. Sent to fight a war that wasn't theirs. Like me. Like Nadus.

"Boarding shuttle is approaching your sector, Lax," Tetra's voice buzzed in my ear. *"Sending co-ordinates to your comms system."*

My wrist computer flared to life. A red dot blinked on a section of the ship a few hundred meters away from me, marking the spot Tetra and her team of observers estimated the shuttle would land to begin boring through the *Aboena*'s hull.

"Cairn's team is catching the second shuttle, a squad of Watchers is on their way to the third, and the fourth looks like it's gonna land in the quarantine zone," Tetra said.

"Keep me posted," I said.

I stared down at the blinking red dot for a few more moments—then took one more deep breath and started walking.

The Vanguard troopers hadn't asked to be here. But I hadn't either. If they didn't die, countless innocent Roamers would. The Paragon would get the ultrarippers. And *everybody* would pay the price.

I broke into a jog, the Icarus's motors carrying me down the *Aboena*'s abandoned hallways.

If the Paragon won, then it really had all been in vain. All the friends I'd lost. All the pain I'd suffered. Lost and meaningless, forgotten in the infinite dark.

I started sprinting, my teeth clenched, my blood hot in my veins. I could see the entry point now where a chunk of the ceiling was glowing with heat in the middle of a long stretch of corridor. In just a few moments it would be breached and a squad of Vanguard shock troopers would drop through, ready to hurl death at everything in their sight via a barrage of explosive bullets. Like I said before—invincible. At least in their minds.

The ceiling exploded inward, spraying flame and debris. Several hulking forms thudded onto the floor of the *Aboena*, hazy through the smoke. They made their formation quickly, forming pairs to cover every angle an enemy could approach at. Ready to destroy any threat that came their way.

Except that the threat they were expecting was a group of Roamers with small arms and a hearty dose of courage, whereas what they were getting—

I grinned and activated the Icarus's thermal blades.

—was *me*.

THIRTY-ONE

I held the twin sheets of incandescent energy width-wise in front of me in a cross over my center mass—right where I knew the Vanguards would be trained to shoot. The charges in the explosive bullets went off as soon as they passed through the wall of heat, bursting in sprays of light and shrapnel that bounced harmlessly off of the Icarus's energized armor.

I triggered the Icarus's thrusters, giving me one last boost of speed, and then I was on top of them. My first two cuts destroyed their Jackhammer rifles, cutting cleanly through the barrels. The Vanguards staggered backward in confusion, their friends turning to help, but the tight hallways restricted their line of fire and gave the advantage firmly to me and my glowing thermal blades.

The Jericho armor was tough, though, and even my ultra-cell-powered blades couldn't slice through it immediately. I had to make slow, precise cuts, listening to their screams as the blades melted through the armor and seared into the flesh below. I knew where the weak points were, though—where the armor was thinnest, and where the most essential systems were located.

I hacked through the first two Vanguards, pushing through until I was standing below the hole in the ceiling. More of them were still leaping down from their boarding shuttle. I fired a concussion grenade upwards into the shuttle's interior and was rewarded with a deafening explosion. It wouldn't have killed any of them, but it might have destroyed some of their equipment and systems, and would definitely have slowed them down.

I kept hacking away at the Vanguards in the hallway. It took them a few seconds to adjust to fighting at such close range. By the time they switched their strategy, though, backing up to give them more room to fire, it was too late.

There. I thought I could see the exact moment SkyCom triggered the Vanguard squad's regulators, flooding their systems with ignicerin. Where there had been shock a moment before, now there was only fury and bloodlust. Which might have worked well enough against a frightened, unco-ordinated opponent. But I was ready for it. I knew that SkyCom wouldn't care what the actual battlefield conditions were like. They wouldn't care that what their troops needed right then was careful calculation, not rabid aggression. As far as they were concerned, the solution to every problem was to press the attack harder, no matter the cost.

And it would be one hell of a cost.

The Vanguard nearest to me was slowly backing up, firing his Jackhammer into my energy-infused armor. The bullets jarred me, but did little else. I saw him suddenly twitch as the ignicerin hit him. He shook himself slightly, as if trying to resist the urge, then broke and charged at me, firing his thrusters for an extra burst of speed as he flung himself at me.

I stepped into and under the attack, blades twirling as I seared his Jackhammer in half, then cut cleanly through the armor on the side of his leg, destroying one of the motors. His right leg buckled, the momentum from his thrusters throwing him face first to the floor. I moved past him, blades never stopping as I met the rest of the charging squad head-on.

One of them shoulder-checked me, sending me staggering backward. I used my thrusters to steady myself then ducked out of the way of a flying fist. One of them grappled me, shoving me against the wall. Seeing how ineffective their Jackhammers were on me they seemed to have given up on them altogether.

One of them was grabbing at my helmet, trying to rip the visor off. The energy-infusion tech in my armor was designed to repel high-speed, low-mass attacks like bullets and ripper claws, not an entire Jericho gauntlet. I felt the Icarus straining behind the force as the Vanguard screamed. I was screaming too, all of our rage mingling into one vast, echoing prayer to whatever primordial gods of war first instilled the love of killing and death in man's heart. I reached up, grabbing the Vanguard's wrists and straining to shove them away while lining the blade emitters up with his arms. His armor started sizzling. A moment later his shout of fury twisted into a high-pitched cry of agony as the thermal blades melted through flesh. I threw him to the side, and started in on the next ones.

More Vanguards dropped from the boarding shuttle behind me. Bullets slammed into my back, sending a spike of panic through my brain. The ultracell powering the Icarus's energy-hungry armor and weapons was housed back there. It was armored, but if something did somehow get through, whether due to bad luck or attrition or a heavy enough armor-piercing round, I'd be incinerated in a blast of white light before I even knew what happened.

I shoved away the Vanguard I'd been grappling with, pivoted, and fired an incendiary grenade. I felt a surge of equal parts horror and satisfaction as I landed a perfect headshot, the grenade fusing itself into the soldier's visor. Poor guy. He started screaming and clawing at it as the intense heat began slowly liquifying the reinforced steel.

There were more where he'd come from, but the delay gave me enough time to finish off the enraged Vanguards who were still trying to pin me down. I turned back to them as they charged. They were fighting recklessly under the ignicerin's influence. I let them push me back until I was back on the other side of the boarding-shuttle breach, stepping carefully over the still thrashing body of the Vanguard with the incendiary grenade attached to his head. They gained confidence as I retreated step by step, a hail of explosive bullets bursting against my armor in a series of white flashes.

Once I was positioned so that none of them could get behind me, I started in on them again. Cut after cut, blow after blow. I lost track of time. Lost track of direction. I let the Icarus do most of the work, trying as best as I could to conserve my strength, but by the time I was down to the last of them I was sweating anyways.

He raised his Jackhammer, firing wildly at me, too hopped up on ignicerin to realize that all his comrades were dead or disabled. I held my thermal blades up defensively as I strode towards him, then swatted his weapon out of the way and punched one blade forward towards his armored neck. My fist pinned him against the wall. He struggled, arms flailing against me, metal screeching against metal as he tried to peel me off. I gritted my teeth and pushed harder. He gave a gurgling choke, then went silent. There was a disgusting hissing sound as melted flesh and liquified steel met. A moment later his helmeted head fell loose from his body and thudded to the floor.

I powered down the thermal blades and leaned against the wall with a groan.

Tetra's voice in my ear. *"Lax? Lax, do you copy?"*

"Yeah." I groaned, straightened. "Sorry. I was in the middle of something."

"We're all in the middle of something. There's another shuttle heading your way. Sending co-ordinates now."

I glanced down at my wrist computer as another blinking red dot appeared. "Got it. Be right there. How's everyone else holding up?"

"About as well as expected. The Wolves have managed to suppress one Vanguard squad with heavy losses. The Watchers have been pushed back and sealed off their sector, but the Vanguards will push through before long. Cairn is sending his special response team to deal with their breach."

"And the last shuttle?"

"See for yourself."

A fuzzy video appeared on my wrist computer's holoprojector. A group of three Vanguards desperately firing into a horde of rippers rushing at them from all sides. One of them went down as I watched, falling to a tailspike to the head. The other two disappeared beneath an unstoppable tide of flesh moments later.

"I'll be damned," I muttered. "Never thought I'd be say this, but I'm glad those rippers are there."

"It's been that kind of day," Tetra said. *"Don't get too cocky. We've got a long ways to go yet."*

"Yeah." I looked at the carnage around me, the floor carpeted with dead and dying Vanguards, then grimaced. One wave down—who knew how many more to go. SkyCom would be adjusting their strategy soon, sending their Vanguards equipped with anti-armor weaponry. I'd have to adjust with them. I reached back and pulled the APMP-17 from where it was slung across my back. "I know."

"Lax, status? We've got another—"

Tetra's voice in my ear was drowned out by the sound of gunshots echoing down the corridors. I jerked behind a corner as a bullet tore past me, cracking into a wall.

"They're pushing me back!" I leaned out of cover and fired

another shot out of my APMP-17. A Vanguard jerked back as a neat little hole appeared in the center of his visor, then toppled over. More Vanguards surged behind him lifting anti-armor rifles of their own. I pulled back into cover just as several bullets tore through the corner, blasting chunks of metal and concrete shrapnel across the hallway.

"How far back?"

"They're not contained, that's for sure," I growled. I crouched next to the corner, waiting in the hopes that they'd creep close enough for me to get at them with my thermal blades. Instead, I heard a thumping sound as one of them fired a grenade. I cursed and retreated as more shrapnel slammed into my armor.

This was the third boarding party I'd intercepted. Each group had fought harder and smarter than the first. And now a fourth was on its way. I glanced down at my computer to see where it was. "I'm not gonna be able to make it to that fourth party, Tetra," I wheezed as I ducked behind another corner. "Not in time, at least."

"We'll send a backup squad to slow them down. This is falling apart fast. Too fast."

I clenched my teeth. She was right. The Vanguards had already taken over multiple sections of the ship. The Roamers were holding their own a lot better than I'd thought they would. Command had broken out the arsenal of heavy weaponry they saved for emergencies just like this, and between that and the Roamers' intimate knowledge of the *Aboena*, they'd been efficient at slowing the Vanguards down, trapping them in ambush after ambush. The Vanguards were undeniably winning, though, establishing foothold after foothold inside of the *Aboena*. It was hard to follow Tetra's running analysis while I was fighting, but it sounded like there were now three ever-growing sectors that were firmly under Paragon control.

And there was about to be a fourth one, unless I could push

these two most recent assaults back. A feat that seemed less likely with each passing minute.

I studied my map, tracing a route for myself, then sprinted down a corridor, taking a series of sharp turns. I emerged in the main hallway this particular incursion had tunneled into on the opposite end of where I'd previously been. Two Vanguards were covering my direction but they still seemed surprised to see me. I fired rapidly, the APMP-17 barking as it fired round after round into the Vanguards. The first two went down along with another who had his back to me. The trigger went stiff and I ejected the mag, slamming a new one home and firing a concussion grenade at the same time. The blast staggered the remaining ones, giving me time to mow down a few more before I had to duck for cover.

"*Cairn wants to play his card,*" Tetra said.

"Tell that—*argh*—asshole," I growled as bullets blasted through the walls around me, "that keeping that card close to our chests is the entire point of this exercise in futility. If he uses his rippers and any of them get captured and taken back to the *Leonidas*, this whole thing is pointless."

"*Futility? This was your damn idea!*"

I heard heavy footsteps stamping towards me. They were charging. Probably thought that I'd retreated again like last time and were hoping to catch a glimpse of my back. Truth be told, the only reason their plan didn't work was I needed a minute to catch my breath. I waited until I heard them just around the corner, then burst out of cover. I lashed out with one thermal blade, destroying the weapon of the closest one, then shoulder-checked him against the wall, slammed the APMP-17 down, and used his shoulder as a brace as I fired several quick shots into the troopers behind him.

His surprise lasted no more than a second or two. He reached up and grabbed the rifle, trying to wrestle it from my grip. The barrel was shoved upwards in the contest. I pulled the trigger, using the recoil to knock it from his hands. The bullet must have hit something important because the lights around us started flickering and a warning siren sounded.

I ignored it, shoving the APMP-17 spear-like into the Vanguard's chest and pinning him to the wall. He reached for me. I pulled the trigger. Once—twice—three times.

Somehow I'd figured that would do the trick. It didn't. He snarled in pain and slapped the rifle out of my hands, then slammed one gauntleted fist into my visor. The blow sent me reeling backward. He bellowed and charged, knocking me against the wall, fists raining into me again and again in fury probably fueled by equal parts pain and ignicerin.

I grabbed his wrist, fired one thruster, and used the combined momentum to spin us around and slam him into the wall, then fired up one thermal blade and made a long cut along the midsection of his already compromised exo. He struggled, gurgled, gasped, clawed.

Something slammed into the back of my shoulder. I jerked my head over my shoulder to see one of the fallen Vanguards had climbed unsteadily to his feet, holding up his anti-armor rifle. The Icarus's energy shielding seemed to have kept the bullet from penetrating, but it wouldn't hold up against shots like that forever—and I was lucky the trooper hadn't hit my ultracell.

I swept my thermal blade to the side, finishing the cut, then grabbed the still struggling Vanguard under the armpits and pivoted. There was a rending sound as the last vestiges of damaged armor gave way and the upper half of the Vanguard's body was torn away, leaving the legs leaning against the wall.

Thud. Thud. Thud.

Bullets slammed into my grotesque shield as I charged, then hurled the remains of my victim with a bellow. He—*it*, now, I supposed—spun through the air and slammed into the shooter, knocking him down again. I scooped another fallen anti-armor rifle up from the floor with the toe of my boot and kicked it up into my hands, then raised it to my shoulder and fired a single shot into the poor bastard's dome as he tried to get up yet again. He stayed down that time.

I heard more gunshots echoing from a distant hallway. No time to rest. I reloaded the anti-armor rifle and broke into a ragged sprint over the bodies of dead and dying Vanguards. "I'm on my way," I gasped to Tetra. "What's their—"

"*Little busy,*" she said, sounding frantic.

I clenched my teeth and redoubled my speed. I saw four Roamers up ahead, running frantically in my direction. A Vanguard stepped into the corridor behind them, holding a Jackhammer at waist height. The Roamers evaporated in a spray of gore as the bullets tore into them.

The Vanguard cocked his head as he saw me, then seemed to panic. Most likely they'd been warned of a rogue Vanguard in experimental armor running around, but this poor bastard had probably figured I was busy with the other squad. He fired hastily at me, the bullets bursting on the walls. I slowed, raising my weapon and firing a shot that cracked through his helmet. He toppled over.

More emerged behind him. I spotted a few with APMP-17s. I cursed and took cover in an adjoining hallway as they opened fire. A moment later I heard more gunshots echoing down the hallway I'd just taken cover in.

"*More shuttles inbound, Lax,*" Tetra said in my ear.

"Just a moment," I growled.

She swore suddenly.

"What?" I growled.

"*Lax, get out of there. Now.*"

I frowned at the urgency in her voice. "What's going—"

I heard shouts of alarm echoing down the corridor, drowned by gunshots a moment later. The gunshots stopped abruptly.

"*Cairn played his card,*" Tetra said.

A chill ran down my spine.

Three Vanguards sprinted around the corner in my direction. They hardly looked at me, though, too busy looking over their shoulders. A moment later, a nightmare burst into the hallway, metallic wings held defensively in front of it. One of the Vanguards skidded to a halt, emptying the magazine of his Jackhammer harmlessly into the biosteel shield. The ultraripper pushed forward through the hail of gunfire, then pounced, landing on top of the Vanguard and tearing into him while protecting itself from the other two with its wings.

Dammit. The entire point of this fight was to keep the Paragon from getting a sample of Ramar's enhanced rippers. I fired two shots into the heads of the two remaining Vanguards, then settled my sights on the nightmare.

"Come on," I hissed. "Show your ugly mug."

"*Lax,*" Tetra said. "*You* really *need to go. You're about to be overrun.*"

"I can't," I growled. "If any of the Vanguards survive that means the Paragon gets the ultrarippers. Which is the entire point of this fight, if you recall."

"*Hurry, then,*" Tetra said.

I cursed and lowered the APMP-17, slinging it over my shoulder. "Rose. How's it looking?"

"*Almost in position.*"

"We're gonna need you real damn soon." I strode towards the nightmare, powering up my thermal blades. "Things are getting hot in here."

The ultraripper finally looked up at me. I still wasn't sure if the ultrarippers could feel emotions, but this one seemed almost surprised—maybe even vaguely amused—as it noticed me approaching. It treated me to a snarling maw of bloody teeth, then pounced.

I ducked under its claws, twisted behind it, then unleashed a flurry of quick cuts, hacking off one limb after another. Flesh sizzled and dropped, slapping against the floor with dull, sullen thuds. I made one last cut that decapitated the beast, then stared down at its ruined remains for a moment.

Amazing how much easier it was to kill those things in a suit of next-generation powerarmor.

More gunshots. More screams. I heard someone shouting something about orders. I took a deep breath, then charged in the direction of the chaos.

I gave a hoarse cry and hacked through one last nightmare's torso, bisecting it diagonally, then staggered and collapsed to my knees, sweat running down my brow. I looked around myself blearily.

The hallway I was kneeling in was carpeted with corpses. Most were ultrarippers, some dead due to the Vanguard's explosive bullets and others from the Icarus's thermal blades. Some of the corpses were Vanguards, their armor shredded by ripper claws or armor-piercing rounds. Still more were the desecrated remains of the poor Roamer defenders who had managed to get caught in the crossfire, half eaten or stomped into gory paste by heavy Jericho boots.

I could hear gunfire somewhere, but it sounded far away. This hallway was quiet, and that was what mattered to me. For now, anyways.

I issued a mental command with my neurotransmitter, popping my visor open and sucking in air that tasted of burned flesh and spent gunpowder. A drop of sweat fell off of my brow and splattered onto the surface of the Icarus, running down its surface and cutting a path through the gore that coated it.

Movement. I looked up sharply, muscles tensing as I readied myself to jump back into action. But I saw no rippers, no fresh Vanguards charging down the corridor. Instead, I saw one of the fallen Vanguards reaching a trembling hand towards his visor, clawing weakly at it. My eyes drifted down to his torso. There was a long, ugly gash in the armor over his stomach. I squinted, trying to remember what had happened to him. He'd been being mauled by a ripper when I'd beheaded it from behind.

His clawing increased. I groaned, climbed to my feet, and walked over. He tensed.

"Hold still," I said, reaching down. I wrenched the visor free.

He blinked up at me with wide, bloodshot eyes. I tried to tell how old he was. Early twenties, maybe. Hard to tell.

"The frigicerin hit yet?" I asked.

He grimaced. "I... I don't know."

"Are you scared?"

He nodded, a tear welling up in one corner of his eye.

"Then it hasn't hit. Maybe your regulator got damaged." I glanced down at the gaping wound in his stomach. "Does it hurt?"

"No." He craned his head, trying to see, but his suit was too heavy. "Is it bad?"

"Yeah. It's bad."

He swore quietly.

I looked down. His Jackhammer had fallen next to his limp left hand. I reached and hefted it, checking the mag. Just a few rounds left. He watched me the whole time, eyes wide.

I held up the gun. "Do you want me to..."

He clenched his eyes shut. Nodded.

I grimaced, then lowered the barrel, aiming at his head.

"Wait!" His eyes shot open.

I lowered the gun. "Yeah?"

"I..." He looked up at me, his expression pleading. "You're Vanguard, right?"

I hesitated. "Yeah."

His face twisted with pain. That'd be the shock wearing off. He forced the words through it, though. "How'd you get out?"

I gave a short, humorless scoff. "Would you believe me if I told you they let me go?"

He stared. Then gave a short, wet cough of a laugh. "No. I don't think I would."

He closed his eyes and gave a short nod.

I did what I had to do, then tossed the Jackhammer aside, trying not to think about how that had been me and Nadus, once upon a time. "Tetra. Situation is clear up here."

"*Define* clear," she asked a moment later.

"Clear as in, Cairn's ultrarippers took the Vanguards by surprise, then I stepped in and cleaned up the leftovers. I think my sector's clear. What's the status everywhere else?"

"*They've been pushed back from all but one sector,*" Tetra said. There was a begrudging respect to her voice. "*Say what you will about Cairn...*"

"... but it sure worked," I finished, nodding to myself in agreement. "As long as we're sure the Vanguards didn't capture any of them."

"*I'm not sure of anything. But it seems like the Vanguard retreats have hardly been organized, so I wouldn't worry about it. Not yet, anyways. We've got bigger problems. They're sending another wave of boarding shuttles.*"

I groaned, feeling a deep exhaustion seep into my bones. I glanced at the clock on my wrist computer. Eight hours down. Sixteen to go.

Might as well have been an eternity.

"Let's play our next card," I said. "We need the extra time."

"*Sounds good.*" There was a beeping noise that indicated Tetra had looped Rose into our channel. "*Rose, has the payload been placed?*"

"*Should be good to go,*" she said. "*We're sneaking our way back over now.*"

I hit a button on my wrist computer, tapping into the *Aboena*'s network to access the external feed. I saw a grainy image of the *Leonidas*, just close enough to exert its threatening presence but too far for them to need to worry about getting rammed by the much larger *Aboena*—as if the Roamers would ever have considered that. There was something strange about thinking of the *Leonidas* as small, especially after everything we'd gone through on the *Revelation*, but, in comparison to the Exodus ship, it was.

I saw several tiny blips appear. Those would be the shuttles, in the process of undocking to head our way.

"Light 'em up," I said.

"*My pleasure*," Rose drawled.

The darkness of space was suddenly torn asunder by a stab of white light near the center of the *Leonidas*. A few of the shuttles vanished. The others paused in their journeys.

"Good hit," I said.

"*How the hell did you get over there without being seen?*" Tetra asked, her voice unbelieving.

"*By moving nice and slow*," Rose said. "*Same way I snuck up on you guys. Only, no offense, this was a hell of a lot scarier.*"

"How long you thinking that'll slow 'em down?" I asked.

"*Well, Rid and Bentley managed to get a lot of the explosive down inside of one of their escape pod chutes near the docking bay*," Rose said. "*So... quite a bit, I think. I guess it's a good thing Cairn had those bombs sitting around after all.*"

"*Looks like we've got a bit of a break, then*," Tetra said. "*We need it. I'll pass the word along and get our squads regrouped.*"

"How're our casualties looking?" I asked, wearily slumping against the wall.

"*Bad. Real bad.*"

"Triages up and running?"

"*They're up. They're running. And they're empty.*"

I winced. You had to be having a hell of a lucky day to survive getting hit by a round from a Jackhammer rifle, no matter where on your body it landed. On top of that, the back-

and-forth guerilla combat the Roamers had been waging didn't leave much time for dragging away the wounded.

"Good news is the Vanguards have stopped pushing out from their established foothold," Tetra said. *"Think they know that reinforcements aren't coming any time soon."*

"Soon's a relative term," I said. "Probably not as soon as they'd like—but a *lot* sooner than we would. Keep an eye on them. How's Command faring?"

"There's some discord," Tetra said. *"Mainly they're conflicted about... well, you. But they're gonna try to reopen negotiations with the Paragon. See if they can slow them down a bit more."*

I nodded. "Tell 'em—sorry, *suggest*—that they wait a bit. Let 'em focus on getting their ship repaired. Then start talks up again. That should give us a bit more time."

"I'll pass them your sage advice," Tetra said dryly.

An hour passed. Then two. Then a third.

"What's the hold-up?" Rose sounded annoyed in my ear. *"I don't like this waiting game much."*

"Guess Command is doing a hell of a job negotiating," I said. "That, or the *Leonidas* is waiting on new orders. Of the two... I'd guess the latter. I'm sure not complaining, though." I glanced down at my wrist computer. "We just need to last another thirteen hours or so."

"Oh, is that all?"

I grimaced. "Yeah. I know."

"Think he'll show?"

"He'll show," I said grimly. "Or I'll hunt him down and kill him myself."

"Quite a list of people you've promised to do that to," Rose said. *"Most of whom are on the Aboena. Probably. You really think Cairn is gonna let all this fly? Even if we do win."*

"Cairn is a problem to deal with thirteen hours from now," I said. "Until then, we are—somehow—on the same side."

"Those rippers of his sure came in handy," Rose said.

I hesitated. "Yeah. I suppose they did. Guess that's why the Paragon wants them so badly."

Tetra's voice crackled in my ear. *"Eyes up. New threat incoming."*

"Negotiations went that well, huh?" I said.

Tetra ignored me. *"Looks like they've repaired the damage—mostly—and are getting ready to launch another wave of shuttles."*

I groaned and climbed to my feet. "Alright. Just point me towards—"

Tetra cursed. I felt a chill.

"What?" I asked.

"They're not shuttles," she said.

I looked down at the feed on my wrist computer. Dozens of long, torpedo-shaped objects were moving towards the *Aboena* at an alarming rate. Except they weren't torpedoes.

Rippers.

THIRTY-TWO

"Here's the good news," I gasped as I sprinted down a corridor towards the indicated dot on my map. "The rippers can't spread unless they find something to eat. Since the vast majority of the crew has been evacuated to the core, they'll just be running around for a while."

"*Until they find a way to make it down to the core,*" Tetra said.

"That won't happen," I said with more confidence than I felt. "Not unless we let them. Remember: rippers—these ones, at least—are stupid. They're predictable. They go where the food is. If we close the right doors, we can channel them like water through a canal right to where we want them."

"*We'll do what we can,*" Tetra said. "*But remember—this ship is old. Most of the doors can't be closed remotely. And the outer decks have taken a hell of a beating. A lot of the usual security systems are offline.*"

I remembered the lights flashing as an armor-piercing round fired into the ceiling during my fight with the Vanguards. "That's fine," I said. "What's important is sticking to choke points and not getting surrounded. You guys know that for your-selves, though."

"*Yeah.*" Tetra's voice was grim. "*All too well. Anti-ripper teams are already on their way to designated checkpoints. We've had to plan for this before.*"

"Good." I skidded to a halt at the area Tetra had suggested a ripper drop pod—*barnacles*, we used to call them in the Vanguard—would be hitting. "I'll stay mobile up top. Keep 'em busy and thin the herd."

There was a heavy thudding sound above me. I unslung a Jackhammer rifle I'd picked up from the floor.

"*Come on,*" I growled.

"*We'll update your map with everywhere we have confirmed hits,*" Tetra said. "*You... won't be able to get to them all. Don't get overwhelmed. If you're getting surrounded—*"

"Don't worry about me," I said. "Worry about keeping everyone else safe. I know what I'm doing."

I heard a grating sound above me. The barnacle had attached and was boring a hole for the rippers to enter the *Aboena* through, just like the boarding shuttles. I raised the Jackhammer, its familiar weight an oddly comforting feeling. After all, if there was one thing in this world I understood, it was killing rippers.

A chunk of the ceiling fell away, landing at my feet. I stared up into a swarm of writhing flesh and gleaming claws as the rippers awoke.

"Welcome to the *Aboena,*" I said, and fired an incendiary grenade directly through the hole.

There was a bright light. I heard flesh sizzling. Burning chunks of ripper fell, splattering onto the floor. I fired a few bursts from the Jackhammer for good measure, then glanced down at my wrist computer to see where the next dot was. *Green dots, flashing red...*

My eyes widened. There were a *lot* of red dots.

I broke into a sprint.

I made it to the next one just after they broke through the ceiling. Rippers were already dropping onto the floor, looking around for a target. I made myself easy to find. I dispatched the first few with the Jackhammer, then tossed it aside and went to work with the thermal blades, making short work of the rest.

Then the next. And the next. And the one after that, arriving just a bit later at each one. Every second of delay meant more time for them to spread out, more time to surround me, and more time to search for ways down to where the Roamer populace was huddled in fear.

Three hit simultaneously. I chose the closest one and ran there first, firing an incendiary grenade through the hole just as it opened and running past to the next one. I stopped short to find a horde of rippers congregated in the middle of a long, wide hallway. *Dammit.* They'd found the leftovers of one of my previous battles and were already digging into the corpses carpeting the floor. One of them finished eating its fill and mitosed before my eyes, splitting grotesquely into two slightly smaller rippers.

I waded into them, thermal blades slashing like a scythe through wheat. They turned on me the moment they realized that there was fresher meat available. Claws scraped against my armor, repelled by a flash of sparks. I dodged narrowly out of the way of a tailspike aimed at my head. I hacked and kicked and stomped and swore until suddenly I was alone, standing knee deep in dismembered corpses.

Movement. More rippers down the hall. More red dots flashing on my minimap.

Damn you, Nadus.

I broke into a run.

. . .

"Defenses at checkpoint three have been overrun," Tetra said, voice hoarse from shouting. *"We're pulling back the other squads too so they don't get surrounded. You better retreat."*

"Way ahead of you," I gasped, shoving open a door that led into a long set of stairs. I slammed the door shut behind me just as a horde of rippers closed in. I heard them throwing themselves against it as I lumbered down the steps, following the directions on my minimap and eventually exiting into a long, dark passageway. I'd managed to last a full hour on the upper deck in my deadly game of whack-a-ripper. Every part of my body ached. And we still had hours to go before help arrived.

If it did arrive.

I heard fighting up ahead and hurried my pace from a stagger to a hobble. I was deep in the dark zone of the ship now, but it didn't feel like the same place I'd been hunted through just a few days ago. The deep, unnerving silence was gone, replaced by echoing gunshots and screams of pain.

I burst through a doorway into one of the larger primary corridors. Rippers were surging past me towards an open doorway at the far end. In the split second I had to assess the situation, I saw that the Roamers had built a barricade there and were valiantly defending it. It didn't take a tactical genius to see that they were on the verge of being overwhelmed, though.

I fired up my thermal blades, gave a haggard battle cry that was more for my own exhausted benefit than anybody else's, and threw myself into the fight, cutting off the flow of rippers like a boulder being dropped into a river.

I fought mindlessly, instincts driving me to duck and weave and hack and slash. My instincts had gotten me through just about as many fights as my mind had, though, and the corpses piled up in the dozens around me.

"Tetra," I groaned. "What's going on outside of the ship?"

"More ripper pods," she said. *"Looks like they're just firing everything they've got."*

I halfheartedly cleaved a ripper in two. "That's fine. As long as we hold these checkpoints, their numbers won't matter."

"Easy for you to say. We might run out of bullets before we run out of rippers to shoot them at."

I grimaced. It was a valid concern. "I—*argh*."

Something slammed into the side of my head, staggering me sideways. Sparks flashed as the Icarus's energy-infusion tech kept the tailspike that had just struck me from impaling my skull. I shook myself, turning to face the threat that had somehow gotten around me, only to feel something else land on top of my shoulders. Claws tore at me, scoring grooves in the Icarus's armor. I spun, swearing and swiping. One of the Icarus's blades flickered. Something caught at my feet and I fell to one knee.

A surge of panic filled me. I roared and fought back to my feet, blades slashing through rippers three at a time. But for each one I killed, more took their place. Another tailspike slammed into my knee and I staggered, and they were on top of me again.

This is it. The thought came to me in a bizarrely matter-of-fact way. *This is how I die.* It felt right, somehow. As if dying in any way *other* than swarmed by rippers deep in the bowels of a ship would run counter to the way I'd lived the rest of my life. My last thought was one of regret, though, as I watched a ripper pin my wrist to the floor and raise a claw to bring down on my visor. *I should have talked to Sev. Should have told her...*

Damned if I knew.

A flare of light. The ripper vanished. Somebody was standing over me, bellowing and swinging a long sword—not a thermal blade, an actual sword, like some sort of old earth barbarian might have used—in one hand while firing a thermal shotgun with the other. It was working, though, the tide of rippers driven back just long enough for me to clamber to my feet.

"Back to the barricade," my rescuer growled. The voice

sounded familiar. I didn't take the time to parse it, though, staggering back in the direction of the Roamer barricade. They parted to let me through and I collapsed onto my hands and knees, gasping for breath.

The sounds of fighting continued behind me. I groaned, closed my eyes. I just needed a minute... just one... minute...

There was a metallic thud near my head. I looked up to see the tip of a long blade embedded in the floor a few centimeters away from my visor. I followed it up, vision blurry with exhaustion, until I was looking up into the face of my rescuer.

Cairn leered down at me, eyes hungry and predatory as ever. His fur mantle was matted with blood. I saw long gashes along his limbs and torso that were healing before my very eyes.

The blade shifted in his hand, while the other tightened around the grip of his shotgun. My blood went cold. For just a moment, I thought he was going to raise his shotgun and blast me in the face.

He stared at me, teeth bared. I could tell he wanted to do it. His finger tensed on the trigger of his shotgun. I braced myself to act first the moment it started moving. My brain felt sluggish, though, and my reactions slow.

He sighed, dropped the shotgun, and proffered me a hand. I stared at it.

"Don't you worry, Vanguard," he growled. "I'm still gonna kill you. But one fight at a time, eh?"

I took his hand, groaning as he helped me to my feet. He picked his shotgun back up, gave me one last glare, and turned back to the fight.

I stared after him, then groaned and reached behind my back for the scavenged Jackhammer I'd placed there.

Not that it came as any surprise, but Cairn could fight. And so could his men.

We held the line until the bodies were stacked almost too high to see over. Until my Jackhammer was out of ammo and most of their guns too. When the time came, we waited for the rippers to try to crawl over the corpses of their companions and thrusted at them with spears or hacked at them with axes. When the rippers seemed on the verge of breaking through, I stepped to the front, sweeping them away with my quickly fading thermal blades

"Your swords," Cairn said. "They're dying."

"I know that," I growled, stepping back behind the barricade and leaning on my knees as I took a short reprieve. "They've been running all day."

"So has this." He held up his bloody sword, giving me a mad grin. "Don't see it running out of life."

"I also don't see it cutting through Jericho armor."

"Oh, it'll run through a Vanguard well enough." He looked over my battle-scarred armor. "Just need to peel off their shell first."

"Don't get ahead of yourself," I groaned. I hesitated, then lifted my visor, letting sweat drop from my face. Cairn gave me an odd look, like he was deciding whether or not to take advantage of my temporary vulnerability.

I found myself studying the most recent set of scars a ripper had given him. The claws had torn right through his tattered clothing along his chest, cutting him wide open, just a few minutes ago. Now the wounds were nothing more than a set of bright red streaks.

"The Stranger," I said, my voice hoarse. "What'd he do to you?"

He looked sharply at me, seemingly caught off guard by the question, and narrowed his eyes. "He?"

"Yeah." I stretched my neck until it popped, groaning. "I met him. Older guy, wearing dark glasses. Wears his hair in a braid?"

Cairn stared at me for a moment. Then he grinned. Then he chuckled. Then he burst into raucous, vicious, joyful laughter.

"You," he managed between peals, "you really thought... you were talking to..."

I blinked in confusion. "What?"

He managed to calm himself, wiping away a tear. "Oh," he groaned. "Thank you, Vanguard. I needed that. Even in the middle of battle, there is joy to be found. *Especially* in the middle of battle, I suppose."

I frowned. "What the *hell* are you talking about?"

He giggled. "Well, if the Stranger didn't feel obligated to let you in on the joke, then I don't think I will, either."

Tetra's voice sounded in my ear before I could retort. I held up a hand as she spoke. "*You need to back up,*" she said. "*More rippers will be coming down the hallway behind you.*"

I frowned. "How'd they get through?"

"*Seems like a surviving squad of Vanguards have been clearing a path for them,*" she said.

Dammit. I looked up at Cairn and his Wolves. "Time to move to the next checkpoint."

Cairn growled. "We keep falling back, we won't have anywhere else to fall to before long."

"Feel free to stay here and hold them off, then," I growled, walking towards the next checkpoint and hoping my exhaustion didn't show too badly. "I'm sure they'd love a light snack before the main course."

I lost track of time. Lost starck of checkpoints. We retreated from corridor to corridor, down one flight of stairs after another. The rippers were endless and our supplies were not. Even Cairn seemed worn down, his breathing haggard and his sword dragging along the floor as we retreated once again.

I barged through the doorway my wrist computer had been telling me to go through, then blinked around in shock as a sea of faces stared up at me. I was standing on a long catwalk over a large, long room that was completely packed with Roamers.

"Ah, *hell*," I muttered.

Cairn filed through the door behind me, leaning against the catwalk railing and staring down at the crowd. "I told you we could only fall back so far," he growled.

I nodded numbly. This was it, then. There were no more checkpoints to retreat to. No more playing whack-a-ripper. As soon as they made it through one of the sets of doors into this room, it would be over. They'd tear into the huddled mass of Roamers and we'd be powerless to stop them.

I glanced down the catwalk and saw a familiar figure. Shell. She was wearing Marshal's armor that was coated almost completely in blood. Her exo must have been compromised at some point in the fight. I staggered towards her. She turned towards me, face haggard.

"You look like hell," I said, forcing a weak smile onto my face.

"So do you," she said. She looked around numbly, as if she was too exhausted to feel any emotion at our plight. "So what happens next?"

"We seal every door into here," I said, "And hold them for as long as possible. We need to last four more hours."

She nodded slowly. "Don't think that'll be soon enough."

"No," I said. "I don't think it will."

Somebody was running up the stairs towards us. Tetra, looking less battle-scarred but every bit as exhausted. "Doors are all sealed," she gasped, coming to a halt next to us. "That should hold them for a good long while."

I nodded. "That's their goal, though. We're trapped down here now. I'll bet good money that we see another wave of boarding shuttles launched any minute. The Vanguards will clear out the rippers deck by deck, then break through into here. And by that time, if the rippers haven't made it in, we'll be happy to see them."

"Not for long, though," Shell said grimly. "I doubt they'll be in a mood for leaving survivors."

Tetra nodded slowly. She blinked heavily at Shell, looking her up and down. "You're wearing a Marshal's uniform," she stated, seeming surprised.

Shell looked down at the gore-spattered armor. "I'm shocked you can even tell under all that blood. I manned my exo until a ripper got the power supply and I had to abandon it."

A tear welled up in the corner of Tetra's eye. She wiped it quickly away. "You wear it as well as ever," she said.

Shell blinked away tears of her own. "Tetra, I'm... glad to be back. No matter how it ends."

No matter how it ends. I turned, surveying the crowd. The room was a sea of whispers, the Roamers too disciplined to fall to panic. Not yet, anyways. For now, their concerns were voiced in quiet mutterings. It didn't matter. They'd all be dead soon, whether by rippers' claws or Vanguards' bullets.

A way out. There had to be one. There always was one, wasn't there?

I triggered my neurointerface and connected my comms channel to the *Orpheus*. "Rose. We've been pushed back into the core of the ship. What's your status?"

"Just waiting outside like you said to," she said a moment later. *"You've got a hell of a lot of boarding shuttles headed your way."*

Dammit. I'd been right, then. "I'm just about out of ideas," I said wearily. "You got anything?"

"There's no escape pods in there? No way out from the core?"

I turned to Shell. She shook her head, face expressionless.

"Doesn't look like it," I said. "And even if there were..."

"The Paragon would just shoot them," Rose finished, her voice quiet.

"Yeah."

There was a long silence.

"I'm sorry, Rose," I said weakly. "But I think it's time for you to leave."

An hour crept by. Then another.

We held the doors and monitored the Vanguards' progress as best we could on whatever security cameras were still functioning. The groups we'd seen flounder before had been caught off guard and surrounded. These ones knew exactly what they were facing. They cleared deck after deck of increasingly large swarms of rippers, working their way gradually down towards us.

I spent the whole time working desperately through our options. Surely there was some ally we hadn't called upon yet. Surely there was some weapon we still had at our disposal. But none came to mind. Nobody had heard from the Shapers or the Stranger, and nobody was sure where they were now. Most likely they were either hiding in some quiet corner of the ship or had quietly slipped away before the siege had even begun. Plenty of other Roamers had. They'd been the smart ones. The ones that were left down here were those either too poor, too loyal, too stubborn, or too stupid to flee. I figured I probably counted as all four.

Another hour passed. The sound of scrambling rippers outside the doors was now drowned out by echoing gunshots. The murmurs spreading through the room grew louder and more panicked.

A cold, helpless feeling clawed at my chest as I realized that nobody was coming to save us. I wondered briefly what I should try to do before the end. Maybe go kill Cairn myself to deny the

Paragon the pleasure. Maybe I should just sit and think, and reflect on my life. Try to come to peace with the fact that in the end, it had been a great, long, bloody trail of bodies leading to absolutely nowhere. The sum total of my life was a black hole, sucking everything it encountered into its destructive depths. Just like the one Ramar had tried to steer the *Revelation* into.

I blinked.

We did have an option left. Just one. The last option that any Roamer would ever consider.

I walked briskly towards where Tetra was talking quietly with Shell. "Tetra," I said. "Does the ship have a self-destruct sequence?"

She looked sharply up at me. "No. There'd be no point."

"Is there a way to get the ship to self-destruct, though?" I insisted.

She and Shell frowned at each other. It was Shell who spoke up. "I mean... sure. If you were to overcharge the null-breacher badly enough, plus if a few other things went wrong, you could destroy the entire ship in one blast. But there are tons of safeguards against it."

"How hard would it be to remove them?" I demanded.

Tetra frowned. "Why would—"

Shell straightened, eyes widening. "Our last card," she said. "The Paragon wants the ultrarippers. They can't have the ultra-rippers if the ship gets destroyed."

Tetra stared at her as if she'd gone insane. "But then the *ship will be destroyed.*"

"No." I shook my head. "All we need to do is break enough systems to start the emergency systems blaring. We just need to scare the Vanguards back. Just for another hour."

Gunshots sounded outside. We all looked sharply towards the door.

Tetra grimaced. "Command will never—"

Shell shot to her feet. "Screw Command. Hell—even if it

doesn't work, and they don't retreat, they'll kill us all anyways. This way we take them out with us. At the very least. Revenge is a piss-poor substitute for victory, but beggars can't be choosers." She held one hand out to Tetra. "Are you coming?"

Tetra studied her sister for just a moment. Hesitated. Then took her hand, letting her help her to her feet.

The gunshots outside of the room grew louder. I unslung my APMP-17 and checked the magazine. Thirteen rounds left. "Go," I said. "We'll see how much time we can buy."

The sisters dashed off. I turned towards the door, taking a deep breath. I glanced over my shoulder towards where Cairn was standing, wearing a grim expression.

"Shame, Vanguard," he called out to me. "I was very much looking forward to killing you myself."

I didn't give him the satisfaction of an answer, instead focusing my attention on the door in front of me. I heard a few more muffled gunshots, then silence.

Hurry, I mentally begged Shell.

"*Attention,*" blared a loud voice through the doors. "*This is the Paragon Vanguard. The bioweapon infestation has been cleared. It is safe to open the doors now. You have been rescued.*"

I grimaced, raising my rifle. *Rescued.* Well, at least you couldn't deny they had a sense of humor.

They waited about a minute before speaking again, this time in a much harsher voice. "*Open the doors. Now. Or we'll cut them open.*"

"*Go screw yourselves!*" somebody shouted, their voice echoing through the large room.

The Vanguards didn't seem to like that. There was a buzzing sound. Sparks began to spray around the edges of the door I was facing.

I lifted the APMP-17, estimated where the saw-wielder's head would be, and pulled the trigger. There was a heavy thumping noise as the bullet pierced through the door and beyond, followed by a crashing sound. The sparks died. I heard muffled cursing.

Another door to my right started to barge inward. I moved towards it. Metal burst as a gauntleted fist shot through the door. I lined up my last incendiary grenade, waited until the gap was clear, and fired it through the hole the Vanguard had made. Screams followed.

"This is your final warning!" The Vanguard was screaming now. *"We will use lethal force to—"*

His voice cut off abruptly as red emergency lights flared overhead. A hush fell over the crowd of Roamers as a voice repeated something in what sounded like an old earth language, over and over again.

Then the Roamers started panicking.

I leaned against the wall, trying to listen to what was happening on the other side. I heard a shouted conversation, but couldn't make out the words. Sounded like they were trying to make up their minds.

Come on. Get out of here. Don't be insane. The thought was almost enough to make me giggle. *Only an insane person would stick around on a ship that's about to explode.*

I heard a shouted command. Braced myself for the Vanguards to make entry.

But they didn't.

A Marshal standing nearby me pointed suddenly at their datapad. I glanced over at it. A security feed showed a blurry image of a hallway full of dead rippers, a few fallen soldiers from both sides—and a full column of retreating Vanguards.

I heard shouts. Looked up to see that Roamers were fighting to get into a door that looked like it led to the ship's innermost core. That'd be where the power generator was. I clenched my teeth and trudged down the stairs into the main floor, wading through the crowd to get to it, then pushed them away.

One of them—Gladen, I realized, with a start—stared at me incredulously. "What are you doing?" he cried.

"Saving the ship," I said, meeting his crazed look.

He stared a moment longer. Realization seemed to dawn on him. He turned and started pushing the other Roamers away.

"Shell!" I said into the comms. "How much longer can we go before we hit a point of no return?"

"*You mean before we* actually *blow the ship?*"

"Yeah."

"*Not much.*"

I pulled up the security feeds on my own wrist computer. The Vanguards were sprinting now, exerting all of their strength to get away. *Go, Vanguards, go,* I found myself silently urging them. They still had a long ways to go until they got to their shuttles. I doubted we'd be able to keep up the ruse for that long.

But we didn't have to.

I heard a burst of static. Then the most grating, lyrical, beautiful voice I'd ever heard.

"*Fear not, my friends—your deliverance has arrived!*"

Relief surged through me, strong enough that I sagged to my knees.

Zathari Renault, King of the Buccaneers, had arrived.

Tetra emerged from the engine core beside me, looking dazed. "Did it... work?"

I nodded numbly. "It worked."

She shouted something down to Shell, then turned back. Voices echoed across the room. A Marshal, shouting out announcements every few minutes. Tetra translated for me. The Vanguards were retreating. Boarding their shuttles. Returning to the *Leonidas* as the battlecruiser braced to face the new arrival.

"*Lax!*" Rose's voice sounded in my ear. "*You still there?*"

I grinned. "Hey! I told you to get out of here!"

"Well I can't go now that there's a show to see! I've never seen a space battle up close. Not like this, at least. Renault brought a lot of ships. The Leonidas doesn't seem like it's super confident in its chances."

Shell stared at me, eyes wide. "Did we just... *win?*"

I looked up. Cairn was watching me from the catwalk, eyes aglow with that predatory light of his. As soon as our eyes met, he grinned. Then turned and nodded to one of his followers.

"Almost," I growled.

Gunshots echoed suddenly, followed by screams. Cairn's grin widened as he stared down at me.

"I'm coming, Vanguard," he mouthed, then vanished into the crowd.

I turned wearily to Shell. "Is everything in place?"

She gave an equally tired nod. "Yes."

I gave a long, heavy sigh, then climbed to my feet. "Then let's finish the fight."

THIRTY-THREE

"There you are, Vanguard."

I looked up wearily.

Cairn was standing a dozen meters away from me, holding his shotgun in one hand and that sword of his in the other. He looked around, eyes sparkling. "You chose quite the dramatic place to die, didn't you? So eager for it I see you even abandoned your suit of shining armor."

I gave a heavy sigh, looking around. The Icarus had been on the verge of collapse, and it wouldn't have fit down the entryway to the engine core of the ship anyways. We were standing in the very heart of the *Aboena*, now. I could feel the humming of the ship's massive, ancient primary power generator, along with its gravity core and its nullbreacher. All of those systems could now be built on a ship even smaller than the *Orpheus* and powered with a handful of ultracells. Back when the *Aboena* had been built, you needed a core three kilometers long to produce enough energy to manipulate gravity or break dimensional barriers.

Above us, I spotted a scarlet tendril creep slowly around a beam.

Cairn took an easy, casual step towards me. "Come now, Vanguard. I know you're tired, but we've unfinished business to attend to. Surely you've got one more fight left in you."

I turned towards him, leaning against the catwalk railing with one arm while letting my other dangle next to Peacebreaker's holster. "That's really what's on your mind now, huh? After everything that just happened?"

He shrugged. "Well, why not? Nothing quite like winning one fight to put you in the mood for winning another. And believe me, Vanguard..." His grin widened. "I've already won. This is just a formality. For my own satisfaction."

"Yeah?"

"Yeah." He took another step. "You didn't think I'd be so stupid as to let you take over my ship like that, did you? After all the work I've done? All the effort and sacrifice I've made to turn my vision into reality?"

I said nothing.

He took another step, letting the point of his sword scrape along the catwalk floor. Ding, ding, ding. "And now, finally," he said, taking another step, "even this calamity with the Paragon has worked in my favor. I don't know how you got them here, and I commend you for the effort—but it was a poorly planned power grab. You thought you could ride the chaos. Turn it to your advantage. But you're not the only one."

"Yeah?" I asked, trying to force some life into my exhausted voice.

"Command seems to have turned against me," Cairn growled. "And so, I'll simply replace them. My soldiers are launching a coup as we speak. They'll kill the Command leaders and their guards. Then your friends. And the best part is that I can blame it all on you, then fill Command with my own followers. Or just do away with it altogether. I've always thought it was an unwieldy power structure."

"Me too," I said.

He stopped, frowning at me. "Why are you... so..."

I raised an eyebrow. "Calm?"

His frown deepened.

"I knew you'd try something," I said, soft enough that he had to strain to hear me over the noise of the *Aboena*'s thundering engines. "You made a few mistakes. One of which was turning the Oathless against you."

He narrowed his eyes. "What the hell are you..."

"Right now," I said, "Oathless hunters who have been hiding like animals from your Wolves are in the process of doing two things: first, intercepting the hit teams you sent to kill Command, and second, incinerating the holding cells where you keep your rippers."

He stared at me. "You're lying. They don't know where they are."

I chuckled weakly. "But Ramar does."

He stood in shocked silence for a long moment, studying me, looking for any indication that I was lying. If I'd been less exhausted, I might've accidentally given away the fact that I didn't know for sure that the Oathless had actually agreed to help Ramar stop Cairn's coup. As it was, though, I was too tired to do anything but stare back at him.

Tetra and I had known that there would be no better opportunity for Cairn to take the power he so desperately wanted than right after the battle concluded, when all of Command's troops were worn down. So we'd sent Ramar to beg for help from the only group that nobody ever thought to account for: the Oathless, lurking in their hidden camps scattered around the ship. They might not have the same martial prowess Cairn's men did, but they knew the ship better than anyone and they were still fresh. With any luck at all, they'd at least slowed the Wolves down enough to give Command a fighting chance.

I gave a heavy sigh, gesturing around us. "Did you really think I brought you down here just for fun? I needed you away from your teams. Someplace they couldn't call on you for help when the Oathless ambushed them. I figure this is about as remote a place as you can find on this ship."

His face contorted suddenly into a mask of pure hatred. He raised the thermal shotgun with one hand, aiming it at me.

"You know damn well," I said, "that if you fire that thing in here, this whole ship could turn to plasma." I jerked my head towards the churning engines below us. The air shimmered with the fumes leaping up from them. "That's some mighty ancient equipment right there. I'm not sure I trust it. Do you?"

He clenched his teeth, eyes bulging. His finger tensed on the trigger. Then he suddenly threw it onto the catwalk with a loud clang.

"Always preferred a real fight anyways," he snarled, holding the point of his blade towards me.

I pushed myself away from the railing, reached back, and drew a long knife Shell had given me.

"I've just got one question first," I said.

Cairn's eyes narrowed.

"Why me?" My voice was quiet. Quiet enough I could barely hear it over the sound of the engines. Cairn evidently heard it plenty, though. His eyes lit with fury.

"Because you killed my *little brother*," he snarled, and leaped.

I jerked backward, barely staying out of his flashing blade's reach.

"You slaughtered him like an *animal*," Cairn hissed, swinging in wide, vicious blows with each sentence. "Ambushed him in our own territory. Killed his escorts. Cut off his *hand*. Stabbed him in the back. Beat. His. Head. Into. *Pulp!*"

I ducked and dodged, narrowly avoiding one cut after another. He was getting reckless, his blows wider and sloppier. I wasn't the only one who'd spent the past day fighting for all I was worth. Touched by the Stranger or not, he was on the verge of exhaustion.

It took a moment for everything he was saying to click into place. *Of course.* Cairn's obsessive hunt for me hadn't started until after I'd snuck into his territory and killed Dak. I'd assumed Dak was simply a second in command. Nobody had ever bothered to tell me any different. Maybe it had been a secret of some kind.

I scrambled back, making a gap. Cairn slowed, just long enough for me to get a few more words in. He was mad—but I needed him to be furious. Blind with rage. Driven insane with hatred.

Breathe, I told myself. *That's where it all begins.*

He screamed and dived recklessly, sword swinging wildly towards my head.

I pivoted, ducked under the blade, and jerked the point of my knife up into his torso. He let out a shocked gasp as the point drove deep into his guts.

"And *you*," I hissed, in his ear, driving the point deeper with each word, "*killed. My. Friend.*"

I lifted him, using the knife as leverage. Every bone in my body ached. Every muscle throbbed. But I managed to lift him over the railing, holding him above the churning, grinding machinery below.

I threw him. Someone was bellowing. Him. Me. Both of us. I saw his face go suddenly white with terror. He fell. Twisted in mid-air. Grabbed at me. I grunted as I was yanked from the catwalk.

We hung in space for a short moment. Then I slammed into something hard, bounced, rolled, grabbed, clung. Gasped for air.

I shook myself, looking around. I'd somehow avoided landing in the twisting mechanics of the engine. Instead I had landed on some sort of narrow platform that ran perpendicular around the circumference of the engine core. Where had Cairn gone?

There. I saw him climbing to his feet with a snarl. He'd rolled to the other side of the platform. With the gravity core so close to us, gravity affected each of us differently. The power of the engines cast an eerie red glow over us. There was something otherworldly about the sight of him standing there, standing at that *wrong* angle.

He reached down, tore the knife out his side, and charged, bellowing.

I summoned every last ounce of strength I had, climbing to my feet and let loose a cry of my own as I knocked the knife out of his hand, sending it clattering to the floor, and shoulder-checked him in the gut. He staggered backward. Shoved me away. Threw a blindingly fast punch that slammed into my temple and made the world spin.

I staggered, dangerously close to the edge. He grabbed me. Pulled me back.

"*Not yet,*" he snarled. "Not. Till I'm. *Done with you!*"

I tried to fight back. Tried to lift my hands to block the blows. Tried to dodge. Tried to counter. Just like Nadus had. None of it worked. I was too tired and he was too fast. I could feel my body crumbling with the strain of the past twenty-four hours and he seemed to be suddenly full of endless energy and fury and raw, unbridled *hate.*

A blow slammed into my temple, sent me staggering. He pulled me back again. Delivered another blow that slammed into the side of my jaw. I felt something crack. Felt my face go numb.

He struck again in the same place. Pain *exploded* through my head. I fell over backward. He was on top of me, his leering, maddened face all I could see. He grabbed me, rolled me over so I was face down. Grabbed the back of my head. Pulled it back.

"*You killed. My. BROTHER,*" he snarled.

THUD.

The metallic surface of the platform slammed into my face. My nose snapped, gushing blood. Lights burst in my head.

He pulled me back again.

THUD. Pain—more of it than I'd ever felt—ran up and down my entire body in a devastating shockwave.

Kessa's face drifted through my mind. *It's alright to feel anger, Lax. It's alright to use it.*

Just don't forget who you're fighting for.

THUD. Something cracked. I was fading. Fading, vanishing into a long, deep, empty nothingness.

I saw Rose. Rid and Bentley and Shell. All depending on me. Or was it me that depended on them?

I saw Sev, sitting at the bar, waiting for me. The thought of never seeing her again was unbearable.

I saw Nadus. Not battered and broken. Smiling. Sitting beside me, sharing a drink and a few words of quiet, humble wisdom.

I heard Cairn laughing as he grabbed the back of my head. Pulled me back up, one last time.

Nadus was dead. And the bastard who had killed him—who had promised that he would kill *all* of my friends—was about to kill me.

A surge of raw, bloody, white-hot fury stronger than any emotion I'd ever felt before *exploded* from my chest, filling every fiber of my breaking body. I threw my arms out, catching myself against the platform as Cairn tried to slam my face down again. I heard him give a surprised grunt before I twisted, throwing him off of me.

He rolled, caught himself on the edge before he could go over. I snarled, sprayed blood and spit and broken teeth from my shattered jaw as I charged. My fists slammed into him. Once, twice, three times. He recovered, swung a wide haymaker at me. I dived out of the way, grabbed the fallen knife, spun, slammed it into his rib cage.

He screamed. I jerked the knife out, then back in again. And again. And again.

He twisted. Tackled me onto my back. We were both screaming and laughing and crying and dying and the knife was going in and out and in and out and it *wasn't. Working.*

He caught my wrist. Shoved the blade away from his body. Moved it inexorably towards the grinding, whirling machinery just beneath the platform's edge. The blade sank into the spinning gears and vanished in a spray of sparks.

His hand tightened around my wrist. Shoved it down. Down, down, down. Inch by inexorable inch. He was staring into my eyes, blood frothing from his mouth. His other hand closed around my throat, clenching like a vise.

My hand inched closer to the spinning machinery.

Cairn lowered his face until it was only inches from mine. His breath was hot against my face. His eyes were burning—completely, utterly consumed in rage and hatred. I saw my death a thousand different times and a thousand different ways in them. I knew he did too. It was *all* he could see.

Focus. Breathe. That's where it all begins. Then you can see the whole picture.

My eyes inched sideways—towards my hand, hovering just above the rapidly spinning engine. And towards Cairn's hand, wrapped tight around my wrist.

There's always a way out.

I gave Cairn one last, broken grin. He blinked down at me in confusion. I reached out with my free hand, grabbed tight to the other end of the platform, and then suddenly *jerked* my other hand—the one whose wrist he was currently gripping—down into the whirling machinery.

My hand vanished. The machinery ate it up, tried to pull me in after it, but my other hand held tight.

Cairn's eyes widened as he jerked sideways, the pressure he'd been putting onto my wrist suddenly relieved. His arm sank into the whirling machinery. He cried out in shock and let go of my throat, clutching at the platform. But it was too late.

He vanished. The engines never even slowed down.

I pulled my hand back up. No—not my hand. Just a torn, bloody lump of flesh, with jagged bone and bits of Vanguard machinery jutting out into nothingness.

I let out a short, broken, triumphant, gurgling laugh. Above me, I swore I could see thick, scarlet, writhing tendrils, reaching down towards me.

Then I was gone.

EPILOGUE

"How long you think we can keep this up?"

Kessa rolled over, putting her head on my chest and looking at me with her infinitely green eyes. I just stared at her.

"I asked you a question, silly."

I blinked. "Sorry. Just got... lost."

She smiled. "How long do you think we can keep this up?"

I thought about it.

"Forever," I said.

She smiled again. Not the same smile, though. Her sad, knowing smile. I felt my heart sink.

"You know that's not true, Lax," she said. "The fight isn't over yet."

"I think it's pretty over," I said.

She pulled my hand close to her—my right hand, the one that I was just now remembering had been eaten by the *Aboena*'s engines—and kissed it gently. "I wish it was," she said. "I really, really do. But you need to go back. You need to move on. And you need to finish the fight."

I gave a long, heavy sigh. "I know."

She smiled again, and then she was gone.

———

I was floating. Drifting in space. Somebody was speaking words in a language I couldn't understand. The voice sounded far away.

My hand was gone. I was dimly aware of the fact. It somehow didn't alarm me, though. Neither did the memory of my jaw shattering.

Hands. One hand, actually. Reaching towards me from the darkness. I frowned at it. It wasn't like any hand I'd seen before. Somehow too big and too long, with slightly bluish skin, as if it belonged to a drowned person. Strange, white, otherworldly light—like the light I had always sworn I could see in Cairn's eyes—seemed to emanate from the hand's pores.

I tried to move. I couldn't. Thick, vein-like vines were holding me down to a table. I caught a glimpse of a ceiling covered in a thick spiral of vines above me.

I've been here before.

One of the fingers rested gently against the stump of my ruined arm.

A deep calm filled me.

I faded away.

———

I woke up.

It took me a minute to convince myself that I had actually woken up. I was lying in a patch of grass, surrounded by a cool breeze. Vines hung over me, laced with strange, golden berries that glowed.

"He's awake!"

"I told you he'd wake up!"

I looked around to see my crew rushing towards me. Rose, Rid, and Bentley dashed to my side, their faces split by wide grins. Shell walked right behind them. And behind her, Sev stood, smirking at me.

I sat up, groaning. "How long have I been out?"

"Three weeks," Rose said.

I felt a jolt of shock. "*What?*"

Rid nodded seriously. "You were... in *bad* shape, Lax. We all thought you were dead."

"You *would* have been dead," Shell said. "If it weren't for the Stranger."

I frowned at her. "The Stranger?"

She nodded. "We went in to find you after everything got resolved. The Shapers got to you first, somehow. Dragged your broken, bleeding body back to their master. Apparently, the Stranger was waiting for you. Not sure what they did, but..." She gestured downward. "It sure seems to have worked."

I frowned. Looked down. My right hand was exactly where it had been—perfectly intact and not looking at all as if it had just been shredded off by a hungry engine. Come to think of it, my jaw had been badly broken. And I was pretty sure Cairn had fractured my skull.

My eyes widened. "Am I..."

"Whatever it was the Stranger did to Cairn," Rose said, "it seems like they've done the same thing to you."

"Zeka said that you Proved yourself," Shell said quietly.

I stared at my hand, rotating it like I was a baby seeing my limbs for the first time. "I... this doesn't feel..."

"Real?" Sev chuckled, kneeling down next to me. "I didn't think so either, at first."

I looked back up at her, blinking. I felt like I was seeing *her* for the first time, too. Maybe it was just the fact that I'd already accepted I'd never see her again, but she looked beautiful. More so than ever before.

"I'm sorry," I whispered.

She put a hand on my arm. "I know you are," she said

quietly. "They filled me in on everything that's happened. It's been a hell of a time. For all of us."

I nodded. "Listen. When I was fighting Cairn... and I thought it was over..."

I trailed off. She watched me expectantly. I searched desperately for words. *The thought of never seeing you again was unbearable. I missed you.*

I... think I might love you.

But none of that came out.

Instead, I just shook my head. "I... never mind."

She held my gaze a moment longer, searching me. I don't know what she found. But for a brief moment, she looked almost disappointed.

The moment passed. She nodded. "Here's the quick rundown of what you missed. Renault and his fleet drove off the *Leonidas.* Shell, Tetra and their teams were able to intercept Cairn's Wolves before they could take out Command."

Another figure approached from behind Sev. Ramar, his face scarred and weary-looking but no longer on the verge of death. "Valley and I were able to find where Cairn was keeping the ultrarippers caged. They've all been incinerated."

I felt a sudden surge of relief, as if a massive weight I'd been carrying without realizing it had lifted from my shoulders. I nodded. "Good. I guess that means—"

"There's more," Sev said.

I blinked. "Oh."

"You've kinda, sorta, slept through the first three weeks of the new Last War," Bentley said.

Sev nodded. "Redhawk has been officially liberated. Several other systems came to their aid. Battlelines are being drawn across the Paragon, and the Paragon itself seems to be flailing in the water."

I raised an eyebrow. "Albeni 7?"

"Firmly under Vatheson's control," Sev said grimly. "But

not for long. We've got a fleet to work with now. This is quite the alliance you've put together, Lax. We'll co-ordinate with Renault and the Roamers to prepare our assault and retake Albeni 7. And when we get there..." She narrowed her eyes. "Vatheson'll regret ever hearing the name Maren Sevani."

I nodded slowly.

Just a few weeks ago, the idea of leading a fleet into battle would have been ludicrous. All I'd wanted was to stay out of the way. But now, it seemed inevitable.

I'd been made to fight. I was done running.

"Damn right," I said.

A LETTER FROM JAROM

Dear reader,

Thank you for taking the time to read *Starship Raider*! I had a blast writing this second instalment and I hope you had just as good of a time reading it. Lax's adventures come to their conclusion in *Starship Rebellion*, available now from Second Sky Books.

If you want to stay up to date with my future releases, you can sign up for my newsletter at the following link. I promise not to share your email with anyone else or spam you, and you can unsubscribe at any time.

www.secondskybooks.com/jarom-strong

Finally, it would mean the world to me if you would leave a review for *Starship Raider*. It's impossible to overstate how important reviews are to the sale of a book in today's market, especially for a debut novel. If you have additional thoughts about the book, I'd love to hear personally from you! I can be reached through social media or you can contact me directly though the contact form on my website.

Thanks again!

Jarom Strong

KEEP IN TOUCH WITH JAROM

www.jaromstrong.com

 facebook.com/jarom.strong.750
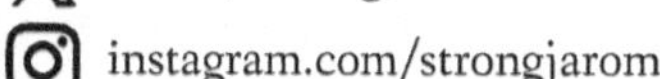 x.com/StrongJarom
instagram.com/strongjarom

ACKNOWLEDGMENTS

To be perfectly honest, I never really expected to write this book. I started *Starship Salvager* as an experimental project to force myself to try something new, not thinking it would go anywhere. I was happily surprised when it got extremely positive feedback from my writing peers and mentors, delightfully shocked when my (now) agent Helen read it and agreed to represent me, and downright flabbergasted when Second Sky Books said that not only did they want to publish it—they wanted me to write two more books following Lax and team and publish them simultaneously.

So—here's *Starship Raider*. And *here* is a sadly abbreviated list of just a few of the people who have helped bring it to pass.

First credit goes to my editor, Jack Renninson, who has been extremely patient as I've worked through version after version of this book, graciously giving me the time I needed to get it to where it need to be and generously offering feedback and ideas to help it along the way, along with the rest of the team at Second Sky: Ruth Tross, Melissa Tran, Mandy Kullar, and Jen Shannon, Helen Hawkins, and Angela Snowden.

My agent Helen Lane was as supportive as ever, keeping me sane as I churned through the first draft and offering much needed feedback and encouragement.

My writing group must feel like they're living in Groundhog Day after how many times they've read, commented on, and helped me improve the first few chapters. You're all champs for sticking through it with me.

Finally, there's no way it would have been even remotely possible for me to write this book without a frankly ridiculous amount of support from my family. Between the birth of our first child and the purchase of our first home, this was a crazy time for our family. My wife Marci bent over backward to make sure I had the time I needed, and my siblings spent hour after hour helping us settle into our new condo.

PUBLISHING TEAM

Turning a manuscript into a book requires the efforts of many people. The publishing team at Bookouture would like to acknowledge everyone who contributed to this publication.

Audio
Alba Proko
Sinead O'Connor
Melissa Tran

Commercial
Lauren Morrissette
Hannah Richmond
Imogen Allport

Cover design
Tom Edwards

Data and analysis
Mark Alder
Mohamed Bussuri

Editorial
Jack Renninson
Melissa Tran

Copyeditor
Helen Hawkins

Proofreader
Angela Snowden

Marketing
Alex Crow
Melanie Price
Occy Carr
Cíara Rosney
Martyna Młynarska

Operations and distribution
Marina Valles
Stephanie Straub
Joe Morris

Production
Hannah Snetsinger
Mandy Kullar
Jen Shannon
Ria Clare

Publicity
Kim Nash
Noelle Holten
Jess Readett
Sarah Hardy

Rights and contracts
Peta Nightingale
Richard King
Saidah Graham

www.ingramcontent.com/pod-product-compliance
Lightning Source LLC
Chambersburg PA
CBHW030520190726

48283CB00006B/1701